P9-DMI-958

- BOOTS AND STARSHIPS

- KEEPING THE FAITH, OR HOW TO LIVE THROUGH A *STAR TREK* CONVENTION

- EVEN MORE *STAR TREK* MYSTERIES SOLVED

- *STAR TREK*'S THIRD SEASON: A WORTHWHILE MIXTURE OF SUCCESS AND FAILURE

From in-depth analyses of beloved characters and enterprising storylines to firsthand accounts of convention etiquette and outrageous parodies of the show that have lasted twenty-five years, this grand collection of the best writing from *The Best of Trek*® books gives exciting proof of *Star Trek's* growth from a favorite TV show to an undisputed American cultural icon.

THE BEST OF THE BEST OF TREK® II

From the Magazine for Star Trek Fans

Edited by
Walter Irwin and G. B. Love

A ROC BOOK

ROC
Published by the Penguin Group
Penguin Books USA Inc., 375 Hudson Street,
New York, New York 10014, U.S.A.
Penguin Books Ltd, 27 Wrights Lane,
London W8 5TZ, England
Penguin Books Australia Ltd, Ringwood,
Victoria, Australia
Penguin Books Canada Ltd, 10 Alcorn Avenue,
Toronto, Ontario, Canada M4V 3B2
Penguin Books (N.Z.) Ltd, 182–190 Wairau Road,
Auckland 10, New Zealand

Penguin Books Ltd, Registered Offices:
Harmondsworth, Middlesex, England

First published by ROC, an imprint of New American Library, a division of Penguin Books USA Inc.

First Printing, June, 1992
10 9 8 7 6 5 4 3 2 1

Copyright © Walter Irwin and G. B. Love, 1992
All rights reserved

Acknowledgments

"Diversity in Combination" by Alan Manning. Copyright © 1986 by TREK®.
"The Brilliant Door" by Joyce Tullock. Copyright © 1986 by TREK®.
"Boots and Starships" by Walter Irwin. Copyright © 1986 by TREK®.
"The Neglected Whole, or, 'Never Heard of You': Part I" by Elizabeth Rigel. Copyright © 1986 by TREK®.
"The Neglected Whole, or, 'Never Heard of You': Part II" by Elizabeth Rigel. Copyright © 1986 by TREK®.
"The Classic Star Trek" by Linda M. Johnston. Copyright © 1986 by TREK®.
"The Journey to—and Beyond—the Search for Spock" by Hazel Ann Williams. Copyright © 1986 by TREK®.
"Star Trek: Odyssey of Salvation" by Sister Mary William David, S.N.D. Copyright © 1986 by TREK®.
"Star Trek Lives in My Life" by Jacqueline A. LongM. Copyright © 1987 by TREK®.
"Tomorrow Man" by Joyce Tullock. Copyright © 1987 by TREK®.
"Keeping the Faith, or How to Live Through a Star Trek Convention" by Ingrid Cross. Copyright © 1987 by TREK®.
"Walking on Water and Other Things James Kirk Can't Do" by James H. Devon. Copyright © 1987 by TREK®.
"The Neglected Whole, Part III: The Engineer and the Doctor" by Elizabeth Rigel. Copyright © 1987 by TREK®.
"Cheaters and Katras: A Short Discussion of Death" by Douglas Blake. Copyright © 1987 by TREK®.
"Star Trip III: In Search of Taxi—A Star Trek Parody" by Kiel Stuart. Copyright © 1987 by TREK®.
"Medical Practice in Star Trek: Cures and Catcalls" by Sharron Crowson. Copyright © 1988 by TREK®.
"Reflections on Star Trek: Past, Present, and Future" by Gail Schnirch. Copyright © 1988 by TREK®.
"A Guide to Star Trek Blueprints" by Michael J. Scott. Copyright © 1988 by TREK®.
"Star Trek Mysteries Solved by Our Readers" with commentary by Leslie Thompson. Copyright © 1988 by TREK®.
"Even More Star Trek Mysteries Solved" by Leslie Thompson. Copyright © 1988 by TREK®.
"Star Trek: The Next Generation—Review and Commentary" by Walter Irwin. Copyright © 1988 by TREK®.
"Same Sexism, Different Generation" by Tom Lalli. Copyright © 1990 by TREK®.
"You Have the Conn: The Star Trek Video and Computer Games" by Dan Skelton. Copyright © 1990 by TREK®.

"The Men at the Helm: Captains Kirk and Hornblower" by Mark Alfred. Copyright © 1990 by TREK®.
"Walking the Decks of the Real Enterprise" by Sally Jerome. Copyright © 1991 by TREK®.
"The Disappearing Bum: A Look at Time Travel in Star Trek" by Jeff Mason. Copyright © 1991 by TREK®.
"Star Trek's Third Season: A Worthwhile Mixture of Success and Failure" by Gregory Herbek. Copyright © 1991 by TREK®.
"Uniforms" by Lieutenant David Crockett. Copyright © 1991 by TREK®.

Library of Congress Cataloging-in-Publication Data

The Best of the Best of Trek II / edited by Walter Irwin and G. B. Love.
    p.   cm.
  ISBN 0-451-45159-7
  1. Star Trek films—History and criticism. 2. Star trek
(Television program) 3. Science fiction, American—History and
criticism. I. Irwin, Walter. II. Love, G. B. III. Best of Trek.
PN1995.9.S694B44 1992
791.45'72—dc20

91-39731
CIP

REGISTERED TRADEMARK—MARCA REGISTRADA

PRINTED IN THE UNITED STATES OF AMERICA

Without limiting the rights under copyright reserved above, no part of this publication may be reproduced, stored in or introduced into a retrieval system, or transmitted, in any form, or by any means (electronic, mechanical, photocopying, recording, or otherwise), without the prior written permission of both the copyright owner and the above publisher of this book.

BOOKS ARE AVAILABLE AT QUANTITY DISCOUNTS WHEN USED TO PROMOTE PRODUCTS OR SERVICES. FOR INFORMATION PLEASE WRITE TO PREMIUM MARKETING DIVISION, PENGUIN BOOKS USA INC., 375 HUDSON STREET, NEW YORK, NEW YORK 10014.

THIS COLLECTION OF THE BEST OF THE BEST OF TREK IS RESPECTFULLY DEDICATED TO THE MEMORY OF GENE RODDENBERRY

As these words are written, it has been only one short week since the death of Gene Roddenberry. As are millions of *Star Trek* fans around the world, G. B. and I are shocked and saddened. Gene Roddenberry not only created *Star Trek*, he personified its ideas and ideals. He stood as a shining beacon of idealism, integrity and intelligence to every *Star Trek* fan, and, indeed, to many millions more who were not true fans but were nonetheless thrilled and inspired by his creation. Gene Roddenberry will be missed, but he will not be forgotten. The universe he created, the good that he did and—most importantly—the many lives he touched, and, in large or small measure, improved, will go on. Gene Roddenberry may no longer be with us, but *Star Trek* will assuredly live long and prosper.

CONTENTS

INTRODUCTION

Many months ago, when writing the introduction to *The Best of Best of Trek #1*, we commented that the collection was unprecedented—a collection culled from a series of collections—and we were a little bit leery of how it would be received. We shouldn't have worried. Thanks to our faithful readers and *Star Trek* fans the world over, that collection became one of the best-selling trade paperbacks of 1990.

For that, we thank you, our faithful readers. We also thank those of you who became new readers because of that first volume. We're awfully glad to have you aboard.

The fact that *The Best of Best of Trek #1* sold well didn't really surprise us; we've known for years that there are hundreds of thousands of literate, intelligent, thinking *Star Trek* fans out there who are hungry for information and opinion about the show that goes light-years beyond the typical fan-magazine flackery. We've been proud to offer that kind of fine, intelligent writing—and, lest we forget, fun writing—in *Trek Magazine* and our *Best of Trek* collections for more than fifteen years.

The response has always been, and continues to be, just marvelous. We've been privileged to communicate with *Star Trek* fans from every continent on Earth, and had the greater pleasure of meeting many of them in person. Best of all, many of them have become close friends. These friendships have evolved into areas and interests well beyond *Star Trek* and science fiction, enriching our lives and helping us to become better people.

Yet as enthralling as the response from our readers is, we never cease to be amazed at the variety and scope of articles submitted to us by our readers. To this day, we are amazed and astounded by the new things our readers can find to say about *Star Trek*. We personally have edited and published—by a very conservative count—more than *two million words* about *Star Trek*. And every single time we feel there is nothing new to say, nothing new to discover, nothing of note to write about, one of our readers sends us an article saying, "Well, what about *this?*" and all of a sudden it is all brand new and exciting again.

We spoke at length in the introduction to *The Best of Best of Trek #1* about the legendary status that *Star Trek* has achieved, and the fact that it is now such an ingrained part of our mythology and culture that it will live forever. But what we didn't speak of is the effect the show continues to have on even casual fans, an effect Gene Roddenberry wanted the show to have more than any other, an effect that makes Star Trek so unique, an effect, that, more than any other reason, may be why the series, in all its incarnations, remains so popular.

Star Trek makes you think.

It is that simple, friends. We see it almost every day: People of all ages, all levels of education, all backgrounds have something unique and individual to say about *Star Trek*. And why? Because it made them think. Think about the future, think about space, about themselves, about morality, about responsibility, about prejudice . . . think about everything.

That is why we continue, and will continue, to receive articles, letters and comments that amaze us with insights into *Star Trek* that never occurred to us, because somewhere out there, right now, *Star Trek* is making someone *think*. And in a small way, we've been privileged to be a part of that ongoing process, hopefully entertaining our readers along the way, but always striving to make them think.

We're pleased to present this second collection of articles from our ongoing *Best of Trek* series. We think you'll find these articles to be just as interesting, controversial, informative and enjoyable as those in the first collection. And if our writers make you think a little bit and you find one of those insights into our favorite show popping into your own head, why not share it with all of us?

In closing, we'd like to express our thanks to our longtime editor at ROC Books, John Silbersack, and his excellent staff. They do a great job and help us immensely. We'd also like to thank the many people who have helped us with research, loaned us books, videos and other materials, and contributed time and effort to making our editing the very best it could be. Thanks, too, to the many convention staffs who have been kind enough to have us as guests and attendees; the opportunity to meet our readers in person is always welcome.

Finally, let us once again give our most heartfelt thanks to the many writers, artists and fans who have ensured the success of our collections over the years through their wonderful contributions. In this instance, it is literally true to say, "We couldn't have done it without you!"

Walter Irwin
G. B. Love
December 1991

DIVERSITY IN COMBINATION

by Alan Manning

We sometimes feel that the philosophy of IDIC is bandied about among Star Trek fandom a little more freely than the concept warrants. Some fans do, however, give it the thought it deserves and ofttimes manage to develop concepts and theories which transcend the original idea. Such examination can be found in the following article, which wonders if the diversity which all too often seems to be lacking in Star Trek's stories is alive and well at the core of Star Trek's characterization.

"Infinite diversity in infinite combinations," or IDIC, is a prevalent motto and ideal in Star Trek fandom. Any individual aficionado of Star Trek had strong personal opinions about its meaning and typically constructs his or her own version of the imaginary universe implied by the series. Their common philosophical acceptance of frequently incompatible views developed by other, equally dedicated fans seems to keep them all from coming to blows with each other. In fact, IDIC may be keeping the peace between this minority and the general population, which considers such devotion to a television program frivolous.

On a higher plane, IDIC encourages diversity for its own sake, implying that contrasting opinions, life-styles, appearances, and so

1

forth are somehow beneficial rather than merely tolerable. It is generally agreed that this was a major message conveyed by the television series, "evidenced" by the racially integrated crew of the *Enterprise* and occasionally positive portrayals of alien creatures and cultures. However, there are visible limits to acceptable diversity; the *Enterprise*, through Kirk, is dominated by recognizably Anglo-American values, and a number of alien customs are changed by Kirk precisely because they violated those values. (See "The Apple," "Patterns of Force," "The Omega Glory," and "A Taste of Armageddon" for examples.)

While infinity is a highly useful concept in a mathematical system or as a philosophical ideal, in actual practice only limited variety and finite combinations shape our experience. By itself, the principle of infinite diversity in infinite combinations has no informative content; that means it allows any state of affairs, forbidding nothing, and experience is as much a matter of finding out *what is not* as it is a matter of seeing what is. Some may recall Spock's advice in "The Gamesters of Triskelion"—if you can't know where someone is, you may at least determine where he isn't. We may choose limitations ourselves, by picking specific qualities from a potentially infinite diversity; examination of all possible combinations of these qualities alone does tell us something: the number of unique combinations, and consequently, the characteristics of each combination due to the possession of certain qualities and the lack of others.

For example, let E represent the quality of *emotion* and L represent the quality of *logic*, our chosen bits of diversity. Since these are qualities and not quantities, it's pointless to use E or L more than once in a combination, and their order of appearance is arbitrary. This disallows combinations like EE or LLL; and EL is equivalent to LE. In the process of combination a quality can either be included or excluded; as was said, it is also important to know what is not, so a zero would indicate that a quality has been excluded. Under these conditions there are exactly four unique combination-entities: $EL, OL, EO,$ and $OO.$ The first entity has both *logic* and *emotion* at its disposal; the second, however, is only disposed to *logic*, and the third only to *emotion*. The fourth entity is the decimal zero, indispensable in mathematics for its place-holding value; it has no overt qualities and so the other three may obscure its importance, but it exists by logical necessity, as background; it is the slate, one might say, on which the next three entities are written.

Readers who have not, by now, begun to detect a familiar pattern in all this should turn in their phasers and have their pointed ears clipped.

Entities *EL*, *LO*, and *EO* clearly designate the most fundamental characteristics of Kirk, Spock, and McCoy respectively—these characters have been referred to countless times as the Three, the Triad, the Friendship, the distinct aspects of a Whole Man. If the world of Star Trek goes around, it is because they turn the crank. However, it is rightly said, and not often enough, that the *Enterprise* is also a character, indeed a key character in Star Trek. It is the background without which there would have been no story. As a piece of machinery, the *Enterprise* is neutral with respect to *emotion* or *logic*, and she is bound to the other three, as an entity complementary with logical and emotional Kirk, in a relationship unemotional and illogical: "I give—she takes. . . . No hand to hold; no beach to walk on," laments Kirk ("The *Enterprise* is a beautiful lady and we love her!" ("I, Mudd"). The fourth combination entity *OO* quite appropriately designates the *Enterprise*.

So, while IDIC in its unlimited sense fails at the level of plot (what with Kirk blasting computers, pulverizing perverse cultures, and quoting the U.S. Constitution), it succeeds at the level of characterization, in finite terms—two elements of diversity, *logic* and *emotion*, have exactly four possible combinations: one, the other, both, and neither. The inherent, complementary pattern of these combinations reflects to a striking degree of specificity the basic characterization pattern of Star Trek.

This diversity in combination produces a special kind of pattern known as a *paradigm* (pronounced PAR-a-dime), an ordered system generated by the combination of a finite number of principles. One paradigm readers are probably all too familiar with is the pattern of verb conjugation English teachers oblige us to learn: *I run, you run, he, she, it runs, we run, they run.* This paradigm has a logical gap where there is no special plural form for *you* as there is for *I* and *he* (*we* and *they*), but this lack tends to be repaired by the increasingly acceptable southernism *you all* or *y'all*. This demonstrates the natural tendency to fill all possible positions in a paradigm sooner or later. Once a paradigm is established, innovations which violate its boundaries are unpopular; things like *me runs* or *them run* are denounced as "ungrammatical."

Commenting on the early days of the series, the cast and creators of Star Trek seem to agree that the complex relationship between Kirk, Spock, and McCoy developed spontaneously, as if by magic, and once "the Big Three" were established it seemed impossible to produce an episode focusing on anyone else. It is as if the positions of a paradigm were spontaneously filled, and thereafter all real activity was limited to it. Structural oppositions in the pattern developed in the character; a bickering feud got started between Spock and McCoy, and Kirk began to manifest a troublesome pseudosexual attachment to the *Enterprise*. Events like these have been described and discussed in detail, but more often than not, no real *explanation* for them is ever offered. *Why* does Star Trek showcase three and only three of its regular cast? *Why* do Spock and McCoy oppose each other literally and symbolically? *Why* is Kirk romantically involved with 200,000 metric tons of metal and plastic? Why do we enjoy watching this so much, in rerun, year after year?

The hypothesis offered here would explain these and many other Star Trek phenomena as the inclination to match characters with a paradigm generated by specific qualities, in all possible combinations.

To continue, then, as the series developed there came to be four regular supporting cast members: Scotty, Uhura, Sulu, and finally Chekov. This would be the natural consequence of adding the quality of support to *logic* and *emotion*, making a total of three instances of diversity. The inclusion or exclusion of three qualities in combination yields 2^2, or eight unique entities: *OOO, EOO, OLO, ELO, ELS, OLS, EOS, OOS*. While this string of figures seems like some arcane religious chant, it is intended to represent the character types which naturally develop given those three themes. The first four designate the *Enterprise*, McCoy, Spock, and Kirk, as we have seen, with the added stipulation that they are non*support*, i.e., supported rather than supporting by nature. This does not mean the Three are incapable of lending a hand to those in need; Spock does show emotion now and then, and McCoy is not incapable of logical reasoning, so the Three occasionally help others out of a jam, too, but it is more typical for them to be helped by others to accomplish their own goals. Naturally, it is Edith Keeler who offers help to

Kirk ("The City on the Edge of Forever"), and Kirk who steals the scene by explaining the poetic significance of that gesture to her.

For Scotty, Uhura, Sulu, and Chekov, all of life's meaning lies in supporting the *Enterprise* and the Three. It seems certain that *ELS* designates Scotty. Of all the supporting cast, this character is the most completely developed. His expertise in techno*logical* matters equals that of Spock, and yet Scotty is quite an emotional character, particularly where the *Enterprise* is concerned. This is expected because *ELS* and *OOO* are paradigmatic complements, each possessing features missing in the other. The old adage that opposites attract is exploited here, just as it is in the relation between Kirk (*ELO*) and the *Enterprise* (*OOO*) at a different, non-support level. Scotty's love for the *Enterprise* is supportive, while that of Kirk is not. That is why she is Kirk's "lover" and Scotty's "baby." Complementary difference between *EOO* and *OLO* (McCoy and Spock) is exploited another way; opposites attract but they also argue a lot.

While indications that Scotty matches up with *ELS* are strong, the correspondence between *EOS*, *OLS*, and *OOS* and Sulu, Uhura, and Chekov seems harder to establish. Throughout the series they are either being upstaged by the Three or they are so busy doing their jobs that their personalities never really develop. This problem solves itself because the jobs come to match those paradigmatic types instead; what these characters do to support the others becomes more important than who they are.

Like Scotty, the communications officer holds a technological position (stress *logical* again) and works with intricate codes and complex equipment. This post also demands the single-minded ability to send messages as they are given, without personal or emotional coloring. *OLS* is probably best matched by Uhura.

The position of helmsman surely requires a special "feel" for the ship in order to execute often delicate maneuvers successfully. Such sensitivity might qualify as an emotion, at least in an extended metaphor relating control of the ship's motion to e-*motion*. The helmsman should take no time to consider the logic of any action. His job is to carry out the captain's orders to move, quickly and accurately. *EOS* designates that position, usually held by Sulu.

This leaves Chekov with the role of just plain *support* (*OOS*), nature unspecified. In the episodes before Chekov was added, this paradigmatic position was probably held by Yeoman Rand, and in her absence it could be filled by assorted crewmen such as Lieutenant Riley. These are characters-at-large, with flexible duties: some days the navigator, some days the assistant science officer, some days part of a landing party, some days toting papers for Kirk to sign. *And* when the script calls for someone to be poisoned (Riley, "The Conscience of the King"), someone to be accosted by strangers (Rand, "The Man Trap," "Charlie X"), someone to be thrown into the agonizer booth (Chekov, "Mirror, Mirror") or shot ("Spectre of the Gun") or frightened ("The Deadly Years") or burned (*Star Trek: The Motion Picture*), this character type is the favorite victim. Chekov seems to fill the role best; as David Gerrold points out (*The World of Star Trek*), he has a great way of screaming.

Given the typology of their duties, Uhura (logic-support), Sulu (emotion-support), and Chekov (unqualified support) could be expected to manifest those traits in their personalities, should these ever be developed. Vonda McIntyre's "Hikaru" Sulu is surely a romantic character in her Star Trek novelizations. A bit of this also appears in Joyce Tullock's comments about *Star Trek III: The Search for Spock* "There is Sulu, the dashing, sexy swashbuckler. . . . There is Uhura, with her warmth, beauty and elegant presence of mind. Here is a dignity which rivals even that of Mr. Spock. . . . Mr. Chekov . . . seems to be the most clearheaded of the crew, in fact, lacking both Scott's rebel cynicism and Sulu's passion for adventure . . . (*Best of Trek #8*).

Majel Barrett fans may perceive a flaw in the hypothesized paradigm because it fails to provide a position for or explain the character of Nurse Chapel, but in fact her lack of "fit" in the eight-member paradigm explains why she is not used in the later Star Trek films. If she matches any type it is *EOO*, as a feminized version of McCoy, complementary and therefore attracted to Spock. Significantly, it is she who temporarily carries Spock's *katra*, consciousness, soul, or whatever, in the episode "That Which Survives," foreshadowing McCoy's service in *The Search for Spock*. Figuratively, these *EOO* characters have room for Spock's *OLO* in their persona; together they briefly make a whole *ELO* being. But in the end, Chapel is not the real McCoy, as it were; when the true Spock/McCoy relationship is portrayed, her role is superfluous.

Because the three-quality paradigm generates exactly eight positions, the number of characters that can be included in the "family group" is eight, counting the *Enterprise*. Guest stars, as aliens, bad guys, love affairs, etc., are no problem, because they come and go, interacting but not intruding upon the *Enterprise* family. With the advent of Star Trek cinema, however, new characters appeared with evident intentions of joining the family. Even Gene Roddenberry must have thought this would work; David Gerrold notes that Decker and Ilia both were first created as regular characters for a new Star Trek television series, but as the script for the aborted series evolved into a feature film, Decker and Ilia were sacrificed to V'Ger and the nth dimension. Harve Bennett then took creative control of Star Trek, and marched out his new generation of characters, Saavik (apprentice-Vulcan) and David Marcus (son-of-Kirk). In *Star Trek II: The Wrath of Khan*, Saavik is acceptable, but David is clearly excess baggage. In *The Search for Spock*, Klingons get to kill David, while rookie actress Robin Curtis never lets her performance of Saavik live.

This all does not mean that characters cannot be added to Star Trek successfully; it does mean that new players cannot be stuck on the old paradigm with thumbtacks, glue, and good intentions. Arangements must be made and prices must be paid.

Star Trek II: The Wrath of Khan pays a price for Saavik which makes her acceptable; Chekov is transferred to the *Reliant* crew, then Saavik, not he, holds the *OOS* position aboard the *Enterprise*. Complementary relations between *ELO* and *OOS* sustain the chemistry between Kirk and Saavik, evidenced by their verbal fencing, just short of being openly flirtatious. Saavik is here the support-character-at-large; she is the apprentice commander, the navigator, landing party member. She gets all the jobs Chekov had, except screaming.

Saavik can take a few liberties here with her ostensible Vulcan background—a little aggression here, a few tears there—because the paradigm only stipulates her *support* quality. Her Vulcan nature is as incidental as Chekov's Russian accent—both interesting, but flawed on several points. Perhaps if Spock had stayed properly dead she might have moved to *OLO* and might have been paid Leonard Nimoy's salary too, thereby inducing Kirstie Alley to keep the role. But in that case Saavik would have to clean up her Vulcan act.

Chekov suffers greatly in the trade to *Reliant*, but Walter Koenig benefits as an actor. As victim-of-Khan he garnered more on-screen time than Sulu and Uhura combined; sometimes it pays to escape the paradigm, but when it comes to long-term survival, there is safety in being numbered among the Eight. *The Search for Spock* returns Chekov to his original support role, and the price for that arrangement is Saavik. It could easily have been Chekov, as senior surviving officer of the *Reliant* (survey ship for the Genesis Project), assigned to explore the Genesis Planet with David Marcus, where they could have had a revealing discussion about the proper role of the military in scientific research. But Chekov was returned to the fold, and Saavik was thrown to the Klingons.

On Genesis, Harve Bennett gathered together all the problem-characters he created in *Wrath of Khan*: the planet itself, Spock's animate corpse, Saavik, and David Marcus. David was doomed from the start. Besides having no place on the *Enterprise*, the script forced him to be a distasteful boob. In fairness to his creators, it is conceivable that he could have evolved as Luke Skywalker did, from fool to hero, but *Star Wars* was structured *a priori* to accommodate such a character; Star Trek was only structured *ex post facto* to dispose of him. On Genesis there were two forces at work, *aging* and *death*. The planet itself ages rapidly and dies. The body of Spock ages rapidly from its regenerated youth along with the planet, but is rescued and lives. Saavik does not age and lives—*AD, AO, OD, OO*—creating another paradigm does make a place for these characters, but it is doomed from the start to dismantle itself.

In some respects, that is also the way the extra characters for *Star Trek: The Motion Picture* neatly remove themselves from the continuing adventure. Decker, Ilia, and V'Ger form a separate group corresponding with the same *EL, EO, OL, OO* pattern which formed Kirk, McCoy, and Spock, with the *Enterprise* as *OO* background for both groups. Decker, Ilia, and V'Ger fuse into a single superbeing; all identical qualities are the same quality, so *ELEOOL* equals *EOLO*, which suggests that both qualities are included and excluded at once. To resolve this paradox the superbeing vanishes into another dimension, leaving the *Enterprise* to its old crew.

Perversely, Saavik is left to the old crew at the end of *The Search for Spock* and the *Enterprise* perishes. This just barely seems a fair trade because a restored Spock is produced in the bargain. Incredibly, after all the action, explosions, deaths, and reshuffling of characters, the paradigm endures. Exactly eight continuing characters remain when the dust settles: Spock, Kirk, McCoy, Saavik, Scotty, Uhura, Sulu, and Chekov. After death, confinement in McCoy's persona, and refusion in his physical body, it is doubtful that Spock is still his former nonemotional, merely logical self. This leaves his former paradigmatic position, non-*emotion*, *logic*, non-*support*, available to someone else. A painfully obvious candidate is Saavik. If few fans liked Robin Curtis's cold portrayal of her, it is because she matched that paradigmatic type too well and *too soon*. Contrasted with Kirstie Alley's warmer, almost seductive *OOS* version of Saavik, Robin Curtis was so cold she made our teeth ache. This leads to a major blunder because her main role in *The Search for Spock* was *OO* in the Genesis paradigm. In contrast to the aging, dying world around her, Saavik should have been shown fighting actively, even passionately, to sustain her youthful attitude and her life; in this context, a textbook Vulcan, wisdom-of-the-ages approach was as wrong as it could be. Failure to match the right paradigm at the right time has cost this character its original popularity and maybe its future.

To fill the *OLO* position, Saavik might get another chance in the future film(s), but there is at least one attractive alternative. The character of Sarek, nicely re-created by Mark Lenard, could be taken up as a continuing character instead; in a vicarious sense, Sarek keeps Spock's old position filled all through *The Search for Spock* by pointing out to Kirk that Spock's soul is still lurking about. As Spock's father, Sarek is a well-established fixture in the Star Trek universe, and hence a more reliable choice than Saavik.

In any case, Saavik, or Sarek, or someone like them, is necessary for the immediate future because Spock has been promoted to *OOO*, the center or background position formerly held by the *Enterprise*. At the end of *The Search for Spock*, Sarek explicitly informs the audience that Kirk's ship was the price of Spock's return. A curious exchange of fates has taken place: Spock's battered remains fall like a meteor into the atmosphere of Genesis in *Wrath of Khan*, and in *The Search for Spock*, the burning wreck of the *Enterprise* streaks across the Genesis sky. Spock is rescued from his fate, but the *Enterprise* is left to hers.

By definition, there cannot be a star trek without some vehicle to travel between stars, so the erstwhile crew of the *Enterprise* must board another starship in order to continue the adventure. Even so, there may never be an *Enterprise II* or any other ship which is also a real character, Kirk's lover and Scotty's "baby." By willfully discarding the *Enterprise* in exchange for Spock, Kirk and Scotty abandoned that disproportionate affection for a material object; to restore it would be a step backward.

Instead, Spock assumes the paradigmatic position *OOO*, which is a convenient pattern for someone recently resurrected to match. There is now as much freedom to redefine Spock's character as there was to redesign the *Enterprise* sets for the Star Trek films. It will also be convenient for Leonard Nimoy, as director of coming films, literally in the background of every scene shot, to play a role which is now figuratively the backdrop of all other main characters in Star Trek.

This outcome of *The Search for Spock* is so convenient for Mr. Nimoy that some might wonder if he planned it that way. We can imagine Nimoy and Bennett plotting together in some dark corner of a Paramount sound stage to assassinate the *Enterprise* and place Spock on the throne. . . . Besides bordering on paranoia, such a scenario ascribes to the conspirators more explicit knowledge of the internal workings of Star Trek than they probably have. In order to succeed, real plotting demands a working knowledge of cause-and-effect rules which operate in the situation being manipulated. These imagined conspirators are the same people who brought us David Marcus and derailed the character of Saavik. How much can they possibly know?

In reality, Star Trek is an art form, and all the people who bring it to the screen are artists, usually just doing the best they can. When a creative decision is made, it is because it "feels right," "looks good," or "sounds like it will work." A sequence of these subjective, noncalculated decisions has directed the evolution of the world of Star Trek to its present point. Paradoxically, the whole purpose of this essay has been to demonstrate a Star Trek paradigm, a tightly organized pattern which dictates the acceptable number of regular characters, the typical qualities each should have, and the complementary associations between them. It would be a good bet that your average writer/producer/director would not realize that such a paradigm even exists in Star Trek. How can such a pattern be used and how can it survive, without the conscious control of its creators?

This phenomenon, while puzzling, is not without precedent. Children learn to use all major components of their native language long before they can be taught any explicit rules of grammar in school, which are rarely learned anyway. People who hear an ungrammatical sentence are more likely to spot it because it "sounds bad," not because they recognize that any rule has been violated. Conversely, they recognize a grammatical sentence because it "sounds okay." Knowledge of language is so basic that we have access to it without being aware of it, and we can learn a language (at least when children) by simply being exposed to it, rather than by laboriously learning the explicit rules. The Star Trek paradigm can be seen as the explicit form of a *paralanguage*, a symbolic structure having qualities similar to a real language (just as a *paramedic* is something like a real doctor, but not quite the same). Like children exposed to a language, people who watch Star Trek episodes long enough begin to sense the typical paradigmatic roles of the characters without being consciously aware of what they are. Some people are more adept at learning new languages than others; so too, the degree to which some people are deeply moved by Star Trek and find meaning in it, while others find it bizarre and insignificant, may be in keeping with their natural ability to learn the paralanguage associated with it. A question: Do Trekkers score higher on language aptitude tests than the general population?

Those who do come to understand Star Trek can detect instances when the proposed paradigm is not being correctly matched in an episode or film because "it feels wrong" at certain points. On the production side, those with creative control over the series make decisions about what the characters will do and say based on what "feels right." Their subjective judgment is hopefully also guided by the same paralanguage, learned by watching precious episodes or reading the series guidelines. If there is anything a fan fears or hates, it is a television episode or film "mutilated by someone who doesn't understand Star Trek," i.e., someone who hasn't learned the paralanguage well enough to be guided by it. Of course, even the most literate among us occasionally make grammatical errors, slips really, with language, that we don't detect until we've said them, so even reasonably experienced people like Roddenberry, Nimoy, and Bennett may try something which isn't an obvious mistake until it's on the screen in the final cut, too late to be fixed. In learning to recognize and produce acceptable forms of a paralanguage, Star Trek filmmakers come to obey constraints of its paradigmic structure without explicit knowledge of it; if they make occasional errors, it is fortunately true that these can be recognized and corrected later, just as long as there is another Star Trek movie in the works.

It was explained at the outset that the Star Trek paradigm originates from a finite application of IDIC, which in itself may explain the popularity of that expression among Star Trek devotees. It happens that diversity in combination is a highly efficient method of generating character types. In television and film, efficiency is always a must, because of time limitations. While a novelist can take hundreds of pages to establish characters and plot, screenwriters have to tell their whole story, with believable characters, they hope, in an hour or two, with a handful of scenes and a limited budget. More characters means less time devoted to plot only, and less time to make each person real to the viewer. Not surprisingly, more programs fail in this balancing act than succeed. But if all characters are variation on the same qualities, then to develop each is to develop them all, directly, by similarity or indirectly, by complementarity.

Consider, for example, the original Spock, unemotional and logical. Time spent illustrating his logical behavior onscreen is also time spent illuminating the logical qualities of Kirk (ELO) and the logical duties of Scotty and Uhura (ELS, OLS). Spock's unemotional behavior establishes the emotional nature of Kirk, McCoy, etc., by contrast. In like manner, portrayal of any and all members of the paradigm reinforces the features they possess in all the others as well. Most of the character development thus takes place in our minds by association, and only a small fraction one-eighth to be exact, is physically manifest on camera. Because the developmental potential for each character is multiplied eight-fold in this manner, it is small wonder that the Star Trek characters become very much alive to those who understand the paralanguage best, the ranks of Star Trek fandom.

A bare handful of syndicated television programs enjoy a level of economic success comparable to that of Star Trek. For some reason, people find these programs watchable even after years in rerun. It is enlightening to count the number of main characters in some of these:

Bewitched—Samantha, Darrin, Endora, Larry Tate . . . 4
I Dream of Jeannie—Tony, Roger, Jeannie, Colonel Bellows . . . 4

I Love Lucy—Lucy, Ricky, Fred, Ethel . . . 4

Gilligan's Island—*Gilligan, Skipper, Mr. Howell, Mrs. Howell, Ginger, Professor, Mary Ann, the island . . . 8.*

These are precisely the number of characters that would match two- and three-quality paradigms $(2^2, 2^3)$. Each of these programs has identifiable theme qualities which will generate patterns that do match its characters quite well. Identification and elaboration of these will fill many more essays; readers wanting intellectual exercise may tackle these themselves.

Diversity in combinations is such an effective characterization strategy that those few programs which are lucky enough to chance upon it should have much greater chances of survival, in syndication if not on prime time. Evidently, characters which are so developed that they seem real are enjoyable to watch, even when the outcome of the episode is well known, as if a *historical event* were being experienced directly, and not the nth repetition of a mere story.

So long as the producers of those cultural artifacts we call entertainment are not consciously aware of IDIC and paradigms, the phenomena described here can work to their advantage only if it all develops spontaneously; but in theory, one could deliberately pick qualities, generate a paradigm, and match characters to it before shooting a foot of film. If this ever becomes standard practice, we may get better programs, and IDIC will have become a first principle of *cultural* engineering, just as Newton's $F = ma$ is a first principle of mechanical engineering. Should that happen, I hope people remember they heard it here first. Nowhere is IDIC and the paradigm principle of characterization more clearly revealed than by the *Enterprise* and her crew—one more discovery made on their epic journey.

THE BRILLIANT DOOR

by Joyce Tullock

Joyce Tullock was one of the few regular Trek *writers that we asked to comment on her personal feelings about Star Trek's twentieth anniversary. She was among the very few to agree—very reluctantly—to do so.*

Apparently, discussing one's innermost feelings about Star Trek was just too difficult a task for most. And as you read the following article, you'll realize that it was difficult for Joyce as well. Trouper that she is, however, she came through—dare we say?—brilliantly.

Back in the third grade, I had to write an essay on the first day of school. It was supposed to be about "what I did on my summer vacation." It was very hard for me to say anything. Not that a lot didn't happen during summer vacation, it's just that the stuff you remember, that really, really is important to you . . . well, it's personal, even to a third-grader.

That kind of thing never changes, so when, for the one and only time I sat down and tried to write a personal account of Star Trek's influence on me, I just got stuck. And kind of angry at a certain someone for even suggesting I do so. I got defensive. After all, it's nobody's damn business what Star Trek means to me. Don't I write about the series enough anyway? Can't people get the point of what I'm thinking?

Anger, as Dr. McCoy might point out, can be a useful tool. If you apply a Spockian logic to it, that is. And so it is that I have found a starting point for my little article.

First and foremost, it seems, Star Trek has always been a very personal experience for me. As personal as my social security number, bank balance, and shoe size. I don't care to flaunt my feelings about it to just anyone. They might misinterpret them. Sometimes I think even *I* misinterpret them. And it seems pretty obvious that the anger I feel about having to talk about it means that Star Trek must have had a greater effect on my life than I'd like to admit. After all, I've spent a good deal of time these past years trying to express what it is that I see in Star Trek. One might ask: "Why?"

I could get real defensive here. I could tell you about all the people I know who have revealed themselves to me, telling me how Spock has influenced, even changed, their lives. Yes, I could just tell on everybody else. It would be easy, and fun. But it would not be accurate. I would not have the whole story, only bits and pieces friends and acquaintances and casual readers have given me.

Not that Star Trek ever taught me honesty and journalistic integrity. There are too many episodes where Star Trek's scientific credibility, for example, does not want to be examined closely. And even moral judgment is left in question from time to time, for it seems as though Captain Kirk is all too ready to impose the WASP-ish Western ways of our society on alien planets. Not that I blame him particularly. I'm as blind as he is about some things. I would never presume to outguess or outjudge the noble Jim Kirk. He is a hero of grand stature. I always marvel at the way he handles so many impossible situations and questions and world-wrenching problems with such grace and adroitness. I've always wondered how he did that, and have never been able to imagine myself handling life so well.

Maybe I've always been a little jealous of Jim Kirk. And if that doesn't give you a hint about what Star Trek means to me, I feel very sorry for you indeed.

Spock, on the other hand, has always been a character I could grapple with. I've always liked his type. Even when his type was Michael Rennie in *The Day the Earth Stood Still*. Now I realize that the good Vulcan is many things to many people, and I don't want to step on toes. But to me, he is . . . oh, what do you call it? . . . *Future*. I've heard him referred to as an emotional idiot. But those remarks don't come from anyone who has studied the series. You have to take time to know Star Trek, after all, just like anything else. You have to learn to know Spock, for after twenty years, he is quite real. And in the context of Star Trek and the Universe it contains—with a Vulcan race which decided on peace over passion and war thousands of years before Spock was born—Spock must be seen as an alien. He must be seen as one who does not follow the "rules" as we know them, and as we demand they be followed in our world. To many people, I suppose, Spock must seem offensive, hence the label "emotional idiot." All because he's an alien. You know, I think I like Spock because of that. Because of his being "alien," I mean. I have been an alien all my life.

Now are we getting personal?

It's all right, though. A lot of people I know are alien. Some are my friends and some are not, but at least we all have that much in common. I bet Mr. Spock would be pleased at something in that statement. After all, look at the fellow: In the series he's a lone alien aboard the *Enterprise*, trying to make do with the likes of Jim Kirk and Leonard McCoy for friends. Now we all know that Jim Kirk, while being a Terran, with many of our rutty Terran ways, somehow has become such a special man, such a diplomat, that, socially speaking, he pretty much passes the Vulcan test for good manners and propriety. Yes, Jim's been around, and maybe, just maybe, I'm a little jealous of that too.

But Spock's other friend, Dr. Leonard McCoy . . . well, he isn't the kind of guy you would expect to see at your average Vulcan social affair. I've said it before, in other articles, but this is my one and only time of being personal so I just have to say it again: I like McCoy because I can relate to him as a real, honest-to-goodness human being. Of the three, his character is the most complete, the most believable, the most "for real." The irony of it being that understanding McCoy takes more work. That statement sounds illogical, but it's true, and I'm sure McCoy would be more than happy to back me up on it.

McCoy is embarrassingly human. Overall, he's a nuisance, and generally annoying. He suffers from foot-in-mouth disease. He is humanitarian in principle, sometimes hypocritical in deed, and forever trying to reconcile the two. He likes people, but he wishes they'd leave him alone. In other words, he's the kind of man who'd love to be a hermit—if only he weren't so busy with humanity.

Leonard is mixed up, and like Spock, he is alien. He is Spock's psychological negative. That is, Spock seems to be an individual with direction, discipline, a sense of future. McCoy, on the other hand, is a tad chaotic. The universe is not all mapped out before him, described in the language of physics and mathematics. One would guess that McCoy had to work really hard to be satisfactorily good at math. To be honest, though, it's just something I like to imagine: that McCoy isn't good at math. It isn't necessarily so.

And if Spock gives me a sense of future, then McCoy gives me a sense of *Past*, But hold on, 'cause this is where the science fiction comes in and ties Spock and McCoy together in the kind of literary symbiosis I love—the past McCoy represents is our present. I like that, because it makes Star Trek more real to me. It's like the hub at the center, the quiet spot, the recognizable, where I can sit and watch through McCoy's eyes as the future happens all around me. I don't think it's going too far to say that I bet a lot of people view Star Trek the same way, whether they are consciously aware of it or not. I don't think you can really help it.

And the fact that McCoy is there too, in that beautiful future, with Spock and Kirk, makes me hope that something of the kind of person I am will make it to a better future, somehow. That's a very selfish feeling, and it is personal.

I remember how things were in the sixties when Star Trek made its first public appearance. Not to reminisce, but we'd been through one hell of a decade. We'd lost a young president who'd promised us a future, and we'd lost others, valuable people who had actually stood for ideals. All of us who were old enough were in a trauma in those days. No kidding, it really was a time when you would sit down to dinner with the TV on and watch young Americans and Vietnamese die. People talk about the young people of the sixties, with their flower songs and peace movements, as being unrealistic, escapists. I don't think anyone, young or old, was escaping in those days; we were all on a pilgrimage, looking for the Holy Grail. And we probably knew more about reality than any generation since Hiroshima.

We were definitely looking for something, and it's no accident that a lot of the things we were looking for popped up in a daring new series called *Star Trek*. For one thing, it was clear that in Star Trek, our own painful, complicated time was history. That is, we had made it through the nuclear age. But we'd been through some nasty times, as characters like Khan of "Space Seed" and Colonel Green of "Savage Curtain" reminded us. These fellows represented everything civilized man has always tried to rise above: racism, fascism, tyranny, cruelty. And in Star Trek, it seemed pretty evident that the men of planet Earth *had* risen above those things—for the most part, anyway. How refreshing it is to learn from Dr. Marcus in *Wrath of Khan* that the Fleet had preserved the peace for one hundred years. Just think of it!

Some fans refuse to accept the movies as genuine Star Trek, by the way. They have all different kinds of reasons, too—from Kirk being too "imperfect" (huh?) to Spock's death and resurrection being too contrived, too "Hollywood," if you will. Well, I don't blame anyone for complaining from time to time, but I can't agree with this authenticity thing. Although sometimes I'd like to. Like everyone else, I sometimes forget that Star Trek is not my own personal property. That's why Paramount has a hard time with people like me.

That's also why Star Trek is still around.

From the time the series was canceled it has been a comedy of errors. Bjo Trimble spearheaded the movement to save it, but some people think we might almost be better off if we'd been left without that last season. I'm not one of them. There were some dogs in the last season, but there were some gems, too. It was worth the pain.

The people who gathered behind Star Trek, seeking to keep it alive in their own writing, if necessary, have become sort of legend to the Trekkers. In the early days of Star Trek fanzines, for example, there was some fantastic talent. Connie Faddis of *Interphase*, for one. She set the pace for the zines we see today.

Of course, that was then and this is now. Since the time of *Interphase* a whole new generation of fans has turned up—and this is not a generation that has to do with age, but with tastes, with talent, with what they see in Star Trek. Fans write more about inner feelings than did the early writers—although there were some fine, introspective writers in the early days as well. But now fan writers, always trying for something different, tend to examine the characters as people, not so much as heroes. It makes it much more difficult to write the relationships and keep them in character. Even Paramount is trying it, giving us a Kirk who makes personal and judgmental errors. A Kirk who is growing old, facing the pain of separation from the people and things he loves. The fallibility and maturity of the man in all three movies is refreshing and wise. Paramount is to be commended. It is to be even more commended for *finally* allowing the other characters to have some time with the audience. Paramount had to learn the hard way, but the last two movies have proved that Star Trek is more than Jim Kirk or any one of the characters.

Unlike Paramount, however, fan writers have known that all along. They *know* Star Trek, and usually work hard at making the science in their material at least marginally credible. The serious writers really work hard, on both the amateur and professional levels. Maybe Star Trek isn't "growing up," but it is certainly growing. While the fan novels still beat out the pros in character development, character relationship, and true "Star Trek feel," we've seen some good professional novels in the last few years, like Howard Weinstein's *Covenant and the Crown* and Diane Duane's *Wounded Sky*. These stories are the genuine article, true Star Trek. No more perfect than the episodes or movies or fan stories, but filled with the warmth and the wonder, just the same.

But an indication of how much Star Trek is growing up is seen most clearly in the works of the fans themselves. Bev Zuk's novels, *Honorable Sacrifice* and *The Final Verdict*, absolutely shine. She treats her subjects with maturity, clarity, and professional prose style. And Laurie Huff of *Galactic Discourse* edits a zine that rivals *Interphase*. She has a gift of putting graphics, story, and artwork together in such a way as to make a zine that is, of itself, a work of art. These people care about Star Trek, and it shows in their work. It is not a living to them, but a nonprofit hobby. No, that's not right, either. To these people, the appreciation of Star Trek is an art. Maybe that makes them and their kind the truest writers of all.

But what makes us do it? That's the real question. Star Trek fans, the creative ones anyway, seem driven to go about a virtually thankless, profitless task. Why?

I think the answer takes us back to that personal stuff I mentioned earlier. You know—the topic of this article, which I so slitheringly avoided. Star Trek is personal. And for those who write and draw and edit it, it is frighteningly so. Because when you write, when you create with pen and ink, you have to call up things inside. When you're creating, it doesn't matter if you're professional or amateur, you're using personal things—some happy, some painful.

On some level, you're discussing and defining things you never knew before about yourself and the world as you see it. And speaking about such personal matters so openly can prove quite dangerous. But that's the point, I suppose: Star Trek works particularly hard on creative people, and draws from them, challenging them to define what it is they see in this world of the future, how they apply it to the world of today. Even the most cynical creative fan knows—when you write, draw, paint, or edit Star Trek you are, on some level, in search of that Holy Grail.

For me, the Star Trek experience has been remarkably rewarding. It helped me come to terms with my own view of the universe. And yes, I'll admit it, with my own view of myself. I've learned, for example, that I've never, ever been able to see the universe around me in black and white. I've learned to live with that and appreciate it. That's gotten me in trouble a time or two, though. For example, I've had people complain that I am an atheist because of my remarks in the *Best of Trek* article "Bridging the Gap." To them I would say, "Read it again, and tell me who is the atheist and who is the believer." I enjoy writing articles like that one, because they allow me to express openly the way I see the world. In analyzing the series, I discovered a lot that surprised me about myself, about Star Trek and science fiction, and about our own society.

I have had to pick the episodes and characters apart sometimes, and in doing so, have found bits of my own personality. It's a very rewarding thing, very exciting, very frightening. So I guess you could say Star Trek has helped me to understand my own perspective. If I learned anything else in watching Star Trek, I learned to give as much attention and respect to my own view as I do to anyone else's. And more important, I've learned that the best way to expand my point of view is to listen to others.

The feelings evoked in and by Star Trek are deep, mysterious. No wonder some think of it as cultist, for there is no good bread-and-butter, black-and-white way to describe to an outsider what Star Trek means to those who number themselves among its fans. It has a lot to do with the mysterious, surrealistic magic of science fiction, of course. And with the powerful literary presence of such ideas as isolation, alienness, of hope for the future, of the imperativeness of human brotherhood. Then, of course, there are the deep, virtually endless meanings found in the trial friendship of the unified personality of Spock, Kirk, and McCoy.

It's the triad that stands out most in my mind. It's the triad, I would venture to guess, that is at the core of the very "personal" nature of Star Trek. Kirk, Spock, and McCoy are the point of center from which I can view a world of imagination. A world that is as alien or as twentieth-century as I care to see it. They are the key, or more correctly, the equation of Kirk, Spock, and McCoy is the key. It is not so much the men, but the relationship they have to one another and their world. It wouldn't have to be a Kirk, or a Spock, or a McCoy—it just happens to be so. It is their part in the equation: the outgoing human spirit of Kirk, the sensible, controlled logic of Mr. Spock, the warm, positively irrational emotions of McCoy. They are us, bits of us, altogether.

Spock and McCoy, with their ongoing battle of emotion versus logic, past versus future, impulsiveness versus stoicism, and on and on and on . . . they are indeed bits of me. They present a challenge for the writer, for in writing them, in understanding them, one must dig deep. For myself, and for many others I know, these characters have opened a brilliant door.

And if I cannot tell you what it means to me, I will tell you what it means to you: Look in the mirror.

BOOTS AND STARSHIPS

by Walter Irwin

There's seldom any problem getting Walter to the keyboard—the problem's more often getting him away!—but in this instance, for once, he proved reluctant. Like many others, he was loath to discuss his personal feelings about Star Trek, feeling that his already published articles and features were more than sufficient. But canny G.B. pointed out that maybe not everyone on earth had had the privilege of being thrilled by Walter's previous writings; more seriously, each volume attracts new readers who've never seen any of the earlier ones. So didn't Walter owe them something, too?

By the time our readers see this volume, it will be 1986 and close upon the twentieth anniversary of Star Trek. A twentieth anniversary is a good time to look back, to take stock, to ask questions and seek answers. Several articles in this volume discuss "What Star Trek Means to Me"; this is supposed to be one of them.

Instead, I'm going to present to you a speech I made at Deltacon in Baton Rouge, Louisiana, last September. The speech is not about my feelings about Star Trek; it is, however, about the way in which I see Star Trek, a view which is unique unto me, and a view which probably says more about me than I could ever say otherwise. I'll also have a few things to say afterward.

By his own admission, Gene Roddenberry's original concept of Star Trek was based, in part, on the Horatio Hornblower series by C. S. Forester.

The image of the seafarer, the explorer, is a powerful one, which has been used to good effect in the legends and fiction of many cultures. From Odysseus to Ahab, the stories of men who cannot resist the lure of the sea are part and parcel of humanity.

Forester, when creating Hornblower, used this tradition to the utmost. His captain is all of the things we expect our heroes to be: courageous, self-sufficient, loyal, handsome, compassionate, steadfast, and just the tiniest bit flawed. The Hornblower stories are also set in that most romantic of seafaring times, the era in which England was stretching her colonial arms around the world, building an empire upon which the sun would never set. It was a time when men set forth upon tiny wooden ships, braving the elements and enemies on every side, simply for God and country. And maybe just a smattering of Adventure.

The Hornblower books, well written and exciting, sold in the millions. By the time that Roddenberry was planning Star Trek, the Hornblower series was an institution, virtually a template from which any seafaring series dared not stray too far.

Roddenberry had no intention of doing so. He envisioned his captain as being firmly in the Hornblower mold. The parallels were nothing if not obvious: a captain in charge of a vessel, weeks, even months removed from contact with his government, required to act as diplomat, governor, general, despot as the occasion arose, an explorer who also served as ambassador of his culture and arbiter of others, and a natural leader of men, but humanized by a dollop of hubris, ambition, and the occasional doubt.

It was around this familiar and romantic theme that Roddenberry built his series. Star Trek wasn't to be "Wagon Train in Space"; it was to be "Hornblower Explores the Stars."

But somewhere along the way, something went wrong.

In each of the early Star Trek episodes, we see a little bit more of this concept lost. The introduction of faster-than-the-ship subspace radio, the establishment of an entire fleet of starships, all seemingly within the same area of space, and mostly the introduction of Starbases and the consequent command structure.

The focus of the "commander alone" concept was first watered down, then completely abandoned. The long tentacles of Starfleet Command reached farther and farther out into space, until it seemed that in many episodes, Captain Kirk and his crew went home every night for dinner.

Thus, the concept became quite something else in execution. Instead of the intrepid explorer, Captain Kirk became a soldier, a keeper of the peace, a patroller of borders and neutral zones.

In short, the *Enterprise* became part of the cavalry. The myth of the seafaring man was exchanged for the equally powerful, and, to American audiences, more familiar, myth of the horse soldier.

Portions of the United States Army, divided into groups of officers and men designated (and numbered) as cavalry, patrolled the American West from after the Civil War until during (and shortly after) the First World War. Their duties included aiding and protecting settlers, enforcing borders, tracking down and punishing marauders, limited exploration and mapping, diplomacy and treaty-making, and law enforcement in the absence of federal marshals. The cavalry operated out of a series of forts established along, and sometimes beyond, territorial borders. The ongoing settlement of western lands, the building of railroads, and the continual expansion of telegraph lines allowed officers to keep in touch with their superiors in Washington.

This era has become part of our folklore. The sound of "Charge" blown on a bugle is known by every schoolchild; the name Custer is synonymous with both incredible bravery and incredible stupidity; when one hears the word "fort" an image of upright log walls and attacking Indians immediately springs to mind.

Although there is enough truth in the annals of the cavalry to supply any television series with material for several seasons, most of our enduring images of the cavalry have come from fiction. Thanks to the stories of writers such as James Warner Bellah, who wrote, among many others, the stories on which the John Wayne movies *She Wore a Yellow Ribbon*, *Fort Apache*, and *Rio Grande* were based, and Ernest Haycox, to name only two, we get a glimpse of what life as a dollar-a-day man in the cavalry was really like. Many other writers, some equally fine, most just hacks, have contributed to the legends. Most persuasive, however, have been the innumerable movies and television shows featuring the cavalry. It is safe to say that a substantial number of stories which we think of as "westerns" are tales of the U.S. Cavalry.

So what, you may be asking, does a series set in space, on a starship, have to do with boots and saddles?

Just this: The duties of Captain James T. Kirk, commander of the *Enterprise*, over the course of the series, included aiding and protecting settlers, enforcing borders, tracking down and punishing marauders, limited exploration and mapping, diplomacy and treaty-making, and law enforcement in the absence of Starfleet authority. The *Enterprise* operated out of a series of Starbases established along, and sometimes beyond, territorial borders. The ongoing settlement of new planets, the building of faster and faster ships, and the continual expansion of subspace radio allowed officers to keep 'n touch with their superiors in Washington.

Sound familiar?

This transmogrification was not necessarily a bad thing. As a matter of fact, by grounding the Star Trek world in a legend/format more recognizable to American audiences, it probably accounted for the (eventual) success of the series.

Star Trek is nothing more than the logical extension of the lusty American creed: "Elbow room!" It is the twenty-third-century equivalent of Manifest Destiny, the promise of a United States from ocean to ocean which stirred colonists to keep moving west. Star Trek, in its devotion to the work ethic and down-home American values, reaffirms the rightness of exploration and colonization—without exploitation—by free men who remain tree.

Little wonder, then, why the series very quickly became a reflection of our own past struggles to capture and colonize our West. In episode after episode, the battle aims were restated, the battle lines redefined, the battles refought. In "Where No Man Has Gone Before," the second pilot (and the first Kirk episode), the aim of the *Enterprise* is to discover what is on the "other side" of the barrier surrounding the galaxy. "Mudd's Women" presents us with itinerant traders, fiercely independent miners, and "mail-order brides," all staples of western fiction. These are but two very early examples, made before the introduction of the elaborate series of Starbases, outposts, survey ships, etc. that made the *Enterprise* ever less alone and ever more dependent upon the chain of command.

Roddenberry was also faced with what virtually amounted to a *fait accompli* in the area of characterization. So vivid were the portrayals of his leads that he was forced to adjust the concept of the series to accommodate them. William Shatner's Kirk was simply too active, too brash, too *American* to be the brooding, introspective captain. And the quick emergence of Nimoy's Spock and Kelley's McCoy required a readjustment of the series which showed them constantly interacting with Kirk as part of the regular chain of command. This resulted, of course, in the development of the classic Triad, or Friendship, which completely refocused the show and further affected the development of each character. This inter-dependence of character called for situations in which the three would be working as a team, thus further removing Star Trek from the original concept.

In short, Gene Roddenberry's dream of a "Hornblower in Space" was not successful. This is not to say, of course, that such a series could not be successful; nor were all of the "seafaring" elements dropped from Star Trek. (Most, however, survived as elements of nostalgia: naval rankings, Kirk's yearning for "the wind at his back," etc.) The lure of firmly grounding the *Enterprise* and its crew in a more audience-recognizable and appealing milieu, one which was also easier to write and act, was virtually irresistible. One might even say, given the time and the place and the people involved, that it was inevitable.

If you read between the lines (and I hope you can), perhaps you realize that, to me, Star Trek came to represent everything that is good about our country—today, in the past, and in the future. Most fans like to say that Star Trek represents hope for the future, a promise that we will overcome our difficulties and differences and build a world of freedom and tolerance. I see it a little differently: I believe that Star Trek represents the best in humanity, as evi-denced in American principles and life-styles . . . *today*, not in some "maybe," Utopian future. Principles and life-styles not perfect by any means, but better than most and damn well preferable to the death of the mind enforced by totalitarianism and the death of spirit caused by socialism. Principles and life-styles which can accept, and have accepted, again and again, new and different cultures, and can take the best from them, tolerate the rest, and emerge ever stronger and enriched.

Star Trek says that all men are better off when free and left to their own devices. As a product of Twentieth-century America, it says this in American terms, to a largely American audience. But the message is nonetheless clear and demanding: Man must be free, he must continue to explore and grow, he must continue to ask, "Is this all that I am?"

THE NEGLECTED WHOLE, OR, "NEVER HEARD OF YOU": PART I

by Elizabeth Rigel

Loyal fans of Star Trek's supporting characters often chide us for not featuring enough articles about their favorites. But when we do run an article about, say, Sulu, we hear complaints from all the fans of Chekov and Scotty and Uhura and Chapel and Kyle and DeSalle and Saavik and Balok and . . . well, you get the picture. They get mighty upset. Although we reckon that our readers will never run out of new and fresh things to say about any of the Star Trek characters, we have to give Elizabeth Rigel credit. In this article (and a sequel to follow) she takes on the herculean task of discussing all of the supporting cast of the original series. We think you'll be as impressed by her insights into them as we were.

Star Trek lives in part by the Vulcan philosophy of Infinite Diversity in Infinite Combinations (IDIC). Therefore it is particularly discouraging that no one told the original scriptwriters about it. If you are a Kirk or Spock fan, life is good. The other regulars (remember them? They run the ship when the stars are captured) have faded into the background. Their supporters are drowned out, and articles are few. A casual viewer would be hard pressed to distinguish them from the extras in less than a month. So, after twenty years of frustration, let us introduce the "neglected whole." First, meet the ladies.

(Penda) Uhura
First Appearance: "The Man Trap"
Rank and Post: lieutenant, chief of communications
Rank and post by *The Search for Spock*: commander, first officer, communications

When Uhura (ably portrayed by Nichelle Nichols) first graced the bridge of the *Enterprise* in 1966, her future looked bright. As introduced, Uhura was a classy, witty, bright young officer who tackled her enemies and her career with a prowess rarely allotted blacks and/or women on television.

Her skills on the bridge are her most neglected characteristic. More than anything, the regularity with which Kirk takes her for granted confirms her status as "one of the gang." The captain will never understand what a pain in the nether region he is when he rants because the galaxy dares to have static in it. Nevertheless, Uhura shrugs off his outbursts, sends the message, pulls it in, coordinates the damage-control teams, and calls the medics. She leaps at the meager opportunities to man the helm in "The Naked Time," "The Corbomite Maneuver," "Balance of Terror," and "Courtmartial." In "Who Mourns for Adonais," she repairs equipment that Spock cannot. Indeed, her efforts made it possible for Spock to contact and rescue the landing party. And of course her brilliant work in disrupting the military's communication system was crucial to the successful *Search for Spock*.

A complaint of her bridgework (no pun intended) is that Uhura is rarely left in command ("given the conn"). In "The Trouble with Tribbles," Chekov was left in charge twice, although his rank and experience were not comparable to hers. In "Catspaw," Assistant Engineer DeSalle was left in command. (Apparently Scotty offers more attractive career opportunities than does Kirk. One season before in "Squire of Gothos," DeSalle was just another navigator.) Even as Spock was dying in *Wrath of Khan*, Kirk left the inexperienced Saavik in charge, although there were three officers of command rank on the bridge. Could it be caused by Kirk's muddled state of mind? If so, it has been muddled for some time. Uhura reminds one of the Vice-President, except that she doesn't even have the diplomatic duty.

Physically, she can more than hold her own. In "Gamesters of Triskelion," she was matched to train with Lars (whom she later fended off when he tried to rape her), though he was a foot taller. When the landing party was originally captured, both Shahna and Tamoon (who struck from behind) were required to subdue her. Both women carried six-foot pikes. Uhura was unarmed. (Lars and Shahna were also among the planet's finest warriors, as both were chosen to battle Kirk to the death.) In "Mirror, Mirror," both Sulu-2 and the phaser-wielding Marlena were finished so easily that the whole thing looked like a game. Uhura is not a person one would expect to see regularly in a fistfight, but she does not tolerate troublemakers.

Unfortunately, the sight of this lady in motion usually brings different images to mind. The men who chase her do not strike one as being interested in her good health.

Lars and Sulu-2 made their intentions clear enough. With sufficient provocation, they might have killed her instead.

In "Plato's Stepchildren," Kirk bestows an unwanted smooch on her, but the Platonians find this tame for a Saturday night's entertainment. They are more entertained by seeing Kirk crack a bull-whip at her head. (It is sad to note that the outcry over the Kiss exceeds that over the Whip.) It is easy to say that Kirk was not responsible, but the memory must still hurt.

Only in "The Man Trap" is it even hinted that Uhura was ever in love. The salt vampire, having scanned her thoughts, adopted the face of a handsome Bantu man for the purpose of luring her into a private conversation, then hypnotizing and killing her. Perhaps this is the face of the boy she left behind. Maybe he died, or he found another when she never told him that she cared for him. Only she knows why this image is so appealing. But the salt vampire's assault on her loneliness and homesickness is very effective. Only Janice Rand's noisy passage breaks the spell and saves her life.

The only "decent man" who ever made a pass at her proved to be a conceited little snob who soon dropped her for a blonde. However, he also gallantly kissed her hand, raved about her beauty in his highbrow way, and taught her to play the harpsichord, which delighted her musical soul. He did not attack her virtue or even threaten her life. So there you have it—in twenty years she has been Officially Kissed but twice (drooling doesn't count), and the nicest man she ever met was Trelane, a six-year-old boy!

The menfolk are not the only ones interested in the lady's appearance. Uhura must know, for example, that Vulcans do not make small talk, but she asks Spock, "Why don't you tell me I'm an attractive young lady, or ask me if I've ever been in love? Tell me how your planet Vulcan looks on a lazy evening when the moon is full." As to her precious lovelife, it is known only that she is not a virgin ("The Naked Time"). Probably the salt creature's disguise. And her romantic adventures in the series are anything but. But is Uhura vain?

Actually, yes. That scamp Harry Mudd figures that out right away. Just as he was the one to describe Kirk as being "married to his ship," he notices that Uhura is nervous of losing nature's best as time takes its toll. In a scene that was ultimately dropped, Harry almost convinced her to sample his Venus drug. (This illegal hormone/cosmetic would transform any plain model into a raving beauty in seconds.) This is enough that Uhura has a bad self-esteem problem, maybe even a screw loose. Male fans have informed this writer that you can't get any better than she is. Uhura is also intensely curious about the artificial bodies used by Mudd's androids—lifelike doubles that would last 800,000 years. "I want to be young and beautiful!" she says, and the androids believe her. The crew escapes, but the temptation was there. Why should Uhura care for such props?

In "The Children Shall Lead," Gorgan employs the "beast within her" (her greatest fear embodied) to paralyze her at her post. If she cannot work, no warning or plea for help can be sent. The "beast" in Uhura is the aged, weak, ugly reflection that appears in her mirror. That subconscious fear of ugliness and helplessness is Gorgan's most effective tool against her. But when Gorgan is undone, the "beast" is overcome, apparently for good.

In fact it seems that both Uhura and Nichelle Nichols have heard enough on the subject. At Kirk's whining that only the "young" (which excludes anyone from the series) belong in space, Uhura whips back, "Now what is *that* supposed to mean?" And Heisenberg the Wag's crack about her encroaching retirement earns him an armed escort to a locked coat closet. For her part, Uhura never could stand a smart mouth. And Nichelle Nichols is no doubt sick to death of hearing about: (1) the command debate (whether Uhura is really good enough to be captain, or if Starfleet is run by male chauvinists); (2) the thoughtless comments of critics, paid and unpaid, who don't care to see the "old guard" anymore and want to meet the "new blood." (As if something is wrong with a mature mind, a distinguished record, and a wise heart.) This is cruelly unfair to all the actors/actresses, but it is particularly senseless for Uhura. Of all the Star Trek performers, past or present, Nichelle Nichols looks the best. *She has not aged a day.* And she probably never will. Maybe Gene Roddenberry and friends found their Vulcanita after all.

Starfleet must have provided some interesting memories, though. Fans and crewmembers will always cherish her talents with vocal and instrumental music. She will be remembered as the one who brought chaos to the Klingon Empire by buying the first tribble puppy or kitten (depending on your allergies). She learns that Nomad does *not* like her singing, but Nomad had a few wires crossed anyhow. She is generous to the faults of others, as when she permits the royal brat Elaan to occupy and destroy her quarters. Uhura even complimented T'Pring as "lovely," which is surely the kindest name any woman has ever had for *that* one. Less appealing, but more common, is her fear of strange places, which prompts the usual "Captain, I'm frightened." At least she has enough confidence to express herself. But she will not hesitate to admit her lack of confidence in Kirk when he leads his valuable officers into yet another fool trap. It is not merely her way, but the only way, to criticize his unsafe work habits. Kirk just yells at anyone else.

There are no other clues to her personal life. How does she feel about her family? What does she look for in a man? (Assuming she ever gets one.) And if she could live life over again, what would she change, if she could? These things remain unknown.

However, there is one last area of concern, and that is her career. Uhura bores easily, and that boredom makes her impatient. It's more than opening hailing frequencies ten times in "Corbomite Maneuver." It's more than angrily informing her boss the-Denevans-won't-answer-my-calls-so-get-off-my-back-sir in "Operation: Annihilate." No, she described the problem on Day One.

In the second pilot, "Where No Man Has Gone Before," the communications officer is a man. Uhura was either a backup or berthed on another ship. But in "Man Trap," the first episode, she complains to Spock, "I'm an illogical woman who's beginning to feel too much a part of that communications console." In less than a year (at most), her new job as department head had become boring and stifling. With some upward mobility, she believes, she would not be bored. (Obviously she chose not to get it through Engineering; Scotty would have gladly made room for her, perhaps as his main assistant.) She is a commander in *The Search for Spock*, so she has followed a fifteen-to-twenty-year command pattern, which is extremely good. True, it isn't comparable to Kirk's less-than-ten-year-climb, but few could match his fanaticism. Many recruits spend twenty-five to forty years trying to attain a lowly captaincy, and some never achieve it. But to Uhura, Starfleet never moves quickly enough. Perhaps her goal is much higher than one starship, so that might explain her fidgets. Yes, it is irritating to fans that she has a small part. But that does not affect her promotion path. Careerwise, Uhura is not terribly put upon, folks. She's impatient (and so are we, but that's life).

The complication in the promotion scheme is the Genesis Experiment. In *The Search for Spock*, the conversation with Heisenberg indicates that Uhura has been a commander for a long time—perhaps too long. After all, no career can be said to be "winding down" when a promotion looms on the horizon. If Uhura is not being penalized for merely *knowing* about Genesis, then why is a ground post at a *deserted* transporter station the best job she can find? Why isn't Chekov joining Scotty on Sulu's ship, the *Excelsior*? No, there must have been a penalty. It is extremely unlikely that Uhura would share duty with Heisenberg (even if she chose to do so), because she is too important. Wouldn't Chekov have been suspicious if she had been the guard or transporter operator when Spock was caught tampering with the equipment in "The Menagerie"? Heroes simply do not sit idle with the diaper set. True, Heisenberg wasn't the brightest lad who ever lived, but his crack about Uhura's dead career makes more sense if he knows that she has been busted. He wouldn't know *why*, but he would know that she was.

It appears that Starfleet prefers quick-wits like Heisenberg and slow-wits like Saavik to run the show. The "yuppies" hit the big time! Ah well, those two cannot be the best representatives of the next generation. But where does this leave our old crew, the "puppies" of the show? ("Puppie," for the reader's info, is the acronym coined by Jim and Jan W. of Michigan, for "Poor, Underpaid Professionals Praying for Increase in Earnings.") Obviously, they're out in the cold. But it's doubtful that Uhura will miss it much. She will shrug it off, repair (and clean) the Klingon ship, and sing for her friends as they sail off into the starlight . . .

(Janice) Rand
First appearance: "The Man Trap"
Rank and post: yeoman, captain's yeoman
Rank and post by *The Search for Spock*: unknown; in *STTMP*, lieutenant, transporter chief
Grace Lee Whitney, who plays Janice Rand, is often left out of the permanent Star Trek family. Although she was billed as a regular character for that magical first season, young Rand saw only half of it. The captain's yeoman, although not crucial to the plot of an adventure series, did have potential for a dramatic series. Her fresh and somewhat civilian viewpoint of her stubborn boss and the military in general could have been quite interesting. The killing blow was the fact that Janice had to get a crush on Kirk to demonstrate more fully the loneliness of high command. In her ten or so episodes, Janice emerges as a surprisingly well-rounded young person and a darn fine worker. But one unrequited love (Chapel's feeling for Spock) was apparently quite enough, and when Janice was written the same way, it was time for her to go.

Her actual duties make her a combination of secretary, time manager, and nursemaid. If the paperwork is cluttered, she organizes it. When Kirk has unwanted visitors, she shoos them off (or warns them they must be accepted). If he is frustrated, she is his whipping post. And when he is overwhelmed, she is a comforter.

She probably did not meet many people during her short stay on the *Enterprise*. Uhura is one good friend whose songs are a fine way to pass the evening. Sulu is her best friend, though. They both have a writing hobby, and both named the plants. Janice probably takes care of them when he is particularly busy or on leave. It is easy to visualize them playing tennis or go; they probably jog, too. He is probably one of the few *Enterprise* crewmembers who have heard her sing, but he could not encourage her to sing in public. (Grace Lee is a fine songstress, but she did not have a chance to sing on the series before she was dropped.) When she appeared in

Spacedock in *The Search for Spock*, it was most likely that she was waiting to board as a member of Sulu's new ship, the *Excelsior*. (The alternatives are that she works either in Spacedock, at the Academy nearby, or on some tugboat-style craft in port at the time.)

Janice also enjoys her work. In this new feminist age, the "traditional" yeoman's job is sometimes considered undignified or worthless. But Janice chose to endure four stressful years at the Academy to get that job. No one could make her endure that environment against her will; no one could make her drop out if she chose to stay. And after the books were set aside, Janice evaluated the opportunities—command, science, medicine, engineering, law, administration—and chose to be a yeoman. Obviously she is one of the best. She was assigned to the finest ship and the strictest commander within weeks of graduation. That's something to be proud of, provided she doesn't rest on her laurels.

At only twenty-two, Janice is mighty young to have such a difficult job. Her youth influences most of her behavior. She has a few faults, like all humans, but many of these can simply be chalked up to inexperience.

It is said that Janice scares too easily. Actually, death is never pleasant (to witness or experience), and it takes time to settle into a job where death is commonplace. There are also many things that are nonfatal but just as intimidating. Even Kirk is occasionally afraid. As he tells Janice in "Miri," "Only a fool has no fear when there's something to be afraid of." Maturity simply means an ability to restrain fears and other sensitivities so that one can better function. Yes, Janice has seen others die, as everyone has—perhaps through an accident, or maybe by a deliberate act or horrible disease. It's just that death is something that happens to someone else, and Janice wasn't personally fond of it.

Janice isn't easily frightened by the dead crewman she and Sulu found in "Man Trap." She is sickened, and even a little fascinated, but not a screaming wreck. The salt vampire has no effect on her. When it takes the salt from Sulu's lunch, she smacks it. When it follows her, she tells it to bug off. Certainly she knows that "Green" is unusually strange today, but she has handled strange men before. (Such is the curse of the beautiful.) She doesn't gasp and faint when she finds out why "Green" was after her, either.

While helmsman Bailey is falling apart in "The Corbomite Maneuver," Janice is making lunch. This might seem an odd thing to do when Balok is telling them to prepare for death. When Kirk is giving up in "Balance of Terror" because they will soon die, Janice wants to know if she should continue making log entries for him. As long as she is preoccupied, she does not panic or quit.

Probably the best example of her excitability is her screaming fit in "Miri." The sight of her pretty, youthful figure being wasted by oozing sores, to be followed by madness and death, overwhelmed her. Death is taking a long time, and there is little she can do for distraction, so she crumbles. Yes, Janice is fearful, but no more so than most young people. She would have outgrown it.

Another way in which her age influences her behavior is in her mannerisms. She is new to the military world and has not had time to blend her individuality into the often faceless mass of the service. Some unity is essential for a smoothly running ship. But Janice hasn't yet lost that bright-eyed ideal that life is fun, even fanciful. She is still very much the teenage cheerleader, the belle of the prom, the one who yaks on the phone (?) continuously; but she has been transplanted to the difficult and sometimes painful life of galactic security.

As Charlie X discovered, Janice is *very* feminine. She loves perfume, and her favorite brand is only available planetside. Her favorite color is pink: her robe is pink and her quarters are flooded with pink lighting. She loves flowers (pink roses, of course) and those useless, harmless ceramic knickknacks all over the dresser. Her hairstyle is of the typical junior miss persuasion—soft, fluffy, and almost too pretty for work. (If she lost a hairpin she'd be blind for ten minutes. It is flattering, though.)

Her feminine ways also slip over into her job. Psychologists know that in a traumatic and ever-changing life, few sensations are more satisfying than a hot meal and the security of Mother's undying devotion. Janice is almost always feeding someone. The snacks and drinks are always welcome after and during a long, boring (or stressful) day on the bridge.

Janice always seems to know when to have the captain's coffee handy. This is more than her mother-hen personality, because she couldn't make him quit if he needed to. Kirk, like many workaholics, depends on his caffeine more than he should, but he is more nervous and disagreeable without it. If he gets intolerable, that's the doctor's area of influence. So she brings the cup faithfully and will go to unusual extremes to get it.

When the power was off in the galley in "Corbomite Maneuver," she went so far as to make the coffee with a hand phaser. After Balok's countdown to destruction, a hot meal and drink would be very soothing and welcome. But it must have been a real nuisance to make. Kirk had not issued phasers to the crew, but Janice was able to obtain one anyhow. Having got one, could she heat the equipment? Oh yes, and Scotty would chase her to the Klingon Empire with the ax of Lizzie Borden—unless he had absolute confidence in her ability. The alternative is that she dismantled the weapon and drained its fuel or power source into the machinery as Scotty did in "The Galileo Seven." Either way, Janice demonstrated a neglected knack for technology. (The only time she was seen to *operate* complex equipment was during her shift on the transporter in *Star Trek: The Motion Picture*.) The coffee incidents underscore her devotion to her boss. How many secretaries on Earth would go to that much trouble for such a whiner?

One thing to keep in mind, though: Starfleet did not train Janice Rand in weaponry to improve her cooking. Kirk usually brings her (or any yeoman) along when he must leave the ship on business, although he may not need her (fat chance). The reasoning behind this is not fondness for his rookies. Kirk is a hero, and heroes have enemies. As the fleet's best, Kirk requires additional protection. If something dangerous gets past his security escort, that innocent little yeoman with the phaser in her garter is the last line of defense. She must be prepared to attack or even die to defend him (even if the chivalric hero, employing a military lack of sense, tries to protect her instead). So much for equal rights.

This aspect of the job is probably distressing to her. Janice is by nature a peaceful and loving person, so it is just as well that she was never thrust into that situation. She loves people, even the misguided ones.

The memory of Charlie Evans will surely be with her for a long time. When Janice took him under her wing, she was unaware of his great powers and destructive temper. When she did realize, it did not intimidate her. To Charlie, her praise is eagerly lapped up, her scolding is like a rain of stones. When the weeping Charlie is taken away, she cries too. By giving him the affection he never had and could never return to, she probably made his lonely life worse. In a way, it's like losing her little brother.

Janice is also concerned for children in "Miri," including Miri herself. They are able to trap her only because she cares for them. (Never mind that after 300 years, only the self-sufficient are left. Children need attention, she decides.) When she tells Kirk, "Miri really loved you, you know," his flip answer brings a sad smile to her face. Amusing as it may be to outsiders, a crush is intensely sincere (and painful). When the adoration is spurned or made light of, the victim feels a thorough fool and never wants to be seen in public again. Janice knows that Kirk does not take Miri's (or Charlie's, or *her*) crush seriously.

How the tune must have changed when Kirk realized that Janice could live without him. In "The Enemy Within," the evil Kirk was shaken to discover that "his" woman did *not* want him, or even *like* him. Finding himself rejected by the crew as well, he "explained" himself to her, asking her forgiveness, understanding, and company. He passed himself off as the "good" Kirk, but Janice was not fooled. "The impostor told me what happened and who he was," she said. With unusual strength and insight, she recognized that even this beast needed to feel loved and accepted. She could have betrayed him when she found him roaming loose, but she didn't. Instead, the Kirks were forced by their freedom to work it out themselves.

However, the near-rape would not have been quickly forgotten. As Grace Lee Whitney indicated in *Best of Trek #1*, the episode "Dagger of the Mind" was originally written for Kirk and Rand. Would Janice actually have planted a "love" suggestion in his mind? Perhaps. But since Kirk already has suppressed feelings for her, the suggestion might prove *too* effective. Recalling her experience with the evil Kirk, she might have panicked at the last moment and said, "Sir, there's a rock in your boot the size of your fist, and it hurts like fill-in-the-blank." When no rock was discovered, the true nature of the "therapy" exposed, but no one would be harmed. She's only affectionate, not stupid.

Kirk does have real feelings for her. But he has set himself up for failure in love. In "The Naked Time," he longs for a "flesh woman" (Janice) to love, but he is "not permitted," he insists. Yes, he knows that his addiction to command turns a woman into a hobby, not a companion. Janice is clearly not interested in that.

Maybe he refers to a regulation prohibiting relationships with his personal employees—not an unwise rule. Should an affair begin and his yeoman's career take off, idle talk will mention her "inside influence." If she stagnates there, a lover's spat or harassment is suggested. The fling would not be worth the shading of their professional reputations. Kirk can afford to be sweet to her when they face certain death, but when they survive, he clams up again.

For her part, Janice only asked Kirk to flirt and look at her legs, as puppy love demands. When she had had enough of his peculiar baiting game, she decided to see some proof that he was (or wasn't) worth a commitment. Janice originally transferred elsewhere to observe his reaction, and also because she was embarrassed by the gossip and teasing. If, now that she was available, he failed to follow up on it, she was well rid of him. Obviously he didn't, so she is.

Janice does not seem to be the type who would join Starfleet to find a husband, as critics would contend. It could happen, of course, in which case she has nothing but our best wishes. Marriage is rather a good goal with the right person, because nothing is more important than love. And nothing is more difficult (but vital) than transforming squalling, selfish toddlers into moral, caring, good human beings. (Or good something-or-other beings.) Any boob can handle them when they've grown. However, a military marriage can be much more difficult than a civilian one. And Star Trek had enough trouble fitting in all the regulars and guests each week. If Janice did marry (particularly if she had children as well), we might never see her again. Even Spock's mother showed up only once and was never mentioned when he died.

Even if Jim and Janice had loved each other enough to marry while in service, it would not have lasted. He sulks, fights, constantly demands his own way. She would hate his tendency to be first in danger. His idea of shore leave would not exactly thrill her soul; hers would bore him. Occasionally he must be given orders to eat or sleep. He would soon cease to be charmed by her crying. She would eventually want a permanent planetside home; to him, home is in space. If they had children, it's a whole 'nother can of worms. To stay with her husband, Janice would have to dump the kids off on the grandparents. But since Janice definitely loves kids and only likes Kirk, she might stay with the little ones instead. (Then, being lonely or restless, his roving eye would grow back.) Taking the kids to Little League or a fourth-grade piano recital would bore him to tears. (He might even say that they needed more practice.) Janice would be the first to leave. He would be the last to care.

It does not seem that any intelligent woman, least of all Janice, would consider the military a good place to attract a husband. There are many more eligible males on the hundreds of (civilian) Federation planets. It doesn't take four years of slaving to reach them, either. True, the armed forces would provide room and board while the gold-digger was looking, but it still isn't worth the trouble. Most people who work in isolated starships must be loners by nature, so that's a waste of time. The comments that Janice is lovesick and feather-brained are unwarranted. After all, Kirk started it, and she was smart enough to end it with her career and self-esteem intact.

So, it was unnecessary to remove Janice Rand so quickly from the Star Trek family. A crush on one's boss, though embarrassing, is curable. Kirk's amorous adventures also tend to be brief and soon forgotten. They would have returned to a professional relationship. Then she could find a more compatible man if she wanted to, while still being Kirk's right arm. Because of the security nature of the job, it would not seem that the captain's yeoman was intended to be a high-turnover position. Clearly Janice was the best help he ever had. He uses up a flood of yeomen in a very short time, and none of them is seen more than twice. And he thinks that Kirk and NBC let Rand go!

What is she doing these days? One could hardly imagine her wasting away at the transporter for eight years. She could, of course, have joined the traditional paths to command—helm/navigation, science, or engineering. With her technical know-how, she might be into equipment design, with maintenance or repair being the bread-and-butter job. Or, employing her clerical and "people" skills, she could be Sulu's personnel officer. If she is not a member of Sulu's crew, she could hold a teaching or management position in the Academy or Spacedock. She was not called upon to be a part of the criminal "Search for Spock," but that's no reason why she shouldn't be involved in the pursuit of *Star Trek IV*. So, for Janice Rand's fans, the future is bright. After all, *someone* has to run Starfleet while the boys are away.

(Christine) Chapel
First appearance: "The Naked Time"

Rank and post: lieutenant, chief nurse, with a doctorate in bio-research

Rank and post in *The Search for Spock*: unknown; in *STTMP*, lieutenant commander, ship's surgeon

Christine Chapel was the only minor character who did not enter the service for its career opportunities. She has never wanted to be anything other than a wife or mother. To her, Starfleet is neither thrilling nor burdensome—it's just a way to make a living until the right man comes along. Her problem is that she cannot seem to select good men. Having lost the dangerous Roger Korby, she then found another marriage prospect in the unwilling Mr. Spock. This was quite a contrast to Majel Barrett's original role as the career-oriented and practical Number One. However, Christine has potential—more than one would suspect from the one-dimensional treatment given her.

She is indeed a good nurse, but her primary job is to assist the doctors. She does little work on her own.

Her degree in bio-research is rarely employed. Probably she was in charge of the frantic study of a neurological disease in "The Tholian Web." She also uses this knowledge for some autopsies, as in "Operation: Annihilate." Having discovered the parasites could be killed by light radiation, Kirk and McCoy were too impatient to wait for her results. She is apparently in charge of (or has access to) the psychological files. She observes that something is wrong with Kirk ("Obsession") and Spock ("Amok Time") as quickly as McCoy does. This is probably a more interesting part of the job, although the subjects usually say that it's none of her business.

Christine must find medicine in the military a peculiar thing. For McCoy, bluffing is often the only out of a dangerous situation. But he might at least warn her. Christine rarely fibs; she finds it distasteful, especially when it is pulled on her. But not all the lessons are lost on this sometimes very confused nurse. The "applied psychology" used against the brooding Ensign Garrovick in "Obsession" is not a bad imitation. It didn't actually work, but it was the thought that counted.

So, Christine has virtually no place in the series as a professional. Even Uhura's switchboard affairs and Sulu's bus-driving had more screen time than Nurse Chapel's work. She was born to be in love, and most of her appearances emphasize her failure to find a man who wants her.

Why is it so hard for Christine Chapel to be realistic? She seems to make her poor choices deliberately, as if punishing herself. She certainly would have a harder time finding a good husband in Starfleet, because most people would not accept an assignment to deep space unless they preferred to be alone.

Roger Korby certainly preferred it that way. One can admire Christine's devoted search for him before he was introduced. He was once a good man, and they had a sincere, if undramatic, love. However, she could not seem to separate the man she remembered from the one who threatened her captain now. Once he has been shown to be unstable and dangerous, it becomes much harder to respect her.

One thing she did not notice or act upon was that Roger did not love her anymore. He made no effort to communicate with or return to society, although the technology of Exo III made that quite possible. He had built a female android which somehow knew how to kiss and dress in skimpy clothing. When Christine finally did catch up to him, his androids attacked the guards and her captain. He also stole military documents and planted an impostor on the *Enterprise*. He lied to her repeatedly and showed contempt for or at least indifference toward her work, and the effort which she had taken to find him did not impress him. The sad thing is that she tolerates all this.

The android Kirk was the first to question her loyalty to Starfleet. And Korby was no doubt pleased by her answer: "Please, don't make me choose. I'd rather that you kill me." Perhaps she was merely saying this to confirm her suspicion that the room was bugged. By pretending to continue her devotion to dear old Roger, she might be able to stop him at his weakest point when he was occupied with Kirk.

From the evidence, though, it would seem that Christine really could not choose. She did not explode at Andrea, or at Korby. Her most bitter response was a mere "I am disappointed in you." A good approach for a sane man, but not against an irrational android. The more he hurts her and her company, the more numbed she becomes. This is her way of handling stress. If she had not prevented Ruk from killing Kirk, Korby would have gotten away with his dangerous infiltrations. It is a great shame that the androids destroyed themselves, thus depriving Christine of the responsibility of facing her problem.

Once Korby was gone, so was the lesson. Christine soon fell in love with Spock, another unrealistic choice. It was not a bad idea at first; Spock could certainly do worse, and Christine was the nicest woman who had ever chased him. However, as it became apparent that Spock would not permit himself to take any woman, Christine, realistically, should have backed off.

Humans and Vulcans marry for different reasons. Christine, of course, would marry for love, which is the primary basis for most Western marriages. Vulcans, and some non-Western cultures, have prearranged marriages which are based on logic. Cross-culture marriages can work, as Sarek and Amanda have shown. The modifications are that the marriage will happen only if both parties are convinced that they can remain happily (human) together for life (Vulcan).

Sarek and Amanda made their marriage work because "it was the logical thing" for both of them. Amanda could adopt her husband's culture without being a burden to him. Neither did she sacrifice her own personality—if Sarek had wanted a doormat, there were available Vulcan women. She did not nag or try to change him, as he did not try to change her. In both work and relaxation she was a support and a benefit to him. Altogether, she was an asset to him, and he was wise to find her. Amanda had the man she loved, and he made her happy. By the standards of either culture, they have a good marriage.

In like manner, if Christine intends to catch Spock, she must convince him that he is better off with her than without her. Spock already had a successful career and a few friends, and he will remain single as long as he can. Unless she can improve on that, he will not accept her.

If Spock did have to marry tomorrow, Christine would not be a bad choice. All his girlfriends have a selfish streak; none seems particularly concerned with the wants and needs of the other person.

Leila Kalomi (in addition to her deceit) would not be a supportive woman. Her major interest in Spock is to expose his emotions. She is rather upset when he declines her invitations, saying, "I can't bear to lose you again!" The fact that he has also been hurt is secondary to her own loss.

T'Pring was much worse. Her anticipation of receiving Spock's name and property while keeping a lover is more typical of human behavior than Vulcan. She scorned the law and was not interested in the possibility that people might be killed to preserve her scheme. Fans can understand why Spock avoided her previously.

The Romulan commander is sometimes called Spock's only "true love." This is not the case, as the woman only wanted a way to control the *Enterprise*, which was the catch of a lifetime. If she could bring the Federation warship home without much bloodshed, the Romulans would have valuable officers as well. Spock goes along with her plotting to buy time for the espionage efforts, and he is more of an actor than a participant. Further contact between them might be interesting, but would also be treasonous and so would not occur.

Droxine had a crush on Spock's looks, and he had learned by then the polite human reciprocations. His main interest here is to procure the needed cargo and convince Droxine that the political and class structures were wrong.

Zarabeth was an intelligent woman, but not a truthful one. She would do what she could to keep Spock with her, but in the end there was nothing she could do. He was also not himself, and even if he had become fond of her in time, he would not have cared for her in the present.

All these women had some selfish motivation for obtaining his friendship. Christine, on the other hand, is so selfless that she cannot stand up for herself. She would adopt his culture, abandon her career, and go anyplace to be with him. The phrase "separate vacations" is probably not in her vocabulary. If Spock wants a devoted shadow, Christine is the woman for him.

However, a selfless woman frightens Spock as much as a selfish one. Christine's emotions could really grate, since they are all concentrated upon him. He is always a little unsure of himself, and he would shrink from the overwhelming attention. True love is the desire to benefit another person, not the expectation of something in return. So, Spock would find her devotion just another form of the fault-finding magnifying glass that humans use on everything except themselves.

There are legitimate strikes against him. For one, Spock had much difficulty breaking the apron strings. A man who has not come to terms with his parents is not mature enough to begin a permanent relationship. So, Christine waited until the feud with Sarek was healed, and she tried again.

Another point is that Spock has become distrustful of human emotions and motivations. Leila (and T'Pring as well) entered his life without his permission, and the scars were not yet healed (he would deny having them). Why should he trust Christine, who after all invades his privacy by entering his cabin unasked, checking his files, and "accidentally" eavesdropping on him? She does these things because she is concerned about people; she means no harm. As humans go, she is not a loud or indiscreet person, but he will be cautious around her. He does not disbelieve that she only wants to please him, but he doubts that her fragile, emotional approach could be binding or lasting in a Vulcan sense. It is easy for her to follow the Vulcan ideal when times are good, but even Amanda finds it painful when the situation demands too great a sacrifice. Spock would rather avoid that stress and just not marry. Too, he understands what it is to be without a name and culture, and he would not wish such pain on his own children, which Christine would insist upon having.

If not for the Vulcan mating cycle, one can rest assured that the Spock of the series would never marry. In "Amok Time" he finally tells Christine to get lost: "If I want anything from you, I'll ask for it!" When he realizes that he will not go to Vulcan, he figures that it is time to ask. Fortunately for Spock, Christine is not one to notice rejection. From him, "It is illogical for us to deny our separate natures" is a seduction. Christine must have kicked herself to find that she had told Spock he was going home to his wife. However, the marriage was not necessary, and Spock went free.

If *pon farr* is fatal, why did Spock survive without a wife? One, it could have been "all in his head"—that is, the body reacted to his mental health with the Vulcan equivalent of a stress-induced ulcer. This seems the likely theory, as Spock would otherwise have married by *Wrath of Khan*, and he apparently had not. Two, it could have been a "false start," which would be followed by the real thing. The human influence probably spared him this. Altogether, Spock simply could not be "got." He would not yield to emotion, and he had no physical need for a wife.

(However, if the incidents of *The Search for Spock* are to be accepted, the Genesis Experiment has disrupted Spock's biology. If he recovers, his mutant physiology may require a Vulcan married life-style after all.)

However, it would seem that Christine has finally snapped out of her trance and given up on him. In *Star Trek: The Motion Picture*, she has proudly taken her post as the new ship's surgeon, which is an admirable advancement. She has evidently come to take satisfaction in her career and become a self-respecting woman. Her goal to be a wife and mother was a good one, but she set about finding it in the wrong way and with the wrong men. It was unhealthy for her to live only for other people and not develop a sound personality of her own. Now she seems a happier and more likable person. She has not been seen since *STTMP*, but she probably has new duties and hobbies (maybe new men) on which to spend her time. In addition to her abilities in practical medicine, she may be studying the many cures and devices she discovered on her first trip into space and introducing them to the scientific community. It is possible that she will turn up as Sulu's ship's doctor, although that remains to be seen. However, now that she has broken free of the flat stereotype originally given her, she can go nowhere but up.

(In the second half of this article, we will examine the other part of the "neglected whole," the gentlemen of the *Enterprise*.)

THE NEGLECTED WHOLE, OR, "NEVER HEARD OF YOU": PART II

by Elizabeth Rigel

We never cease to be amazed at the insights our writers find in the characters of the Star Trek regulars. Last volume, Elizabeth took a closer look at the female regulars, and offered some startlingly new opinions and observations about their characters and their place in the Star Trek world. Now she turns her attention to the two junior officers, with equally fascinating results.

In Part One of this article (*The Best of Trek #10*), you met the supporting ladies of Star Trek. Now let us introduce two of the gentlemen:

(Pavel) Chekov
First Apppearance: "Amok Time"
Rank and post: Ensign, navigator, backup Science Officer

Rank and post by *The Search for Spock*: commander, First Officer/ Science Officer.

Pavel Chekov first appeared among the Bridge crew of the *Enterprise* in Star Trek's second season. The *Star Trek Guide* outlined Chekov as "reliable and dependable, with a good head on his shoulders in spite of his youth." He was one of the few minor characters given adequate (if not overwhelming) screen time to live up to his description, surviving despite the rigors of Starfleet and fickle television rating systems.

Chekov was born to a middle-class family near Moscow and is an only child ("Day of the Dove"). He has apparently always been their "nice boy," the one who still cries after receiving his mother's proud letters and fruitcakes. Thus he was well prepared to assume the pecking-order position (vacated by fellow youngster Janice Rand) of "the Bridge baby." He bears the common burden of youth: no respect. He lacks maturity, so he will be made better by being watched, bothered, and left behind. He has talent but is too green to understand it. If he does a job right, another person receives credit. And if he does something wrong . . .

He is introduced in "Amok Time," but his earliest filmed episode was "Who Mourns for Adonais." And according to Khan Noonian Singh, Chekov was around as early as "Space Seed." This identification must be accurate. The *Enterprise* was alone in "Space Seed," and no ship visited Ceti Alpha V thereafter. Chekov was indeed aboard the *Enterprise* at that time or they never would have met. Chekov was already twenty-two by the time of "Who Mourns for Adonais?", so he could have graduated from the Academy early.

However, raw genius alone cannot earn a starting position on Kirk's "crisis bridge" team. Kirk requires additional on-the-job training for rookies and transfers, which is why he has the finest ship in the fleet. He required it of Sulu and Uhura sometime between "Where No Man has Gone Before" and "The Man Trap." For everyday duties such as navigation, the training period is brief. But Chekov has been personally groomed by Spock to be the backup Science Officer. Because Spock is the best Science Officer in the fleet, it is entirely reasonable that it took Chekov a year of training (in one of the two (eight-hour) or three (six-hour) off-shifts on the Bridge) before he was allowed to relieve Spock of the position. In an emergency he would be in charge of auxiliary control. He was also never seen off-duty because he was up to his eyeballs in "homework." (Obviously, Spock learned his teaching methods from his mother.)

There's no question Pavel learned his lessons well. As Kirk said in "The Ultimate Computer," "Chekov could do his job with his eyes closed." There are days when Spock is not even missed. Chekov adopted the science duties with complete confidence in "Catspaw," "The Immunity Syndrome," "Friday's Child," and "The Enterprise Incident," to name just a few.

He is equally skilled on ground assignment, as in "Who Mourns for Adonais?" This show in particular emphasizes Chekov's logic and talent. (He didn't scream, either.) First, he made the connection between Apollo and his mechanical energy source. Second, he volunteered himself into danger to protect his superiors. Third, his task was complicated by the fact that no one, especially Scotty, did anything useful. And fourth, Chekov was probably scared to death. Apollo had threatened several times to kill the landing party. (And the crew, as well; the ship could not be contacted, so how could anyone know he had not already done so?) Until the final commercial, it looked like Chekov was on his own—he would have to destroy Apollo himself. Now, logically, the expendable ensign should have been the one to bear the brunt of Apollo's anger. Chekov tried to point this out to Kirk, and encountered Kirk's actual modus operandi: "If I don't do it, it isn't done right." The captain is willing to die to prove his point. So although Chekov was presented well in "Who Mourns?", it is a shame that he looked so good only because everyone else did so badly.

Although Chekov was never intended to make his screen debut in "Amok Time," the episode is an indication of things to come. One of his first lines is the eloquent, "I think I'm going to get spacesick." Don't doubt it—Chekov is forever falling victim to the malice of man and nature. He is first to become ill in "The Immunity Syndrome," "The Tholian Web," and "Day of the Dove." A particularly painful moment is the bewildered, trusting expression on his face just before the coldhearted Kelvans evaporate him into a teething toy.

It has been truthfully said that if McCoy is loose when the action starts moving, he is going to get clobbered. But it's even worse for Chekov, who is frankly expendable in story terms, regardless of how popular he became. Now and then a writer may generously nail both of them, as in "The Deadly Years." (Chekov was spared from deadly radiation so that McCoy could pull him into taffy in Sickbay, instead.) This is not the only similarity between Chekov and a major character. His struggling imitation of Spock is obvious, but as a person he is much like his other heroes, McCoy and Kirk.

McCoy has been called the embodiment of that chaotic element, emotion. Chekov is even more emotional; his spirit is young and not yet very organized. McCoy has the advantage of maturity and a stable career, plus self-control—which, admittedly, he doesn't always use. He has come to an age and viewpoint that enable him to channel emotions to definite goals. Chekov cannot do even this much; and the only thing he's learned so far is that when he acts like Dr. McCoy, either the enemy or the boss whales the tar out of him. Maybe McCoy torments Chekov, not because he objects to his exposure to Spock, but because he reminds the doctor of himself in younger days.

The education of the ensign must be an interesting hobby for his stern tutor, Spock. When Chekov is feeling logical, he drives even McCoy nuts. Yet Chekov is hopelessly emotional, by Vulcan standards a lost cause. It must please Spock no end that someone even worse off than McCoy is being successfully "rehabilitated."

In the long run, though, Pavel is much more like Jim Kirk. They share a particularly fascinating problem: a powerful love/hate relationship with authority and The Job.

Kirk's contempt for Headquarters and Federation bureaucrats is well known. When he encounters an alien race, he educates them until they suit him. He takes badly to a power that proves stronger and/or more ethical than he is. Kirk *must* be in charge; he craves power, and with a starship at his command, he usually gets it. This is when he loves his job. But there are days when things do not go his way. Perhaps he has orders he does not want, or his friends are mad at him for doing something stupid. Some nights he lies awake hating the long hours and missing the loving women and happy homes he's thrown away. At such times, he hates his job. He does not quite know how to solve his problem, but when presented with a solution, he cannot go through with it.

Apply this to Ensign Chekov. Pavel is proud to have an envied posting on the heroic *Enterprise*. The work is stimulating, his folks adore him, outer space is breathtaking, and the people are the best.

At times he feels the invincible, "what, me worry?" life is upon him ("The Apple," "Friday's Child"). He enjoys the company of Sulu the gossip and Uhura the big spender. And Chekov's favorite commander has got to be Scotty. Scotty is a party on legs—for instance, he starts bar fights with Klingons. But the best thing about Scotty is that he lets Chekov work in peace. He doesn't do babysitting. If Kirk lets Chekov on his Bridge, the fellow must know his job. Scotty (gasp!) respects Chekov. So do Uhura and Sulu. Their support is his only comfort.

However, a disturbing thought must occasionally cross his mind: Is it better to be highly regarded on a mediocre cruiser led by nobodies, or to just be nobody on the *Enterprise*?

Is "just being there" worth all the baiting and condescension? What reward has he gotten so far for his hard work? He is afraid of the kind of "blood brother" friendship that Kirk has with Spock and McCoy, so he doesn't open up to anyone. Oh, Uhura and Sulu *seem* to like him, but they probably just feel sorry for him. He is, after all, their inferior. Kirk and Spock have told him so. Everyone he works with is in the chain of command—how important could the pressures on a mere ensign be? If Uhura is as calm as Spock, and Sulu never takes that blasted grin off his face, then what could his "friends" know about loneliness? He is frankly afraid of them. Even the temporary help, like DeSalle of "Catspaw," treat Chekov as if all he really needs is a bottle and a diaper. As for Kirk or Spock, Chekov seems resigned to his belief that he will never please them, and resigned to their belief that they are doing him a favor by teaching him patience. He bottles up his feelings too often, hoping to please them, but he ends up hating them and himself. He can't even attract female companions, with the dubious exceptions of yeomen, security, or some alien's leftovers. Is it any wonder he fights Spock ("The Tholian Web"), Kirk ("The Children Shall Lead"), and the Klingons (any opportunity) so fervently?

An excellent example of the contrary Kirk/Chekov relationship can be seen in "The Trouble With Tribbles." After a minor error draws a lecture, the friendly captain informs the ensign that his memory stinks. ("Ivan Burkov/John Burke" obviously was like "Jeanne d'Arc/Joan of Arc," common in American textbooks) a convenience of the Russian translator, and no excuse for Kirk's bad manners.) Later, when the Klingons insult Kirk, Chekov is the first (and only) one who defends him. Scotty holds back because Kirk isn't worth the trouble. But when the captain lines up the transgressors, he first blames loyal old Pavel for starting the fight. Nice guy, huh?

"The Gamesters of Triskelion" were obviously aware of Chekov's suppressed anger. If they could tap and channel that aggression, they could have a truly brilliant gladiator, one who might even defeat Kirk someday. They selected him out of a crew of 430 capable crewmembers, gave him a woman of his very own, and severely punished his uncooperative boss. If Chekov really hates the service, this should have been enough to win him over.

It is not. The military may stink, but it does issue paychecks, promotions, and doors that lock from the inside. One of the reasons Kirk seems to like Chekov so is that the ensign has a short memory. They decide to escape.

Chekov has an amusing relationship with his woman, Tamoon. She seems a nice enough young gladiator, but she's not his type. He does not like her any more than he does captivity, but he doesn't take it out on her. He never lied to her, and he made a point of politely tying her up during his escape attempt. (Kirk, however, cracked Shahna's jaw.) Chekov also didn't care for Sylvia ("Spectre of the Gun"), but he defended her to the death. It is Chekov, not Kirk, who "doesn't go around beating up beautiful women." True, Chekov isn't much exposed to beautiful women. But he will defend himself.

This incident was still not enough to resolve his love/hate problem with authority. By the time of "The Children Shall Lead," it was once again volatile enough to become dangerous. This "beast" was ideal for Gorgan's plans, which require getting rid of the meddlesome Kirk and Spock. Chekov has heard from Starfleet Command, he says, and the Captain and First Officer are to be arrested. It is something he has always fantasized about doing. If only, just this once, he could get back at them! Never again would he feel inferior or intimidated; now someone would respect his abilities and needs. To his credit, Chekov admits that he does not wish to kill them, although he will if he must. If anyone on the *Enterprise* has the capacity to kill Kirk, it would be Chekov—and Gorgan, who has killed before, would send the most dangerous person for the job. However, Kirk saw that even then Chekov was not controlled deeply enough to succeed, and he was able to stop him

It is ironic that Kirk has assembled the best crew in the fleet by giving no more than a pat on the head for effort. He has been warned by now that the natives are restless, and it is surprising that he hasn't done something about it. Chekov has once again made clear that he wants better, and again he is ignored. Compare this with the ambition of Chekov-2 ("Mirror, Mirror"), who wanted a raise so badly that he would kill Kirk to get it. (From what we saw of Kirk-2, we almost hope he got it.)

Probably Chekov's most controversial role was in "The Way to Eden." Fans complained vigorously that their teeny-bopper hero had turned into just another stuffy military man. Pavel was supposed to attract young viewers—in this show he sounded like their parents. True, this is not how Pavel Chekov was first introduced, but that is because he has outgrown the description. He is entirely the Chekov we have recently seen.

Pavel originally loved his job. No doubt his family did, too. For all we know, it may have been their idea. But because Chekov was the one who had to live with it, the starry-eyed idealism finally faded. He discovered that the outwardly glamorous *Enterprise* was a real drudge factory. His bosses (and many crewmembers have only one) proved to be perfectionists and workaholics. They did not understand why he did not share their passion for solving problems or "work as play." The conflict developed and he did not, could not, solve it. On top of all this, he had served only three years. There was no legal way to get out of the military. He is wondering whether he has made a mistake.

Into this troubled scene strolls a serene soul named Irina, an Important Person from his past. He had broken off their relationship when she dropped out of the Academy to become a swinging hippie. He did want to continue the relationship, but on his own terms. Pavel Andreivich Chekov would never be associated with a hippie, no matter how much the free life-style might appeal to him. His common sense (or traditional pressures) won out, and he was convinced of his own correct position, all the way through Starfleet Academy.

Pavel used the same arguments on her that his parents would have used on him: The work ethic (industriousness, loyalty, paying taxes for services) is a good thing. If she would not work, she would starve. On a primitive planet, she would have little medical care. She would find the morals of the hippies degenerate, their goals selfish and shortsighted. He knew that he could not bear to see her inevitable final decline, such as befall the dregs of society. Instead, he would go forth into the galaxy and become a hero.

Imagine how Chekov felt when Irina met him again on the *Enterprise*. His dire warnings have come to nothing. All his emotions come crashing down on him: envy for her simple life, and her happiness. Shame, that he was afraid to follow. Anger, that she makes her living by sponging and stealing from people like Chekov who earn their bread. But above all, pride. He was wrong. He would like to escape this crushing career and make peace with her. But not on his life would he admit it.

He feels cheated. He has done everything he was supposed to do, and it doesn't work. It is all garbage.

However, Irina too has changed. She did not accept his word as a friend that he would find her Eden, because he was no longer a friend. He loathed it, and it humiliated him, but he tried. She responded to his assistance by taking over the ship. She gave the *Enterprise* and the lives of her crew into the hands of a thief, a lunatic, and an attempted murderer. Irina knew fully well what she was doing, and what her unstable leader would do. Well, Chekov may have been wrong about her the first time, but he was right in the long run.

He does choose to bid her farewell. He can now distinguish between Irina and her life-style, though he hopes she will practice it legally. And he has learned that environment alone does not make a person err, but the choices he makes do, as well. It's no different from the understanding that Kirk is temperamental because he chooses to be, not because he's Irish.

"The Way to Eden" was crucial to Chekov's self-esteem and the solution to his problem. He is no longer on the *Enterprise* because he "should" be there, but because he wants to be there. He is still young, but he has grown up.

By the time of *Star Trek: The Motion Picture*, Chekov has become a lieutenant (note that Kirk was *not* there) and secured an additional post as weapons officer. And in *Star Trek II: The Wrath of Khan*, he is a full commander on the *Reliant*, all ready to assume the "Jim Kirk School of Strategic Thought." Of course, *Captain* Terrell and *Commander* Chekov are the ones to beam down on a routine survey to be caught by Khan. It would seem that after Chekov's eyewitness observations of what happens to valuable *Enterprise* personnel who beam down into danger, he would never leave any ship again. Some things never change: Chekov being tortured and screaming himself blue; Chekov being in a position to blow Kirk's rear end off and then somehow not doing it. Even under Khan's influence, Chekov refused to harm Kirk; Terrell's will was not as strong, so he killed himself. Pavel never lost his weapon or was attacked, so nothing could have prevented him from killing Kirk. But Chekov still had his will, and he simply would not do it.

(It would be interesting to see how Chekov would actually run operations if he had his own ship. Would he turn cautious? After all these years, it must have occurred to him that the "Jim Kirk School" does not have many living followers.)

It is logical that Chekov would so quickly join the renegade *Search for Spock*, no questions asked. Chekov owes as much to Spock as he does to Kirk, and he would prefer to express his gratitude in the typically silent but active Vulcan manner. Chekov also respects McCoy, mostly because Spock did. Pavel and the doctor never did get along very well on their own; both thought Spock had some bad effect on the other. As the reviewers in *Best of Trek #8* pointed out, (1) Chekov does not need a reason to do the right thing, so long as there is a right thing needing to be done, and (2) the man is sick. He should be home in bed. The Ceti Eel supposedly derives nutrition as a parasite, so either his poor brain was starved for food and air, or it was just chewed a bit. If McCoy had been the least bit well, he would never have let Chekov run loose, but he must have believed he could call the commander back to Sickbay later. No question, Chekov did not need the extra aggravation.

It was up to Chekov and Scotty to almost re-create a battered, *big* ship. Their talents were less emphasized, and far more important, than any other effort in *The Search for Spock*. After all, you can't exactly walk to Genesis. Everything else done, although important, cannot be considered to be in the same league. As Star Trek proved countless times, Kirk can bust out of jail anytime. Characters are invincible and immortal. Ships are honest to their nature and break down. Ships die.

Chekov is in a delicate position, though, one that may be to Kirk's advantage in the fourth film. Unlike Scotty and Uhura, Chekov was not on duty when they left for Genesis. And unlike Kirk and Sulu, Chekov got onto the *Enterprise* early and undetected. This means that *no one saw Chekov leave Earth and/or go to Genesis, therefore no one can charge him with anything*. Legally, that is. And only Saavik and the Vulcans of Mount Seleya know how he got to Vulcan.

Can the Federation convict him of conspiracy on circumstantial evidence? It isn't impossible—McCoy was being sent to an asylum without so much as a hearing—but just this once he might get away with it. Kirk may badly need a spy in high places in the months to come. (Of course, there's always Saavik, but she has not learned to keep her mouth shut; her honesty could put him away.) However, Chekov does stand a better chance of being acquitted than Uhura does. Too many fans are making the assumption that "Mr. Adventure" will keep *his* big mouth shut.

One more thing: Consider poor Pavel's clothes. "Buster Brown," they've been called (although in 1985 his stirrup slacks mysteriously came into fashion among junior high students). Chekov may not be quite as flamboyant as Kirk, but it is generally believed that the man does have taste. Obviously he was dressed blandly in order to ditch Petty Federation Officials in Charge of Two-Month Debriefings and the everloving *Federation Enquirer*. So don't shoot anyone in Wardrobe, unless it happens again. Chekov may look good in Klingon armor.

(Hikaru Walter) Sulu
First appearance: "Where No Man Has Gone Before"
Rank and post: Lieutenant; astrophysicist, helmsman
Rank and post by *The Search for Spock*: Captain of the USS *Excelsior*

It is astonishing that Sulu has been given so little attention on screen and in print. Surely a young man so elegant, so dashing, so essential to the safe operation of a Federation starship deserves better.

His history is certainly unique. The closest he ever got to a romantic encounter was his, ah, welcome of the Deltan Ilia, but he is not lonely. When he is insulted, he can shrug it off; but challenge him to a contest and he will win it, without malice or pride. Unlike some of the regulars, he takes care of himself and enjoys doing it— exercising, eating properly, taking recreation. He has no fear of dying, and he isn't afraid of living. He not only strives to be happy, he *is* happy. Perhaps his lack of exposure arises from the problem some writers have to relating to characters who are at peace—it is far easier and more fashionable to expose a person's weaknesses, or even choose a villain as the target for sympathy. By this standard Sulu's only fault is being too nice to possibly be considered interesting. So Hikaru fires the phasers, steers the ship, and similarly stays out of trouble that would help his popularity.

It isn't obvious how much Kirk appreciates Sulu. For one thing, Kirk rarely says so. His steady hand can easily be taken for granted, so it is. Indeed, the helmsman is one of Kirk's favorite targets when something goes wrong. Originally, the fact that Sulu was a lowly lieutenant was excuse enough, but now he is a convenient scratching post for another reason: he doesn't care. He knows his work is good and Kirk is not mad at him personally. Even if he was, and had good reason to be, Hikaru would mend the situation without fuss. Sulu is able to humor the captain, and he acts as a buffer between Kirk's unthinking temper and those crewmembers who are sensitive to it. It is not a pleasant position to be in, but as long as Kirk acts as he does, it is necessary. No one else will play this game: McCoy and Scotty yell back, Spock coolly informs the captain that he's being silly, and the others grind their teeth and slink away. Kirk needs Sulu desperately; without him he would lose every friend he has. The helmsman's patience, tact, and acting are nothing short of amazing.

He utilizes his ease with people in another important task—breaking in the rookies. Bailey, Stiles, Kevin Riley, and Pavel Chekov are just a few of those left in his care. He knows all the front duties better than anyone, and he makes it clear that there is no embarrassment in asking his help. Of course, the youngsters look to him for cues as to when the captain's anger is to be taken seriously and when he's just blowing off steam.

Even in life-or-death situations, Sulu is an uncommonly stable presence for the rookies to cling to. From "May the Great Bird of the Galaxy bless your planet" to "Don't call me tiny," he always has a succinct observation, soothing their nerves with lively chatter, gossip, and wag, but in turn he absorbs a good deal of information from them. Sometimes his gossip's tongue is required to save lives—Hikaru knew in "Day of the Dove" that Chekov was an only child (he claimed to be avenging his dead brother), and therefore that Chekov was dangerously mad.

Sulu was almost ready for a promotion in the series. As an astrophysicist in "Where No Man Has Gone Before," he had little screen time, but enough to establish his competence. He was qualified to command the *Enterprise* in an all-out war against the Klingons ("Errand of Mercy"). This indicates that Sulu is more highly trained in fleet operations than is Scott—which is no slur against Scotty, who is as capable in solo engagements as he is with his engines.

Sulu proved quite competent in handling security in "The Man Trap." To his good fortune, Kirk never followed up on it by appointing him security chief, for if he had, Sulu would have: (1) been killed; (2) been regularly in hot water until he was removed; (3) been brilliant, which would destroy a convenient plot device.

The Sulu of "Mirror, Mirror" is predictably everything the real Sulu is not. In that other reality, he has a position worthy of his talent, but not his ambition. Sulu-2 has no intention of waiting twenty years to be the captain of his own ship, and dastardly as he was, one certainly could sympathize with that. Had his selected targets not been from another universe, his well-laid plans might have worked. (Perhaps not . . . Kirk-2 must be pretty good himself not to have killed a single security chief in two years of Federation-reality, and most certainly he can take care of himself.) Had Sulu-2 not been so bloodthirsty (not to mention a twin to the crewman Kirk already had), he might have made that ideal security chief that Kirk was always looking for. (But, if our Sulu couldn't get the job, perhaps Kirk subconsciously didn't want a good one.)

Incidentally, Sulu-2 had a ladyfriend, or at least he thought he did. In the canon universe, Sulu and Uhura are affectionate friends, so whatever the other fellow did to earn the woman's enmity, he certainly did a good job. The real Sulu never even gets far enough for offense to be taken.

In "The Enemy Within," Hikaru assumed leadership of the stranded landing party. Having completed a survival course taught by Spock, Sulu was able to save all his people despite their lengthy stay on the planet. Sulu made light of the difficulties, limiting his complaints to, "Where's room service? The rice wine is taking too long." Also, because he sent up the doglike animal, the problem was revealed to Scotty before other people could be harmed.

Sulu also has advanced engineering experience, as indicated in "Day of the Dove." Because Klingons have cut off life support to the Bridge, Kirk sends him to auxiliary control to *repair* it. Kirk did believe that Sulu actually fixed it, so he must have had the experience to do so. So we'll postulate—when George Takei disappeared during the second season to film *The Green Berets*, Sulu was Scotty's apprentice in Engineering. At this time, Scotty was losing his old hands and assistants (such as DeSalle) to promotions and transfers, but the Academy graduates were not enough to meet his personnel needs. Thus Scotty asked for and received Sulu's help in breaking in *his* new kids. The opportunity was also good for rounding out the helmsman's skills for future command.

Surprisingly, Hikaru really doesn't care much about his work. He gives every effort to ensure the best possible job, but when the deed is done he forgets it. He is not a victim of one of Star Trek's (and America's) greatest neuroses—addiction to his career. He never lets a mere job become a prop for his identity. When he is on duty it is his top priority, but when it is time to relax, he relaxes. He is free of the snake pit that workaholics such as Kirk or Spock throw themselves into.

Kirk and his followers developed as people as their positions demanded. Sulu, though, brought a stable and satisfied personality into his worldly circumstances, and the result is that circumstances have no control over him. He will not gamble with his sanity by investing his identity in the effort of his hands or in a job that could be gone tomorrow. Take Kirk or Spock off the *Enterprise*, even for a vacation, and they are bereft of their purpose for existence. *Star Trek: The Motion Picture* proved that conclusively. Without the specific place of the *Enterprise* and the time "prime of life," they melt away, because they've persuaded themselves they are good for only that. Sulu, on the other hand, would be happy as a stockbroker or a dishwasher. He is more mature than either of them in that he does not limit his head and hand to what he is paid for.

To a great extent, this gives him his appearance of agelessness. This does not mean that he will never grow old, but that he has no fear of growing older. Age may someday fetter his ability to work and play, but it will never rob him of his enthusiasm for life. A far cry from Kirk and Uhura, who will do almost anything to keep their fair faces but distressed minds frozen in time, as if this is a good thing. In reality, denial and stalling set them up for a cruel shock later.

There is a lot of little boy in Sulu. He plays harder than he works, but his play does not exclude family, friends, or happiness, as work often does. Recreation develops the character, refreshes the mind, gives one grace in both winning and losing, and attracts curious company. Janice Rand shared his love for plants; although to his amusement, she insisted that they would one day prove (upon her person) to be carnivorous. Kevin Riley would hang around despite his voluble objections to Sulu's repeated attempts to "educate" him. The helmsman is generally believed to be precariously off-balance, but he has never lost an audience. If the others would rather be boring or bored, or work too much and goof off, this is their problem. Since they are dissatisfied now, when "work" is all they live for, what will they do in retirement? Is this maturity? Then children are far wiser. Sulu, for one, has not let maturity evict his childlike curiosity, freedom, and playfulness. It is appropriate that Sulu sees the value of "play" in "Shore Leave," although he doesn't get to enjoy much of it. Ask him how he can always be so happy (and Chekov has probably done so many times), and he will quote, "My friends, you stress very unimportant matters" (E. Sandoval, Omicron Ceti III) and go on transplanting his weeping willows. Sulu is mentally healthier than most, and he is far from crazy.

Fortunately, even when he *is* crazy, he is rarely dangerous. "Return of the Archons," "This Side of Paradise," and "Wolf in the Fold" show a loopy Sulu, or as George Takei describes it, "with pongs." In these instances he is no more disturbing than usual. As Sylvia's tool ("Catspaw") he was less help than she thought him to be. When Sulu is sane he can wipe the floor with anyone in the gym. But Sylvia knows nothing of the martial arts, so he loses his "edge," his control, and his struggle with Kirk. Sulu was unstable in "And the Children Shall Lead" only because Gorgan played on his fear of responsibility; what would happen to 430 innocent people if he fell asleep at the wheel? He dares not travel into "unsafe" space, so Gorgan has him under control.

For an insanity that is truly close to his character, review "The Naked Time," wherein he believed himself to be d'Artagnan of Dumas' *The Three Musketeers.*

D'Artagnan was a young Gascon gentleman who went north in 1625 to seek his destiny among the Royal Musketeers. On the day of his arrival, he gracelessly offended all three musketeers of the title and found himself challenged to three consecutive duels of honor. The Inseparables were highly amused by this turn of events, and when he stayed to fight their common enemy, the Cardinal's

Musketeers, the three accepted him into their friendship. All of them looked forward to the day when he completed his apprenticeship and became their true comrade-in-arms.

Athos was the eldest Musketeer, a solemn nobleman said to be embittered by a lost love. Porthos was a babbler and a self-proclaimed ladies' man. Aramis considered himself a churchman at heart and insisted that someday he would sheathe his sword for a Bible. They served the King against the forces of Cardinal Richelieu, the real power in the land. It was d'Artagnan who approached the Inseparables with an unfolding adventure that finally involved the governments of both France and England. The four Musketeers thwarted the plans of the Cardinal by capturing his agent, Lady de Winter, who was revealed to be Athos's thought-dead wife. For her international crimes she was put to death by the public executioner of Lille. Athos gave the letter of safe conduct she carried, signed by the Cardinal, to d'Artagnan. When d'Artagnan was brought before Richelieu as the ringleader of the executioners, the letter was produced and his life was spared. Impressed by the gentleman's cleverness, the Cardinal granted d'Artagnan a lieutenancy in the Musketeer corps. Soon after, Aramis disappeared to a monastery, none knew where, and Porthos married a wealthy widow. Athos served under d'Artagnan for seven years, then returned to his estate.

In some ways, Sulu is very much like d'Artagnan. Certainly he is skilled in the sword, and his position in Starfleet often involves the safety of many lives. He interrupted a circle of three great friends, but was accepted because of his daring and integrity. (However, it took the three longer to accord a junior officer more than professional respect.) The "Big Three" friendship fell apart in *Star Trek: The Motion Picture*, even as d'Artagnan's friends separated.

So it's not surprising that he should fall into the role when affected by the virus. When the crewmen first ran from Sulu, he knew them for the cowards of the Cardinal. When Uhura rejected his offer of protection against them ("Sorry, neither"), he recognized her for the villainess Lady de Winter, the fair-but-no-maiden who spurned d'Artagnan and was executed. (Apparently, "woman" is as unpredictable, and therefore deadly, in Star Trek as in romantic France.) Good thing for Uhura that d'Artagnan had never had a Vulcan nerve pinch before.

For some reason, Sulu was never again seen to wield his swords.

He turned his attraction to guns ("Shore Leave"), and Kirk took that away from him. No doubt this explains why the normally fearless helmsman was upset when an enraged samurai (also created out of his own thoughts) charged after him. Sulu's yearning for the gun did make it possible to stop McCoy's black knight, but aside from that no one saw fit to let the man enjoy his hobby.

Sulu is rarely upset by anything, but when he is, it usually involves the safety of others, as in "The Children Shall Lead." He told Janice Lester/Kirk that she could execute Starfleet personnel literally "only over my dead body." And Khan's surprise attack was all the more upsetting to him because the expletive-deleted shields would not go up.

But personal danger rarely distresses him. This doesn't make him unrealistic—on the contrary, he is far more realistic than some. Kirk, for one, believes that if he bluffs death, stares it down, then it will go away: Sulu, though, has come to terms with the possibility that he really might die at any moment. His console could electrocute him, life support might fail, Klingons might make a sneak attack, or he could drown in the bath. All life is borrowed, so why cry about the inevitable? Why not simply enjoy each day and be thankful to have made it this far and seen so much? Sulu is the only one who looks forward to birthdays, and he'll continue to celebrate as long as he can afford to buy the candles with his pension. If death is no longer feared, there is no harm in tossing off jokes about Balok or Khan—they can't hear, they don't care, and it makes the children feel better.

Sulu and Kirk will have a better chance to become friends if they end up cooped up in the Bird of Prey. Sulu already has quite a crush on that small batlike ship, and even if Starfleet exonerates them, it's doubtful he would let the designers touch it. Let's hope Kirk at least lets him keep his toy and stays with something he knows, like convincing Maltz to join them. It would be a golden opportunity for Sulu, easily replacing his loss of a ship with talking turbolifts.

Sulu's source of inner peace is never mentioned, nor are many of his interests, achievements, or goals in life. It is possible that he has a strong religious faith to strengthen him both in health and hot water. By circumstance he has an American accent, admires a French musketeer, and is presented to an audience that began as approximately half Christian. There is no solid evidence that Sulu holds a Christian faith, but from his attitudes and actions, he could. His life is dedicated to doing good and not expecting good in turn. He does not have many vices, and he tries to eliminate those he does have. Hikaru Walter Sulu would sacrifice his own life to protect another, and he would do so without regret or (usually) fear. He is "in the world but not of it" and knows where to place his priorities. And he observes the phrase, "Be ye kind to one another, tenderhearted, forgiving of one another, even as the Lord hath forgiven you." Above all, Sulu is good with people, often kinder to them than they are to themselves. He might be Christian or Buddhist or Shinto, but unless he says so, there is no way to know. There is Oriental and Filipino blood in him, and there are many other beliefs in the world (not to mention the many other worlds known in Star Trek's time).

Whether or not Sulu has a religious conviction, he plays an important part in understanding man in Star Trek's (and our) time. Kirk and company are not the only ones capable of making profound statements, but as they are the stars, they get the attention. Thus, something very important is neglected.

If Kirk/Spock/McCoy represent the spirit of man, then Sulu/Uhura/Chekov are the source of man's strength: faith, hope, and love.

Faith is Sulu. Faith is the unshakable conviction that nothing can stand against a being that is right with its Maker. A man can have hopes without faith, but they will not be *hope*—they will be unworthy of his true nature and destiny. And he cannot have the *agape*, the love for all beings regardless of their worthiness, without faith. Faith is the bridge between the world of sinful, stumbling mortals and the holy eternity where they belong. Faith is a creature of this life, ceasing at life's end; but in its domain it is supreme among men. Sulu heads this forgotten triad: His strength and purity are the powerful link between the purely-mortal and the purely-eternal impulses of man.

Hope is Chekov. Hope is transient, a product of fleeting man as he struggles to achieve his goals. In timeless eternity, hope, which implies a progression in measurable human time, has no meaning or being. Hope is active; it takes action to achieve its desires; when the object of effort is gained (or lost), hope ceases and a new goal is chosen. Yet without love, hope's goals are often frivolous and without benefit. Chekov is the active, even impatient, driving force, that must have results while still in the mortal world.

Love is Uhura. Love is the whole being of Almighty God. This *agape* force does good to all men; but men, because of their impurity, are unable to truly return it. Therefore love, although the final word in the soul, does not translate well into the realm of mortals. Love needs faith to be welcomed into a man, and love needs hope to be its hands, building that faith. Uhura, like the power she represents, had difficulty "translating" into her imperfect world, and she will take longest to come into her strength. But in the end, she will command the forgotten triad. "And now remain these three, faith, hope, and love; but the greatest of these is love" (1 Cor. 13:13).

Star Trek III: The Search for Spock was one of the better vehicles for expressing the unity of Sulu/Chekov/Uhura (not to mention putting the tense, electric, shattered threesome in the spotlight). Sulu was tempted by the splendid if odd-looking *Excelsior*, truly a once-in-a-lifetime chance, and in his faith he let it go. Kirk was called upon to sacrifice his ship, and he did so, but considering his misery in *Wrath of Khan*, it's hard to believe he was losing much. What would he have done if called upon to give up the *Enterprise* at the *beginning* of his career, when that career had some meaning for him? Sulu had reached that marvelous point in time. All his dreams were finally coming true. Yet he let it all go to do what he knew was right. He didn't have to; despite his concern, this mission had nothing to do with him personally.

Chekov was the force of hope's power for action when he aided Scotty in repairing the crippled *Enterprise*. As ever, Chekov needs a concrete goal, one that he can reach in a reasonable period of time, to be satisfied. Kirk, like Chekov, is mostly a creature of hope: creating, striving, achieving (or failing), and living throughout in great impatience. But Chekov has the talent to repair the ship as well as command it; and Kirk, frustrated with idleness, envies him. His own hands ache to take action, but command will not permit it.

Uhura demonstrated her love for the others in both of these ways, with mixed results. In choosing McCoy's life over duty, she showed her faith in Kirk's task. By sabotaging Starfleet's communication system, she gave the crew the hope of success. But she had to remain behind to do these things, and it is very obvious that given the chance, she would have gone with the men. It was indeed love that caused her to endanger herself, when surely Janice Rand, Winston Kyle, or some other such loyal soul would have volunteered to take that position—and be turned in by Heisenberg. Rather than cause another to be punished, Uhura took the questionable honor upon herself.

Oh, the friendship of Sulu, Chekov, and Uhura still needs major development, but even now it is clearly more affectionate, peaceful, and stable than that of Kirk/Spock/McCoy. Chekov still needs some patience lessons, but not just now. Why take all the life out of him? Uhura is rather too shaky for her role and will take some years growing into it. Sulu for now is their natural leader, but it is a comfortable, almost lazy leadership. When Uhura has grown up a little, there will be some dynamic changes, and Sulu with be then content to follow her vision.

Even Kirk is beginning to notice the strength of these people. Until now, he has shied away from showing affection for them because it would be unprofessional, too intimate for a great captain and his meek underlings. Never before would he have considered joining them for a drink for any occasion, let alone invite them to his home. But he is beginning to understand that they are not children any longer, and that perhaps he still is. It is disturbing to him, but he is doing his best to work it out. It is his last hurdle in aging— the "calendar syndrome." (This is the tendency of parents never to see their children as growing up, or the mental rut of an employer who sees his employees as never older than the day they were hired, because if they age, then so do their elders. It's a curable ailment but still quite persistent, especially in somewhat vain persons like Kirk.) Yes, it hurts Kirk in some small way that his "kids" don't need him anymore.

This article will conclude in *The Best of Trek #12* with Part Three— "The Engineer and the Doctor."

THE CLASSIC STAR TREK

by Linda M. Johnston

The word "classic" is bandied about pretty freely these days . . . The word has even popped up in these collections from time to time. But what is a "classic," really? How is it defined? Who decides? And, most importantly, can Star Trek truly be termed a "classic"? Linda Johnston answers these questions in the following article, as well as offering a short course on what "classic" actually means.

Thanks to a local independent television station, I've been watching some of the old shows I watched when I was a teenager or thereabouts, shows like "Mod Squad," "Combat," and "Star Trek." Even in my youth, Star Trek was my favorite, but the three were more equal in my esteem then than now. This second time around, twenty years later, I began to wonder, personally, why the older I got the better Star Trek got, and the less satisfying the others were. And, by extension, I began to wonder why Star Trek seems to be quickly becoming a classic and other shows apparently are not.

I teach English in college, so the word *classic* is quite familiar to me, yet that a work is a classic is, like a lot of religion, simply to be taken by faith because it has stood the test of time. *Antigone* is a classic because it has survived since mid-400s B.C. *Canterbury Tales* is a classic because it has survived since the 1300s. *Huckleberry Finn* is a classic because it has survived since the late 1800s. But is Star Trek a classic because it has survived since 1966? Is

65

twenty years enough time to establish something as "a classic"? How does one predict what will survive the test of time or know when classic standing has arrived?

"Now wait," you may be saying. "You're comparing apples with oranges, written literature with visual television. Star Trek already is a classic within its own medium, having survived almost half as long as television itself." That may be true, and I, personally, believe it is. But comparing one TV show with another seems somewhat pointless when we try to capture *classic* in the classical literary sense. A classic is, by definition, something "of the highest rank or class; serving as an outstanding representative of its kind; model; having lasting significance or recognized worth." How can one call any television show a classic" when (1) the medium is so new that there have been devised only recently standards by which to judge what makes a good series (I am, for the moment, excluding old movies made before the advent of TV, and do not include in this discussion technical matters such as editing, directing, special effects, etc.); (2) something so novel cannot yet have proven lasting significance; (3) there are so few apples in the barrel—what other science fiction TV series, exactly, are you going to compare Star Trek with?

So, in the traditional sense, Star Trek cannot yet be called a *classic*. But when it can be, fifty or one hundred years hence, whatever that vague and arbitrary number of years is that something must survive, will it have survived? Will it be a classic?

I think the answer is yes, and I have several specific reasons for this belief.

First, a classic is something that, like influenza, spreads throughout the world, unstoppable, affecting rich and poor, educated and uneducated. And, like the flu, some get a mild case, others a bad case. Nearly everyone has heard of *Huckleberry Finn*, for instance; whether they've read it or not can tell you the author, at minimum, they've heard of it. The name pops up in the oddest places—there's no immunity.

We saw this invasion of Star Trek begin to happen not long after the last episode was aired. In *The Star Trek Compendium*, Allan Asherman states, "By 1978 Star Trek had made syndication history. The series was being seen over 300 times per week worldwide in 134 markets in the United States and 131 international markets located in 51 countries. Star Trek was being seen translated into forty-two languages. At the start of 1978, there were 371 Star Trek fan clubs and 431 fanzines being produced, and approximately thirty Trek conventions were being held each year."

Today, Star Trek references have spread to the general population. In 1983, Nena, a German secretary, recorded "99 Red Balloons," an extremely popular song that has an explicit Star Trek reference: ". . . every one a Captain Kirk." For me, the clincher came last spring. I hate to admit it, but when I choose a textbook, I don't always read every word of it. I had two new texts and, much to my amazement, found that both had one or more specific references to Star Trek—and these for 1984 college freshmen!

Let me clarify a point here. Contemporary popularity is not necessarily a harbinger of classicism, often just the opposite; what is "popular" is often critically poor. However, when something popular also becomes pervasive through various media, especially through allusion in scholarly literature, it is well on its way to becoming "a classic." Star Trek has entered this stage.

In the humanities—music, art, literature, theater (television?)—another test of what climbs to classic stature seems to relate again to the very word classic. "Of or in accordance with established principles and methods in arts and sciences" is another dictionary definition of classic. Just where were these principles and methods established? The first body of material to be considered classic in the Western sense was that of ancient Greece and Rome. A "classic," then, conforms to what ancient philosophers and critics themselves said an exemplary work should be.

It is not my intention here to get into a lengthy discourse—as the Greeks would say—on ancient philosophy, nor am I going to take every Star Trek episode and movie and try to explain how it conforms to the ideal of Greek thought, though I will say, there are some episodes and some movies more "classic" than others, Star Trek II: The Wrath of Khan, for instance, being almost a perfect Greek tragedy, with Khan as a tragically flawed man not all evil like Kruge and whom we can simultaneously admire and despise (i.e., creative tension, a major Greek standard for drama).

There are, however, two Greek principles of literature/drama/art against which Star Trek can easily be measured because one is so obvious to any fan and the other is so much discussed in Star Trek literature.

Greek playwrights believed that to be effective a play should be cathartic, figuratively cleansing the emotions. That is, one should be so drawn into the play that he laughs, cries, rages, and so on, at the appropriate places. Vicariously, he becomes part of the action. He forgets that he is seeing a play, an illusion. Any fan will tell you that more episodes than not pull the viewer into them—to laugh or cry or rage. Is there anyone who did not shed a tear at Spock's death?

I often find a kindred spirit among my students, someone who loves to come in and talk Trek. It always amuses me when he begins to speak of Kirk and Company as if they actually existed in the flesh. Sharron Crowson's *Best of Trek #9* article "Speculation: On Power, Politics, and Personal Integrity" is a perfect example of this real/unreal confusion that marks a classic. She asks, "whom and what did the Federation send to deal with the most explosive crisis of the century?" as if the Federation actually existed to send anyone anywhere. Writer Harve Bennett sent the *Grissom*, yet we are so drawn into the *Enterprise* world that we forget it isn't real. The first rule of reading a short story is that nothing exists before the first word or after the last one, or, in the case of Star Trek, between episodes, yet fans are constantly filling in the gaps, speculating, about the "actions" of nonexistent beings in a yet-to-be world. I'd find the tendency ludicrous—if I didn't do it myself.

Realism, thus, is one classic method for developing cartharsis. Another is concealment. An artwork must be so well crafted that one forgets it is contrived. Good art never draws attention to the artistic process. Seldom in Star Trek does anything spoil the illusion. The smoking operating table in "Journey to Babel" and the elevator scene between Kirk and Saavik in *Wrath of Khan* are the only exceptions I can think of, and they are technical problems more than plot or character development. (How many takes did they do in the elevator, anyway, that Shatner and Alley were in stitches?)

Character development is another technique for assuring catharsis. We identify with a filled-out character. In talking with fans, I, like Joyce Tullock, in "Brother, my Soul . . ." (*Best of Trek #9*), have found that every person has a favorite character, usually because that character has qualities the fan himself lacks. This "opposites attract" theme is central to Greek, specifically to Platonic, philosophy. The degree to which a work of art successfully handles this "incomplete man" theme seems to me directly proportional to the degree to which that work will attain classic stature.

Plato believed that man strove constantly to live the "good life." To him, the good life had nothing to do with leisure or money. A man was living the good life, or was *virtuous*, when he fit into the purpose for which he was created in two areas: society, and his own totality of soul. In Star Trek, we see the Triune characters—Kirk, Spock, and McCoy—and, to a lesser extent, the other characters—constantly seeking this classical "good life."

In Plato's ideal society, there were three basic functions that needed to be fulfilled. These functions are typified by the teacher, the soldier, and the worker. I do not find it by chance that at the beginning of *Star Trek II: The Wrath of Khan* Spock is a teacher. He has always functioned as the one who acquires, preserves, and imparts knowledge. Kirk, of course, is a natural-born soldier. He is often also the diplomatic arm of the political system, a part of the classical soldier function he does not really enjoy but performs adequately. McCoy, though not an artisan who crafts metal artifacts, nonetheless functions as the worker. His skilled hands are always busy.

Without stretching logic too much, we can see also that the other characters have found their ideal places within the *Enterprise* microcosm. Chekov is Spock's protégé, and on the *Reliant*, he is the knowledge-gatherer. Sulu, with his love for weaponry, is the soldier, who, if Genesis had not intervened, would have been captain of the *Excelsior*; with his warm, ready smile and humor, he could easily act as diplomat. Uhura and Scott, both members of the engineering section, are workers, constantly using their hands to keep vital ship functions operational. As a nurse, Chapel, like McCoy, is also a worker. Rand's position is difficult to explain in Platonic terms—perhaps he forgot the category I shall euphemistically call "companion," although that certainly falls into the worker class. No wonder her role did not survive.

Philosophically speaking, the crew of the *Enterprise* is living the good life: everyone is performing the task he was created for. No bickering, no shoving, all harmonious. Plato's ideal society.

Until a niche is jeopardized. Many of the episode plots are based on a disruption—from within or without—of this ideal society. In one show after another, each Triune character is offered a chance to change his role in the *Enterprise* society. In "The Galileo Seven," "The Tholian Web," and "The Paradise Syndrome," Spock moves from second in command to become the highest ranking officer present and, though he always saves the day, he is never comfortable with this higher role, nor is he very good at it. More than once, he reminds McCoy that he has no desire to command a starship. McCoy, of course, is quick to let everyone around know that Spock is in over his head.

In "For the World Is Hollow and I Have Touched the Sky," McCoy is given the opportunity to live out his dying days in a different society, doing nothing. At first, he thinks this would be wonderful, especially because he is in love, but he realizes, even before he's cured, that medicine is his whole life and that his place in society is as Chief Medical Officer of the USS *Enterprise*.

Kirk's position as captain is the one most often threatened, either by other men, aliens, machines, or by strife within Kirk himself. "The Enemy Within" is the first episode in which we see Kirk losing control of his ship as the splitting of his own personality in two makes him incapable of leadership. Immediately thereafter, in "The Naked Time," Kirk's position is again jeopardized from an internal personality change. Charlie X, Harry Mudd, and Khan are some of the people who try to dispossess Kirk of his rightful social position. The most powerful displacement episode, though, is "The Ultimate Computer," for the other enemies he could at least fight. But his position is within Starfleet and it is this very system that is trying to replace him. Fortunately, machines, although valuable in their own places within society, as Spock says, are not ready to rule humans. "There are certain things men must do to remain men," said Kirk. (Perhaps Star Trek's adherence to this classical standard of "the good life" with each community member contributing his unique talents explains why Kirk seems always to be destroying paradise societies, for example, "The Apple" and "Return of the Archons.")

But by far the most obvious enactment of this theme of man's place in society comes at the beginning of *Star Trek II: The Wrath of Khan*. Captain Kirk is now Admiral Kirk, and for once McCoy and Spock agree—Kirk is a man out of his societal niche. "You should never have given up the *Enterprise* . . . Get your ship back. Get it back before you really do get old," advises the doctor. "Logic does reveal . . . that you erred in accepting promotion. You are what you were: a starship commander," says Spock. Kirk is absolutely miserable with a desk job. Despite all the horrors of Khan and Kruge, Kirk is happy commanding the *Enterprise*. His place in society is the command chair. I shall be extremely surprised and disappointed if Kirk is not demoted right off in *Star Trek IV*. He deserves the reward of being captain again, of returning to "the good life."

Two other themes based on Platonic ideal of society should be mentioned. Plato believed in equity of wealth. There should be no extremes of wealth or poverty. "The Cloud Minders" emphasizes this theory. Plato was also an advocate of women's rights, believing they had a legitimate right to hold any position they were capable of, even the top political office. Unfortunately, there is never a female captain in Starfleet. "Poor Janice Lester," "Turnabout Intruder" seems to say at the end, "If only she'd been content with her place as a woman obviously inferior to men." Even Uhura never gets to lead an expedition. Only in the last movies do we see that Saavik has a shot at her own command. Vulcans, however, have apparently read Plato's *Republic*, for T'Pau obviously is in her rightful place. In *Star Trek IV*, I hope we see some women wearing pants figuratively as well as literally.

Not only must man seek his intended place in society, but, Plato says, he must also seek harmony among the parts of his own being. Throughout his life, Plato tried to define the pieces that comprise the thing we call *man*. Basically (and I mean bare-bones basic, for no one can pretend to condense Plato's ideas into a short essay), Plato said that man could be divided into two major parts, the body and the soul. Somewhere in between the two is the intellect, which could itself be divided into reason and the senses. Together, reason and the senses gain knowledge or wisdom. When all is working in harmony, man is said to be *virtuous*. The four chief virtues of the soul extending from the man as a whole are wisdom, justice, courage, and temperance.

Many protagonists in classical literature are incomplete. They are always seeking some missing part of themselves. Much has been said about the relationship of the Triune. This relationship, this interdependence, is a symbolic literary representation of Plato's philosophy. It takes Kirk plus Spock plus McCoy to make one complete man.

If we can't compare Star Trek with another science fiction series, we can compare it with something fairly similar, the fantasy, *The Wizard of Oz*, which, with little argument, has established itself as a classic, having passed all the aforementioned criteria. In *The Wiz-*

ard of Oz, we have a heroine who is a complete human being. She is wise, just, courageous, and temperate. She is, thus, virtuous. However, classically, and literally, she is displaced. She is looking for the way home, for her ordained place in the universe. It is the other three major characters—another Triune—who are each fragmented. The scarecrow lacks reason (a brain). The tin man lacks feeling, senses (a heart). And the lion lacks courage (a brave-acting body). At the end, each receives the missing ingredient, and the three taken together represent one unified whole.

Again, without consideration of technical aspects of film, *The Wizard of Oz* is a classic partly if not entirely because it so beautifully interweaves these two classic ideas of man's search for his place in society and his search for his whole self. Thematically, this classic is closely paralleled by Star Trek, a potential classic.

We have seen that on numerous occasions plot conflict arises because someone's place in the *Enterprise* society is threatened. Now let us see how plot and theme make use of man's search for completeness, for virtue.

Like the Oz characters, within the Star Trek Triune, each person represents only a part of Plato's complete man, but instead of having a fourth person who magically supplies the missing parts, each Star Trek person supplements the other two.

Spock, as has been well documented, represents reason. He deals in abstractions, in theories, in the invisible, the universal, the changeless. He relies primarily on logic, both deductive and inductive. (Logic, by the way, comes from the Greek word *leg-*, meaning "to gather.") In "Shore Leave," for instance, Spock gathers evidence that suggests someone is fabricating reality from mental images. In "Courtmartial," he gathers evidence, including a test of the computer, and concludes that someone has tampered with the computer's program and that Ben Finney is not dead. He enjoys gathering information.

Often, though, Spock cannot see what is plainly under his nose: that the primitive creatures in "The Galileo Seven" had no logic of fear; that Minerva Jones ("Is There in Truth No Beauty?") is blind.

McCoy, on the other hand, is the senses of the Platonic Man. Much of Star Trek literature states or implies that McCoy is the embodiment of emotion. To Plato, however, there was a distinction between sensual and emotional. To him, the worst sin against mankind was an act of unbridled passion (emotion). Such a "wild" man was called vicious. Even at his most caustic, his most agitated, McCoy never loses control (often because of his dependence on the other two). He is never Plato's evil man. If he were, he would never have killed the creature in "The Man Trap"; he would have wallowed in self-pity in "For the World Is Hollow . . ."; and so on. By *sensual*, Plato meant the use of the five senses and worldliness of experience. McCoy is of Southern gentility. He enjoys fine drink and fine food, and he has an eye for beautiful women. Whereas Spock deals in abstractions, McCoy deals in concretes. McCoy is a "seer." His gift is not logic but intuition, a word based on the Latin *intuere*, "to look at or toward."

Because McCoy relies on the tangible evidence of his senses, he has a difficult time believing that the creature in "Man Trap" is not Nancy Crater. His faith in what he sees also makes him the first victim of the illusionary world of "Shore Leave."

Plato recognized a certain antithesis between reason and sense. Much has been made in Star Trek literature of the feud between Spock and McCoy. True, they seldom agree on anything, primarily because their incompleteness makes each view the world differently. They are not so much men in a mirror (as Joyce Tullock stated in her article "Brother, My Soul: Spock, McCoy, and the Man in the Mirror," *Best of Trek #9*) as pieces of a shattered mirror angled differently. Yet Plato says that reason is dependent upon the senses for data, and that the senses are dependent upon logic for self-control. In the series we see the feud, but we also see the mutual dependence. It is evidence of the senses—McCoy's white sound device—that proves Spock's deduction right in "Courtmartial," that knows how to deceive those very senses in "Amok Time," and that provide inspiration for illogic in "The Galileo Seven." Conversely, it is logic (Spock's urgings) that causes McCoy to shoot the deceptive salt creature, that convinces McCoy that Kirk is alive in "The Tholian Web," that is able to depose Decker when McCoy cannot in "The Doomsday Machine." Constantly we see the feud between reason and sensation, but we also see their classic cooperation, and it is this last which is so often overlooked in Star Trek analyses, yet so vital to predicting a classic.

Both reason and sense are part of the intellect. Intellect is for Plato the highest natural faculty of Man, guiding and directing the body. Kirk is very definitely the body in Plato's complete man. Undeniably, he is the sex symbol of Star Trek. Being both naive and a McCoy fan, I was not aware just how many women had wild fantasies about Kirk until I saw the near-brawl over very explicit pieces of Kirk artwork at a recent Star Trek convention. Kirk is definitely a lover (remember the boots scene in "Wink of an Eye"?) He takes every opportunity to remove his shirt. Also, he does physical battle with the Squire of Gothos, the Gorn, the Klingons. He acts.

But Kirk acts only after consulting Spock (reason) and McCoy (sense). There's an old cartoon that shows a character with an angel on one shoulder and the devil on the other. Although Spock and McCoy may not be quite that extreme, though the direction is Platonically right, there are countless scenes of Kirk caught (by choice, usually) between Spock literally on his right and McCoy on his left.

Triune, meaning three in one, is a perfect appellation. The Triune is one Complete Man, having reason, sense, and body. Thus, all combine to make the soul, which, in harmony, has virtue. If one character is missing, the soul becomes unbalanced. ("Plato's Stepchildren" is, of course, an explicit rendering of this theme.) That is why Spock's death is not only emotionally upsetting for Kirk and McCoy; it shakes their very essence. They are hopelessly incomplete without reason. It is not only Spock's soul they seek to reunite with his body but also their own soul which has been shattered. It happens to be Spock who died, but the search would have been necessary were it Kirk or McCoy.

In the *Trek Roundtable* secton of *Best of Trek #9*, some fans could not understand Kirk's decision to destroy the *Enterprise*. Others felt that Kirk had "matured." Here we see a classic dilemma: The Klingons are trying to usurp Kirk's social position, symbolized by the *Enterprise*, and, in so doing, are thwarting his effort to reunite his soul. It is not strange, though it may be sad, that Kirk chose totality of being over social standing, truly the good of the one for the good of the many (a concept that will be vindicated in *Star Trek IV*).

Thus, if the use of classic philosophy as a basis for theme, plot, and characterization is one more mark of a future classic, Star Trek is well on its way here, too.

Now, if this crash course in Greek philosophy was confusing, let me take the one episode which, to me, epitomized the best use of man's place in society and man's search for completeness as thematic material. Instantly, several fans will say, "Oh, 'The City on the Edge of Forever.' " This episode seems to be the most critically acclaimed, and I cannot think of a better tabloid of the Triune as perfect Platonic symbol than the final old Earth scene: Reason (Spock) standing behind and directing the Body (Kirk) to willfully and deliberately act to restrain the Senses (McCoy). The scene is virtuous because we vividly see wisdom, courage, temperance, and justice.

For me, however, the episode most true to Platonic ideals is "The Empath." It is often criticized for its excessive, senseless violence. And I suspect that, because of the ending lines, the episode is often misinterpreted as being a statement of the value of emotion *over* logic. McCoy says, ". . . with all their scientific knowledge and advances, it was good, ol' fashioned emotion they valued most." Scott then wonders if the Vulcans know that, and when Kirk asks if Mr. Spock will take them the news, Spock says, "I shall certainly give the thought all the consideration it is due," and it truly isn't due much. The point of the episode, just like *Star Trek: The Motion Picture* is not that one part of man is better than another but that all parts—reason, sense, and body—must operate in harmony.

Let's begin at the beginning, for even before Gem is introduced, we wee Platonic philosophy in operation.

First and most obvious, it is the Triune only that is brought underground by the Vians, totally isolated from the *Enterprise*—Spock first, then McCoy, then Kirk. But Kirk (the Body) wakes first; then he "comes to his senses by awakening Spock and McCoy.

The three stumble upon Gem simultaneously, but each immediately reacts differently, and almost exactly as they did in "City." McCoy impulsively approaches the girl—ahead of the others. "She seems (looks) harmless enough," he says. Kirk acts to physically restrain him as Spock, again slightly behind the two, gives a logical reason: "The sand bats of Maynark IV appear to be inanimate creatures until they attack." The Man is in perfect harmony.

Immediately the Body demands information. At least half of Kirk's lines in this episode are questions. "What is it, Spock? Analysis."

Spock gives a logical answer. "From what we know," he begins, ". . . a life form such as hers could not have evolved here."

Then Kirk turns to the doctor. "Bones, what's wrong with her?"

From his examination of Gem, McCoy "jumps to the conclusion" that all her species are mutes. "That's my observation, for whatever it's worth," he says, denigrating his input.

To act rightly, the Body must have the input of both reason and sense. Only after this exchange does Kirk move toward Gem.

Not surprisingly, it is Kirk, the physical man, the soldier/diplomat who receives the first three physical abuses—the cut from his fall in the surface laboratory, the jolt from the Vian weapon, and, later, the "torture experiment" (with his shirt removed, of course).

The next part shows Spock and McCoy operating on different levels of reality. The three men find the underground laboratory. "Fascinating," says Spock abstractedly. "*Look* at this stuff," says McCoy. The Vians appear and McCoy says, "We've just *seen* the results of your tests." (italics added) Outside, McCoy *sees* Scotty and the search party. When they disappear, the doctor, mystified, asks Spock, "Where did they go?" "I believe they were never present," says Spock. McCoy believes in what he sees. Spock does not. In a later scene, he and Kirk are surrounded by a force field. It is Spock who is able to get around "reality" to a higher abstraction. "In spite of what we see . . ." he begins, then suppresses all emotion to kill the force field and walk out. Here, then, we have *three* scenes in one episode that show the interaction of sense and reason.

Then, as if that isn't enough, the Vians state the parameters of a test: there is "an 87 percent chance the doctor will die—sensory function will cease; there is a 93 percent chance Spock's brain will be damaged, resulting in insanity" —the reasoning function will cease. Notice that the chances are about equal that each will lose his function, thus, logically, that each one contributes an equal but totally different element to the complete Man.

Plato's theory of man's place in society disrupted is demonstrated in the scene where a choice must be made as to who will be the guinea pig. At first, each man is in his proper role. Kirk, as captain, will go and, because he is rightfully in command, that is his prerogative. No one can argue with him because his decision is within his right as commander. In his proper role as physician, McCoy unintentionally upsets society by knocking Kirk out. It is important that the action is unintentional, for he can be forgiven for upsetting the societal balance.

Now Spock is in command, so he will go with the Vians. Because the displacement is accidental, Spock's succession is just, and

McCoy should not question it. However, McCoy, deliberately and premeditatedly, knocks out Spock. Before he succumbs to "the good doctor's hypo," Spock makes a statement Plato himself would have said: "Your decision is highly unethical." McCoy's deliberate disruption of the law of man's place in society is, indeed, highly unethical, and, in a sense, he is now to be punished for it, and it is this impulsive, intuitive, sensual part of the Triune which was immoderate who suffers most.

If this "decision" scene shows Man out of harmony in society and the subsequent punishment, the "dying" scene shows Man's internal discord. When one member of the Triune seems hopelessly lost, the others attempt to compensate. Instantly, Spock becomes more sensitive ("good bedside manner"); Kirk becomes more logical, deducing that Gem is the focal point and solution to their problem.

In my opinion, the final scene with the Vians is the best summary of what Star Trek is all about and why it will become a classic.

Here we have the Total Man—the Triune—juxtaposed sharply against the Incomplete Man—the Vians. One Vian gives Plato's definition of virtue (harmony of soul). "You were her teachers," he says, having taught her "the will to survive [courage], love of life [wisdom/The Good Life], passion to know [temperance/justice]. Everything that is truest and best in all species of beings has been revealed by you." The Vians recognize the Triune as the ideal, complete, Total Man.

To the Vians, Kirk says, "You've lost the capacity to feel the emotions you brought Gem here to experience. You don't understand what it is to love [the Platonic "good life"]. Love and compassion are dead in you. You're nothing but intellect." Despite McCoy's illogical remark at the very end, it is not that intellect per se is evil. It is that any part—reason, sense, or body—without the others causes imbalance of the Man.

Few of us real live humans are "virtuous" in the Greek sense. Perhaps we have not found our niche in society. Or perhaps we are weak in one of the key areas of the Complete Man. We are, thus, forever searching for our perfect place in the universe and/or for our soul. The *Enterprise* is a world in harmony and, together, its characters represent the ideal man. We have, if only temporarily, found the Good Life. That is why we have such an insatiable appetite for anything related to the show, why we spread its message of brotherhood like the gospel to the world, why we identify so strongly with the characters, why we want to serve on the *Enterprise*, why we laugh and cry as we watch the show, why we hate to come back to anything less than that good life.

Of "the will to survive, the love of life, the passion to know," the Vian says, "these are the qualities that make a civilization worthy to survive." A firm foundation on this premise of virtue is also what makes Star Trek worthy to survive, worthy to become a classic. I am convinced that it will be—or is.

THE JOURNEY TO—AND BEYOND— THE SEARCH FOR SPOCK

by Hazel Ann Williams

Why did events in the last two Star Trek films unfold in the fashion they did? What were the forces that shaped the death and resurrection of Spock, the destruction of the Enterprise, *and the trials faced by Admiral Kirk? In the following article, Hazel Williams takes a look at some of the behind-the-scenes machinations that possibly could have made it inevitable that both films turned out the way they did. And she offers a few speculations on the direction* Star Trek IV *will take.*

From "The Cage" through *Star Trek III: The Search for Spock*, the world of Star Trek has been through many changes. New characters have been introduced, only to die off or disappear. The *Enterprise* has been redesigned three times, and the uniforms are as change-able as the weather. Change is the essence of life, but nothing wreaked as much havoc as the drastic events of *Star Trek II: The Wrath of Khan* and *The Search for Spock*. At the end of *The Search for Spock*, the *Enterprise* has been destroyed and most of the major characters are at grave risk. How did we get into this situation?

Where *can* we go from here? Since the future is grounded in the past, let's look back and analyze the findings.

Star Trek II: The Wrath of Khan began by putting the characters in perspective to their universe. When Kirk was Captain of the *Enterprise*, he was portrayed as brash, daring, brave, and in all ways extraordinary. A man sure of his abilities and confident of the people around him. He ably led a group who proved they could think their way out of every situation an unpredictable universe could present. Why Kirk considered, much less accepted, an Admiralty position is not revealed in *Star Trek: The Motion Picture*. That he hated the job, hated being away from a command position and the *Enterprise*, is painfully obvious. The Kirk who takes a new *Enterprise* out against the threat of V'Ger is a desperate, driven man who bears only the slightest resemblance to the self-confident Captain of the episodes.

Slowly, over the course of the movie, Kirk regains most of those well-remembered qualities. *Wrath of Khan* picked up ten years after V'Ger. Again, we are faced with a desperate Admiral Kirk, but this is a quieter, bleaker desperation. He is fifty years old and in the grip of a devastating midlife crisis. Looking back, the Admiral sees all his best and brightest years behind him. To Kirk, his questions about his own future seem sensible. What more could—or in his view of reality, should—he do? Kirk's line, "Galloping around the cosmos is a game for the young" isn't sarcasm, it's his new belief, or what he feels he *should* believe. It is this attitude that causes his friends' concern, and inspires McCoy's warning, "Get back your command before you turn into one of these antiques, before you really do grow old." In this disoriented state of mind, Kirk must face some of the greatest challenges of his life.

Spock, too, has changed, but this is the change of growth and maturity. As the episodes progressed, Spock showed more of his humanity. Yet, when *Star Trek: The Motion Picture* begins, we see he has retreated to Vulcan to purge his human half. Spock's way has never been easy; as Amanda explained to Kirk, "Neither Vulcan nor human; at home nowhere, except Starfleet." Whether in reaction against his own "weakening" to emotional humans, or simply tiring of the constant struggle to control his feelings while denying he had any, Spock was driven to Gol and *Kolinahr*. He is just as desperate as Kirk to find, or rediscover, something neither can, or will, name.

STTMP gave Spock a vivid picture of logic and the sterility of the Vulcan Way carried to extreme. His experience with V'Ger allows Spock to accept that he no longer must hold his Vulcan and human heritages in dichotomy. He can merge both to create a greater uniqueness that *is* Spock. The complex simplicity of IDIC (Infinite Diversity in Infinite Combinations) is a lesson Spock can now fully appreciate. *Wrath of Khan* shows us that Spock used the years since V'Ger to apply that lesson to himself. The tense rigidity of his battle stance and the quick, tight, stress-revealing movements are gone. This Spock can relax, even to the point of lighthearted word play with his protégé or closest friend. He is sure of his place in the universe and the placement of his soul. All the best facets of Spock are now combined into a mature being.

Except for the quiet aura of competence created by experience and survival, the rest of the *Enterprise's* regular senior officers are comfortably familiar. McCoy, with his feet still solidly planted in his belief of humanism. Scotty, still a devil on shore leave and bursting with pride at his engines and his nephew. Sulu, bright and wonderful, happy to get back to the *Enterprise*, whatever the reason. Uhura, more beautiful than ever and secure in her own abilities. Chekov, now first officer of the *Reliant*, but still Chekov. They provide a solid background to bounce back the shattering reflection of a shaken Admiral Kirk and the solid, concerned Captain Spock. An almost happy family reunion, but then the real problems begin.

Instead of rehashing the plot, let's look at five major events. Because both *Wrath of Khan* and *The Search for Spock* depend deeply on Kirk's actions/reactions/decisions, we'll deal with these events as influences upon him.

The return of Khan is a master stroke. The cataclysm that struck Ceti Alpha IV made survival almost impossible, and advancement of Khan's "master race" merely a pipe dream. The deaths of his wife and people and his own terrible sense of failure combine to put more pressure on that great mind than it can tolerate. The arrival of Terrell and Chekov, with the chance for escape and a return to power, pushes Khan over the edge. He becomes evil and madness personified.

Khan's thirst for vengeance exceeds the boundaries of quest. It becomes an all-consuming obsession. Even with Genesis aboard (and there's little doubt that these brilliant people won't understand it and be able to duplicate the process), and Kirk supposedly entombed in Regulus, Khan must finish the task personally and destroy the *Enterprise*, Kirk's ship and love. Khan is more than a physical threat, he becomes a symbol of past sin and past error that haunts the future, Kirk's future. Khan is the ultimate random factor in Kirk's one-time orderly universe, and it is he who starts the chain reaction of events that ends in tragedy.

Where would evil be without power? *Star Trek II: The Wrath of Khan* provides power to spare in the form of Genesis. As proposed, it would help alleviate the problems of population and food production by force-evolving life-giving conditions on lifeless planets. Yet it has military potential, too. The "discussion" between Spock and McCoy of the Genesis Effect aptly points out the vast potential for a novel form of destruction that would create new life as it was destroying the old. To control this power is to control the universe, and the struggler for control is the battle line of the film. For Khan, it is not only the key of release from his own personal hell, but the key by which he can avenge himself upon Kirk, and to once again be Master. Kirk, again on the side of the angels, must keep Khan from possessing the device and save the Federation from Khan's evil domination. A classic confrontation, and one that intensifies the final Khan-Kirk showdown.

The person responsible for creating Genesis is Dr. Carol Marcus, Kirk's one-time love, and the mother of his son. Although we know very little about this relationship, Kirk's reaction to her name shows that the parting, at least, was painful. She and her project are threatened by Khan's madness. Kirk arrives too late to save the rest of the research team, but just in time to help Khan get Genesis, and without enough preparation to spare himself an abrupt and painful introduction to his son, David. With blood and death behind them, and the threat of Khan and Genesis before them, Kirk and Carol's bittersweet reunion is necessarily brief. In many ways, this scene raises more questions than it answers, but its effect on Kirk is unmistakable. He feels even older and more confused than he did at the beginning of the movie.

The introduction of Kirk's son, although not of major importance to the plot, is an event in Kirk's life. David, with his strong aversion to the military and Starfleet, is almost a stereotype of the brave scientist doing battle glorious with the nasty, evil armed forces. His shock and resentment at finding out one of *them* is his father is therefore understandable. Kirk is hurt by his son's rejection, and this feeling adds to his growing list of problems. By the end of the film, David has vividly learned what real evil is, and the price that must be paid to stop it. He can then begin to accept his father as a human being, a man, and not a false image of a Starfleet authority figure. Before this change, Kirk bears a heavy burden of guilt about David's reaction to him, and grieves for their life that could have been.

Hunted by a madman with the potential to destroy the universe, embroiled in personal problems, trying to fight with a crippled ship managed by "children," Admiral Kirk manages to beat the odds again. Even when a dying Khan sets off the Genesis Device, Kirk and the *Enterprise* survive to witness the birth of a new world. Yet Kirk still has to face his biggest crisis: the death of Spock.

Spock, with his slightly higher tolerance to radiation, has done what no one else (*almost* no one else) could have done—repaired the main engines and saved the *Enterprise*, Kirk, and the trainee crew. This time the price of salvation was Spock's life. Kirk witnesses his friend's final agony and death, but is cut off by a wall of glass, unable to touch, unable to give or receive the comfort of embrace. The sacrifice, grand and noble as it was, is almost too much for Kirk. Spock was more than a friend. He was Kirk's right hand, his balance in all things, especially rash and foolhardy things . . . almost Kirk's other half. For the first time, Kirk must face the harsh lesson of mortality. As he explains to David, "I've cheated death . . . and patted myself on the back for it . . . but I've never faced it, not like this," Kirk listens to David's words of comfort without real acceptance, although he allows himself some joy at David's gesture of conciliation and embrace.

Something happens to Kirk on the way to the Bridge—he loses the hard edge of his grief. When faced with the new planet, he is filled with wonder; he feels young again. In Engineering and at Spock's funeral, Kirk grieved, but now something is numb, something vital has been stilled. Even with his moist, shining eyes and the throwaway line of, "I can't believe his questing spirit is at rest . . . ," something is missing. Kirk has too quickly seemingly accepted Spock's death, something that should happen at a very late stage in the grief cycle. The voice of Spock and the final scenes of the movie give fans hope for our favorite Vulcan, but what of Kirk?

There is no real ending to *Wrath of Khan*, for very little has been resolved. Khan has been blown to bits along with the *Reliant*, and that threat is removed. Genesis works better than expected; it was intended to develop a lifeless world or moon, not create a new planet. Genesis is more potent than ever and this can only lead to controversy. Who can be trusted to administer such power? Can the Federation survive the moral, economic, and military side effects? How can it be adequately protected?

Because Doctors Carol and David Marcus are the only members of the Genesis team left alive, it's reasonable to assume they will take charge of whatever group explores the new Genesis Planet. Kirk and Carol seem to have made a tentative step toward renewing their relationship, but that was in the midst of crisis, when people cling to each other out of desperate need. They still occupy different worlds. Do they *want* a relationship of that nature, or are they more motivated to part as friends? David has begun to change from childish stereotype to human being. It poses interesting possibilities for the future. Can he establish his own personality?

The biggest problem is, of course, Spock. As was noted earlier, the final scenes of *Wrath of Khan* gave hope for Spock's return. It has to be tied up with the Genesis Effect, of life from lifelessness. Related to this is Kirk's strange reactions. Will he suppress the pain he must feel and slide through the rest of his life? Will he come to grips with his feelings, and problems, and face the future, taking his friends' advice to follow his own first, best destiny. No, *Star Trek II: The Wrath of Khan* does not end, it merely pauses.

Fandom circulates many stories that should more fairly be called rumors. One such states that, at the cast party after the premiere of *Wrath of Khan*, Leonard Nimoy said he couldn't wait to see how Spock would come back in *Star Trek III*, and Harve Bennett almost had a coronary. As James Blish says in his book of episode adaptations, *Star Trek 4*, a writer should not inflict his technical problems on his readers. However, fandom explores every aspect of the Star Trek Universe, and to understand the direction *The Search for Spock* took, it seems we have to seek a partially technical explanation.

Except for a gifted few, most writers must begin their work with clear and definite goals in mind. Then either the characters or the circumstances will dictate how the writer accomplishes these goals. An examination of *Star Trek III: The Search for Spock* seems to reveal three major objectives. First, as the title states, Spock must be found and revived. A second goal is to completely discredit

Genesis. If, as further analysis will bear out, the Genesis Planet must be destroyed, an easy explanation is that it exceeded its programmed parameters and we're damned lucky that it held together this long. A functioning Genesis would raise too many problems. It would pose as big a threat to the Federation as Khan, albeit a more obscure and insidious one. Genesis is too well-known to ignore, as so many new devices and discoveries were in the episodes. Although it is the obvious key to Spock's resurrection, it must be discredited and destroyed. The third goal, even though it seems cruel to fans, is the destruction of the *Enterprise*. It could have been avoided, written around, if it was not a goal. The "why" is unknown. Mr. Bennett's supposed explanation that he simply wrote himself into a corner is totally unacceptable. The written word has always been vulnerable to erasers.

Star Trek III: The Search for Spock acknowledges the nonending of *Wrath of Khan* by revamping the important final shots of *Wrath of Khan* in its opening sequence. However, we do see changes. Kirk says most of his trainee crew has been reassigned, and David and Saavik are on the *Grissom*, en route to the Genesis Planet. Because the *Enterprise* has not yet reached dock, this must have been accomplished by a ship-to-ship transfer. Another ship has gone to Ceti Alpha, gods know where Carol is, and Kirk now feels the full weight of Spock's absence. Now he is uncomfortable, even morose, saying he has left the best part of himself behind, and that they have paid for their victory with their dearest blood. Kirk notes the crews' obsessive reaction to Spock's death, but he doesn't associate it with his own. McCoy is acting strangely, although we later understand his change, and more than enough clues are provided. Everyone is burdened by Spock's death, an event no one ever conceived as possible.

To further complicate the picture, certain conditions are imposed. First, every other member of Starfleet must appear dull of wit—to put it kindly. Admiral Morrow, if he is the friend the film implies, must have realized Kirk would not take calmly the retirement of the *Enterprise* and the refusal to allow them to return to the Genesis Planet. Even if he knew Kirk only by reputation, did Morrow really believe he'd so easily dissuaded Kirk from an obviously important task, especially one that involved Spock and McCoy? When Kirk left the officer's lounge, Morrow should have had red alert sounding in his head loud enough to deafen him. Another point: Just because

Morrow "never really understood Vulcan mysticism," is that any reason to brush it aside as if it didn't exist? Does the Admiral *really* understand human (or alien) psychology or physiology, warp physics, theoretical mathematics, or stellar evolution? If not, do these too not exist?

As an officer, Styles is a bit more believable. His overbearing pride in his ship, and his own abilities, will never make for a happy ship. His crew will obey him, or suffer the consequences of a blotted permanent record and a rough trip, but they'd never follow *him* into the mouth of hell. Styles's reaction to yellow alert in space dock is a nice theatrical bit, but ludicrous. The alert could have been sounded as a drill, due to a fire or accident on his ship or another ship, or the dock itself, due to sabotage, outside threat, a ship coming in disabled or out of control, and so on. If we can think of all these things, why can't a trained Starfleet officer—the *Captain* of the Fleet's fastest, newest, and most powerful ship— think of at least one?

There are two ways to make a character, or a set of characters, appear extraordinary. The first, and admittedly the most difficult, is by careful choice of dialogue, action, and reaction that *is* extraordinary. The second, easier and simpler, way is to play down all other characters in the film, making them dull and vaguely stupid. Unfortunately, *The Search for Spock* used the second method. The character of Esteban, the Captain of the scientific exploration ship *Grissom*, is entirely unbelievable. He and his crew must be experienced, and have seen quite an array of the strange and unusual, or they would not have drawn this assignment. Esteban is so stiff and by the book, it's easy to understand his poor showing as a battle commander—it's his refusal to take any initiative that's ridiculous. Only the character of "Mr. Adventure" has any link to reality. His behavior can be written off to inexperience, youth, and a phaser pointed at his chest.

Besides making everyone at Starfleet imbeciles, a second condition is, that in order to place Spock's essence at rest, Spock's body must be returned to Vulcan. The reason for this is not brought out in the movie, except that it is responsible for further narrowing the possibilities. The novelization cites the duality of mind and body, good enough for a plausible cover story, and fairly reasonable philosophy. A point to mention: Sarek must have known Spock's tube had been found or he'd simply have asked Kirk to bring McCoy to

Vulcan, or even simpler, have done it himself. Kirk believed Spock's body burned on entering the Genesis Planet's atmosphere. Remember David's line to Saavik: "The gravitational fields were in flux. It could have soft landed." Sarek had read Kirk's report, which surely included the disposition of Spock's remains, so Sarek knew it was Kirk's intention to burn his son's body. Sarek would not have asked Kirk to return a body that no longer existed. Whether the process would have worked without Spock's body is unknown, but apparently as long as the body existed, it was as necessary to the ritual as the essence in McCoy's mind.

This brings us to the third condition, McCoy's reaction to the death meld. Although it would have been safer to bring McCoy to Vulcan first, and thus protect Spock's essence, the good doctor's mind was in confusion. Parts of Spock's needs and thoughts kept sliding into McCoy's consciousness. McCoy's reaction led him on a desperate path of indiscretion and, finally, imprisonment as a nut case. Even at this point, the story could have developed along different lines had an alternate route to Spock's revival been sought. Sarek could have appealed to the Federation for McCoy to be brought to Vulcan for "treatment." Surely the Federation Council couldn't have been as bigoted as Admiral Morrow. Sarek could have also used his enormous influence to get Kirk to the Genesis Planet, or simply requested the return of his son's body with the greatest possible speed, citing Federation laws and Starfleet regulations guaranteeing personal religious freedom. The only way to negate these possibilities is the fourth and final condition. Simply stated, it is "time is of the essence," and needs no further explanation.

In consideration of the story goals and imposed conditions, what results is a precise series of events that constantly narrows Kirk's choices until the final result is achievable through no other means. The Klingon threat has been a slowly tightening coil during the whole movie. Beginning with a theft of basic information, it progresses to violation of Federation space, discovery of the Genesis Planet, and the "accidental" destruction of the *Grissom*. With the *Grissom* gone, David, Saavik, and a living Spock are alone and vulnerable on a spectacularly dying planet. The second story goal, discrediting Genesis, is fulfilled by David's admission to having used protomatter, a wonderfully vague catch-all substance able to hide all problems under a scientific umbrella. Although tying the aging of Spock to the aging of the planet stretches science fiction almost to the border of pseudo science-fantasy, it presents an interesting, if not well handled, set of side-bar problems.

Kirk arrives at the Genesis Planet to find the Klingons already there. The brief battle leaves the *Enterprise* burned out, unable to maneuver, run, or fight. She is, to all respects, dead and trapped in orbit around a dying planet. That the Genesis Planet is going to explode very soon is vital, or the threat is lessened to a degree where the destruction of the *Enterprise* is not a necessity. Kruge, the Klingon commander, plays a hunch and reveals his hostages. For Kirk, finding his son, and a living Spock in the hands of the Klingons on a dying planet, raised the stakes to almost impossible heights.

To force Kirk's surrender, and prove his ruthlessness (an unnecessary gesture, fandom knows the Klingons don't play around, and the movie has more than proved the point by having Kruge kill his spy and her ship, kill one of his own crewmen for disobeying an order, and kill a giant worm with his own hands, just for fun), Kruge sacrifices one of the hostages, secure in his knowledge that Genesis can be found in the *Enterprise*'s computers, or at least in the surviving hostages. David, jumping the Klingon about to kill Saavik, is killed instead. Why David instead of Saavik? Neither, to this point, is indispensable, but David's death provides goals that would not be accomplished by Saavik dying. First, David is the scapegoat for the failure of Genesis and his own stupidity. Now there will be no disgraceful trial, investigation, and so on. It was all David's fault; David is dead, therefore the case is closed. Second, it also closes the questions of Kirk's responsibilities toward his son. Third, it adds a touch of revenge and another notch of desperation to Kirk's actions, as if that were needed.

David is dead, Saavik and Spock are held by the Klingons on a self-destructing planet, the Klingons have more of an advantage than they realize in the impotent *Enterprise* and Spock, and Kirk is left with few options. Making the only real choice that enjoys even the slimmest chance for success, Kirk sets the *Enterprise*'s self-destruct, invites the Klingons over, and beams everyone down to the Genesis Planet. This plan has several things going for it: It greatly reduces the number of Klingons, it protects the hostages—now Kruge's only link to Genesis, the hostages can be freed with relative ease—Kruge won't be expecting a rescue force, he believes he just saw 400 plus crewmen and his own boarding party destroyed, and the shock of *Enterprise*'s destruction should stun Kruge to inaction for a few precious minutes. The basic problem now is to rescue Spock and Saavik, and get aboard the Klingon ship, preferably in a position of control. As McCoy says, Kirk has turned death into a fighting chance for life; not a guarantee, a chance. If it had not worked, they'd be no worse off, for they were dead men without the Klingon ship.

Disposing of the remaining Klingon guard is child's play. The next step is more difficult. Using words sharply reminiscent of his futile challenge to Khan, Kirk dares the Klingon commander to beam up his party. Kruge answers by beaming down to face Kirk and bring the brilliant pacing of the Klingon threat to its inevitable and very final conclusion. With all but Spock, Kirk, and Kruge safely aboard the Klingon ship, Kirk joins Kruge in hand-to-hand combat—a brief, violent melee that brings the level of the movie back to basics. Kirk has offered his career, his son, his ship, and now offers his life for a chance to recover his friend.

Killing the Klingon in a satisfactory manner, Kirk escapes with Spock to the refuge of the Klingon ship. The finale of a reborn and whole Spock is almost anticlimax to the sheer beauty of the final scenes of the Genesis Planet. With all hell literally breaking loose, Kirk holds Spock in a safe, sure embrace as they beam up at the last possible second. After that, no one believed Spock would not be fully recovered. Anything less after such great sacrifices from so many would have been ludicrous, if not violence-producing.

The destruction of the *Enterprise* is a thorn in the side. As the story is written, Kirk could have done nothing else once the Klingon demanded his surrender. Examination of a few alternatives proves that point. What if Kirk wiped the memory banks (if it's possible to do so in their limited amount of time), killed the Klingons as they beamed up, and had then gone to the planet? This would reduce the number of Klingons, but doesn't necessarily protect the hostages. If Kruge killed Spock and Saavik before he had the *Enterprise*'s Genesis tapes in his hands, he would not be the first Klingon to jump the gun. Also, when his boarding party didn't call or respond, Kruge would realize he'd been tricked. He'd probably then destroy the *Enterprise*, and take his hostages, leaving Kirk and crew stranded on Genesis. This is not a good plan.

Kirk could wipe the memory and simply beam down, leaving the

Klingons to find out as best they could that they'd been tricked. This has all the disadvantages of the first plan, with the added problem of leaving a larger number of living, angry Klingons to deal with. We've already established that Klingons aren't the most tolerant race in the universe. This would give Kirk and party time to get to Spock and Saavik, but leaves them in a bad bargaining position. Kruge has all the good options, and that makes this another bad plan.

A third alternative is that Kirk could refuse to surrender, but that is irrational. The trouble with aliens is that they think differently than you do. Kruge might kill the hostages just to prove he could or would, he might attack the *Enterprise*, and in her condition, kill them all. If Kruge was willing to play out his hunch on the *Enterprise*'s condition, and feeling he couldn't get Genesis from Kirk, he would have simply taken his hostages and gone home. The *Enterprise*, unable to follow or escape, would have been destroyed with the Genesis Planet. Good-bye, everybody . . . not a satisfactory ending.

Finally, Kirk could have tried one of his infamous bluffs. Something to the effect that if Kruge kills the hostages, Kirk will wipe Genesis, or blow up the *Enterprise*, and so forth. It's not even improbable that Kruge would then feel justified in his estimate of the *Enterprise*'s battle abilities by this ultimatum. The Klingons' most obvious move, because they believe the *Enterprise* holds over 400 people—a number his small group could never overcome by force—would be to take his hostages and go, again abandoning Kirk and the *Enterprise* to its fate. Kruge, indeed any Klingon, would like to bring home an intact Federation starship, but Genesis is clearly the more important prize. Even incomplete information is better than nothing.

Even with the chosen plan there were a few problems. Kirk took a chance with the delicate timing of the rescue by pausing to watch the fall of the *Enterprise*. We must, however, concede that it would have been almost impossible for Kirk to *be* Kirk and not watch. He must have bet that Kruge would not react instantly and that they had a bit more time to effect the rescue and still finagle a way onto the Klingon ship. Also, at any given point, Kruge could have taken the hostages and left. It seems unlikely that he would have risked taking the whole *Enterprise* group, as there are only two Klingons to guard the other seven. These points can be easily set aside by

Kirk's always extraordinary luck, and Klingon psychology and cultural training. This way we are treated to a couple of moving, potent scenes.

At the end of *The Search for Spock*, Kirk's nether parts are grass and all of Starfleet eager lawn mowers. Sulu, Uhura, Scotty, and Chekov are in similar shape, although McCoy may be excused by pleading temporary insanity, an out it's doubtful he'll use. Genesis is exposed as a sham and a failure, and can be safely relegated to never-never land. David is dead and the *Enterprise* has been destroyed. Now it's time to speculate what might happen next.

Although David's admission to the use of protomatter and the inherent instability of Genesis have made it useless in providing worlds to colonize and exploit for minerals, food, and other production, it is still a potent weapon—or is it? What remains of Genesis, the device and the research?

If the material detailing Genesis had been in Regulus I's memory banks, Khan would have found it. The actual device would have been icing on the cake, for Khan and his people could have developed a new device from the complete research material, just as they could've reconstructed the material from the device. Therefore, the lab's banks were wiped clean. The *Enterprise*'s memory banks had the bare bones on Genesis in its proposal form. When Regulus's banks were wiped, Carol or David must have kept at least one copy, and they might or might not have supplemented *Enterprise*'s tapes. It doesn't matter, because the *Enterprise* is gone. The Klingon information could not have been very complete, or Kruge would never have risked entering Federation space on such a desperate search for information. Carol may have had a copy with her, or there may be a required depository for top secret scientific projects. The latter is highly unlikely, because the more copies of anything that exist, the harder it is to guard or keep secret. So the only probable complete set of information on Genesis is with Dr. Carol Marcus, wherever she is. Being a sensible, bright lady, she may (and probably will) choose to hide or destroy it. Genesis has brought only pain, death, and destruction. It did revive Spock, but only his body and only under a set of unique, impossible to re-create, circumstances. Genesis's only use now is military. Further research will be impossible without complete records. It may prove impossible to fix all of Genesis's problems even with Carol's records. Other teams may rediscover Genesis after many years of painstaking research, but my impression of the original team is that they were the best and brightest. Genesis is now only the vaguest of possible future threats.

For the *Enterprise* there can be no future. She is gone and an era is over. Technically, the ship was dead when Kirk and party beamed down to the Genesis Planet. They could not have repaired her in time and still have completed their desperate mission, but her final death throes gave them life. It was a poetic balancing of Karma, for as Spock gave his life for *Enterprise* and her infinitely precious cargo, so *Enterprise* gave its existence for Spock and his rescuers. Her death was glorious, bright, and beautiful, much preferable to scrapping or mothballing. But to me, *Enterprise* was the embodiment and soul of Star Trek and fandom, my own personal vehicle to the stars. I neither apologize for my tears, nor look forward to a universe populated with pregnant guppies.

We must also consider Spock. Here the only acceptable result is for him to recover completely and be the Spock we know so well. Whether he returns to Starfleet, stays on Vulcan, or finds another course for his life path will probably depend on the fate of his friends, who did so much on his behalf. Logically, he should not approve of their actions, but neither Spock nor his responses are totally logical. While McCoy carried Spock's essence, Spock occasionally spoke through the good doctor. It is my belief that McCoy's line, ". . . what you had to do. What you've always done, turn death into a fighting chance for life," is not McCoy's alone. It is a statement from both McCoy and Spock, trying to comfort their anguished friend, Jim Kirk. This has always been one area where Spock and McCoy could agree. As Spock sorts out his memories, he will find all the times of his joining to McCoy, and he will find this time. He will continue to give Kirk comfort and support, friendship and honest love, in whatever the future holds. Even if this is not the "proper" interpretation, Spock is logical enough to realize that the deed is done and he can't change it. He is Spock enough to feel the irrational warm glow of friendship, and the lengths we will go for that bond. Whatever track is taken, Spock will be there for all his friends.

Kirk and his faithful crew have saved Genesis from the Klingons, brought home an intact Klingon ship, and returned McCoy to sanity and Spock from the dead, but they broke, or severely dented, almost every Starfleet regulation doing so. Kirk's future seems to hold only three possibilities:

First, he may be court-martialed and publicly disgraced. This seems unlikely. Starfleet would have to make Genesis and the Klingon violations public. Because Khan's actions also deal with the proceedings, his taking of the *Reliant* would also come out. None of this is likely to please Starfleet's PR department. Public opinion would, in all probability, shift to Kirk and his friends as the people who saved the Federation. Even in the military, public opinion, and funding, are important enough to make a difference.

Second, Kirk may be "allowed" to quietly retire rather than face a general court. Although Kirk may feel his actions are wrong and deserve punishment, he may still demand a court-martial rather than let his friends sink into oblivion. Again, this is something Starfleet would want to avoid.

Third, Kirk may be bumped upstairs, promoted to a strictly advisory, noncommand position. Here Starfleet benefits from Kirk's experience without having to air its dirty laundry. Kirk can't protest a promotion, so he can choose either to accept this exile or resign. (This is similar to the "court or grounding" choice Kirk was given in "Courtmartial," but they're unlikely to offer a choice this time. Also, Kirk *was* innocent in that instance.) Whatever happens, it seems that Captain Styles's warning, "Kirk, if you go through with this, you'll never sit in the center seat again" seems all too true.

The future of Kirk's co-conspirators is tied up with his. If there is a general court, for whatever reason, they will stand it together. If Kirk retires, they may be allowed to resign their commissions, or they may also be placed in safe, advisory, or simply boring positions. It seems most likely that Starfleet would want to keep the experience of Scotty and McCoy available, but the simple fact of having survived a five-year mission may keep Sulu, Chekov, and Uhura in the service.

There are a string of less likely, and more bizarre possibilities. *Star Trek IV* could start with, "Having been completely exonerated by a little known Starfleet rule, the crew of the *Enterprise* gets a new ship and . . ." They could all quit and join the twenty-third century version of the merchant marine, or start their own fleet, or . . . On the slightly more serious side, they could stay on Vulcan. Starfleet might be persuaded to leave them alone if they stayed there in exile. Perhaps Vulcan could refuse to extradite them. Of course, that would effectively end the series, and then there's Vulcan logic and Kirk's sense of honor and duty to deal with . . .

Here's my personal favorite, and the only scenario I can come up with to keep Kirk and friends in Starfleet as fully functioning individuals. Starfleet, in order to keep various and sundry eggs off its collective face, looks the other way and Kirk, and such are allowed back into the big, happy Fleet. Pressure could be brought to bear by certain Vulcans, and others, threatening to make the entire affair public. Or perhaps Admiral Morrow isn't as dumb as we thought. He had read Kirk correctly, but could see no official way to sanction the act. His silence was tacit permission. Styles must have been in on it, too, for he knew it was Kirk on the *Enterprise* and seemed to know what Kirk was up to. Thus, Admiral Morrow only has to say "*secret mission*," or at least claim that was the case. Very secret, even Kirk didn't know (or did he?), but he and his crew can be trusted to keep the secret—for the good of the Fleet, of course. This way they are returned to the Fleet without prejudice. Their official records won't carry the real story, for the secrecy must be maintained, and they will therefore be just as eligible for promotion and duty positions as any other member of the Fleet.

There is precedent for this. If you will recall the only two-part episode, "The Menagerie," *Spock* stole the *Enterprise* and violated the only General Order that still carried the death penalty by taking it to a proscribed planet. All was forgiven because Spock's actions gave a valued Starfleet officer the only possible chance for a viable, tolerable life. Yes, he broke the rules, but no real damage was done, and good came of it. Spock was not disciplined in any way; he retained his rank, his position as first officer, and eventually became the captain of the *Enterprise*.

The only negative result of Kirk's actions is the destruction of the *Enterprise*, and she was to be scrapped anyway. The pluses include the capture of a Klingon ship and the repulsion of a clear and present danger in the form of the Klingons and Genesis, the returning of two very valuable Starfleet officers to active, productive duty, and the incidental rescue of Lt. Saavik. This is an even better score than Spock racked up. If Kirk, Scotty, McCoy, Uhura, Sulu, and Chekov are to appear in any future stories, some variant on this explanation must be used, and having a precedent in an episode only makes it easier and more attractive.

Star Trek, like V'Ger, must evolve. As the actors portraying the major characters age, we must prepare ourselves for their gradual replacement and eventual demise. I've always favored moving the senior officers up to advisory positions and familiar junior officers taking over the command duties. This will be accomplished by introducing new—but interesting and competent—crew members. I want to see these people replaced with love, not disposed of and tossed aside. Yet the ongoing fan (and fun) argument of replacing Kirk versus replacing Shatner may be canceled out by the next movie. Will *Star Trek IV* simply tie up loose ends and explore another aspect of the Star Trek universe with a new ship and new characters? Will it be the final chapter for people who have loved and faithfully followed the series for twenty years? Something in my mind, my heart whispers no. Where *can* we go from here? Anywhere. There *are* always possibilities. This article brought up a few, but more exist. I will wait to see Mr. Bennett's magic, humbly suggesting he remembers Star Trek is love, friendship, and all the best man is and does . . . But most of all it is the people who hold these values dear, and follow this life-style.

STAR TREK: ODYSSEY OF SALVATION

by Sister Mary William
David, S.N.D.

We receive a surprising number of articles and letters which have a religious orientation: apparently a great many fans find an appealing similarity in the pro-humanistic viewpoints of Star Trek and their chosen religion. Below, Sister Mary William David takes a look at how the events in the first two Star Trek films (this article was written before the release of The Search for Spock) *can be interpreted in relation to events in the life of Christ . . . with special emphasis, of course, on Mr. Spock.*

"Trekkie" is the term affectionately applied to a person suffering from video addiction to Star Trek. I have just lately become a "Trekkie." Why? Adventure and Imagination, yes, but there's something more. When I first began watching the science fiction program, the characters touched a responsive chord in my own life, in my own thoughts, desires, and struggles. So, I looked forward to seeing the two feature-length films. What I found there was a more universal message, a parable of redemption echoing the life and mission of Jesus.

The crewmembers of the Starship *Enterprise* represent all persons confronted with the mystery of being, of good, and of evil; persons in search of their meaning. Captain James Kirk, authority figure, represents the official in each of us, tied to duty and responsibility, patriotic, aware of the rules of the game of life—sometimes challenged to break the letter in order to fulfill the spirit. Doctor Leonard McCoy, the healer, concerned to alleviate human pain, angered at the waste of human life, is the most often argumentative and emotional. "Bones" is that side of us that would do away with all suffering, that becomes enraged at the lack of feeling in others, that longs to return to the soil, the life of nature, that believes in the innate goodness of unspoiled creation. Mr. Spock, First Science Officer with the unpronounceable and unpronounced first name, the head, the brain, the computer of the Starship *Enterprise*, cannot understand let alone enjoy a good laugh, or love, or any of the emotions because they are illogical. Yet a single raised eyebrow reveals a depth of emotion held in check only by a stronger Vulcan pride. Spock represents the thinking and reasoning side of human nature; the calculating logical side which, although invaluable in times of crisis and dilemma, is by itself a terrible emptiness and loneliness.

The interrelation of these characters in the episodes is a human parable. The characters are part of us all. Their challenges are ours as we move within the microgalaxy of our daily lives. Therefore when the characters are transported from the everyday planet of video into the galaxy of the theater for two full-length motion pictures, it is not surprising that they also take on a more cosmic meaning. Because of my background as an English teacher and a religious sister I found myself paralleling both films to the whole drama of salvation. This is not to say that the screenwriters and directors hoped to produce a Gospel According to Spock; only that beauty is sometimes in the eye of the beholder even if it may not have been in the camera of the creator. Each movie taken separately has a death/resurrection theme. However, if the character of Spock is traced through both films, the Christ-figure is more clearly detailed. The following is not meant to be a technological exposition; simply one person's thoughts and responses after seeing both films.

The Direct Experience: In the beginning of *Star Trek: The Motion Picture* Spock enters the Vulcan desert to discipline himself, shed all emotion, and complete and secure his Vulcan heritage. He goes in search of his meaning—"who is he and is this all there is to life"—as he later verbalizes it. At the end of his desert trial he is called out of the wilderness to accept the symbol of his successful completion of this Vulcan discipline. He refuses the Vulcan insignia because he already knows what the Matriarch will speak after reading his thoughts: "He will not find his answers with us." He must follow the call which he senses vaguely (even if illogically) from outer space.

Jesus, after his forty days in the desert, refused the easy salvation offered him by the devil: "Man does not live by bread alone." He will not find his answers here, but only by going out into the desert in response to the call and mission of his Father.

Spock is drawn to the mission on which the *Enterprise* has already embarked in order to answer his own questions about life's meaning, as well as to save both the alien creature and the human race. We may also believe that Jesus' understanding of the meaning of his life grew gradually as he fulfilled his mission of salvation.

Mind Meld with V'Ger: At a vital point in the conflict with V'Ger, Spock decides he must go alone to study the alien. He joins in a Vulcan mind meld with its transmitter in order to gain information about this creature of perfect logic. Recovering in Sickbay from the damage to his central nervous system caused by the powerful energy of the machine-creature, he comes to a realization that changes his life. In uniting with the alien, Spock experiences the emptiness of its pure logic. He comes to an appreciation and acceptance of his human companions and, more important, his own human capabilities to experience that which is not "illogical" but "beyond logic": beauty, love, mystery, the simple feeling of a friend's handclasp of support. He discovers the meaning in his own life and at the same time, recognized that this meaning will grow as he continues on his journey; the answer are not "found" but "lived." He is no longer surrounded only with the cold, unfeeling questions, but with living and caring companions on a similar quest into the mysteries of life.

This could parallel Jesus' baptism in the Jordan where he accepts and comes to understand his identity as Son of the Father, where he is given a glimpse into the true meaning and power of his existence. It could also be seen as the experience of Christ's Transfiguration, a step into the fuller than human existence which was

Jesus'. It takes place before his passion and death. It is not the end of the struggle but an experience that can give meaning to that suffering.

Tears over V'Ger: Possibly the most unexpected moment of the film comes shortly after the Captain has given the standby order for self-destruction, a measure both to prevent the alien from collecting their data and to destroy it along with the Starship *Enterprise*. (Note: I personally cannot understand why this scene was cut from the movie and only shown in the TV version because it is so important to understanding the growth in Spock's character.) Kirk's surprised response to the unlikely (and most illogical) Vulcan tears—"Not for us, Spock?"—is as much an admonition as a question. However, Spock's reply is that he weeps for V'Ger as one would weep for a brother, for it was as such a brother that he first joined this mission. He weeps that V'Ger will never find the answers to its questions; will never experience, as Spock has just experienced, the value of the supra-logical; will be condemned to death having never experienced true life.

Jesus' words as he wept over Jerusalem come to mind easily. "Would that you understood the time of your visitation. How I longed to gather you as a mother hen does her chicks, but you would not."

Life from Death: At the end of *Star Trek: The Motion Picture*, it seems that Decker takes over the Christ-character that up to this point was Spock's role. Still, death-resurrection is accomplished in the union of V'Ger with its creator, man. That death has not been triumphant is borne out in two ways: Doctor McCoy's reference to the birth of a new life form, and Kirk's final lines listing the two crew members as "missing" instead of dead.

However, this need not be the redemption yet; rather let it be a foreshadowing of the new life to be given to man. The Raising of Lazarus to life was such an event in the life of Christ. Preceding the passion and death of Christ as a sign of hope, this miracle restored Lazarus to earthly life, not the eternal life that Jesus would give by his death. Interpreting the end of *Star Trek: The Motion Picture* in this way allows Spock to keep the role that he will fulfill in *Star Trek II: The Wrath of Khan*.

The Teacher: Spock's role at the beginning of *Wrath of Khan* is that of a teacher—in charge of passing on the command of the *Enterprise* to the younger generation. So was Jesus in his public life, the teacher, the Rabbi, eager to pass on life and leadership to his apostles and disciples. Albeit that makes Lt. Saavik a feminine St. Peter, but all analogies hang loose at some point. Actually, Spock's training of the half-Vulcan, half-Romulan orphan girl—now the young commander trainee—reminds me more of Jesus' redemption of Mary Magdalen. Here the novel based on the movie is helpful in filling out the details of their relationship and explaining how Spock has saved Saavik from a life of total barbarism. And by the end of the story she begins to understand and accept the mystery of love and death along with a future of hope for herself.

I have called you friends: During a birthday visit when Dr. McCoy tries to convince his friend and patient, Admiral Kirk, of the importance of returning to command the Starship *Enterprise*, he only succeeds in angering him. Spock, on the other hand, shows genuine sensitivity to Kirk when he presents the Admiral with an antique copy of *A Tale of Two Cities* for his collection. Later, when Spock tries to explain that the good of the many outweighs the good of the few "or the one," he turns to Kirk and states simply that no matter what his decision, "I will always be your friend." Jesus, at the Last Supper, on the night before he was to die for the good of the many, said, "I call you friends."

Passion, Death, and Resurrection: Spock's death must be seen as an act of redemption. It is obvious that he weighs the consequences before leaving the Bridge; he makes a decision to give his life for the life of the *Enterprise* as Jesus made his surrender in the garden. Jesus forgave his enemies before he died. Spock finds the way barred at the door of the reactor chamber by Dr. McCoy. After overpowering his constant antagonist with the Vulcan nerve pinch, Spock touches the Doctor's head and speaks softly, "Remember," paralleling Christ's words at the Last Supper: "Do this in remembrance of me."

Once locked in the radiation chamber, Spock knows there is no turning back, although death will not come until after the reactors are back on line and the *Enterprise* well out of danger. Visually the scene is one of beauty and transfiguration before death. A halo of radiant energy envelops and fans out from Spock's body as he struggles with all the strength that only he as a Vulcan can call forth to pull the off-line cables back into place.

Just so, Jesus was the only one who could save the human race. Although his death was one of unspeakable horror, Christian art often represents it as a scene of triumph: Jesus reigning from his cross. A true picturing needs to include the resurrection glory even amid his agony. He himself said that no one took his life from him, but he laid it down willingly only to take it up again on the third day.

Beneath the cross of Jesus stood his friends, who listened to his final words of love. At the end there is a trio of the Vulcan's friends present: Kirk, McCoy, and via the intercom, Saavik. Spock uses his last strength to pull himself up to full stature and speak words of friendship and consolation to the companions who look on helplessly from the other side of the sealed door. "Do not mourn . . . The good of the many outweighs the good of the few . . . I will always be your friend." His burned and withered hand forms the sign of Vulcan blessing on the glass. "Live long and prosper."

Before he dies, Spock experiences the resurrection through the words of Lt. Saavik, who calls over the intercom the beauty of the newly formed Genesis World. In the novelization of the movie, it is clear that Saavik realized where Spock was heading when he left the Bridge and what the consequences would be for him and for her. She accepts his sacrifice and only wants him to know that it does have great meaning and consequence. Pardon me for seeing in this Mary, his Mother's acceptance and participation in her son's death on the cross and her faith in God's ultimate triumph.

Before Spock's body is launched from the *Enterprise*, Kirk says of the Vulcan: "Of all the souls I have met . . . his was the most human." This serves at least as a faint reminder of the Centurion's words of Jesus: "Truly this was the son of God."

Finally, both McCoy and Kirk make references to resurrection as they watch the torpedo casing with Spock's body orbit around the new planet. The doctor states that "he isn't really dead as long as we remember him"—an echo and perhaps an effect of Spock's parting words to the unconscious McCoy—"Remember." And the admiral? When asked by his concerned physician, "Jim? Are you all right? How are you feeling?", he responds, "Young. I feel young."

Perhaps it seems a bit much to put a pointy-eared half-breed side by side with the Lord, no matter how many comparisons can be drawn. The Gospels, however, so lead me to believe that Jesus wouldn't have objections. He who was friend of sinners and outcasts, and who promised that these followers should expect their lives patterned after his, might feel right at home. Star Trek appeals to me because if Spock is Jesus, so are we all called to be. The human personality parabled in the TV series, through the two motion pictures, led to its Christian fulfillment: sacrificial death leading to new life. Popularity ratings notwithstanding, here is certainly worthy material for eternal reruns.

STAR TREK LIVES IN MY LIFE

by Jacqueline A. LongM

Walter had the pleasure of meeting Jackie LongM at Swamp Con in Baton Rouge in February of 1986, and being interviewed by her for the public-access television program she hosts and coproduces (also titled Star Trek Lives in My Life.*) The following excerpts are from Jackie's ongoing series of personal reflections on Star Trek, science fiction, fandom, and life and the world in general. We enjoyed them immensely, and found ourselves nodding in agreement and empathy; we think you'll feel the same way.*

The Great Bird of the Galaxy

When I was a young child growing up in a suburb of Washington, D.C., all I knew was that my daddy worked for the government. (He still does.) Later in life I discovered that he actually worked as a drafter-designer for the National Security Agency and was not allowed to talk about his job when home. However, during those years it never dawned on me to ask; Daddy just went to work in the morning and came home at night. We would have dinner, then Daddy would read the paper and watch news, a documentary, or some sports event on television. Nothing of real interest, at least not to me.

My two sisters and one brother were very close in age and had to do everything together. Therefore, Daddy took us all to the circus and to the park. He took us all to the doctor and shopping for Mother's Day. When we all missed the bus and got stranded after school, Daddy came and got us.

He was blessed with only one son, and for a brief interim he took my brother aside to teach him sporting skills. Unfortunately, Mama insisted that we all play together. So the next day following each session, my brother would show us what Daddy had taught him the day before. For two years in a row, my brother got to attend the opening game of the professional baseball season. My sisters and I cried until an unprecedented move for women's liberation took place (considering it was the late 1950s): My mother said, "You have to take the girls."

In what now seems like a brilliant revelation for one so young, I discovered that excitement did not come from seeing the Washington Senators lose to the Baltimore Orioles. The thrill was telling my classmates that my daddy was coming in the middle of the school day to get me, and seeing their faces light up trying to sneak a peek at my handsome father.

As time marched ahead, I late-blossomed into a Star Trek fan. I say "late" because my viewing began during the third season. The movie theater closed at 9:00 p.m., and I was underage for clubs, therefore Friday nights at 10:00 p.m. were fine for me. Plus, my parents had purchased a second TV set by then. I'd simply shut their bedroom door and enter my own private world of the twenty-third century.

Another four or five years passed. I was home from college for the summer. One afternoon my mom sashayed into my room and dropped a *Washington Post* ad page on my bed. By this time she had established an intimate, one-on-one communications relationship with each of her children; words were not necessary. I gazed at the particular ad she had turned up. It read, "The World of Star Trek: Featuring Creator and Producer Gene Roddenberry." My excitement was spontaneous. "The Great Bird of the Galaxy appearing fifteen minutes away at the Capital Center. I can't believe it! Of course I'm going!"

As the family gathered for dinner, Star Trek became the topic of

conversation. My daddy asked me questions about Gene Rodenberry and I shared the limited information I had. Out of the blue,
Daddy remarked, "He sounds interesting. I think I'll go too."

Noah Webster has yet to catalog a word to describe the emotional
enthusiasm that remark aroused in me. When the big event came,
my daddy followed my lead as I explained what conventions were
and how Trekkies act. I whispered background information on inside jokes and comments that Roddenberry made. I even stood up
and asked an intelligent question. Needless to say, I was happily
beaming with pride and joy.

After the affair, we went to eat and talked about our thoughts
and feelings stirred by the presentation. Star Trek incorporates such
a broad scope of subjects that we talked politics, religion, social
science, psychology, the military, and relationships—as well as science and fiction. Our discussions and debates ran on for weeks.
Suddenly there was really something to talk to Daddy about. Also,
talking to him now seemed to be easier.

As a black female, I could give several accolades to Gene
Roddenberry, for I truly believe Star Trek played a part in the
acceptance and advancement of both my race and sex. However,
major changes are made only after a lot of minor encounters where
people sit down, talk, understand each other, and relate.

Therefore, my real thanks go to Roddenberry for creating Star
Trek, which provided the opportunity for me to better relate to the
"Great Bird" of *my* galaxy—my daddy.

The Chekov Psychology

I was deep into "black tow," penning a difficult Spock scene in my
unpublished Star Trek novel. Shockingly, from the bedroom came
cries of "No! No! No!" My characterization supervisor, J.B., barged
out waving an earlier Chekov/Sulu chapter in midair: "Chekov is
wrong!" she wailed. "I won't let you do this to him. It's wrong!"

Hardly offended, I mildly remarked, "I call it like I see it," then
proceeded to accuse her of identifying with the situation, not the
character, since she had endured a similar real-life incident. Out-
raged, J.B. called me a heartless, unfeeling Vulcan and yelled
"Spock!" in an offensive tone as she slammed the bedroom door.

After the slow count to ten and the deep breaths, I went to

apologize. While J.B. remains constantly a female "Bones," she caught me in a moment of "Spock." Still, the confrontation brought home one painful revelation—I did not truly know Chekov.

Two months later: Delta Con '85 in Baton Rouge, Louisiana. Special guest: Walter Koenig. Yes, I was there! Koenig's presentation opened with an original dialogue between himself and Pavel Chekov. Dropping into a Russian accent to play Chekov, Koenig comically debated the fantasy life of his created character versus the actual life of himself, the talented actor.

The extraordinary presentation revealed two facts. First, Walter Koenig is a remarkable actor. The rigid, proper, often hyper and intense chief navigator of the *Enterprise* is not the playful, easygoing, conspicuous, sexy personage of Koenig. *He acts!* The second point made clear was that both what we are perceived to be and what we are can coexist simultaneously. When the perception is our own, we often debate ourselves.

For example, I say to myself, "Self, I want to be a writer."

Self says, "If you want to be a writer, you have to write."

"How can I write when I have nothing to write about?"

"You saw Walter Koenig this weekend. What did he say that struck you the most? Write about that."

"What struck me most is that he has a degree in psychology, but, of course, says he was never a psychologist."

"Well, what does a psychologist do?"

"A psychologist makes a person think and then act on those thoughts."

"Hasn't he just made you think and act?"

"Self . . . you're right. Walter Koenig is a psychologist."

"Yes . . . and you are a writer."

I Am Not Spock

I am not Spock . . . but I'd like to be.

I long for the practical discipline of logical thinking, the certainty and stability of structured life, the understanding that accompanies scientific, mathematical, and technological knowledge. I want to use reason as my motivating force and have order as my ultimate goal. However, my limited existence has been marred by emotionalism, chaos, and a D in math! Regardless of my longings, I am not Spock.

I am not Spock . . . but I try to be. I attempt to evaluate each situation on its own merit without interjecting unrelated personal influences. I strain to render fair decisions without prejudgment and prejudice. I subscribe to the high ideals of dignity, honor, and truth that form the basis of the Vulcan society. Yet it is difficult for me. There are times and situations when I discover that I can tell a lie. This only reinforces the fact that I am not Spock.

I am not Spock . . . but I need to be. I need the loyalty and certainty that results from the mental linking of true friends. I desire the total abandonment of mind, body, and soul immersed in the onslaught of ecstasy, fantasy, brilliance, and boundless energy that accompanies *pon farr*. I would gladly sacrifice countless nights of sexual sparring and social role-playing for one night of unadulterated, honest bliss once every seven years.

During my later college years I served as secretary to my Greek organization. The president was a strong-willed, flamboyant Scorpio with significant leadership abilities. The vice-president was a Leo—cold, quiet, calculating, and expressionless. At a national meeting we recessed for a chapter caucus. I heard myself argue animatedly for the feelings of our members and the perpetuation of our spirit and goals at all costs. All I needed was a hypo, medical scanner, and DeForest Kelley's voice. Dr. McCoy would have been proud! Although my cause was just and I made my point, in retrospect I wish I had been more logical, like Spock . . . but then, I am not Spock.

Back on campus I worked as the first female chairperson of a particular special committee. After thorough preparation I stormed into the Dean of Students' office wheeling, dealing, and negotiating for the decision most advantageous to me and my organization. Upon returning to the dorm, I related my recent triumph to my roommate. The "Jim Kirk" gleam in my eyes did not go unnoticed by her; she pointed out the parallel: Kirk vs. Starfleet Command. While proud of my accomplishment, I questioned my procedure. Could a more controlled, logical approach have worked?

I confessed my hidden delusions to a close friend, describing my ability to act totally on instinct without forethought. Although my actions yielded the appropriate results, I still wanted to be like Spock!

He replied, "You are like Spock, Jackie. You have so attuned your emotional instincts with your mental abilities that you now 'feel' what is the logical thing to do."

I wasn't sure I completely agreed with him, but it was food for thought. I've since realized that I am not Spock, nor am I Kirk or McCoy, either. I'm just me.

Yet, that is the true beauty in the Star Trek universe: Infinite Diversities in Infinite Combinations.

Death and the *Enterprise*

Captain Spock's death at the climax of *Star Trek II: The Wrath of Khan* brought silent, solemn tears to my eyes. But the self-destruction of the *Enterprise* in *Star Trek III: The Search for Spock* caused a churning in my stomach as if my guts had just spilled out. My lungs gasped for air as if I were hanging in the vacuum void of space, clinging to my last fragments of life. For a few seconds, I sat in that movie seat literally sick.

A couple of years ago, I purchased my first automobile, a Volkswagen Rabbit I called Crusader. The two of us zipped up and down I-95 between New York and the Carolinas, boldly going where this woman had never gone before. If there was a friend in need, a crisis to solve, an important ceremony, or a meeting to attend, Crusader and I were there. Finally, after five years and 180,000 miles, Crusader gave out. My husband peered into my eyes, shaking me by the shoulders, and cried, "Give it up! She cannot be repaired!" Although devastated, I yielded to the logic.

I can't help but compare the death of the *Enterprise* with the loss of my car. Fortunately, I have yet to endure a close personal death. My parents, intimate friends, even my grandparents are still alive. When my puppy was struck by a car, I was 1,000 miles away. However, I have come to accept what happened to the *Enterprise*. She was a machine, the same as my automobile. Machines break down or become obsolete.

They will someday build another *Enterprise*, just as they resurrected Spock and Volkswagen built more Rabbits. Still, through it all I have a learned a very important Star Trek lesson: Not only do you turn death into a fighting chance, but you accept death as part of life.

Someone to Scream With

There is always someone to scream at. There are times when there's someone to scream to. Often, there is someone to scream about. But rarely is there someone that you can really scream *with*. Usually, when the need to scream arises, pride, public image, responsibilities, or circumstances make you overcome the natural urge.

Take for example the case of James T. Kirk in *Star Trek III: The Search for Spock*. Pretending calm, he sat in the Starfleet Officers' Lounge awaiting a response to his personal request of Fleet Commander Harry Morrow. The body of Kirk's dearest friend, Spock, had been left on the newly formed Genesis planet. The soul of Spock, his *katra*, had been placed in another of Kirk's friends, Dr. Leonard McCoy. The separation was killing both friends.

"Harry, give me back the *Enterprise!*" he pleaded. Morrow refused.

You could see the scream anchored with Kirk's chest hammering to be hauled up. But high-ranking officers of a superior fleet are not prone to emotional outburst. Therefore, he curtailed his anger and converted it into determination.

There can be no greater anguish than to survive the earthquake, then get hit by the aftermath tidal wave. That is how Kirk must have felt when Saavik's voice sputtered, "Admiral . . . David is dead."

That was a moment truly worthy of screaming, but Kirk had no time to mourn his son. He faced a deadly Klingon enemy and the safety of Project Genesis rested squarely on his shoulders. Balling his fist and violently cursing, Kirk turned the anger into an act of desperation.

The final self-destruction of the Starship *Enterprise* struck a blow for human endurance. Reformed on the surface of Genesis, Kirk, unwillingly, looked up. He saw his life. One minute, a glorious blaze; the next, black and empty.

Have you ever been so consumed with an internal scream that your vocal cords refuse to vibrate, your lip muscles won't conform to the proper position, and your mind can't issue the appropriate command to deactivate your nerve endings? All Kirk could do was whisper, "My God, Bones . . . what have I done?"

I can identify with James T. Kirk because I saw *The Search for Spock* at a strange theater, in an alien state, with unfamiliar people and a newlywed husband. In my effort to maintain the proper public image, I held in my screams each time Kirk held in his. After the film, my husband placed his arm around my waist to escort me from the theater. He thought he was being chivalrous, but I knew my body lacked the emotional strength to propel itself out. The latent screams were still trapped inside me.

Days passed, but the kinetic screaming remained. Then I remembered my former roommate. We had seen *Star Trek: The Motion Picture* together and talked all the way through it, happy to see the *Enterprise* and our old friends again. We saw *Flashdance* and sang the soundtrack together as the movie progressed. Also, we watched a little-known film named *The Fish that Saved Pittsburgh*. It was about basketball and starred Julius "Dr. J" Erving. My roommate and I stood up in our seats, yelled, jumped, screamed, and cheered as if we were in Madison Square Garden. It was she I needed.

Although I had moved five states away, I knew she had not seen *The Search for Spock*. She was saving every available dime to return to school, and the local theaters in her area had increased the price of admission because of Star Trek's vast popularity. Also, there was no one with whom she could see it because her new roommate hated science fiction. Therefore I sat at my desk, addressed an envelope, stuffed cash money into it (which the post office discourages), and wrote this note:

"Take this money and go see *Star Trek III: The Search for Spock* on your Wednesday day off. When you see it you will want to scream. I saw it with the husband and couldn't. I will call you Thursday night, 9:00 p.m. sharp, so that we can scream together. Love, J.L."

That Thursday at 9:00 I dialed her phone number. At 9:01 she picked up her receiver and immediately started screaming. I joined in. We screamed and screamed and screamed! She was standing— I could hear her jumping up and down. I was on my bed, rolling around screaming. Our screams turned into hysterical laughter, then tears of relief. We eventually settled down and discussed the movie after my husband declared us both terminally insane.

A lot has been written in the annals of Trekdom concerning friendships and relationships. Is it the primary motivating factor in the characters' lives? How will they develop or affect the future? How much strain and pressure can our heroes' bonds withstand?

I can't begin to answer or analyze these deep matters of friendships and relationships. All I can do is offer a piece of wisdom derived from my personal experience. I'm sure James T. Kirk can relate.

"Once you find the someone you can truly scream with, you will have found your *t'hy'la*."

Amazing Grace

"With love, we commit his body to the depths of space." Captain Sulu moved from the line. "Honors: hut." The ships company saluted. Mr. Scott began to play his strange musical instrument. It filled the chamber with a plaintive wail, a dirge that was all too appropriate.

Star Trek II: The Wrath of Khan

Every Sunday evening at six my mother would turn on the inspirational gospel radio station and listen to *The Mother's Hour*. It was an hour of popular religious hymns played on a single organ. Once, when my sister and I were home from college, the song "Amazing Grace" came on the program. Mama began to hum along and finally remarked, "You know, I really love hearing that song. It is truly one of the best songs ever."

This brought on quite a negative emotional reaction from my sister and me. "Ugh! I hate that song!" "Every singer who's ever sung has done that song, and ninety percent of the time done it wrong!" "That song has been played on every instrument including bells, zithers, and kazoos!" "I am sick of that song!" "If I never hear it again, it will be too soon!"

Having survived our teenage development stage, Mama was used to having us disagree with her. Still, the magnitude of our reaction to her simple comment surprised her. Indignant, she stated, "Well, you might as well prepare yourself to suffer through it one more time because I intend to have it played at my funeral before they put me into the ground!"

Fortunately she is still alive and we have yet to endure that scene. However, we were party to another shockingly unexpected one more than ten years later.

By the time *Wrath of Khan* was released, we had both married and I had moved to another state over 1,000 miles away. We saw the film separately in our own home towns with our respective husbands. A few months passed before I visited for a holiday. When the initial greetings were over, Star Trek become one of the first topics of conversation.

"I could not believe it," my sister exclaimed, "After Spock gave his life for the *Enterprise* and crew, and Admiral Kirk gave his most deeply moving eulogy, Scotty had the audacity to pick up the bagpipes and play 'Amazing Grace'!"

I responded with equal horror. "Just think, two hundred years from now, people will still be playing that song."

My mom is not a Star Trek fan; she considers it to be like the weather, something that's there all the time and that people talk about. So when we told her that "Amazing Grace" was used in a Star Trek movie, she mildly replied that it was probably appropriate.

Still, as the pallbearers lifted Spock's black coffin into the launching chamber and the missile was fired, I did not wish to hear the national anthem. Nor would a modern "I love you, baby" tune have filled the emotional void of that cinematic moment. Somehow, "Amazing Grace" did.

I have been known to be dogmatically stubborn at times, but when reviewing centuries of past religious culture and faced with its obvious reality in the future, I yield to the logic. So when I die, "Amazing Grace" can be played at my funeral, too. If it's all right for Mom and Spock, it's okay for me.

TOMORROW MAN

by Joyce Tullock

It suddenly occurred to us that we, and our readers, have been enjoying a unique privilege. Over the past few years, we have been witnessing, firsthand, the evolution of one individual's philosophy about Star Trek and its worth, meaning, and ultimate significance to we "real" humans. As Joyce Tullock continues to delve into and refine her thoughts about Star Trek and its universe in each successive article, she takes us along with her on her journey of discovery. How suitable, then, that she now turns her attentions to comparable journeys of Kirk, Spock, and McCoy.

All the universe surrounds us. An infinity. In this galaxy alone, there are more things to see, to wonder about, to discover, than we can know in a thousand lifetimes. But we feel driven to continue to try, because experience and discovery are so essential to our kind. It is our nature to seek. And so we travel the roads of outer and inner space, constantly in search, as if to verify or even justify our existence. It is the human way.

Star Trek's journey through outer and inner space has become symbolic to a whole generation. And as it moves into its second generation, it expresses humanity's need to grow beyond the being it is now, to discover its own greatness. It is a journey to adulthood, perhaps, a quest of the highest sort. In fact, it may well be that

Star Trek's major theme involves man's greatest adventure—the discovery of himself.

In Star Trek, nothing is greater than the individual human being—except, perhaps, what the human being can become. Those who need a label would call it the humanistic approach, and that fits, for science fiction as a whole is the genre of humanism. It tends to put humanist questions of every nature to the forefront. Are we greater than the animals? Are we animals? What is the nature of the human soul? Is there some absolute code of conduct by which all human beings should abide? What is the "moral" thing? Are we the subjects of some greater, unknown being? Or—could it possibly be—are we creation become self-aware?

Those questions can be frightening; for some, even threatening. But they will not go away. We can hide from them, as some do, behind theological, sociological, or political doctrines. We can ignore them if we want to, or we can even deny that such questions exist. But they will continue to exist, as ideas tend to do, beyond all the walls we build around them, waiting for the day when one person will have the courage or innocence to ask a question.

The creative minds behind the evolution and production of Star Trek know about these questions. They can't help but know for two reasons: They are versed in the themes of science fiction; and they are human beings.

Humanity was cooked from the same brew as the stars. Everyone knows that. But through the eons we became different from the stars, and that is what sent us, in the fictional Star Trek, at least, on the road to self-discovery in space—like children looking for the place from which they came. But first off, we have to overcome some prejudices. We had to evolve as a species and get some things out of the way.

Star Trek begins with an assumption. At the time of the *Enterprise*, racial prejudice does not exist on planet Earth. That puts us one big leap from the starting point of our own time. While the theme of racial prejudice apparently does exist in Star Trek, it does not seem to thrive where Terrans are concerned. Not on the literal level, that is, but it is surely discussed time and again when Kirk, Spock, and McCoy encounter alien societies. But, on the *Enterprise* itself we can at least assume that racial prejudice is pretty much a thing of the past (excluding an occasional "throwback").

In Star Trek we're dealing with another kind of prejudice, worse than racism, worse than sexism, more ridiculous and difficult to overcome even than religious bigotry. It is the feeling man has, the one he has been brought up with from the infancy of humankind, that he is somehow not "worthy." It is a fear, really. Man's biggest enemy. We see it expressed in many different ways, but always at the root is the theme that man is "inferior," either because he is inherently so, or because someone or thing wants, quite frankly, to lord it over him. And each episode that deals with this fear directly helps overcome it a little bit more.

In a goodly number of episodes we see this theme approached in various ways. "All Our Yesterdays," "The Apple," "Bread and Circuses," "The Enemy Within," "The Empath," and "The Return of the Archons" are just a few, a cross section of the type of theme that relates to man's discovery of, first, his prejudices about himself, and then, ultimately, the revelation of his own value. It is a slow process, like a theme-journey that travels through virtually every episode of Star Trek, culminating, in different forms and on different levels, in the movies. It's highly unlikely that it was a conscious effort on the part of Roddenberry or anyone else. That simply isn't necessary. The topic of man's inner conflict and self-discovery is such a vital theme in science fiction that it really cannot be avoided. It is always there, like the spirit of some haunted, disembodied soul. It cries for attention. And it has many voices, many faces. Sometimes, to see it, you have to look very carefully, and with love.

There is what we might call the "reversionary" man, the Jekyll and Hyde. We see this approach to man's inner debate about his worth in episodes like "Mirror, Mirror," "The Enemy Within," and "The Alternative Factor." Each of these stories dissects the very nature of man in an effort to explore his dual, good/evil existence.

In "Mirror, Mirror" we have an alternate-universe *Enterprise*, and what we call a "distorted" image of our crew; their opposites, or, some might argue, their inner, darkest selves. Kirk, caring, insightful, and clear-thinking in the Federation's universe, is shown to be a cruel tyrant in the alternate universe of the Galactic Empire. Perhaps "tyrant" is too kind a word, for this Kirk seems to have no conscience. He is willing to kill anyone who gets in his way, without hesitation. In fact, we may assume he does so with glee. The Kirk of the Galactic Empire is greedy for power.

But he isn't alone there. Everyone on the alternate-universe *En-*

terprise is greedy for power. They're even worse. We know, for example, that the alternate McCoy's sickbay is nothing less than a torture chamber. It's all very appalling to our kindly Federation McCoy, and it leads one to wonder what kind of vile demon lies within the body of that Galactic Empire McCoy whom Spock has locked up aboard the Federation *Enterprise*.

In fact, Spock is the only one of the "mirror" characters who seems to have any redeeming qualities at all. Strangely enough, or predictably enough, both Spocks figure out the transportation and eventually cooperate in a kind of separate unity to make things right. In the meantime, we are treated to glimpses of the savage Kirk, Scotty, McCoy, and Uhura snarling in their cell while their kindly mirror personalities try to make their way back home.

It's a curious point that while the mirror Spock looks sinister enough and sports a devilish beard, he is not all that different from his Federation-universe counterpart. Kirk and McCoy recognize this, and at the moment of escape, McCoy risks his only chance of returning home in order to save this mirror Spock from death. Kirk understands McCoy's compassion, acknowledging that this Spock does "remind" him of their own Mr. Spock. So the similarities are striking, and the mirror image is incomplete. At worst, it is a flaw in storyline; at best, it is a paradox. Of course, *someone* had to save the day, and that is probably the reason for the kindly alternate-universe Spock. But it could also go to prove what Spock has maintained for so long, that Vulcans truly *are* different from humans. Vitally so. Perhaps, even in a mirror universe, they respond differently than humans, with greater control, striving to find logic in a chaotic world? How compelling. For the negative world of the Galactic Empire hardly seems the kind of place to nurture any creature devoted to order. And yet "Mirror, Mirror" ends by telling us that there is hope, even in the dog-eat-dog universe of the Galactic Empire. Hope, that is, if logic and honor are allowed a formative hand.

"Mirror, Mirror" is a good story. It is fun, it is nasty, it is vigorous and strangely compelling to watch. Both the episode and the topic it discusses are popular material for fan writers. There have probably been volumes written in the fan literature about the Kirk, Scott, or McCoy of that dark universe. Not simply because it is fertile ground for the amateur writer, but because of the almost hypnotically enthralling nature of the subject. All writers, whether they admit it or not, write in part as a means of self-discovery. Writers need to understand what makes people the way they are, and there is no better way to do that than to look at people as they are not. From the Bible to Milton to Stephen King, we have marveled at evil, perhaps even been secretly enchanted by it. Perhaps that is because evil, for all its destructive power, is something we need.

Which brings to mind another Jekyll/Hyde episode: "The Enemy Within."

In this episode, there is no temporizing; we *need* evil! Or at least, to be fair, we need the qualities of human nature most of us would equate with evil. We need our darker side, our aggressive side (which the creators of this episode equate, rightly or wrongly, with our animal nature). According to "The Enemy Within," this is the side of us that makes us build skyscrapers and spaceships and venture to the stars. The animal, aggressive side is the part of man that makes him forge ahead, unendingly, almost without forethought, into new territory. Very much like Milton's Satan, come to think of it. Very much indeed.

Kirk has another transporter accident in "The Early Within." Only this time, instead of being shot to an alternate universe, unwelcomed and mistrusted, his atoms come back home a little, shall we say, readjusted. He gets split in two. We will not dignify the science in this episode with a discussion of the possibilities or impossibilities of such an accident occurring. Somehow the set number of atoms it takes to make one Jim Kirk come apart in a most miraculous manner and fashion themselves together again to form not one, but *two* starship captains. We will suspend disbelief, if we have any doubts, and venture on to the greater good. For this story is a honey. And the accident had to happen if it was to be told.

There are two Jim Kirks, then. One is good, one is evil. That's the literal interpretation. Let's start again. There are two Jim Kirks. One is animal, one is spiritual. Oops! That's not quite right, either. One more time: There is one Jim Kirk, and he is split into two tenuous, unsuccessful entities. He will not be truly human until he is put back together.

For the sake of discussion, let's borrow from a statement above, from our bank of ideas about the human creature, and find a way to discuss the two independent and conflicting halves of Jim Kirk. Let's call the negative half his "animal" half (though in the course of our discussion we may find that it is not as "negative" as it seems) and let's call the positive half his "spiritual" half (though in the course of our discussion we may find that it is not so positive as it seems). Language can be confining, especially when we're dealing with paradox. And the more we get into man's discovery of himself, the more "paradoxical" it all becomes!

Jim's animal half appears on the *Enterprise* alongside his spiritual half, and all hell breaks loose. The distinction between the Kirks is immediately apparent, but the implications of their differences are not quite so clear. At first, the spiritual Kirk seems normal enough. A little lackluster, perhaps, even boring, but certainly the concerned, caring Jim Kirk we have all loved so long. He is very worried about being split in two, plus other worries concerning a landing party which is freezing to death on the cold planet's surface because the transporter doesn't work.

The spiritual half gradually becomes aware that his ability to make command decisions has become strangely impaired. He has lost his usual emotional vigor and drive. Before long, he recognizes that he needs what the other half has—aggressiveness, animal drive, the will to prevail.

But there's a problem. The animal half is dying. And he is dying in an angry, animal, wild-eyed rage. He virtually storms the *Enterprise* while he is still able, jealous of the spiritual Kirk, even murderous toward him. Where the spiritual Kirk is sensitive and caring, the animal Kirk is insensitive and totally unconcerned with his fellow man. He is a lusty fellow, and his animal passions lead him to attempt to rape Yeoman Rand. No doubt had he been allowed, he would have destroyed Kirk's beloved *Enterprise* and everyone on it.

The important thing about this story, though, is how Jim Kirk comes to know and appreciate himself. He had to get over some prejudices about himself, too. This is something which only the spiritual Kirk is capable of doing. And it is an excellent example of man's need to understand and overcome the unthinking, destructively aggressive side of his nature. For Kirk, the only way to survive, to be the person he was before the accident, was, ironically, to regain that part of his nature which had become so repulsive to him in the personification of the animal Kirk. He goes through a great deal of soul-searching in this episode as he tries to reconcile himself to the fact that the "animal" Kirk is just as much a part of him as is bone, muscle tissue, and blood. He must understand, respect, and thereby control that in himself which is repellent to all he holds dear. And if he and those he loves are to survive; he must learn to use it, as well.

It is nothing less than human destiny. In discovering the mysteries of space, time, and all the universe, we must also discover the richness and complexity of what we are. We can't turn away from it and survive.

"The Enemy Within" provides us with a very gentle, human discussion of the value and beauty of being human. Kirk discovers that humans, not only himself but all humans, are neither pure nor inherently righteous. Neither are they evil or simply naturally wicked (the odious teaching of original sin). They are a mixture— a *good* mixture. The tiny atom is an innocuous thing, until it is split. When its whole is divided, havoc ensues in the form of fantastic energy. On a less powerful scale, that is what happened to Jim Kirk. And in "putting himself together again" he learned to value and channel those qualities, both animal and spiritual, which make him a man. He was a fortunate man, in a way, for he was forced to come to a point of truce with himself; face to face, he met and conquered the demon in his soul.

But before we become bogged down in clichés, let's look a little deeper. Kirk did more than face the "animal" side of his nature. At the very end of the episode, when Kirk takes that last daring chance on the transporter (we aren't sure at this point if it will bring back a whole Kirk or a whole "dead" Kirk) he embraces himself, soul to soul, as a brother would embrace a brother. He feels love for that being he had earlier despised. And in doing so, he comes to love and value all that he is.

Often unnoticed by the fans, it was one of Kirk's most courageous moments. And it pointed the way, early on (the fifth episode), to the path Star Trek would take in its entirety.

"The Alternative Factor" deals with the Jekyll/Hyde theme as well, but with an important difference. The "evil" double in this episode is more than just warlike and aggressive. He is mad, totally insane. And he is a fanatic. His name is Lazarus, and unlike Kirk in "The Enemy Within," really two people. One, the lunatic, is from our universe, and he is obsessed with killing his mirror Lazarus (a sane, kind, decent being) who is from an alternate, antimatter universe. If the two should meet it would mean the destruction of both universes.

It should not go unnoticed that the fanatic Lazarus from our universe has become mad through the simple knowledge that he has an exact likeness in another parallel universe. Like some bold, single-minded crusader from another time, he ventures out in his spacecraft (which is also sort of a time machine) in order to annihilate this one human who is his double. That says reams about hate. And it is an unmatchable commentary on the process and rationale of prejudice.

As an episode, "The Alternative Factor" moves slowly, mostly because what it has to tell is so concise, and the rest of the story must be padded out with action and the "winking" in and out of the two alternate Lazaruses. Like the other Jekyll/Hyde stories, it is heavy with paradox. The crew of the *Enterprise* is once again experiencing the results of positive/negative behavior in mirror beings. Only this time, they are the observers, confused at first, trying, and almost failing, to understand. But the ultimate answer to Lazarus' problem is not so different from the mirror Spock's answer to his universe or the split Kirk's solution to his divided essence. The good Lazarus had to find a way to restrain his mad alternate self from destroying two entire universes.

"The Alternative Factor" is much like the stories of old mythology, and Lazarus becomes a godlike being, cast into a lonely void between universes where he must eternally fight the good fight of sanity over madness. It is a lonely battle indeed. And whether we are aware of it or not, it is a fight experienced by every human being since the beginning of time.

The mad Lazarus was filled with many negative qualities: anger; fear; hatred; prejudice. He was the embodiment of all destructive human drives. He would wipe out two universes so that he could be the only Lazarus. He was filled with ultimate prejudice—against every living thing. The good Lazarus' positive answer to the problem involved tremendous love for all existence. And he made the grand sacrifice of spending all time in the void with a madman.

Symbolism is the name of the game when viewing and discussing "The Alternative Factor." But when viewed symbolically, it reveals ideas very similar to "Mirror, Mirror" and "The Enemy Within"— the key to life, to human existence itself, lies in the ability and downright *need* to come to terms, or at least control, all aspects of human nature. To respect the enemy in some cases, to even go so far as to love him in others. The eternal struggle of the two Lazaruses is realistic, when viewed as the human struggle with self. Kirk's answer offers more hope on a personal level. He is saying, essentially, that control (like Spock, like Lazarus) is necessary, but that it can be taken yet one step further . . . to love.

Before we leave the Jekyll/Hyde episodes, we should mention an interesting side note: "The Enemy Within" is considered by some to be a kind of starting ground, or establishment episode, for the Kirk, Spock, and McCoy friendship. There is so much interaction and character examination going on in the story that it brings them all closer together. In this episode, they become solid friends, and their affection for another is most apparent. For that alone, we owe Richard Matheson a great deal, because the Kirk-Spock-McCoy friendship has become the very cornerstone of Star Trek. The way they complement each other and their collective desire to understand and deal with the unknown are also essential elements in the humanistic theme that runs through Star Trek. And with Kirk at the head, the triad friendship is certainly busily doing the job of discovering just what it is to be human.

And don't they do it well! Twenty years of Star Trek has brought a great seasoning to the relationship of what we have now come to call the Big Three or the Triad. We have come to look at them as the collective man. And as the collective man, Kirk, Spock, and McCoy have had a few prejudices to overcome themselves. About themselves. And about one another.

What, you say? Kirk has prejudices about Spock or McCoy? Look back on the episodes and see. You might be surprised at what you find. Kirk *does* have his doubts from time to time. His opinion of McCoy in the series' first episode does not exactly reflect confidence. Nor does it display a great understanding or insight into what the man is all about. In "The Man Trap" he is angry with McCoy, more than once implying that the doctor's behavior is less than professional. Not that Kirk is particularly wrong, mind you. Only that he—well—doesn't know or doesn't quite trust the physician yet. He seems to see him as a good enough doctor, not a bad Joe, but perhaps too involved in his own feelings. This is a good example, though, of the kind of internal prejudices wrapped up inside every human being. We call them self-doubt, and they are not necessarily a bad thing. As long as we know how to approach McCoy's "feelings"; that is, his very emotional nature.

McCoy is *always* involved in feelings, as we discover during the series' unfolding saga. But never again, after "The Man Trap," does he reveal anything about his personal past to Kirk. At least, not for us to see. But then, if we'd been allowed to see more of his personal friendship with the captain and less of his professional one, it would have been a different series, wouldn't it? A little more soap than space. There are other times throughout the series, of course, when Kirk and McCoy come to harsh words; "Friday's Child" and "A Private Little War," to name a couple. And they show their relationship has been through great strain at the beginning of *Star Trek: The Motion Picture*. Soon enough into the series, however, we find that although they may be at odds, with squabbles and even a kind of peevish mistrust, it is primarily the healthy kind of contention that must exist from time to time in solid friendships.

As late as *Star Trek: The Motion Picture*, Kirk is challenging McCoy's opinions, perhaps feeling the doctor should keep his own "prejudices" to himself. When McCoy dares to question Kirk's motives for rejoining the *Enterprise*, the admiral darn near throws him out of his quarters. But this has more to do with Kirk's independent nature than with his friendship for McCoy. Kirk and McCoy are both completely human, after all. And they can both be very pigheaded, when it suits their own prejudices. Like anyone, they have their blind spots.

What about McCoy's prejudices? He has a slew of them, especially about the Spock part of the collective friendship. And he has more squabbles with the good Vulcan than we'd care to relate here. Everyone knows about the great Spock/McCoy logic/emotion debate. It's common knowledge, too, that the famous debate is lodged in a unique, powerful friendship. From the view of the collective Kirk, Spock, McCoy friendship, it can be seen as being not so different from the Jekyll/Hyde paradox discussed earlier. (Most likely Spock would like that allusion, since he was the rational side of the Great Internal Debate. But maybe we'd better keep the analogy from McCoy.) The two, as part of the symbolic human personality set up with the Big Three, must of necessity *always* be a little bit at odds. It's healthy psychology, good writing, and just plain fun. We wouldn't have it any other way. But, oh, how the two do squabble at times! No doubt Spock could feel great sympathy for the eternally struggling Lazarus.

But the "prejudices"? They entail McCoy's view of humanity: what it should be; what he'd personally like it to be; what he believes it is. McCoy is something of a cynic, on the surface at least. At times he seems a little embarrassed by the human race. Perhaps, when upholding its virtues to Spock, he feels a little defensive. Whatever the case, from the collective friendship standpoint, the McCoy/emotion part of the friendship is always nagging the Spock/logic part to ease up a bit, enjoy itself. Maybe McCoy sees in Spock too much of himself, as well. All the more fitting that the debate goes on. None of us *really* feel comfortable about confronting ourselves with total honesty.

But in Star Trek, the characters work at facing one another—practice for facing themselves. It's part of the process of discovering their own worthiness, which, let's not forget, is what this whole "prejudice" thing is all about. Self-doubt, actually, of the worst kind. The kind that has been "taught" and "learned" throughout the ages. Humans are brought up with it from the time they first begin to understand that they are greater than the other animals. It supposedly works to keep them in their place. At least as far as religious training is concerned. *Like yourself, human, but not too much.* To be too happy with what we are is somehow against all that is holy and good.

If that's the case, our Vulcan Mr. Spock has been a good human. From the collective-friendship point of view, he is the one who holds that naughty human nature—you know, the part that lusts and carries on—in contempt.

And so we have Mr. Spock's "problem." He has some trouble accepting the likes of Leonard McCoy. No one really blames him, either. It's hard to get a handle on the kind of personality who says one thing while actually meaning another. It takes Spock some time (perhaps all the way to "The Empath," or even beyond to his encounter with Vejur) to fully understand what makes McCoy tick. He is so alien to the Vulcan. And as part of the collective personality, he represents the part of "self" most commonly held in mistrust.

McCoy, who constantly derides Spock's love of logic and emotional restraint, knows, as any human must know, how important Spock is to the *Enterprise*. But here's a question for someone to answer: Does McCoy *know* how important Spock is to the friendship of the three of them? How self-aware is that collective personality? Or is it aware at all?

One thing is certain: If the friendship *is* in any way self-aware, it is through the personality of James T. Kirk. He is the overruling mind, the living spirit, not only of the Friendship, but of the *Enterprise*. And there's a good reason for that: Despite any problems he may have with Spock or McCoy, he is able to maintain an overall objectivity that neither of the two can quite achieve. They aren't "allowed" to do so, if they are to represent the struggling elements of logic/emotion.

And as the "overseeing" mind of the collective personality, Kirk is at a level where he can see them both most clearly. His early "prejudices" about McCoy gradually evolve into an understanding of and affection for the man. He knows that McCoy, for all his sometimes caustic human ways, is responsible, loving, at times even heroic. Kirk is the part of the collective mind which is able to most easily "forgive" McCoy his cynicism and sharp tongue. As a fellow human, Kirk is the cerebral "crossover"; he knows through conscious experience what Spock must gradually learn through a trial-and-error friendship.

Kirk, too, knows about Spock. He understands and respects and has affection for that stupendous, logical, ordered mind. He worries sometimes about Spock's detachment, but for the most part he leaves that job to McCoy. After all, as ship's physician and as the fire-spitting emotional aspect of the collective mind, McCoy is most suited to the task of gadfly. Kirk tends to stay out of the fighting for the most part, acting as mentor for Spock and referee for McCoy. It seems to work.

Kirk has no prejudice where Spock is concerned. He lets McCoy do the doubting while he does the encouraging. He knows how vital Spock's contribution is to the *Enterprise* and to the Friendship. And he is not wrestling with himself to the extent that Spock and McCoy must. In a figurative way, he is more complete. He has to be, as a leader and as the man cast in the role of supreme adventurer. When he does doubt, he is able to turn to Spock and McCoy for help. It's a true symbiosis.

So although the collective friendship of Kirk, Spock, and McCoy has its usual prejudices about itself and its motives, and, at times, even its worthiness, the strong, willful mind of Jim Kirk leads it on, defying old traditions of self-doubt. *He* trusts himself. He trusts his friends. And so he is able to move forward, one of those rare, dynamic individuals who dares to trust the future.

The Friendship has a life of its own. And a new kind of measure is set up. Not just the measure of a man, but the measure of combinations. It is a matter that is finally discussed openly in *Wrath of Khan* and *The Search for Spock*. Which is greater, the part or the whole?

Depends on what you're talking about. If you're out to solve a problem, it'd be handy to have Kirk, Spock, and McCoy working on it collectively. One of them alone, or even two of them, might have some blind spots, develop a little trouble in finding the right answer. But if you have all three . . .

They don't work by committee. That's good, too, because nothing ever gets done (or at least done properly) by committee. What happens in the collective mind is this: All there make their contributions, then the one whose field of expertise dictates action makes his move. In a sense, he uses the other two to gather information for him and offer support. But when the point of decision-making comes along, he is usually on his own.

We've seen all three of them work this way in different episodes. Many is the time that Kirk and Spock have served as "aides" to McCoy, keeping the ship and crew in line or gathering scientific data while the doctor went about the business of developing an antidote for the disease of the week. This is the case in "Miri," "The Tholian Web," and "The Deadly Years." In these episodes (and many more), McCoy's knowledge and decision-making abilities come to the fore. The ultimate answer to the *Enterprise*'s problem rests in his hands, because the solution is a medical (or emotional) one. Kirk and Spock can act as support and advisers, but they must also stand back while McCoy uses what he knows to figure out an answer.

Sometimes, as in "The Empath," he makes a decision totally alone, even against the overt advice of his friends. Sometimes even against orders. But it is still clear that his decision is the result of the Friendship and Kirk's and Spock's influence on him.

The influence of one friend for the other is always strong. While Kirk wasn't present in "The Tholian Web," his advice and guidance lived on to help the other two. Interesting to note, isn't it, that the collective mind seems to have the power to almost outlive the individuals who make it up? (We see this again in *Star Trek: The Motion Picture*.)

At other times, McCoy and Spock have stood by while Kirk was the man of the hour, giving his advice, making their services available according to their talents. This is what we see in episodes like "A Private Little War," "The Devil in the Dark," and "The Ultimate Computer." In all cases, the ultimate resolution is in Kirk's hands, but it is the advice and support of his friends that leads him to that point.

McCoy's part in "A Private Little War" was that of devil's advocate. In a balance-of-power situation, McCoy, as the emotional one and the physician, sees only that more weaponry will bring more pain and destruction. He tells Kirk so in no uncertain terms. Very much a humanist viewpoint, it is perhaps Star Trek's sanest moment, a cry for help from our own times.

The irony of it is that Kirk, though he agrees in principle, cannot agree in fact. If he were to step out of the situation and do nothing, it would mean the ultimate destruction of the hill people, and it would mean that the Klingons would eventually establish power over the planet. So in this case, while Kirk listens to McCoy's views, and probably respects them, he can use them only as feedback. The ultimate decision is his and his alone. It is a military decision.

In *Star Trek: The Motion Picture* and *Wrath of Khan*, Mr. Spock has to make some decisions on his own. The first Star Trek movie finds all three of the characters "alone," struggling once again to discover their friendship and build it into a unit. They accomplish this by the end of the film, but before that happens Spock must make a personal decision. Without the overt support of Kirk and McCoy, he ventures into the loneliness of Vejur, the living machine. He is on a journey of self-discovery. And though he goes it alone, it is only after the fact that he discovers just how vital his friendship for Kirk and McCoy has become. If it were not for those two, it is unlikely that Spock would have been so instinctively "driven" to discover what it was that seemed to be missing within himself. It is his friendship that drew him to Vejur. We are told that he somehow "sensed" a danger to his friends, and to his mother Earth. Sensing strange emanations from the area in space occupied by Vejur, he left Vulcan and joined the *Enterprise*. We can only assume that the investigation of Vejur was always on his mind. Once he enters the alien's territory, he experiences the questions which are tearing Vejur apart. "Is this all I am? Is there nothing more?"

In an awe-filled moment, Spock understands. And it is at that time that his friendship for Kirk and McCoy reaches full maturity. Their human, dynamic influence on him had changed him during his five-year tour of duty. When he sensed the threat to their lives and world, he responded, just as though he were a part of them. Even the distance of time and space and personal differences had not separated them. He had tried to run from them once, but found, through Vejur's loneliness that he was running from himself. His decision to meld with Vejur, however, was a personal one, guided by the influence of his friends. Never, not even in *Wrath of Khan*, would he ever be alone again.

He made two vital, solitary decisions in *Wrath of Khan*. One was to give his life for the ship and its crew. The other was to give his essence, his *katra*, to McCoy.

"I'm sorry, doctor, I have no time to discuss this logically."

Uh-huh, Spock. Bones is sorry too.

Wouldn't it be great to have just two minutes with Spock, to ask him about that time in his life, and about what led to the two decisions he made that day. No doubt he would tell us they were both totally logical solutions to two distinct problems, one of a military nature, one of a personal nature. And if we caught him in the right frame of mind, we might even dare to ask, "But what *moved* you to rest your essence within the mixed-up, irrational, sometimes chaotic mind of Leonard McCoy?"

The answer he would give, if he deigned to respond to such a forward question at all, would go something like this: "It was a practical decision, based more on what was convenient than what was purely logical. I assure you that there was nothing emotional about the matter."

There is nothing emotional about wanting your essence to live on after the body's death? There is nothing emotional about choosing as the vessel for your soul a human being who has been your friend for twenty years?

But Mr. Spock has us just the same, for his decision is such a clever combination of logic and feeling that we can never untangle it. It is the best kind of decision, perhaps. Balanced, sensitive, productive. It's the kind of decision-making he learned from Captain Jim Kirk. And it's tempered with the quality of insight seen so often in Leonard McCoy.

So we've seen what the individual can do. We've seen what the whole can do. Which is better? Which is most productive in the search for understanding? Which is of the greater value to human society?

It's a paradox again. Or perhaps, as we said earlier, it's a matter of perception. The question is raised in *Wrath of Khan* and *The Search for Spock*. In *Wrath of Khan*, Spock says, "The needs of the many outweigh the needs of the one." Kirk and friends disagree in *The Search for Spock*, and the admiral explains in answer to the Vulcan's question "Why would you do this?": "The needs of the one outweigh the needs of the many."

For Kirk there is no longer any separation between himself and Spock and McCoy. They are a unit. We cannot even be absolutely certain who the "one" is: Spock or McCoy? They are both in big trouble. As individuals, they are important. That's what Kirk means by "needs of the one." In that way, then, the parts are each considered to be greater than the whole.

It's the humanist idea come full circle. A sort of fundamentalist approach to a liberal-minded concept. And it gives the Friendship a symbolic and surrealistic maturity. It puts it on a grand scale and allows the science-fiction approach of Star Trek a greater depth and breadth, so that, if we want to, we can examine each episode in retrospect, allowing ourselves an imaginative and interpretive freedom which is seldom provided in science fiction, fantasy, or any kind of episodic adventure.

In Star Trek the questions of the needs of society and the value of the individual are essential. They make up the bulk of material, covering a wide range of stories and storyline "types," from the banished Zarabeth of "All Our Yesterdays" to the happily stagnating subjects of Vaal in "The Apple" and the brainwashed followers of Landru in "Return of the Archons."

Often the conflict between the inner "needs" of the one and the practical requirements of society play a part. These stories sometimes involve class struggles, such as we see in "The Cloud Minders." Here is a classic example of a stratified society. The citizens of Stratos oversee the Troglytes, who are miners and farmers of the planet. While the symbolism is so obvious that it rather rudely hits us over the head, it still makes a good point and reminds us that we are only fooling ourselves if we don't recognize the same problems in our own society today.

Most real cultures are stratified, of course, whether we like it or not, whether they proclaim themselves to be communist, socialist, fascist, capitalist, or somewhere in between. But in the case of Ardana things have gotten a little out of hand. The Troglytes are little more than slaves, and the pseudo-intellectuals of Stratos have managed to rationalize the whole situation—believing in their own way that the Troglytes are best suited to the working-class life through some kind of inherent intellectual inferiority. Of course, we know better, but it takes the imagination of Kirk and the medical skill of McCoy to figure out that the Troglytes are suffering from—are you ready?—pollution of their environment. The Troglytes mine a substance called zienite. Somehow during the extraction process a gas is released that impairs the intellectual capacities of the brain and can even cause one to become violent (as if the conditions under which the Troglytes lived were not enough).

Eventually Kirk proves this to the leaders of Stratos and they begrudgingly come to understand that all Ardanans are created equal. Would that it were easy! Nevertheless, it is an excellent example of how Kirk and his crew work on a humanist level. Suddenly, through interaction with the *Enterprise*, the "lower classes" of Ardana are able to celebrate their equality and self-worth. We can imagine that the Ardanans' society will have some rocky times after the *Enterprise* moves on, but such is the pathway of growth.

Kirk meets many elitist cultures along the way. Some are small, such as in "Plato's Stepchildren," where the planet Platonius is ruled by Parmen, another pseudo-intellectual who, by virtue of his greater psychokinetic powers, rules as a kind of mad-hatter philosopher-king. The only true "unequal" on Platonius is the dwarf, Alexander, who is made to serve as court jester and all-around scapegoat. He has no special powers, you see.

Once again McCoy and Kirk work together to make things right. McCoy discovers that Alexander lacks the psychokinetic powers only because of a difference in how his body assimilates a substance called kironide. After Parmen and company prove to us how sadistic and childlike tyrants can be, Kirk and Spock turn the tables on him, allowing themselves to be injected with enough kironide to have powers of their own.

The true humanist hero of this episode is Alexander. He refuses

McCoy's offer to inject him with the power-engendering substance, because, quite simply, he doesn't want to "be like them." Not only does he discover his self-worth, he understands the responsibility and power that go with the discovery. As the episode ends, Alexander leaves Platonius and begins a new life. He is eager to experience new worlds. He has left hatred behind.

In "Who Mourns for Adonais?" we come across a very small elitist society indeed. A society of one. The lonely, tyrannical god Apollo is in search of subjects. He is an outdated creature, however, unable to come to terms with the equality of peoples (as are the citizens of Ardana, or even, to a minor extent, the pitiful "philosophers" of Platonius). When Kirk and company prove to him that it is their inherent right and will to live as free individuals, poor old Apollo just gives up and casts his spirit upon the cosmic winds. The world of human self-esteem and equality is not for him.

The story of Apollo opens up another area of discussion where the needs of society and the needs of the one come into conflict. Religion.

In Star Trek, as in all science fiction, religion—organized religion, not the belief in a superior being—is a negative. Like it or not, that's the way it is. Look at just the most obvious episodes where Kirk, Spock, and McCoy are confronted with real or sublimated religious questions: "Who Mourns for Adonais?"; "The Way to Eden"; "For the World Is Hollow and I Have Touched the Sky"; "The Apple"; and *Star Trek: The Motion Picture*. Each of these episodes deals with the tendency of religion or high-held religious leaders to rule their subjects through hypnotic, charismatic, or just plain heavy-handed means. In every case, the "god" or religious ruler may have been at one time well-intentioned, but has become outdated, stagnant, even cruel. Any attempt to excuse their behavior always finds itself limited to the literal or surface interpretation of the episode. It is quite a different matter when observed under the powerful, multifaceted lens of science fiction.

"For the World Is Hollow and I Have Touched the Sky" is the most classic, most undilutedly obvious example. It's a classic in that sense, complete with McCoy as the "runaway" who is searching for solace in the face of death (he's just diagnosed himself as suffering from a rare, incurable blood condition). He finds his solace, he thinks, on the seed ship *Yonada*, where he falls in love with the beautiful priestess Natira. He quite frankly abandons ship. Whether this is proper or not, considering his condition, we do not know. It may well be that the diagnosis of a fatal illness allows an officer to resign from the fleet. But McCoy does jump ship in hope of finding some last days of "happiness" by marrying Natira. He is looking for paradise, and for a metaphysical answer to supposedly unsolvable physical questions. The secret of religious obedience on Yonada *does* have a physical answer, however: To be a member of the society ruled by the all-wise computer Oracle, McCoy must allow himself to be implanted with the Instrument of Obedience, a small device inserted above the temple. He does allow it, and eventually pays the price.

Religious obedience, it seems, just isn't in the ol' Southern boy's blood. Out of necessity, he finally rebels. He finds a way to change Yonada's orbit (it's heading for a crashing rendezvous with a heavily populated Federation planet) and contacts Kirk about it through his communicator. With all the good intentions and earnestness of a religious zealot, the Oracle tries to kill him. Disobedience is not allowed, even for the consort of a priestess.

Kirk and Spock, of course, come through. They risk a lot to save him, too, because Kirk has just been ordered to speed *Enterprise* along on another mission. When they enter Yonada's secret control room, they also discover a cure for McCoy's disease. We find out later, by the way, in Gene Roddenberry's novelization of *Star Trek: The Motion Picture,* that the whole experience will have a profound effect on McCoy's life and on his influence in Starfleet medicine.

So McCoy makes some self-discoveries here, as do the people of Yonada. Once the outdated, superstitious bonds of the Oracle are broken, they can move on to find their destined homeland. And they can live as a growing, productive, free society. Once they are freed from the brain-controlling influence of the Oracle, they are able to discover their own potential and self-worth.

There are other episodes which deal with the theme of blind, unthinking obedience to some master being or master plan and its tendency to destroy the society it was supposed to protect. Tyranny is tyranny, whether it be clothed as religious, military, or political government. But in every episode where we encounter this kind of oppression, we find that the story wants to focus on one or two individuals who have the courage to break away. Again, the needs of the many versus the needs of the few. The individual is important, not only for his contribution to the whole, but for who and what he is as an entity.

Whether it is Kirk, himself, outwitting a machine—as he so loves to do—in episodes like "The Apple," "The Ultimate Computer," and "The Changeling," or whether it concerns nonregular characters who desperately seek their freedom, like Alexander in "Plato's Stepchildren" and the underground freedom fighters in the Nazi episode "Patterns of Force," no storyline pretends to put the value of the individual beneath the needs of his or her society. But episode after episode does show us circumstances under which such extreme "prejudices" exist.

Star Trek seems obsessed with showing us the individual's struggle for identity and freedom. The day may come, as every human suspects, when the struggle against the computer-god Landru in "Return of the Archons" does not seem so farfetched. "Return of the Archons" is an interesting study, in fact, because it embraces any kind of oppressive society you choose to name: religious, political, scientific, what have you. Somehow, they're all wrapped up in the same package as far as Landru is concerned. He/it doesn't care about the fine line of definition. You're either "of the Body" or you're not. And if you're not, don't worry, you soon will be.

The bottom line in "Return of the Archons" parallels those of other stories we've discussed. The people who are the victims of the highly "prejudicial" society or tyrant are ultimately given a choice. They can remain as they are, ofttimes rather contented (but not always, and not everybody), or they can dare to learn what is wrong, try to correct it, and go on from there. We leave the people of Beta III in a mess, but a very healthy mess, according to Kirk. And we might as well take his word for it; he knows a good bit about growing pains. He's grown a great deal through his adventures, and as part of the Kirk/Spock/McCoy friendship, participated in the painful growth of others. And he's learned to be careful about how he assesses his friends.

He's learned, for example, that the sometimes abrasively emotional McCoy who "thinks with his glands" in "The Man Trap" is also the McCoy who thinks with his heart in "The Empath." When McCoy defied the wishes of both Kirk and Spock and offered to trade his life for theirs, he demonstrated to the Vians that humankind, with all its supposed "inferiority," has the very enviable ability to love. The Vians said of McCoy, "His death is not important." They implied it was for "the greater good."

They were fools. They didn't understand the value of the individual human being. How could Kirk explain? Is there even a language that has the capacity to describe what we all instinctively know? McCoy had already explained it, by showing the kind of love one human can have for his friends. In "The Empath" Kirk learned to respect the power and great stature of that kind of love and to value the emotional personality behind it.

He has also seen how Spock's drive for logic and order eventually led him to journey deep into the cold, lonely heart of Vejur. Only Spock could have done it. And the information Spock gleaned on that fact-finding journey not only helped to save a world, it helped to save Spock himself, and the friendship of the three. The Vulcan learned, finally, that his own fearful prejudice against human emotion was what kept him from being a complete individual. The learning process was painful, but not nearly as painful, Spock discovered, as the emptiness of the entirely logical machine-god Vejur. It's probably quite true that had Spock not journeyed into Vejur and come face to face with the transcending value of human emotion, he would not have been able to entrust his own spiritual essence to McCoy in *Wrath of Khan*.

Everything is tied together in Star Trek. Or it can be, if we care to examine things closely. But nothing compares to the complementary alignment of the Kirk, Spock, and McCoy personalities. They have overcome a multitude of prejudices in order to direct their attention to the larger questions humanity is destined to ask. Their adventures are ours, because where one leaves off, the other takes up, giving us a complex, well-rounded view of humankind's journey in the universe. And its discovery of its own value and potential. In discovering their own self-worth, their inherent *right to be*, our fictional Star Trek friends have found the key, unlocked the door, and taken the first step into man's future. Through their experiences, we can examine who we are and why, we can look objectively at others, we can even dare to challenge ideas which, rightly or wrongly, rule whole worlds. We can defy definition. It's a human breakthrough, really, a journey into a universe of ideas and exploration. And it never ends.

KEEPING THE FAITH, OR HOW TO LIVE THROUGH A STAR TREK CONVENTION

by Ingrid Cross

If you are among the fans fortunate enough to have attended a large Star Trek convention, you know how much fun and excitement is generated during the course of a weekend. Everything seems to go so smoothly, and everyone seems so happy, that you may have been struck by the thought that you could organize and put on such a convention yourself. If you're seriously thinking of doing so, take heed of the following article. And if you wouldn't dream of organizing a convention yourself, perhaps reading about the difficulties involved will cause you to appreciate the next con you attend all the more.

The idea to put on a Star Trek convention in Baton Rouge, Louisiana, was actually born in Omaha and St. Louis. Joyce Tullock and I had attended conventions in those cities in 1983, and, while we were there, one of those deceptively insane ideas crept up on us when we weren't expecting it.

Why not put on a Star Trek convention in our own city?

Both Joyce and I had attended several Star Trek conventions through the years, ranging from informal "fan-oriented" cons to those with one or more of the series actors. We thought we had seen everything: soaring successes; raging disasters; cons where an actor was supposed to attend, but hadn't been paid and therefore quite logically didn't show up; committees that cared about the fans and put themselves out for them; extravaganzas promising the moon and delivering a meteor; cons where professional investors became involved and absconded with the money. As fans we had been enthralled when meeting other fans; we had enjoyed innovative events; and more often than not, we had been bored by routine programming. We had thrilled to the chance of seeing those people who had made Star Trek possible, who had given a tenuous concept life and breath.

We had seen it all, we thought. And then people who knew us as McCoy fans started asking when we were going to put on a convention and have DeForest Kelley as a guest.

First we sneered at the idea. Or we simply smiled politely, ignored the question, and walked away. But the idea simmered in our minds until the fateful drive back to Louisiana after the marvelous St. Louis experience.

Why couldn't we put on a convention? We were smart enough to pull it off, we had a lot of friends around the country who seemed interested in attending a con in the Deep South, we even knew people who might be interested in appearing as guests! And we knew how to advertise.

These were key concerns to us. There were others, of course: money (the biggest of our worries at the beginning and the nightmare beast to plague us until the conclusion of Delta Con), the time required to put a large convention together, the necessity of having enough staff members to help, et cetera.

Looking back, it seems as though we spent more than a year and a half working with the project. We enjoyed it, in the end. But would we do it again?

Perhaps that's the essential question to use as a starting point.

Star Trek conventions ("cons") have been around since 1972,

when a group of New York fans thought, "Hey, wouldn't it be great if we had a gathering of other Star Trek fans? We'll get together at a hotel with a hundred or so people, talk about the show, swap ideas for stories! It'll be wonderful." A lot of people know the rest of that story: Several hundred fans showed up. And a new trend was born.

We shouldn't blame early organizers; they meant well. But they started Star Trek fandom on a path few convention organizers should have followed. Conventions have since been held all over the country—indeed, all around the world. The number of attendees totals in the many thousands (there are no accurate attendance figures). Cons have been held at universities, in hotels of all sizes, and even in huge convention centers. Their success has been measured mostly monetarily (by organizers), but by other factors as well: Did the convention live up to the committee's expectations, and to the attending fans' expectations? Was the programming interesting enough? Did the guest actors live up to the crowds' expectations?

Conventioneering is largely a matter of expectations. Committees set out with some sort of objective (although this is questionable at times), and the fans attending also have hopes, realistic or not. (From our experience as organizers and attendees, these hopes are generally unrealistic.) And when the hoopla is all over, idealistically all these expectations should have merged together and been accomplished.

Idealistically. A lot of things can go wrong between the instigation of an idea and the realization of it.

Perhaps you're one of those people who has thought about organizing a convention. Maybe you've been to other conventions and had the idea creep up on you that you could do a better job than others did . . . that you could put together a convention that would blast everyone's socks off.

We won't discuss sanity at this point. To make the decision to put on a convention is to invite yourself to the nearest mental institution—speaking from experience, of course.

On several levels, the convention we put on, Delta Con, was a success. People enjoyed themselves, the programming went off as planned, and a lot of wonderful things happened to us while planning it and during The Weekend.

Joyce and I had several objectives when we planned the convention. We estimated attendance at 600 to 800 people—a good medium-sized convention. DeForest Kelley and Walter Koenig were our invited main speakers. Other guests included Walter Irwin and Edward Spiteri, a NASA scientist. Connie Faddis, a fan writer/artist/editor, was our guest of honor.

Why do people commit themselves to such a project? You have to be motivated by *something* in order to make the decision in the first place. Let's be straight about one thing immediately: Anyone who does it for the chance to make "big bucks" had better get out before starting.

Money is not a good enough motive. But more on that in a moment. Trust us on that point for the time being.

Fame? What fame? Organizing a convention is sheer backbreaking, exhausting work, if you want it to come off halfway decently. There is no "fame" associated with being a convention organizer. How many convention chairmen appear as guests on a network talk show? How many work the lecture circuit or get interviewed by Dan Rather? If you're motivated by the notion of being "someone," you're in for a big disappointment. When it's all over, you'll look around and say, "I'm the one who did the convention! Aren't you impressed?" If you're lucky, people around you will yawn. More likely, they'll say, "What's a convention?"

In short, in the real world outside of fandom, having organized a convention means nothing. It might look great on a résumé—if you want to own up to it in the "mundane" world. You have contributed nothing of lasting value to the evolution of mankind and the pursuit of world peace.

Most of the people who attend a convention could care less whose name is behind the project. The majority of people want a party and you supply it. Like any host, you'll be fortunate if they pick up their trash as they leave.

To this day, we're not sure we had any tangible reasons for putting on a convention, short of promoting Star Trek in this part of the country. Baton Rouge is a long way from the Midwest, which is where most of the better conventions take place. Part of our motivation was that a purely Star Trek convention had never been done here before.

And part of the motivation was the challenge of doing something

we had never done before. We wanted to prove we could do it.
(It's not clear to whom we were trying to prove this point.) And we
wanted to prove we could do it in ultraconservative Baton Rouge.

Partly we wanted to share the enjoyment in Star Trek we had
experienced with others around us in the city, and around the
country.

We'll assume those were good enough reasons. They sufficed for
our purposes.

So one of the first steps is to make sure you know *why* you're
putting on a convention.

You have to make several key decisions as soon as you decide
to do the convention. What kind of weekend do you want to have?
Do you want to pay actors to come and speak, or will it be a
weekend where fans just get together and talk Star Trek? Do you
prefer programming that is laid-back and loose, or do you want to
program an event or several events concurrently for twelve to eighteen hours? Will it be an extravaganza, complete with a huge dealers' room, charity dinner, parties, autograph sessions, and so on?
Or do you envision your con to be an intimate, quiet three-day get-
together?

If you lean toward the quiet get-together, you're better off invit-
ing several Star Trek friends to your house and playing videotapes
for seventy-two hours straight. But if your visions take you on a wild
extravaganza replete with actors and the entire freewheeling experience of a major convention, your needs will be accordingly greater.

One of those major needs is money. Money, as some wise philos-
opher once said, makes the world go around. It also fuels a successful convention. Conventions are like dinosaurs: They need a lot of
food in order to survive. Except in the case of cons, read "money"
for "food."

The first step when planning a convention is to work up a budget.
Let's say you want to invite two actors, two writers, and a NASA
representative. The actors do not come free. This is only right, since
the convention circuit is a part of their working life. They appear
at conventions in order to enhance their visibility to the public, of
course, and they do it because they love Star Trek. But they also
do it for money. Whether or not you agree with the idea—and there
are a lot of people who can't quite grasp it—it is a fact of life. In
addition to speaking fees, you'll probably be paying for their air
transportation and hotel costs.

Your other guests have requirements, as well. The writers and NASA rep will have to sleep somewhere. Even if they don't charge you for their speaking services (after all, a writer generally makes public-speaking appearances to promote his work and name), you will most likely be responsible for their hotel costs and perhaps meals. Some things can and should be negotiated—but some items in a speaker's contract are immovable.

Okay, you'll need money for speakers. Let's use a ballpark figure of $15,000 to cover speakers' fees, hotel rooms, and incidentals (food and so on).

Did a collective "gulp" just resound from the audience? Probably so. Wait until close to the convention when you get phone calls from people wanting to attend and they balk at the ticket price, which ranges from $10 to $40 for an entire weekend. Try explaining to people that the speakers cost money. One trial of a convention organizer's patience is listening to that refrain—even from friends—over and over again. But it gets worse.

Your initial estimated figure was $15,000. That won't quite cover it. As one chairman of a successful Midwest convention told us, take that figure and double it, or you'll be in for a terrible ordeal when it's all over and you're in bankruptcy court. When planning for a medium-sized convention with professional actors, a budget of $30,000 is adequate. Barely.

So in order to decide whether or not you should make the commitment, what's the next step? Realistically estimate your attendance. If you are a hard worker and you can hustle enough, you might feel you can pull in 800 people. Now divide your total budget by the number of people to get the ticket price you should charge.

And then you need to really think. Expect to stop and think about any major step in planning a convention. The question to ask yourself here is: Would *I* attend a convention that costs as much as what I need to charge? If you can honestly answer yes, go on to other considerations.

If the answer is a shaky maybe or no, perhaps it's best to bow out immediately. Either drastically rethink your plans or scrap them completely and plan on attending other people's conventions . . . but please keep that experience of budgeting firmly in mind as you enjoy yourself at their conventions.

How do you get your hands on the $30,000 you'll need to put on your convention? If you're a property owner, you can mortgage the house. If you're a hustler, you can probably get a lot of your up-front money by getting people to pay admission early. You'll still have to come up with more money, though, as most people don't plan a year and a half in advance when going to conventions. And most of your income will come from "at the door" attendance. You will have bills to pay long before then, so you'll need cash flow, and the best possible way to get it is by talking to a banker. A business loan is another big commitment—another opportunity to think, as you leave the loan officer's office, about whether or not you really want to go through with the convention. If the answer is again yes, keep going.

There are a lot of *major* concerns involved with putting on a convention, as you have probably already guessed. For example: Who will be in charge? If a club is planning to put on the convention, someone will have to take ultimate responsibility. If individual fans are putting it on, the same applies. It is helpful to have a core committee that oversees the entire operation and makes all the decisions. The smart con organizers will realize that the person or persons who put up the money should have the decision-making power. Otherwise, you run the risk of losing friends—especially if the person who is given major responsibility is not the person who signed on the dotted line of a legal document.

Something else to consider is that should you make any money on the convention (highly unlikely), the persons who put up the money should be the first to be repaid, after all outstanding bills are settled.

The ideal delegation of responsibility is to give the core committee the ability to make those tough decisions and be able to enforce them. Some friends who had put on conventions before told us the chances of breaking even were practically nonexistent on a first-time con. Since we were the ones who would have to make up the difference after it was all over, we were the ones who made the decisions. It was that simple. It goes without saying that you have to know yourself and your partners well enough before you give them a sizable responsibility, especially where money is concerned.

Each person on the core committee should have a job description. In other words, each key person's role must be delineated. Think of the major categories required in the project and assign each to a specific person. They will probably have others under them to help carry out the objectives, but someone has to be in charge of each committee.

A good example is programming. Decide what you want fans to do during the weekend and go from there. At Delta Con, we had speakers, video rooms, an art show and auction, a gaming room, panel discussions, a charity dinner and auction, and more. We did not divide up the work so much as check on one another constantly to make sure that each item was being followed through on. As we made our plans known, several friends around the country were tapped on the shoulder (or begged) to be in charge of something.

This caused some problems, however. For example, the person in charge of the art show and auction lived in Virginia. She could not attend any committee meetings with us, which might have made her job easier. Instead, she was thrown into the situation the weekend of the convention. And while the art show and auction went very well and was a successful, integral part of our overall programming, it was not fair to her.

So another key to success is to have local people who can help you.

And that brings up the subject of workers. You will need warm bodies when actually running the convention: people to assist the committee chairmen or to relieve them once in a while to eat or sleep; security people to keep overenthused fans from whatever dangers might lurk around the corner (e.g., excessive partying that threatens to demolish the hotel); and gofers, to take care of just about everything else.

A good rule of thumb is ten ancillary people for every one hundred people you expect to be attending. And, of course, those seventy or eighty people working during the convention cannot work twenty-four hours straight (as the convention organizers seem to), so you will need some scheduling genius to help get everything covered at the same time.

A good way to find people is to check out local clubs—Star Trek and science fiction. If you can find fans in your area, half the battle is won, because there is a good chance you and they will be speaking almost the same language. And if there is some common interest you all share, it makes it easier to work together during The Weekend, with all the other pressures crushing everyone involved with running the convention.

And by the way, the persons who are running the project should be prepared to deal with every kind of person. Diplomacy and tact unfortunately go only so far sometimes. A con organizer needs to have a strong backbone. It's difficult to coordinate forty to seventy people and make sure they're doing what needs to be done. You'll have to worry about personality clashes between the committee and the workers, and among the workers as well. If you make it clear up front who is taking the ultimate responsibility and who has the final word, things should run more smoothly.

Money, core committees with responsibility, and ancillary people to work the convention. What next?

Where are you going to hold this wonderful event? Let's assume you'll be holding the convention in a hotel. First step: Find a hotel that is willing to host the group. This involves examining *your* needs, as well. How many meeting rooms will you need? Does the hotel have a ballroom that will hold the number of people you're expecting? How much does the hotel charge for using its facilities? Does it have special convention rates for its guest rooms?

Finding the answers to these questions requires research; and after talking to many (or all) of the hotels in your city, you'll have a better idea of where to hold the convention.

We were lucky with Delta Con. There are five major hotels in Baton Rouge. Two contenders were eliminated after simply looking in the Yellow Pages, where we discovered their convention facilities were limited to 400 people or less. One hotel was crossed off the list for various reasons, among them the fact that it was stuck in the middle of nowhere, with no restaurants or tourist attractions nearby. (After all, most people are using vacation time to attend a convention; why not give them the chance to explore your city?)

We scouted out the fourth hotel and discovered we didn't care for the atmosphere; the hotel caters mostly to businessmen. It was nice, but *cold*; we wanted a place with the Southern charm that Louisiana lays claim to.

The fifth hotel had many things going for it. It was located on the Mississippi River, was close to the airport, had enough meeting rooms for our programming, and was possessed of old-world charm and history aplenty. And—almost too good to be true, according to friends who worried about our sanity at times—the sales staff were a joy to work with. We worried needlessly about silly things, and the hotel staff graciously laid those fears to rest. After all, they have dealt with conventions since the 1930s. In other words, they had experience.

Still, they had never hosted a Star Trek convention and were probably blissfully ignorant of what to expect. We kept trying to warn them about the costumed fans, excitement, and strange things that would happen. They would just smile. So despite our worries that they didn't know what they were getting into, we worked out negotiations and moved on.

It is essential that you can talk with the sales staff and that you get along with them. If they seem inflexible from the start when you're checking them out, they will be inflexible during The Weekend—something you can do without, considering all the other problems you will encounter. Make sure you are comfortable with them, that you can ask them anything. And treat them with respect.

There is only a limited amount of negotiating you can do with the hotel. You can argue over prices all you want, but the sales staff must go along with management's price list. The hotel is in business, too. There are other points which might be more negotiable—for example, the price charged for meeting rooms.

With conventions, hotels make their biggest money on the number of guest rooms booked. Usually, the more rooms you book, the less you will be charged for the meeting rooms. As with anything else in the discussions, get everything in writing. That way, you will face less headaches when you settle the bill and you won't have to rely on word-of-mouth deals made a year or so before.

Nothing involving the hotel is too minor. You will need to know if it has another major convention booked the same weekend as your con. If it does, consider selecting another date. You don't want to have mass confusion reigning, plus the worry of checking more badges at the door than is necessary. And you want to make sure your attending guests will be able to get a room at the hotel. Ask the hotel about its policy on security personnel. Do you need to "rent" a guard for the weekend, or does the hotel take care of it? (And who pays for the service?) Is there a doctor on the premises, or at least someone who knows first aid and CPR?

In short, you need to know if you can work with the hotel staff. You're going to be involved with them for at least a year, and you'll practically be living with them during The Weekend. The weekend of the convention is not the time to find out they're impossible to deal with. An excellent way to ensure good working relations is to meet with them on a regular basis, increasing the frequency of the meetings as the convention date approaches. Just calling them every other week or so helps. It shows you care about your project—and it will help them care, too.

So you have a budget, a committee, an idea of programming, workers, and a hotel. You're ready to set a date and let the world know about it.

There is nothing minor about these details. In fact, you're probably getting the idea that nothing at all is "minor" when putting on a convention, aren't you? Good. That's what you should be thinking.

It *sounds* simple, "setting a date." Far from the truth. Somehow you have to know when other major conventions are taking place and where they will be held. To start off our consideration of dates, for example, we ruled out November through February. November and December are holiday months; not many people are in the mood to go to a convention around Thanksgiving or Christmas. Besides, they generally don't have enough money to spend on air fare, admission, and in the dealer's room. January and February are bad months for bills; everyone is paying off holiday debts. We wanted to be able to draw students from nearby colleges; that ruled out the summer months. That left March through May, and September and October.

We had two other major reasons why we didn't want the summer months if we could avoid it. First, there are a lot of conventions in the Midwest and on the East Coast during the summer—we would be competing with established conventions. That was a dangerous prospect. In addition, the summer heat in Louisiana is devastating to people who aren't used to it. And since we needed to bring people in from around the country—not just our state—we didn't want fans collapsing in the streets from heatstroke.

That narrowed it down to September and October. September is not as rainy as October—if you've never attended a convention over a rainy weekend, take my word for it: It's depressing. And college kids would have more money available to spend earlier in the semester. Plus, WorldCon was held over Labor Day and other conventions had been held during the summer, so maybe fans would be ready for another convention.

We thought we had settled every angle. And we were pleased with a late-September date—until we realized that the first home football game of the local university (LSU) was on the same week-end. Normally, we don't worry about things like that; sacrilegious as it sounds, neither of us is into football. But in our city, football is *sacred*. Especially the first home game.

It affected our attendance on Saturday, but it wasn't as bad as it could have been. Believe me, when we first found out about the game, it was a frightening notion to think we had spent eighteen months planning and maybe no one would show up.

This just goes to show that you cannot plan for every contingency. But we darn well tried. Sometimes we came up with reasons why we shouldn't use a specific date that now seem ridiculous. But if they sounded good enough at the time, we decided on the bais of our gut reaction. (Another good quality for convention organizers: If you can't trust your own visceral reaction to an idea or potential problem, you will face worse problems all the way down the line.) All of this leads to the fact that you need to think about the date and all possible problems involved. For example, you don't want to schedule your convention—especially a first-time con—for the same weekend as WorldCon, the biggest science fiction convention of all, because it's been around a long time and you'll be competing against its reputation.

Now you know when you want to hold your convention. The next step is to let people know that you're going to have a convention.

By this point, we were accustomed to the idea of the convention. We had a good idea of what was going to happen that weekend, but we had to translate it to paper and advertise it; several major chores had been taken care of before we committed ourselves in print.

First, we had signed contracts with DeForest Kelley and Walter Koenig, and we had made agreements with two of our other speak-ers. Not many people seem to do things in this order. If someone is flying in to attend your convention, he is making the conscious decision to come based on your guest list. Putting an actor's name on a flyer and other advertising is making a commitment; if a con-tract has not been signed or a definite agreement in writing made before that advertising goes out, it is, in my opinion, tantamount to lying. You are leading people on and getting them to commit their time *and money* to a fiction.

An example: If a fan decides to attend Con X where William Shatner and Leonard Nimoy are billed as attending guests, that fan has an interest in seeing one or both of them. If a convention committee accepts money from a fan before contracts are signed, and then negotiations happen to fall through, the fan will be disappointed.

There are other repercussions beyond disappointed fans. The word has already gone out that these actors will be at Con X. When they don't show up, you can bet the committee is not going to take the blame. The organizer will not come out and say, "Well, we didn't have them under contract in the first place." That would be admitting to lying and false advertising. More than likely, the *actors* will be blamed by the committee. ("They just didn't show up" has been heard about more than one actor in just exactly these circumstances in the past.) Such actions damage the actors' credibility, and affects every other convention that legitimately went through negotiations and signed contracts. Con X's greed smears every other convention organizer and causes general distrust among fans.

Another tactic for attracting fans is a bit more nebulous. This involves the practice of putting out a flyer with a long list of "invited guests." This is not outright lying, of course. These writers, actors, or other speakers probably have been *invited*; the implication is that these "invited" guests will be signing a contract and are expected to attend. While it's not a deliberate falsehood, it is still misleading. Major companies would be called up before federal agencies for "false and misleading" advertising if they were to engage in such practices. Convention organizers using this ploy should wait until contracts are signed; negotiations don't have to take forever. But they *should* be started early!

So before you put out a flyer, you'll want to have a very definite idea of what programming you are offering fans. We could have used the invited-guest routine; we certainly approached enough people about speaking at Delta Con. The list would have been impressive to a lot of people, perhaps more impressive than our final guest list; it depends on your perspective. But our reputation was important to us. If we were going to take someone's money, we wanted to make sure that person knew exactly what would be happening that weekend.

It seemed as though a lot of people had been burned before by less savory tactics. We received many letters from people wanting assurances that Mr. Kelley and Mr. Koenig would definitely attend before they sent their money. So it was with a clear conscience that we could reply, "Yes, we have them under contract."

Negotiating with the actors was an exciting, interesting process, but, as we'd heard from other people, there were no major problems dealing with them. They each have idiosyncrasies and requirements. Each Star Trek actor has a set price for his speaking fee and each requires payment of the hotel room. Most of them require air fare. From there on, everything diverges according to the individual. Meals and other considerations are negotiated on an individual basis.

We knew we were under way for sure when we received the signed contracts back in the mail. It was a heady feeling. Now we had committed ourselves and the convention was a reality. Now we had to tell other people about it.

There is nothing simple about designing a convention flyer. Everything has to be on that little piece of paper—without boring everyone who reads it to tears. The same rules apply to a con flyer that apply to any other piece of advertising. You ask yourself the basic questions, then answer them: who, what, when, where, and why. Include clear and accurate directions to the hotel. Put it all together in an attractive manner and mail it out. Of course, this description of the entire matter is rather brief; I won't go into the headaches of editing material to fit onto the page. (Of course, there is always more you could tell . . . but you have to get the reader interested. Anyone can read about a convention. You have to make fans want to *attend* the convention and see it for themselves.) Make the flyer *enticing*!

Probably the most difficult part of getting ready to do the convention flyer is choosing a name for the event. There are no rules about this procedure, except that you don't want to use someone else's name—you don't want to trade off of some other group's good reputation, or bad reputation, if its con happened to be a bomb. The majority of the conventions around today use something about their geographical location to describe the convention. The New York Star Trek Convention sums it up nicely. Or Coast Con, the Gulf Coast convention in Biloxi, Mississippi. Also, some Star Trek terms lend themselves to good convention names: Archon, Con-stellation, Nova Con (although why anyone would want to have a convention named after a catastrophic astronomical event is beyond me). As with any other product, you want a name that catches the imagination, pulls the reader into the concept. There were a lot of choices available to us, most of which were too silly or too difficult to pronounce. We finally settled with Delta Con because Baton Rouge lies in the Mississippi Delta region, and it *sounded* strong and substantial.

After you have the flyer prepared and printed, you figure you're ready. Well, as long as you have someone to send them to, yes, you are ready. Now you have to find your market (something you should have considered before this point, really). You could advertise in different genre-oriented magazines (*Starlog, Twilight Zone*, etc.). You could also ask local bookstores to distribute your flyers. (A national chain store probably will not, since it usually has a policy against endorsing products. This is a shame, but understandable, since such stores don't want to lend their reputation to something that could be, as far as they know, of questionable integrity.) You could even plaster them against windshields at a local mall parking lot.

But the best bet is direct mail. And that entails a mailing list or two. If you know a lot of other fans around the country, you could ask them to send your flyers around to their friends. Ask nearby conventions if they would be willing to let you use their mailing lists. (This can be a touchy matter—we found one well-known convention group to be jealously uncooperative.) Also, mail batches of your flyer to other conventions; after all, if people attend *that* convention, you have found part of your market, right? At least they know what conventions are. And check with Fandom Directory (Post Office Box 4278, San Bernardino, CA 92409); it has a mailing list service at a reasonable cost.

We found that direct mail worked best. With current postage rates, though, mailing out 10,000 flyers first-class was an unbearable expense. After talking to different people who used bulk mailing, we decided to get a permit. We saved 9.5 cents on each flyer that way.

Nothing was more pathetic than seeing our small group doing the first major mailing of about 3,000 flyers. We spent the money to have the printer fold the flyers for us (saving us about three to four hours of labor), but we had to put labels on each one and then sort them by zip code. The living-room floor was a hopeless cause—as it would be for many weeks to follow. Five of us sorted flyers by zip code destination, tried to figure out the postal regulations, and somehow managed to put the right labels on each bundle.

Then we dragged the bags to the post office and worried while they checked the forms. Thankfully, we had guessed correctly at the sometimes vague wording in the regulations. The first bundle was off!

What celebration! It sounds easy enough doesn't it? And yet, one of our earliest concerns was becoming a reality. That first mailing took approximately one hundred hours to complete, when you consider the time spent by the artist to design the flyer, writing, typing, and laying out the copy, pasting labels on each flyer, and sorting and bundling. With everyone involved in the convention also holding down a full-time job, you can see how the time required to do things right would begin to mount up and eat a hole into our lives.

And that was only the beginning of advertising. Starting a year before The Weekend, we took out ads in both professional and fan-oriented publications. We printed a total of 15,000 flyers, all of which were mailed out, sent to other conventions, or distributed locally. We ended up with maybe 300 left over.

Four months before the convention, we began working with the media. One of the most critical phases is sending out the press releases at the best time—in other words, not too early and not too late. Anything more than four months before the convention is too soon; the media won't care. And if you haven't let them know you're around with less than two months left, you might as well forget it. By that time, you'll have too much else to do to give enough attention to local publicity. About three months before the convention is the right time to *begin* with your publicity, but don't forget to follow up right until the day of the con!

We sent releases to every newspaper and radio and television station in Louisiana, eastern Texas, Arkansas, western Mississippi, and a lot of major colleges in the country. After all, this was a Big Event in our area—the first time in this part of the Deep South that a Star Trek convention would be held. And with two of the actors attending, it made for good news copy.

There was some excellent early response, mostly from small-town newspapers. We didn't sneer at any of the coverage; even if it was a three-line blurb, it was free publicity. (The word "free" is what counted most.) Most of the media people worked well with us. There were, as always, some exceptions.

One of the biggest problems a Star Trek convention faces is the public's ignorance of what is involved. You may have noticed, if you're a hard-core fan, that if you mention the words "Star Trek fan," most people will visualize a person who wears poorly made pointed ears and carries a phaser. The media are no different. So you have to try and keep things in perspective. The most common question we heard when talking to reporters was "Is Dr. Spock coming?" Second most common was "Well, what do you do all weekend? Watch reruns?" As they say in politics, we had an image problem. Some media people never did quite catch on to what was happening; we saw some reporters aimlessly wandering the hotel halls with blank expressions. But on the whole, the media treated us generously. We managed to set up radio and television interviews with some of the guests and had a large group at a press conference.

We also bought radio time on a local station. We booked one week of spots; we should have booked two, but even the one week helped immensely. Walter Koenig graciously agreed to tape the spot for us in Los Angeles, and it was put together in Baton Rouge. We managed to get a lot into a thirty-second spot: time, place, what a convention is, and our phone number.

The phone calls started about two months out and steadily increased. We took it as a good sign that the phone was constantly busy; it meant the message was getting out. Overall, we had excellent advertising.

So we were pulling in the people who wanted to come see the strange events. At the same time, we were trying to hustle around and get dealers to come in as well.

Dealers are a strange breed. You can't put on a big convention successfully without them, but some are a pain to work with. Dealers are usually people who sell memorabilia full-time. They go around the country to a different place almost every weekend peddling their wares—an extremely competitive, cutthroat business.

We wanted a large dealers' room, which meant selling fifty tables. The cost of a full table included a three-day membership. We made sure we mailed flyers directly to dealers. And those we didn't reach saw our flyers at other conventions.

We got the number of dealers we wanted. But we also got a lot of headaches. There should be a booklet on the care and feeding of dealers, because handling them was a challenge. As I mentioned, they're in a competitive business; after all, there are only so many

Paramount-licensed Star Trek items to sell. As a result, despite our pleas to bring other items, nearly every dealer showed up with what everyone else had.

This did not make them happy. While we could appreciate their dilemma (some of them had come from as far away as New York State and weren't moving a lot of merchandise), it was difficult to be sympathetic with a group of grown men and women who whined and complained.

Overall, the majority of them were well behaved. But there were a few that the committee and some of the fans attending the con wanted to restrain with a chair and a whip. Of course, I hasten to add that these characters are in the minority. Unfortunately, they are a very vocal minority and tend to give you the impression that all dealers are obnoxious. Most of the dealers at Delta Con were helpful and cooperative.

If you're putting on a convention and want dealers, be prepared for every possible problem. Just keep reminding yourself that you are sane, and that you are doing them a favor by holding this convention so that they will have a market for their wares.

For a year and a half you are working toward one goal: The Weekend. Time rushes past in a blur and you find you are becoming quite adept at working late hours and learning to constantly worry. The strangest details are a source of worry before a convention. I was worried about getting the actors in and out of the ballrooms safely. That went well. But there were other surprises.

For example, I hadn't anticipated the incident of the lost pants. I walked into the gofer room to hear someone asking, "What happened to [the actor's] pants? Who has them?" With remarkable calm, I asked what was going on. When they saw my furrowed brow, they made it clear that no one knew which dry cleaner his pants had been sent to. Fortunately, the actor wasn't out walking the halls in his underwear.

By a month before the convention, a lot of details should have already been settled. First of all, your contractual obligations should be fulfilled at specified times. The actors and other guests usually set up a payment schedule. You should have paid first and possibly second installments on those contracts by this time. (Otherwise, you might not have some of your promised guests. Why should they show up if they have not been paid as promised?) Most notably, you should have mailed out press kits, scheduled as many of the interviews and television appearances as you possibly can, and made sure that your guests have been kept up to date on the convention's progress.

By this time, you should be planning and practicing a lot of things. Don't use this valuable time for something you could have taken care of much earlier.

Registration is a big concern. Do you know how it will be set up to get people in as quickly as possible? Is there someone you can trust in charge of the money? (Don't laugh. People at other conventions have learned the hard way.) When will you be open? Go to the hotel and walk it through. Fix problems you can foresee. But practice it!

Program books should be completed by now, ideally. There is no excuse for collating and stapling program books two nights away from the convention.

Convention badges can be ordered and printed months ahead of time. Your preregistration system should have been ironed out and working smoothly. Letters of inquiry should have been handled as they came in. As mentioned before, the press should know what's happening by this time.

What's left, less than two weeks from the con?

Well, all the thousands of details that couldn't be taken care of earlier than this. Final arrangements with the hotel (finalizing any banquet arrangements, if you have one, floor plans; chair setup requirements). Interviews with the press. Getting your radio spots to the station(s) on time.

I don't remember the final two weeks before Delta Con. Well, I know they happened; I just don't remember what I actually did. I know we were busy all the time with final concerns. Last thing I knew we had three weeks to go and then it was the day before.

Moving into the hotel was a mess. Living about twelve miles from the hotel created problems. Not only did we have to get the actors and other guests from the airport, we had to get everything from our living room into the hotel. This ended up happening Thursday night from 9:00 p.m. until about 1:00 a.m. Despite all the checklists we had made up, we still forgot things.

Like the convention T-shirts. We got everything to the hotel and someone realized the shirts weren't there. We looked everywhere for them all day Friday as people were coming in and registering.

They were back at the house, waiting patiently in the back room.

Friday was a nightmare. We had plenty of people to help set up the convention, it was just that some major problems developed. We had difficulty with art display flats for the art show. The poor art show director wrestled with inferior and decrepit flats and managed to get them in order by late Friday afternoon. No one will tell me with certainty, but I think they were building those flats as artists were entering their work.

The hotel people had neglected to tell us about fire regulations in the dealers' room. The arrangement we had set up to keep everyone happy had to be changed two hours before the room was to open for setup. Then when we did open the room, dealers were arguing about their locations. I was lucky; I was about to scream when our chief person in charge of the gofers stuck his head in the door and offered to help.

Joyce and I were halfway to the airport to pick up one of the guests when we realized a local TV station was going to be at the hotel for a live spot at the time we had to be at the airport.

That worked out well; Walter Irwin saved our necks and handled the press very nicely.

Every time we turned around, someone had a problem. I had not foreseen having so many problems—after all, we had been planning this for so long. The object lesson here is that there is no way we could have planned for *everything*. That's why it's a good idea to start working on a convention so early. At least we had managed to plan on possible contingencies in certain emergencies. We had something to fall back on, even if we hadn't actually gone through a specific crisis that weekend. In addition, we were lucky to have an excellent working staff and guests who were willing to pitch in and help solve problems.

Friday is a blur, and mercifully will remain that way until the end of my life. Saturday and Sunday went very well; the major problems we had anticipated months before didn't materialize (of course, others did, but they weren't as bad as they could have been). People at the convention kept telling us they were enjoying themselves, and that was what counted. Registration was very good, and that was important, as well.

The convention workers seemed to have a good time. The key committee members appeared to be moving with the flow of events, for which we were grateful. The guests were happy—they kept telling us they were, and that was nice to hear.

And yet I remember looking at some of our main workers and saying very calmly, "Never again." They didn't take me seriously . . . then. They could see no particular reason for me to say that, and so they laughed.

I was deadly serious.

The idea started creeping up on me early Friday morning (at about 6:30, sitting in a local television studio); a mutinous thought, really, that didn't take full form until Sunday afternoon. Little sleep for three days before The Weekend, very little sleep and no food to speak of during The Weekend . . . and that mutinous thought burst into full flower.

"Never again" was a private motto for some of us that weekend. Sure, it was fun for everyone—except that the organizers were running out of enthusiasm. Neither Joyce nor I operate well with two to three hours of sleep a night and maybe two solid meals all weekend. Plus we were the ones who heard the complaints and handled the problems. Don't get me wrong—we had not expected to be able to enjoy the convention at the time. (We began to realize this about six months before.) But we also didn't realize how much of an overwhelming experience it would be.

But we managed to pull it off. The people standing in the registration lines were proof of that, as well as the constant media coverage all weekend. We had "done it." We had put Baton Rouge on the map for a very new, different, and positive reason.

But was it worth it?

Even before the convention we asked ourselves that question over and over and we could not find any convincing reason to answer yes. We ran up against a lot of people who wanted something for nothing; we weeded those people out.

We also met many people who wanted to attend the convention for free. We simply could not make certain fans understand why we had to charge admission. I guess they felt it was their divine right to see the actors for nothing. (By the way, we found there are a *lot* of people out there who think the actors owe them something.)

By the end of the convention, we were in awe of all of our guests: their patience, diplomacy, enthusiasm, overwhelming kindness, and courage. By the end of Delta Con they had become like a family, devoted not only to the task at hand but to the ideal Star Trek represents. They acquired a deep mutual respect for one another, a kind of warm comradery that may be rare in most cons, but was beautiful to see. It was our greatest personal reward for Delta Con.

We had so many problems behind the scenes that at times it tried our patience; and we had been developing enormous amounts of patience all along. We simply started to run out.

It is impossible to total up the time Joyce and I spent on Delta Con, beginning with the very early vacillating discussions ("Should we or shouldn't we?") all the way through The Weekend and even after (writing the final checks). We didn't work twenty-four hours a day on the preparations, true. But a conservative estimate shows that we probably spent a total of five months preparing the convention, including all the detail work and the actual running of the weekend.

And so, you might ask again: Is it worth it to put on a convention? If you measure success in terms of fame and fortune, no. But if you're looking for other things (if you're still thinking of putting on a convention, please pay attention to this), the answer is yes. There were many things that made it all worthwhile.

We met a lot of people who are the salt of the earth; we wouldn't have had the opportunity to meet and work with such fine people if it hadn't been for Delta Con. We learned a great deal, as well: how to borrow money, how to work within a tight budget, how to beg for materials at times, how to talk to reporters, how to organize thousands of details and shape them into a three-day extravaganza.

You can't put a price on those things. I wouldn't want to try. But, in the balance, was it worth it?

Well, here is a list of what we accomplished:

1. We wanted a convention *for the fans*. Joyce and I had been to a lot of conventions that seemed to be put on for the benefit of the committee. We wanted to do one where the fans were the important people.

We succeeded. We were told over and over that Delta Con was the friendliest, warmest convention people had ever attended. And nobody got kicked out of the autograph lines.

2. We wanted to gain the experience of managing something like a large convention.

We certainly succeeded there, as well. The convention is something we can put on our résumés, an event that might someday help us in our professional lives.

3. We wanted to celebrate Star Trek.

Delta Con was more than a party. It was a gathering of friends, people who shared a common interest and love of Star Trek. There was a spirit that weekend of pride in being involved with something as positive as Star Trek . . . and that attitude seemed to come through even to the media.

4. We wanted to bring the Star Trek experience to the Deep South.

Again, this was accomplished. Nothing like this convention had ever been seen in our part of the country before. It set Southern fandom on its collective ear, without any apologies. A lot of people in other parts of the country don't understand and therefore are a little afraid of the South. We made it possible for them to look at us a little closer and realize that the South has a lot to be proud of.

5. We learned—and watched as our friends learned—to give without stint.

We saw many heart-warming examples of this; our workers were by far the best group of people brought together to work on a convention. They proved themselves over and over again, going beyond what was asked of them. There was the worker who knew someone who wouldn't be able to attend on Sunday and get her autograph on that day. Rather than saying "tough luck" (which happens at other conventions), this worker stood in line on Saturday—using her assigned card and giving up the chance for her own autograph so that one of our attending fans could get the actors' signatures.

There were the gofers, who were assigned to specific time schedules, coming back for extra duty when they thought they would be needed—without being asked.

There was the guest speaker who took care of an attending member's rambunctious kids so the mother could listen to DeForest Kelley's talk without distraction.

There was everyone's quiet determination to see that everything ran on schedule—unheard-of at a majority of conventions—so that when an event was to start, it started *on time*.

Those accomplishments mean a great deal to us. They are what Delta Con was all about. They were its reason for being. And to be frank, they are probably the most tangible rewards anyone receives from a convention. Those who might think being a con organizer gives them prestige are only kidding themselves. And eventually they will pay a heavy price in sweat and money with relatively little thanks in return.

Putting on a convention is one of the few things a person can do that reveals humanity in black and white. At cons you'll meet some small people, true. But you'll also have a chance to meet and work with the best of people. For us, Delta Con was a sharing between guests and staff. We wish everyone could have seen what we saw, and felt the warmth of caring between participants. They really were all a family.

If you do put on a convention, we wish you the best of luck and hope that your experience will be as uniquely rewarding as was ours.

WALKING ON WATER AND OTHER THINGS JAMES KIRK CAN'T DO

by James H. Devon

*James Devon's article "Beneath the Surface: The Surrealistic Star Trek" (*The Best of Trek #8*) was extremely popular and well liked by our readers. It was also extremely unpopular and vehemently disliked by our readers. Why this mixed reaction? We think it's because James says not only what he thinks, but what other fans think, as well . . . whether or not they* know *they think that way or want to think that way. Strong opinions make for strong reactions, as they say, and we're getting ready for another flood of mail—on both sides—about this article. But that only makes sense, because James himself* takes both sides.

It's amazing. James T. Kirk has become a complicated phenomenon. He isn't the simple, good-against-evil Mr. Nice Guy character we all used to know and love; he's someone else. That's the way some fans would tell it, anyway. Some people have become quite vehement, claiming they've lost interest in Kirk because of a change in his character in the movies. All this despite the fact that he is undoubtedly the most "popular" character in the show. Maybe that's his problem—maybe his massive popularity has done him an injustice as far as Star Trek is concerned. Some fans are discouraged by the "flawed" Kirk they see on the movie screen, constantly bemoaning the fact that he's no longer the twenty-third-century King Arthur they imagined him to be in the series.

By the way, if James Kirk is "no Boy Scout," neither is he a King Arthur. He never was. That vicious rumor was started by some early, sweetly naive fan who evidently had no idea what medieval writing and the Arthurian legends entail. No, Kirk was no Arthur in the series and he is no Arthur now. Thank God. He was and is—at least according to the man who should be credited for creating him—a very imperfect, but idealistic human being. A man who could lust, who could be jealous, who could even let his prejudices get in the way of his decisions once in a while. A man capable of making mistakes.

Those who don't believe that might enlighten themselves by putting their hands on a copy of Gene Roddenberry's writer's guide to the series. In it, he outlined what the characters should be like. True, all of the characters developed according to what this or that writer or producer or actor did to them, but that does not fully explain what I can only call the "Mary Sue" version of Kirk. I will say what few fan writers have the guts to say these days: If it were up to the fans—and I don't just mean the lady fans out there—James T. Kirk would have nothing to offer Star Trek as a character. He'd be a wimp, a goody-two-shoes, or even worse, a King Arthur. (Thank goodness we have at least been spared a "chaste" Kirk. Then it would indeed be "King Artie, step aside!")

Jim Kirk is a man of honor, sure, but with limitations. The morals of the twenty-third century are not all that clear in Star Trek (regardless of what the K/S people, with all their convoluted skips in logic, like to maintain), but we are given no reason to expect that it is customary for a man to have quite so many women (just about one every episode) over the span of a year as does our lusty captain. I'm not knocking it, I'm just saying it isn't very "Arthurian." Of course, his loves are usually presented to us as deep, true loves (or, in some cases, old flames, as in "Shore Leave"), but even that is kind of kinky, and more than a little unbelievable on such a grand scale.

Then, of course, there are those he plays along for the sake of getting out of a fix. That's even worse. You know the story, and more than a few would-be Kirk fans find it offensive that Kirk so often finds it necessary to stoop so low. One would think a man of his brilliance and military imagination would be able to come up with a more sophisticated means of solving the problem than trying to charm, bed, or otherwise infatuate the "enemy" female in a story. Still, he does it time and time again.

But at least his behavior *does* prove that he's not entirely the white knight of the *Enterprise*. He is shrewd and tough, and if he has to play the lady along for the sake of saving his ship and crew, he'll do it. And, interestingly, he always seems to enjoy it!

The crux of it is, Jim Kirk may have nerves of steel, but his glands are quite something else. It's great that his libido is so active, but all in all it's done more harm than good as far as the *Enterprise* is concerned. He almost lost everything in "City on the Edge of Forever" because of his love for Edith. In "Elaan of Troyius" he nearly causes an intergalactic incident. (And let me pooh-pooh right here the idea that we can blame it on Elaan's magic tears. Why should Kirk always be excused for his failings? This guy is supposed to be *strong*, right? Had one of Kirk's men fallen for the old magic tear trick, Kirk would've had him court-martialed) In "Requiem for Methuselah" Mr. Spock and Dr. McCoy are just about to go crazy trying to save the crew from a deadly plague while Kirk spends his time being goo-goo-eyed over an android! (Kirk, incidentally, has trouble distinguishing androids from real ladies. Rather curious, as we all know he is a man of considerable experience. See such episodes as "Shore Leave" and "What Are Little Girls Made Of?")

So let's once and for all put an end to the myth that a macho Kirk is a sign of strength. And don't get me wrong . . . I like the Kirk who gets "tricked" by ladies with magic tears and microchips for brains. And I can even understand why the ladies in Star Trek fandom find it endearing—but don't, please don't insist upon *excusing him* for it. He flubbed, and that's that. He's human. As inferior to Mr. Spock, in certain ways, as is Dr. McCoy.

So much for the macho Kirk. In Star Trek, machismo is not necessarily a positive attribute. It's just *an* attribute, like brown hair or hazel eyes. And sometimes a hindrance as far as our beloved captain is concerned. When we get to see Kirk this way, as a man who puts love or affection or glands or whatever above his duty—however momentarily—we see a fellow who maybe isn't quite the perfect Arthur we thought he was. Arthur is a Christ figure in literature, after all, and sexual purity was something for which he strove.

Was Kirk's *Enterprise* Camelot?

I never saw a round table. That is, at no time are we able to consider that the opinion of all the characters in the series or movies are treated with equal respect. Look at the times McCoy's advice, good though it is, was rejected ("Obsession" and "Return to Tomorrow" are prime examples). In the series Kirk is, and should be, the only boss. His ship—like any military establishment—must be run by dictatorship. There are checks and balances, fortunately. We learned in "The Deadly Years" that a commander can be removed from duty. And we know that McCoy, as ship's surgeon, has perhaps the single most powerful position of authority, in that he can declare Kirk medically or mentally unfit for command. But we also learned in "Turnabout Intruder" that doing so isn't necessarily easy. It involves a military tribunal and a whole lot of hard proof.

Kirk tries to be fair, of course. He is fair, for the most part. That is the sign of a good commander. But there are times (again, "Obsession," again, "Return to Tomorrow") when his judgment is clouded by good old-fashioned prejudice or ambition. In "Obsession" he risks all in a vendetta against the deadly cloud creature, partly because he is consumed with guilt from a supposed failure (again, macho Kirk fans—is this possible?) to stop the thing in a previous encounter when he was under the command of Captain Garrovick. He chases the creature, remember, in what is really an obsessed, blind determination, and all the time he's supposed to be elsewhere, delivering desperately needed medical supplies to another planet.

And to make things worse, Garrovick's son is now serving on his *Enterprise*. The young Garrovick, an ensign, pulls the same trick Kirk had pulled years before when he meets the blood-consuming cloud creature—he fails to fire at it immediately, which means it has time to kill a fellow crewman. (Kirk's failure was much bigger, by the way. His flub cost the life of Captain Garrovick and half the crew of his ship, the USS *Farragut*.) So now Kirk has double blinders. He's really mixed up. With extreme prejudice, he sees in the boy's failure a reflection of his own past sins. It's the only real father/son relationship Kirk has in Star Trek, and it's good writing. (The father/son relationship of *Wrath of Khan* and *The Search for Spock* was an absolute failure. Due not to Shatner or Butrick, or even their characters in the films, but to the high and mighty "don't change my captain" attitude of the fans.)

Well, the captain will change, my friends. Because he is a good character. All the hero worship in the world won't alter that, but it does color it, even in the eyes of Shatner himself. He seems obsessed himself, these days, with making sure that he gets full, uncontested attention on the big screen, as if, like the admiral, he feels insecure in his middle age. It is ironic that the fans, much as they love Shatner and Kirk, have been instrumental in helping to change that by responding (however unaware of what they're doing) so favorably to the movies in which there are somewhat fewer Shatner scenes and a bit more of Chekov, Uhura, Scotty, or McCoy.

So in *Wrath of Khan* and most especially in *The Search for Spock*, we have a bespectacled, somewhat rusty and confused Admiral Kirk. To those who enjoy the more realistic view of Star Trek, it is refreshing to see Kirk make a mistake, as he undeniably did in *Wrath of Khan* when he failed to raise the *Enterprise*'s shields on approaching the hijacked *Reliant*. Please, let's not try to excuse it by saying he knew the *Reliant* to be a Starfleet vessel. He *also knew* that there was something amiss in space by that time. Precautions were in order!

But, oh, how the fans love to defend Kirk on that one. It's those hopeless thinkers who remark quite angrily that "Kirk wouldn't do that!" or "Kirk would know better!" who keep Star Trek down in kiddie land and chain Kirk to the role of superhero. *Of course* Kirk could make a mistake or forget something about the refitting of his ship (*Star Trek: The Motion Picture*) or could be lax with a rule (getting "caught with his pants down" in *The Search for Spock*). Not just because it's necessary to the plot, which it is, but also because he is not Spock, either. He is human, and maybe, having been stuck much of the time on planet Earth, he's just a bit rusty. It could be he envies people like Scotty and McCoy who know what they want, and don't allow prejudices about age or the lure of ambition to run their lives. Kirk has hang-ups; why shouldn't he? And one of them is that he can't make up his mind if he wants to run Starfleet or sail the adventurous, starry skies. Until *The Search for Spock*, Kirk doesn't really know himself. He's been struggling with his desire to achieve more and more success and his almost greedy need for adventure.

In *The Search for Spock*, though, he finds out something about himself, and it is virtually his journey into manhood—at this late date! He discovers, like Dorothy in *The Wizard of Oz* and Spock in *Star Trek: The Motion Picture*, that happiness lies in his own backyard, at home. The difference for Kirk is that home is not what he thought it was. It isn't Earth, it isn't the Fleet, it isn't even the *Enterprise*. It's friendship.

As Joyce Tullock is so fond of pointing out, Kirk belongs with Spock and McCoy. He's part of them, they're part of him. Not in any altruistic, mumbo-jumbo spiritual way, but in a real, human, no-nonsense fashion. They are his friends. It's simple.

That brings to mind another of Kirk's attributes that many fans seem to resent. Occasionally, about certain things, he's not so bright. He has to learn the hard way. He has to take his time to discover that career and prestige and success are the least of it. In *The Search for Spock* he had to make a decision that literally might shatter his life. He's done similar things earlier in his career (disobeying orders in "Amok Time" so he could get Spock to Vulcan; trying to stall moving on to his next mission in "For the World Is Hollow" when McCoy was in need of his guidance), but somehow they were not of this stature, and certainly never before was he confronted with the kind of loss he faced in *The Search for Spock*. In "For the World Is Hollow" he was perhaps ready to move on; it was a matter of obeying orders. And even in "Amok Time" he worries about the repercussions of his actions.

But in *The Search for Spock* he took a gallant stand, and we must assume at this point in the story it was primarily for McCoy. McCoy was the one who was dying, in case anyone forgets. *Katra* or no *katra*, as far as Kirk knew, Spock's body was dead and gone. But McCoy was alive and suffering and it looked like it was going to be a pretty messy business. So Kirk, now a seasoned, respected and trusted admiral of the Fleet, has reached the point where he throws it all over without hesitation, for the sake of a friend.

That is a Kirk who has grown. And that is a Kirk who, in the eyes of a lot of people, has done a very dumb thing. It's the kind of guy I can admire. But to almost anyone, he really messed up on this one. He hijacked a Starfleet ship, took her to a forbidden area in space, and blew her up. Not something that will look particularly good on his record.

I've heard from many people who don't like the James T. Kirk of the movies because they think he's overblown and arrogant. Their complaints surprise me, because Jim Kirk was *always* overblown and arrogant. It's one of his many charming flaws, and if he swaggers a bit too much for the average American science fiction fan, then maybe they should take a look around. There are a lot of swaggerers in the world. They're for real. To expect a man who can do the things Jim Kirk does to be humble is like expecting a test pilot to be afraid of heights. Kirk is gutsy, lusty, abrasive, and annoying. Those who insist this observation is just a kind of prejudice are kidding themselves, possibly because they identify with the good captain and don't care for the negative connotations of his extremely self-assured nature.

Maybe audience identification has been a lot of Kirk's problem since he found the big screen. When he was on the itsy-bitsy TV screen, we could watch and admire that glowing self-confidence and could identify with it as a sort of alter ego. His mistakes in judgment—and he did make them—weren't quite so glaring. We could always just kind of wink at them and blame them on someone or something else. Or we could even ignore them entirely. But now when Jim flashes his brass, argues with his chief medical officer, makes a mistake in military judgment, or becomes just plain pushy and manipulative (his eagerness to take over the *Enterprise* in *STTMP*) on the big screen, its a bit more than the would-be heroes in the theater audience can take. To them, Jim Kirk has been a reflection of themselves—or how they fancy themselves—and here he is, making an ass of himself in 70-millimeter. For some, it's unforgivable.

And all the time he is just being the same old lovable Jim Kirk of the series. Only, well, bigger.

If many of these complaints about the "imperfect" Kirk have reached Bill Shatner, it hasn't made him change his attitude so far. Shatner is playing the swaggering Kirk to the hilt, and he thankfully hasn't been too concerned about the good admiral's occasional lapses into imperfection. His contract allows him some script control, but the stubborn, self-centered, midlife-crisis Kirk swaggered right from Movie One into Movie Two. Only, in *The Wrath of Khan* he put on the glasses to show the underlying vulnerability of the man. And to show his vanity right there out in the open.

Lest we forget, Kirk is part of the Spock and McCoy relationship. Spock and McCoy both came to the friendship more or less unsure of themselves. But Kirk's ego taught them to like themselves, and his association with them gave them strength enough to grow to the point where—just maybe—they have even grown a bit beyond him. We have Kirk's ego to thank for that, so let's not put it down.

He was and is a man who, on the final count, forges ahead, does what he wants, and damns the regulations! Need we list the episodes in which he ignored the Prime Directive and instilled (or even forced) on an alien planet the good old tradition of the white Anglo-Saxon western world? On such occasions Kirk is hardly the open-minded man-of-the-universe. Hardly the deep, sophisticated, sensitive thinker many prefer to imagine him to be. But his behavior, in its straightforward simplicity, is refreshing. It's honest.

Now that the word "honest" has come up, it's time to explore that aspect of our non-superhero. Kirk isn't always completely honest. Not with himself, that is. We learned that in "Obsession," we learned it in *Star Trek: The Motion Picture*, we certainly learned it in "Requiem for Methuselah." Each of those stories present Kirk at a delicate time in his life, show him stumbling for a time (don't worry; Spock and McCoy will get him out of it in the end), staggering between what he knows to be true and what he wishes to be true. If he were perfectly honest with himself at all times, he'd be a bore. And he'd certainly be of no use to the feel and storyline of Star Trek. Remember, Gene Roddenberry wanted him to be *human*. Not a blunderer, certainly, though that's how those identifying fans we mentioned earlier evidently classify any mistake he might make. In their desire to worship him, they absolutely cannot forgive him an error, so they feel compelled to explain it away, or more childishly yet, blame the writer! But Kirk can be seen as a real person who has blind spots just as we all do.

Jim's blind spot, as we've noted before, primarily involves his manliness. He has trouble in two major areas: women and ego. Three, if we count his midlife crisis, but let's hope that's a passing thing. By ego, of course, I can and do mean a lot of things. In "Obsession" he felt that he had failed, and his ego was injured; happening once again upon the killer cloud had opened old wounds. In *Star Trek: The Motion Picture* he wanted command of the *Enterprise* again, when he might have served the cause better by allowing Captain Decker to hold the center seat while he himself concentrated on the overall problem of V'Ger and the immense military decisions that had to be made.

Kirk's flaws remain Kirk's flaws, too. Nowhere do we see him trying to change his nature when it comes to women and ego. These "problems," as they've been called, are not really problems in the sense of something to be corrected. Not where the character of James T. Kirk, adventurer, captain, admiral, and man of the world comes into play.

They are traits, features for us to recognize, analyze, appreciate. (And to an extent, Shatner has been typecast by the macho image of Kirk. It has not helped his career. It certainly hasn't encouraged him to grow as an artist. It's ironic that because of his typecast "Kirk" image, his best performances consistently come as Kirk.)

The flawed Kirk of the movies is honestly no different from the Kirk of the series, except that he has grown into a more well-defined, believable individual. Kirk's ego and his lusty, almost cavalier attitude toward women have not changed. But his view of himself has matured. In *Wrath of Khan* he comes face to face with himself. It takes Spock's death to show him what his life has been about. And he recognizes at last, in *The Search for Spock*, his own mortality. He's seen Spock die. And now, McCoy. In *The Search for Spock* he is very much fighting for his own life, and for a friendship that represents life.

What is he doing in *The Search for Spock*? He is being his old egotistical, swaggering, macho self. Because it works for Kirk to be that way. It's the way he keeps himself—and his friends—alive. There is nothing wrong with ego if it is well placed and used in a positive manner, as its influence on the friendship proves. Kirk's ego is very positive. He thinks he can steal the *Enterprise*. He does. He thinks he can return to Genesis and retrieve Spock's body. Well, he does. He thinks he can defeat Commander Kruge and his crew, though the odds are tremendous. He sure does that.

But Kirk pays a price in *The Search for Spock*. He makes a great sacrifice. Not his son, contrary to what Sarek tells Kirk at the end of the film. Poor David would no doubt have been killed whether Kirk had come along or not. No, the real price for saving Spock and McCoy is the *Enterprise*. And it is a fair price to pay. A good deal, in fact. A bargain. A piece of scrap metal in exchange for the lives and souls of his two best friends. (Let's not forget in our sentimentalism that *Enterprise* was about to be put in mothballs. How much better that she should die to spare the lives of her crew! How poetic! How *grand*! Would she have it any other way?)

There are those who criticize Kirk for his destruction of the ship. And they criticize the writers of the script. But to be fair, a script, when it reaches a certain point, writes itself. No, the *Enterprise* had to die. And here is a lesson for Trekkies around the world to learn, though it's surprising that they haven't learned it already: Human beings are more valuable than things. Beyond comparison.

If the Jim Kirk of the movies is a difficult character for some people to grasp, it is because he is simply more of the same Kirk we've always known. On a larger scale, Jim Kirk is seen many ways by many people, of course. And we can always expect children to see him as something of a superhero, beyond reproach. We can expect some people to see him, whether they realize it or not, as the ideal of white Anglo-Saxon Protestants, too. A sort of Aryan dream boy, cleansed of the sins of prejudice and racism. There's no real harm in that, I suppose. But to those who look deeper, he has more to offer than that. He is a man, a real, fallible human being who strives with the tools of his own nature to find a better way in the universe. He is complex, filled with love, filled with ambition, driven by a lust for life and sincerity of will. He has come a long way and made a lot of mistakes. He has argued with his friends and he has learned from them. He has lost them and regained them. He has loved women, begotten children, and found himself alone. He could not be a good father, because he was too good a sailor. He could not be a good husband, because he cared too much for a career that spanned not only years of life, but space itself. It's ironic. Jim Kirk could be true only to the *Enterprise*. And he sacrificed her for his friends.

Jim Kirk is no saint, no god. He certainly can't walk on water and he has never pulled a sword from a stone. Holiness has never been his interest, purity never his ambition. And when it comes right down to it, Jim Kirk can't do a lot of things that a lot of ordinary men can do. He is too much of a renegade, almost blasphemous in the face of authority and convention. Home by the hearth and family tradition just don't suit him. They never will. But we can say this of him, and celebrate the great measure of his human success: He is a man who understands what it is to be human, to make mistakes, to be hurt by them, to learn from them. He is a hero, but he has come a long road to reach the form of heroism which is most noble. He has learned to give and give well. Most of all, he has come to know, without hesitation, the value of a friend. And he has learned all this by being the man he is, not the man of perfection, but the man of life. One of those rare men with the guts to make a decision, he has made mistakes along the way, and he has bounced back with vigor and with love.

Go ahead and swagger, Jim Kirk. You deserve it. You earned it. And most of us wouldn't have it any other way.

THE NEGLECTED WHOLE, PART III: THE ENGINEER AND THE DOCTOR

by Elizabeth Rigel

This is the final installment of Elizabeth's series on those regular crew members which she refers to as "the neglected whole." This time around she takes a long and detailed look at both Scotty and McCoy, two characters she feels belongs together for a number of reasons. Oh? You say you didn't expect to find McCoy in this series, and why in the world would Elizabeth include him among those "neglected"? And what about Kirk and Spock? Read on. You may not agree with all that you'll read, but we can guarantee it will make you think.

(Montgomery) Scott
First Appearance: "Where No Man Has Gone Before"
Rank and post: lieutenant commander; chief engineer
Rank and post by *The Search for Spock*: captain of engineering, USS *Excelsior*

Engineer Scott is one character who has never been left hungering for action. His reputation as a "miracle worker" was earned by many long hours of experience. He has seen his beloved vessel, as well as his own heart, repeatedly scarred, but he still presents a fine example of a man satisfied with his life's work.

He was never developed much as a person; perhaps it was considered enough to have him visible and preoccupied with some technical problem. As fond as Scotty is of his "bairns," they are far from his only hobby.

Like Kirk and Sulu, Scotty is a collector of antiques. Some of his finest pieces are ancient weapons and restored armor, or other crafted metals. Unlike Kirk and Sulu, however, Scotty does not pretend to be relatively skilled with them. He prefers to admire them on display, which is wise, because Sulu might challenge him to a duel. Other antiques Scotty also enjoys are relics of his Scottish heritage, such as the woven family kilt and traditional bagpipes. As his coworkers aren't all fond of the latter, he brings them out only when he isn't expecting company, or on special occasions. It would be interesting to hear him play a duet with Spock's harp, perhaps with Uhura singing along.

Scotty has a one-track mind which excludes frolic from work, and work from leave, to better enjoy both. He has no time for nonsense when in the engine room, but when he is off duty, Scotty is quite the party animal, a veritable connoisseur of liquors and establishments which serve them. He created his own palatable beverage from McCoy's medicine stores in "The Tholian Web," and he had some success in getting the alien Kelvan invader Hanar drunk in "By Any Other Name." Unfortunately, he couldn't stay awake long enough to take advantage of it. Since Scotty doesn't have any dependence problems with alcohol, Kirk probably doesn't mind his social drinking and even joins him for an occasional nightcap.

Scotty's only problem with shore leave is that when he doesn't want it, Kirk often forces him to go anyway. The captain would never force Spock to take unwanted shore leave, yet obviously feels that Scotty, frail human that he is, cannot possibly know what is good for him. So Scotty goes on leave, and by the time he returns, Kirk is kicking himself for sending him.

For example, within hours of his arrival on the pleasure planet Argelius ("Wolf in the Fold"), Scotty was the prime suspect in several savage murders. Within the day, the entire *Enterprise* was endangered.

In "The Trouble with Tribbles," Kirk told Scotty to go mind the men in the bar with the Klingons. And naturally it was Scotty who started the fight he had been instructed to avoid. But, as he explained, he had good reason: The Klingons would not respect them if they did not defend their ship. (Kirk, of course, should be able to take care of himself.) The result is that Scotty is pleased to be punished, because he now has time to catch up on the pleasure reading that Kirk so unwisely interrupted.

Another leave Scotty did not want to take was the trip home for the funeral of his nephew, Peter Preston. To a great extent, Kirk was responsible for that death, and it is a slap in Scotty's face that Peter was not mentioned in *The Search for Spock*. It implies that Spock's death was more important that Peter's.

There is another interesting aspect to the previously-mentioned "Wolf in the Fold." McCoy stated that an accident caused by a woman brought about a temporary personality change in Scotty, with the result that he suddenly hates women. This is not necessarily logical. It is far more likely that the accident would cause an otherwise healthy man to hate only the woman responsible for the injury. It is quite possible that accident caused his subconscious to tap into a painful romantic encounter from his past, equating it with the "attack" by the same woman in the present. This affair could have ended so badly that it clouded all his personal relationships with women for a long time thereafter. Preoccupation with his work may not be the only reason Scotty has not had many lady friends.

Scotty has apparently always been work-oriented, straightforward, and somewhat naive about the ways of the opposite sex. His lost love was probably subtle, romantic, demanding, and insecure, as well as intelligent and attractive, if rather vain. He would have considered her a fine catch and thought that their love was secure. When she broke it off, he would have been stunned by her "treachery" and deeply hurt. Bitterly, he'd vow that it would never happen again.

Carolyn Palamas probably resembled his lost love, but seemed less scheming and cruel. Scotty was immediately infatuated with her, perhaps seeing in her a second chance to regain the woman he loved. Carolyn found him polite and charming, but hardly her ideal of a romantic partner. He became less involved in his work to spend more time with her; and the dignified engineer suddenly began shedding his no-nonsense exterior, showering her with unwanted affection and protection. When she abandoned him for Apollo, his possessiveness was roused to fury. Once again he was abandoned, bewildered, and bitter. This incident intensified a subconscious anger against the so-called gentle sex that remained suppressed until McCoy discovered it in "Wolf in the Fold."

Fortunately the good doctor was able to clear up the problem, and Scotty soon fell in love with the gentle Mira Romaine ("The Lights of Zetar"). Mira was realistic, shy, and equally in love with Scotty. He apparently learned his lesson, for with Mira he was less possessive, more supporting, and happier in her company. He's not so anxious this time to prove his macho fearlessness and brawn, and she does not require it of him. She would suffer any fate to protect him from the malevolent creatures that have invaded her mind. He also would risk death to save her, and his love proved instrumental in her cure and recovery. She was equally good for him—probably one of the best things ever to happen to him.

Without question, Scotty's pride and joy is his *Enterprise*, particularly her engines, the heart of her being. Often when Kirk and Spock must leave the ship and Scotty is left in command, an emergency arises. He does not possess all of Kirk's cleverness or Spock's logic, but that makes him the most realistic when commanding. Unlike the others, he knows better than to overestimate the ship. It infuriates him that Kirk and Spock are sometimes, in perspective, downright careless or foolhardy with "his" ship. The feeling leads to an annoying problem: He wishes they had to clean up after themselves and gain some wisdom about how much damage can really be avoided. Yet he fears if they do learn his job, they will try to do it for him; they have their hands into his area often enough as it is.

Security (or Kirk's occasional lack of it) affects Scotty's work. Mad crewmen are not locked up, "guests" prove to be saboteurs, or necessary parts are stolen or damaged. But the fabled Kirk charm works on men, too: Somehow the enraged engineer is always placated, and by the end of the day things are at double efficiency. Even so, Scotty years later admitted that he "multiplies his repair estimates by a factor of four" in order to keep up with Kirk's demands.

Spock is even worse. His logic falters where the engines are concerned. He has picked up two attitudes from Kirk. The first is "I don't believe in the no-win scenario"—that is, the ship can actually do everything that is required of it, and Scotty is just pulling my leg. The second is "I know your job better than you who are trained for it; I only keep you around because I can't be everywhere at once." Scotty is always afraid that this time the meddlesome Vulcan will goof and blow up the ship. As Scotty said in "The Paradise Syndrome," "That Vulcan won't be satisfied until these panels are a puddle of lead!"

Scotty certainly hasn't earned such cavalier treatment. In all other matters he has shown great respect for Spock. If Spock insists that Captain Kirk is actually Janice Lester, then it must be true because Spock is a reasonable man. Scotty had faith that Spock could produce a formula ("The Naked Time") that a row of computers would have to work on for weeks. But the engines are Scotty's domain; nothing makes less sense to him than to have Spock try to do something he could do as well, if not better.

Scotty's weak spot, if he has one, is in those engines. His rage in "Day of the Dove" and "The Children Shall Lead" demonstrate that he can be pushed over the brink. In both episodes he is deeply distressed that either Klingons or careless tinkering are trying to destroy his ship, which is bad enough, but there is also the prospect that they will simply drain her to helplessness ("We would all be lost, forever lost"). Scotty longs above all for security and stability, for established routines and well-beaten trails. He doesn't want anyone else doing his job as if he were incompetent or unnecessary. He can't bear to leave his routine and friends even for a post on the *Excelsior*, however coveted. It's not a killing fear, as Scotty is willing to part with his beautiful *Enterprise* if there is otherwise simply no hope. But while there *is* hope and life, the ship is to be well treated and protected. Clearly the careless whims of Kirk, Spock, and Starfleet are threats to that security.

It has been said that Scotty would make only a fair starship captain because his heart would not be in it. This would be true only if he honestly did not want the job. As captain, though, he would be enormously pleased to provide the prudent and considerate leadership that could prevent his engines from being damaged in the first place. Given these conditions, he would be an excellent commander.

It is primarily through happy, satisfied characters like Scotty and Sulu that one realizes how troubled Kirk and Spock really are. Sulu is a bright-eyed, swashbuckling Peter Pan, a boy who never grows up and is therefore untouched by the woes of sober adulthood.

However, he is happier and more responsible than the Peter of literature, and his cheer and curiosity are his most endearing traits. Scotty is his spiritual opposite, the happy adult. Scotty loves work, devotes all his waking hours to it, and brings forth worthwhile results. But he is not crushed by work, either. He sees it as an adult's way of play, and has chosen a career that expands his natural talents and potential. To him, work that is not play is a sad and unnecessary burden.

Kirk is a negative image of Sulu and Scotty in that he has a small-boy selfishness with his toys, but very little satisfaction for his efforts. Kirk is frankly obsessed with the *Enterprise* (at least until Spock's death). He loves the power, but often stumbles under the tremendous responsibility that comes with it. He apparently believes that this is the best he deserves.

Spock, too, lacks Sulu and Scotty's contentment and sense of self-acceptance. He does gain some satisfaction from solving scientific riddles, but that is the closest he gets to happiness. He hides in work, preferring circuits and gadgetry to the unstable, uncontrollable realm of people. The *Enterprise* is both his refuge and self-imposed prison. A refuge because she has no other Vulcans, and bothersome as humans are, they obviously cannot compare to Vulcans when it comes to *real* peer pressure. But the ship has also become a prison because Spock is now afraid to leave it. Among his own people he is thought of (and thinks of himself) as a John Merrick, an "elephant man," a freak unworthy of dignity or respect because of his defective, even monstrous genes. Even his own family and betrothed wife are dissatisfied with him. So it has always been; now that the opportunity to change this pattern of thought is in his hands, he is afraid to take it. The *Enterprise* is just another battleground for him.

Scotty loves his ship in a way that feisty, grabby Kirk, and timid, refugee Spock may never understand. He loves her as a father loves his only child, not because she is a product of his life, but because of the life that is her own. Although Scotty will never abandon her while she lives, it is a mutually gentle and protective relationship. He rages against Kirk and Spock and Starfleet and the enemy because they are literally, maliciously attacking his beautiful but delicate daughter. If Scotty didn't have so much respect for the first three, he probably would have punched them all out long ago. He has no patience at all with the fourth group.

The *Enterprise* commanded such a "long look" in *Star Trek: The Motion Picture* mainly to demonstrate the different viewpoints of Kirk, Spock, Scotty, and Vejur. Scotty made his opinion quite clear by his slow cruise past her, as if to say, "Isn't she a beauty? Let me show you why I love this lady like my own kin." Shots of him here are bright, colorful, alive. And it's infectious—even a crewman flips in space with the joy of being near her.

Kirk's view is dark, animalistic, hungry, saying, "*Mine*! Only mine! Why can't I leave you? Why did I? I wish I could hold you in my hand, I'd put you under lock and key and you'd never get away from me again." His scenes are sharp and bold, but heady and disorganized, like Kirk himself.

Spock's scenes are harsh, impersonal, and infrequent. Once his refuge, the starship is now a purgatory, where his sinful nature must be purified before the religious leaders of Vulcan will accept him. He has let himself be manipulated by the opinions of other Vulcans into an "I'll show you!" struggle, which he thoroughly failed in the test of *Kolinahr*. Now, rejected and overwhelmed, he must consider the illogic of going back to a society where he has never been truly welcome, merely to "show them all"—a very emotional response to pain. He is very confused and weary, and he wants mostly to be left alone. Some of his shots are beautiful; but they only serve to emphasize what Spock is trying to ignore or hide from.

Vejur, through the probe Ilia, considers *Enterprise* a living being like itself, although physically and mentally impaired by its long illness (the infestation of carbon units). The *Enterprise* is the first "living" being Vejur has met in some time, and after its fashion, it is extremely lonely. Ilia is shown all the areas that would indeed be the heart, if not the soul, of the starship. Of course, as James Doohan noted, even Vejur has a better way to run the engines. "It is illogical that this carbon-based unit should be in charge of warp engines," the Ilia probe stated to Commander Decker, her guide. Scotty, properly miffed but enchanted by her mechanical design, tolerantly answered, "Lassie, if I were being logical right now, I'd be showing you the inside of a trash-metal compactor!" Nonetheless, Scotty and Vejur agree on the "personhood" of Lady *Enterprise*, and this proves to be an important part of determining what Vejur is and what it wants.

Surely the eighteen months Scotty spends refitting the ship is one of the happiest times of his career. It's the equivalent of escorting his teenage daughter to her first dance. The only snag is that he has to be 100 percent ready when Kirk comes back, because if he is not, Kirk will leave anyway. Kirk gets a hard lesson via the wormhole incident that he has been overly optimistic. Scotty has never and never will claim that the *Enterprise* can do more than she can. He simply works around her weaknesses, and this gives certain overeager bridge personnel the illusion that she is invincible. Indeed, she would be if everyone followed Scotty's methods.

Of course, since Scotty knows how it feels to be upstaged, he never belittles anyone else. The junior officers adore him. He never questions their efforts or muddies their boards with his hands. Their devotion allows him to better educate them in the proper way to respond to Kirk's unreasonable demands: "The such-and-so isn't working, sir. Why don't you ask Scotty about it?" (Smirk optional, but preferably well-concealed.)

Dangerous women, weird aliens, and exasperating superiors are far from the only trials Scotty has endured in Starfleet. Probably one of his most bitter moments comes when his nephew Peter Preston is killed.

Peter died as a direct result of Khan's attack—he did not desert his post. But Kirk is equally responsible because he didn't suspect the *Reliant* enough to raise shields against her. Nor has he ever bothered to check up on Khan, not even for curiosity's sake. When Scotty watches young Peter die in sickbay, he weeps, not caring about the ruined engines or poor Admiral Kirk's troubles. He asks the universal rhetorical *"Why?"* and hears an unexpected and unwelcome answer. Khan wants revenge, he is told, and he doesn't care who stands between him and Kirk. Apparently Admiral Kirk doesn't care either.

The death of Peter was obviously an afterthought, a device to raise the tension of the postbattle scenes. Peter was proud, but not smug; spirited, but not mouthy. He loved the people and the engines his uncle did, and he would have devoted his lifetime to them. His uncle beams with pride, particularly when the youth defends him even against an admiral. He was a joy to his uncle, and could have been so to the fans—certainly more so than any of the limp personalities foisted upon them in *Wrath of Khan* and *The Search for Spock*.

Instead, we are stuck with David, the paranoid brat; Saavik (actress #1), the bewildered, whose finest quote was surely "I don't understand"; Saavik (actress #2), the babbler, who let Kruge trace her transmissions, and who thinks that *pon farr* is everyone's business; and Heisenberg, "Mr. Adventure," who confuses humor with insult. It isn't surprising, considering the rise of such mental elephants as Admiral Morrow and Captains Esteban and Styles, that Kirk is being turned out—too dangerous to the establishment. Peter was killed for the same reason. It must grieve Scotty deeply that most of those mentioned above are still alive and prospering—even Spock is back—but Scotty's ship and career are gone, and his nephew is still dead.

Scotty knew before the quest in *The Search for Spock* began that he could not possibly make eighteen months of repairs in two days. With a full house of engineers, he had predicted two weeks of work to have the *Enterprise* whole again. He has no time to make her combat-worthy, or even capable of using sleeping-gas and vacuum-pressure security measures against the Klingons. So Scotty has to let her go, and she dies in the atmosphere of the Genesis Planet. It's better than having her captured, but it is still a great loss. Somewhere in his heart he probably wishes that Spock's *katra* had been found earlier, to everyone's greater convenience. There is nothing to be done about it, but since Scotty loved the *Enterprise* as a person (and not, as Kirk did, as part of his ego), he will cherish her memory and recover. The destruction of the *Enterprise* puts him in a new and uncertain position, since he is a man of routine, but McCoy and Spock's recoveries are worth such a minor sacrifice.

So Scotty's creative juices will now turn toward the Klingon vessel. He couldn't actually learn much from it, as there are only so many ways to design a standard matter/antimatter warp drive star vessel. Indeed, he should have some free time for additional study and design work, making him happy and a more valuable officer. The only foreseeable difficulty ahead is if Scotty and Sulu, cooped up together in the same fascinating ship, get cranky and refuse to share their toys with each other. Problems, problems.

(Leonard) McCoy
First appearance: "The Man Trap"
Rank and post: lieutenant commander; chief medical officer
Rank and post by *The Search for Spock*: commander; chief medical officer

Thanks to the efforts of writer Joyce Tullock, Leonard McCoy is certainly the most well-developed of our neglected characters. She points out his important place in the symbolic mind of ego/logic/ emotion, and brings out his power to represent humanity in all its glories and weaknesses. Yet, McCoy is his own person, one who has profited most from a home in Starfleet.

He has changed little during his years aboard the *Enterprise*; most of his growing pains had passed before he joined the service. He had married, become a father, and then lost his wife and child through a painful divorce. Whether his marriage died from anger, third parties, or indifference, it was probably a marriage that never should have happened in the first place. The grief and bitterness of this divorce is presumed to be the reason McCoy entered Starfleet. After experiencing a full life cycle in a few years, a post in space was literally a chance for McCoy to start afresh. But despite his complaints, the young doctor began to like Starfleet a great deal, and there he remains today.

From a professional viewpoint, serving in deep space is a marvelous opportunity. Although space travel forces the doctor to discover and deal with many new diseases, he has made great advances in research because of them. Now and then he might even stumble across a civilization like the Fabrini which has stores of medical information priceless to modern society. And, yes, although he has lost patients to mayhem, delay, and "the unknown," his track record in this strenuous field is one of the best.

McCoy isn't much of a hobbyist. He's not a collector, except of rare or vintage beverages. (These he immediately consumes with fellow connoisseurs Kirk and Scotty.) He reads only a little, less than Kirk does. He plays few sports, although he makes a superior backseat strategist (particularly at chess, and especially if it bothers someone). Teasing Spock (or Chekov, if he's desperate) is good for both hectic days and rainy Sundays. But McCoy's favorite recreational activities are simple: a cool drink and a doze in the nearest sunshine, talking, or strolling about people-watching.

Scotty was probably his first friend on the *Enterprise*. They had no barriers of rank, profession, or culture to overcome, and they are often of like mind. If nothing else, Scotty was the most sympathetic ear when details of the haunting divorce first came up. Scotty is closer to McCoy's age and interest group, and he understands the trials of self versus commitment. He also has nieces and nephews he loves but rarely sees (Vonda McIntyre believes that he has had trouble with some of them, similar to McCoy's situation). Scotty knows more about McCoy's past than anyone, but no one will hear it from him. He is one of the few characters with the courtesy to avoid gossip and keep silent. He and McCoy also both have positions involving the well-being of ship and crew, which often puts them at odds with Higher Up. McCoy and Scotty have very little time to carry on research and development of their own, because the ambitious and slightly careless Kirk always keeps them running.

James T. Kirk was the next person with whom McCoy became well acquainted. Both men tend to be, ah, uninhibited, off ship or on. Despite the low points now and then, they also have great respect for each other's work. But even though they are only a few years apart in age, they are worlds apart in temperament. McCoy complains more, but Kirk is a nitpicker. The doctor gets along well with children; Kirk is a lousy father, even father image. Ask Charlie, or Miri, or the Triachus gang. Or David Marcus.

In fact, Kirk is little more than a boy himself. He tends to act spoiled, a condition aggravated whenever he gets what he wants, episode after episode. Although he has had some disappointments in his career, he's learned little from them. He is clever but not wise. Much of his ego is dependent on his image as a young, virile he-man, and aging terrifies him.

McCoy has accepted himself as a father, even though he's a father without his child around. Like Sulu, McCoy isn't afraid of aging. After his beginnings, nothing worse could happen to him. He worries about Kirk because Kirk hardly has enough maturity to take care of himself, and he certainly isn't mature enough to be a parent surrogate. Was McCoy that self-absorbed when he was younger? It would certainly explain his personal interest in Jim Kirk, perhaps to help Kirk avoid the mistakes he made. So if McCoy lectures him about being unprofessional, it's to protect him before Jim finds— and loses—someone important to him. Yet, by trying to shelter and shape the ambitious Kirk, he deprives him of the *need* to mature. If their friendship sometimes seems stormy, it's because McCoy has changed signals on Kirk. One moment, he's a friend and equal, and next he's a father/mentor, laying down the rules before an unwilling subject. Kirk is then prompted to respond by pulling rank, which leads to more advice, then more pulling rank, and so on. Fortunately, such spats are also easily mended over a bottle of something that Kirk never bothers to find for himself.

From a military point of view, however, many of McCoy's personal rebellions are justified. It is good for Kirk to be confident, and he can usually get himself out of trouble, but those are different things from the presumption that he is invincible. He rarely admits to mistakes (although McCoy often causes him to get his back up), and he repeats one mistake in particular: placing valuable officers in danger. Of course lives will be lost on hazardous missions, but Kirk's should not be one of them. When Kirk goes, McCoy tries to go along with him, knowing he will be needed. When McCoy cannot talk Kirk out of something, he at least offers moral support, but he has no sympathy for Kirk's belief that any suffering sent his way is unwarranted and merely the whim of cruel nature. It is hard to reason with such a person; it's harder if one takes the direct approach. McCoy is a very direct person. His famous quote "I recommend survival" shows where his priorities are. To him, no military or scientific need is great enough to cause loss of life. Kirk's philosophy, "Risk is our business," may or not be correct, but it is the prevailing belief of Starfleet Command. A man like McCoy would not be satisfied anywhere in such an organization, but he keeps trying. As Edith Keeler said, "It's necessary."

It is a great paradox to consider James Kirk a good soldier. He is constantly on the wrong side of headquarters, because he does what he wants when he wants to. Yet Kirk is but one pawn on a board of indoctrination. Training as well as personality causes him to side against "weak" powers of diplomacy and negotiation. The result is that many alien societies find themselves being remade to fit Kirk's ideas. McCoy certainly espouses the belief that some societies "have the right to develop normally."

Probably the best example of the clash of philosophy between Kirk and McCoy is seen in "A Private Little War." The Klingon-backed villagers are decimating the unarmed hill people, among whom Kirk has friends. McCoy didn't want the hill people to be annihilated, but he doubted that equalizing the balance of power would solve anything. Arming the weaker (our) side would only stretch the skirmish into a long, hopeless war. He believed that negotiation would bring the two sides together, and the villagers would either become wise or no longer fear to break off their association with the Klingons. The planet could then become a Federation protectorate and be free of Klingon retaliation. Since anything Kirk does will violate the noninterference directive, why not do so in a way that peace will result?

Kirk, on the other hand, distrusted either the villagers or the negotiators—or both. He was convinced (whether correctly or incorrectly has never been seen) that only armed force would keep the villagers true to their word. This sort of thinking trapped the villagers in the hands of the Klingons in the first place—the notion, without proof, that the other fellow is untrustworthy. Kirk was not at all pleased by McCoy's input, although he had insisted he wanted "advice I can trust as much as Spock's." That is indeed what he got, for Spock would have said the same thing. So Kirk presents McCoy with this question: If overwhelming force, no aid, and negotiation are not being considered, what is McCoy's solution? McCoy doesn't have one. Spock would not have had one. Few indeed are the situations to which Kirk gave so much thought before bringing change down upon a people.

Given such conditions, Kirk shouldn't have been surprised that McCoy quit the service when the captain was promoted to admiral. Only friendship and duty had kept McCoy there, but his friends were now going off in new directions. Also, the many new things he had for study after his tour of duty would keep him busy for years. Certainly he did not intend to watch Kirk make a major mistake which would probably ruin his life. If Kirk no longer cared to listen to him, why bother with him anymore?

Years later, after all his friends had gone, Kirk realized that he needed to go back into space. And he recognized immediately that no matter how much he might edit, loathe, or ignore McCoy's opinions, he couldn't handle a starship without him. And McCoy noted in *Wrath of Khan* that Kirk had been sulking too long—he had better go back into space before he really did run out of time. Kirk has made this mistake so often that McCoy is almost getting used to it. (And Kirk is only fifty when he calls himself "too old." McCoy was almost that age when he *started* the *Enterprise*'s first five-year-mission.)

McCoy no doubt had better luck educating Christine. She is excellent help, and his unorthodox approach to medicine is slanted toward increasing her participation, and thus her understanding and skills. She even takes his advice! What more could an employer hope for?

The one thing he never becomes involved in is her tenuous relationship with Spock. He knows from experience that there are some things, especially concerning love, that are nobody else's business. Indeed, McCoy never teases Spock about it, or even mentions it to him. Neither of them wants or needs his opinion about the matter.

Spock prefers to be single. That's understandable. He has the right to remain so, if his genes will permit it. It's just as well, because he is not mentally mature enough for a commitment with a woman, least of all Christine. All the audience sees of her is that she knows how to eavesdrop, sigh, smile sadly, and be lonely. If she acts that way in private as well, then, frankly, Spock deserves better. If, however, she is actually a supportive, understanding, worthy candidate when alone with him, and he still refuses, then *she* deserves better. McCoy never gives unsolicited advice on this point, but he has been known to give Christine special, interesting assignments to take her mind off her troubles. Apparently it works, because in *Star Trek: The Motion Picture* she has taken control of her life and become a full-fledged doctor. No doubt she hasn't been seen since because she doesn't need the *Enterprise* anymore.

As far as companionship goes, McCoy obviously considers Scotty, Uhura, and Sulu the most adult officers on the ship. All of them are responsible, alert, quiet, peaceful people. They can be reasoned with, and, in turn, they can reason with him. None are known for temper, queer fits, or nuisance-making. His major regret is not having more time to spend with them.

As for the rest, McCoy was dealing with a "boatload of children" long before *Wrath of Khan*. Kirk and Chekov, of course, are well known for their keen noses for disaster, whether accidental or well-earned. McCoy teases them to keep them out of trouble, because they remind him of himself. They are both still young enough to resent it.

As for Spock . . .

All his life, Spock has been insecure. He was never good enough for his parents, his peers, or his society. Even his wife, T'Pring, did not reject him because he was a *hero* "legend" but because he was a *half-human* "legend." Though many human females would leap at the chance to be "that half-breed's wife," T'Pring did not. Vulcan had no place for him, so Spock left it. Vulcans have only two types of behavior (in addition to logic): grim and not so grim. On a human starship there is a wide variety of behavior, all of which is healthy and normal. Spock could easily be accepted on the *Enterprise*. Why then does McCoy bait Spock constantly? Isn't he good enough for him?

McCoy's brand of torment is actually kinder than Kirk's, because Kirk is an unmerciful tease, and sometimes he misses hints. McCoy notices these hints and tries to figure them out. For example, Spock calls himself a Vulcan. Yet, according to Vulcan society, he is a failure as a Vulcan. Therefore if Spock calls himself a Vulcan, he is calling himself a failure. McCoy isn't trying to cleanse Spock of his logic—there are many logical humans, like Scotty—but he does not want Spock to pretend he is something he is not, merely to please some narrow-minded Vulcan neighbor. He wants Spock to accept himself.

Of course, such self-help courses bring out McCoy's own fault. Under his benevolent goals there is a tendency to dictate changes, rather than suggest them. Thus when Spock slips up, McCoy can crow a victory and take the credit for "improving" him. It's the same mental bullying that Spock has faced on Vulcan. He *can't* change, even if he wants to, because McCoy has him backed into a corner. If he gives in, it indicates weakness. By ignoring McCoy, he provokes a renewed attack. Spock will lose face in either case, by looking like a stubborn fool or a gutless wimp.

Fortunately, there is a difference between McCoy and a fellow Vulcan: With McCoy, Spock can fight back. Indeed, McCoy has been known to deliberately lose a quarrel for that very reason. Spock needs the opportunity to realize that he can say something critical, even insulting, to one of his persecutors and walk away unscathed. Eventually he will no longer fear the opinions of others, although he would still respect them.

Spock may be a genius, but he is still a *boy* genius. After fifteen years on his own, he still has not cut the umbilical cord, particularly from his father. McCoy, by virtue of his years of experience, is a surrogate Sarek for Spock, but one who can apply only noise, not pressure. To finally have his views heard, even to win a fight, is a wonderful lift to Spock's self-esteem. He does not need to run from this problem anymore. Yet he has a grudging respect for the cantankerous doctor, who has spent his life *living*, while Spock has struggled to manage *existing*. He is learning that McCoy does not urge him to be more human because humans are superior, but because being a Vulcan hasn't worked. And he realizes that he too has something of value to contribute: Under his influence, McCoy has gradually become more tolerant of others.

How ironic it is that such as Kirk and Spock think that McCoy needs *their* protection. It is true that an unarmed physician will be more vulnerable to danger; however, it is hard to endanger a doctor if neither he nor the aforementioned valuable officers leave the ship. But if they go, he goes. (He will follow them into a dragon's lair.) How else will he be there to say "I told you so"? How else can he dream up his impossible cures for their carelessly spread diseases? How else can he stand in a field behind four hill people and still get shot by the villagers? Only in Starfleet.

As a doctor, McCoy is realistic about his limits. He has never pretended to be brave, but to spare others pain or misery he can find the strength to take their pain and misery upon himself. Pity and love cause him to give himself over to the hostile powers that would harm Kirk and/or Spock in "The Immunity Syndrome," "Miri," "The Empath," and "Plato's Stepchildren." He is willing to sacrifice anything of his own if it will save those he loves. And the primary role of Kirk and Spock, while he saves their lives, is to try to stop him.

Joyce Tullock did such a wonderful job describing this peculiar if affectionate setup in "The Empath" that readers are referred to her articles for that discussion.

However, it must be said that her interpretation of the events of "For the World Is Hollow and I Have Touched the Sky" leaves several major questions unanswered. In this episode, McCoy discovers that he has a terminal illness at the same time an asteroid-sized spaceship is found to be on a collision course with a densely inhabited planet. McCoy insists upon beaming over to the "world" of Yonada, where he meets and marries the beautiful head priestess. He refuses to come back to the *Enterprise*. While on Yonada he finds a way to reverse the spaceship's course. Spock does so, at the same time finding a cure for McCoy's illness. McCoy comes back to the ship. Happy ending. Now for what *really* happened.

Certainly McCoy was shocked and afraid when he realized that he was going to die. He delayed telling anyone else until he felt the time was right. Then he and affected parties could rationally sit down and discuss the necessary adjustments. But he would do none of these things until he could disgest the information himself.

All that changed when Christine found out about it. She immediately called down the captain, who, having other things to do, did not have time to discuss the matter with McCoy. No doubt he was hurt that McCoy hadn't intended to tell him right away, and he determined that his friend was already too ill to function correctly. Christine tells him to cheer up; a year is a long time. He knows it; she knows it; Kirk and Spock are the ones who don't know it.

Suddenly McCoy feels as if he's being phased out. The problem is that he isn't dead yet. Deemed too frail to leave the ship, McCoy had to force his way onto the landing party. Kirk then immediately told Spock. McCoy would have told him himself, but only at the appropriate time; as McCoy's illness has no effect on the first officer or his duties, Kirk had no right to tell him. Spock responds with smothering politeness, as if to agree with Kirk: "Let's not tire or upset him. His last days should be as comfortable as possible." Christine, Kirk, and Spock are convinced that the poor doctor has but hours to live—they had better be kind while they have the chance. This hardly takes McCoy's mind off of the situation. Indeed, it only emphasizes that he really doesn't have long to live. After an ordeal like that, it's no wonder he's irritable.

Perhaps the last straw is when Spock states that by staying on Yonada with Natira, McCoy is being illogical. Balderdash! Have Kirk and Spock forgotten that McCoy agreed to do so to get them out of an execution chamber? Natira agreed in good faith to let them go because she believed McCoy when he accepted her marriage proposal. Obviously, it never occurred to Kirk that McCoy might keep his part of the bargain. He thought the good doctor was lying to her. McCoy's statement "Is that too much to ask?" shows that he realizes that marrying a kind and loving woman like Natira is not a great price to pay for their lives. In fact, if he noses about a little, surely he can find the ship's directional controls before the planet Daran V is destroyed. . . .

Kirk interpreted McCoy's statement quite differently. He thought his friend meant, "What's wrong with being her husband? Don't I have a right to be happy?" McCoy was afraid of death, yes, but his intentions were not all selfish. Kirk simply considered McCoy's rebellion a sign of trauma and a refusal of the cruel fact of death that everyone else had accepted so reasonably. After an encounter like that, McCoy must have wondered if he was losing all that much. If Kirk wants to attribute selfish reasons to McCoy's motives, let him. The reasoning is not false; it's just not the whole truth.

McCoy's duty was to return to the *Enterprise*. He disobeyed. But he was fulfilling his long-term obligation: to find the control room when the others had failed. He needed time and the trust of the woman he would marry to do so. And he succeeded. He was also, although he did not describe it as such, pulling medical rank to find a cure for his deadly illness. He couldn't be the only person in Starfleet afflicted. He is a doctor—this disease must be slippery indeed if it could catch him. Starfleet (and Jim Kirk) would certainly overlook a little insubordination if it resulted in a cure for this killer disease. But he would not find such a cure in the Federation. But what about among the Fabrini?

The Federation is far from being the most advanced civilization seen in Star Trek. Consider that the *Enterprise* was less than fifty years old when it was considered old, worn-out. The colony ship *Yonada* has functioned smoothly for *ten thousand years*, with many more to spare. Now, surely a society that can design such a spacecraft must be vastly superior to the puny Federation. Their knowledge must seem magical in comparison to the primitive Starfleet society. Perhaps they have a cure for many things . . . including McCoy's xenopolycythemia.

Even if all these opportunities turned out to be duds, McCoy would have a home. Kirk scolds him for his decision, forgetting that not everyone is as indestructible as he is. McCoy couldn't have won the argument either by staying or by leaving, because Kirk thinks he's lost his mind along with his health. Can McCoy be blamed for seeking refuge with a beautiful woman who loves him? Natira admitted that this was her first love, but (callous as it sounds) McCoy would have died long before she could "fall out of love." The romantic aspect must have appealed to him enormously; the realization that not everyone would abandon him when he became too ill to care for himself was greatly comforting. Once Kirk and Spock understood *all* of his motives, their simpering treatment of him changed. And McCoy realized that, if he could, he would want to have his friends near him in his last year. Fortunately, McCoy found not only the control room but the library as well, in which was found a cure for him.

And what of Natira? She rightly perceived that McCoy had never intended to hurt her, and that his true motives were kind. "You came to my people with a great mission," she said, awed but thankful for his success. Then she let him go. By the time he returned to her (when the Fabrini reached their proper destination), Natira would have come to terms with her feelings of first love. They might have strengthened, in which case they could have revived the marriage. Indications are, though, that they became "just friends," and had the marriage annulled.

The good doctor, unfortunately, had but one thing to do in the first two motion pictures, and that was to lecture someone. (True, he's very good at it.) In *Star Trek: The Motion Picture*, he lectured Kirk about the foolish mistakes he was making; he pressed Spock to find his true motives for joining the mission to Vejur. In *Star Trek II: The Wrath of Khan*, he debated briefly with Spock about Genesis: Spock felt Genesis could be programmed to do great good; McCoy feared that it could do great evil. Whether good or evil, the device is activated, and Spock sees how it could be used for evil—it kills him.

Yet this tragedy gives McCoy a moment to shine. *Star Trek III: The Search for Spock* demonstrates that Spock is not overfond of death, and that he respects McCoy much more than he can admit.

Why did Spock dump his *katra* on poor, unsuspecting McCoy? He did so because the two men are so different that even if something goes wrong, everyone would know that McCoy had "company." Also, McCoy could be trusted to take care of it—or die trying (it never hurts to give someone a selfish reason to do the right thing). On top of all that, everyone else was needed to take the ship to Vulcan for the *karta* final ceremony. Failing that, they would all need their wits to take him to Vulcan illegally. Kir, in particular, would have been unsuitable for the trust; if his political clout failed, he would need a clear head to find another way.

There can be no doubt that the events of *The Search for Spock* have made an indelible impression on McCoy. Perhaps if all had gone according to plan, there would be no difficulty. But McCoy's and Spock's minds have been mixed together for some time—how hard would it be to separate them? The priestess T'Lar had a difficult task, and no one could blame her if she could not finish all of it. . . .

Did she? Don't ask this writer . . . wait for the fourth movie.

CHEATERS AND KATRAS: A SHORT DISCUSSION OF DEATH

by Douglas Blake

This is an unusual article, to say the least. Originally penned before the release of The Search for Spock, *it was recalled by Douglas for complete revisions once he had seen the film. We were delighted to have him do so; it was excellent before, but in the context of events in* The Search for Spock, *could only be better. Unexpected problems caused Douglas to take over a year to complete the rewrite. (Now his greatest fear is that* Star Trek IV, *which will be released several months before this sees print, will affect the article just as much as did III.) We think the wait is well worth it, but fully expect some negative comments from our readers used to straightforward, linear articles. As we said, this article is unusual. But if you like it, please let us know, as we'd like to run other articles of a more experimental vein.*

Man with the burning soul
Has but an hour of breath
To build a ship of truth
On which his soul may sail—
Sail on the sea of death,

> For death takes toll
> Of beauty, courage, youth,
> Of all but truth.
>
> —John Masefield

What, then, are we to make of this return from the dead, this newfound life which has been granted our Vulcan friend? Does his resurrection from a noble death and well-earned rest thus invalidate our treasured conceptions of heroic sacrifice and eternal friendship?

Perhaps the deed is too new upon us, too stunning in its impact and immediacy to be easily absorbed by minds which have been conditioned by life and legend to believe that that which is dead is forever dead, and that to die well is one of the goals of living. Perhaps we cannot comprehend the alien way in which our favorite alien, the alien we always *understood*, has defied, perhaps even defiled, many of our most cherished beliefs.

Spock the Vulcan, arisen.

> That which is the most awful of all evils, death, is nothing to us, since when we exist there is no death, and when there is death we do not exist.   —Epicurus

Sentiments strangely Vulcanlike in their logical structure. Almost an equation: If life equals existence, and death equals nonexistence, life cannot equal death. Or to put it more convolutedly: If life equals existence and death nonexistence, then death cannot exist.

Specious logic indeed. Spock would patiently point out the fallacy. But fallacy in logic is not always a fallacy in philosophy. A fallacy in logic is especially not a fallacy in fact. We have seen that for Vulcans, at least, there are times when death does not exist. Does this, then, mean that death cannot exist?

Of course not. Vulcans, like all living humanoid creatures, do age and die. Vulcan flesh, hardy though it may be, will wither and corrupt, and death, the silent companion to all that live life as we know it, is not unknown upon Vulcan.

It is the denial of death as a force upon life which marks the difference between human and Vulcan. Like Epicurus of old, the Vulcan feels that while life *is*, death cannot be, and once our bodies have died, that life which was no longer is, so why fear the death of the body when the spirit no longer exists?

Sarek told Kirk, and us, that we know nothing, nothing about the Vulcan. As much as the intracacies of Vulcan life are a mystery to us, so much more of an unfathomable dilemma is Vulcan death. Indeed, we poor humans cannot even recognize when a Vulcan, even a half-breed Vulcan intimately familiar to a human doctor, is truly dead. If our powers are so poor as to not even be able to glean a simple fact from physical evidence, how then may we expect to fathom the psychological?

Much has been written and much has been said about the intellectual capacities of the Vulcan. Much ado is made over the use of logicality as a guide for day-to-day living; even more ado has been made over the legendary (and erroneous) absence of emotion in the Vulcan makeup. But little or nothing has been said about the Vulcan's feelings or attitudes toward death. The only evidence we have been presented which suggests that Vulcans even think about death is the respect in which they hold their ancestors. Why is this so? Does the Vulcan simply consider death a natural ending to life and therefore hardly worthy of consideration as an event of importance?

We could readily accept this view. Many of us humans are more than willing to believe that the Vulcan, being emotionless and caring only for aesthetic pursuits of logic, would simply note the passing of a parent, spouse, or close friend as a matter of course, and then get on with his business, perhaps pausing a moment to express a regret for the loss of a great mind or a person of accomplishment, et cetera; as we might pause to glibly solemnize the passing of a species of bird that was rare, but unimportant to our daily lives.

This view, is, if course, incorrect. We have reams of evidence to support the fact that not only do Vulcans feel and appreciate emotion, but they do share love and feel grief at the passing of one close to them.

And now, it seems to me, the meaning of the evolution of culture is no longer a riddle to us. It must present to us the struggle between Eros and Death, between the instincts of life and the instincts of destruction, as it works itself out in the human species. This struggle is what all life essentially consists of and so the evolution of civilization may be simply described as the struggle of the human species for existence.

—Sigmund Freud

How, we may ask, could a Vulcan culture have developed if they were without emotion? Without emotion, without the ability to see beyond one's self and view beauty, pathos, honor, and all the other myriad facets of the human condition, it would be impossible to make aesthetic judgments about these facets; aesthetic judgments which, in fact, serve as the laws, customs, and building blocks of a society. Without emotion, one cannot point a finger and say, "This is good and this is bad," for the truly emotionless are without conscience or care.

Freud understood that emotion is the basis for all human action. He preferred to express it in terms of sexuality, but it may also be expressed in terms of simple emotional experience. Experience and experiences which, once having been felt, cannot be forgotten nor ignored, and therefore constantly influencing each decision and judgment we make in our daily lives.

The Vulcan, too, experiences this Freudian gestalt. As the Vulcan has achieved a successful and prosperous civilization—a civilization built upon the ashes of an older, more belligerent, more vital, yet ultimately self-defeating civilization—we may easily dismiss the charge that the Vulcan is without emotion.

Emotion among the Vulcans is, of course, carefully controlled. Such iron control is taught from infancy, and any public breach of emotional control is thought to be the height of poor taste. And, most likely, poor breeding as well.

Freud postulates that the eternal battle between the lust for life and the fear of death has led to the development of our civilization. In simpler terms, it is the feeling which drives man to create, the desire to have something endure beyond his lifetime. Most individuals achieve this desire, however unconsciously, through the act of birthing children, for our children are the best and most visible evidence we leave behind us to prove that we once existed upon this earth. By our own very existence, we are irrefutable proof of the existence—the lives, loves, hopes, dreams, sorrows, triumphs, failures, and eventual death—of many long-ago and otherwise forgotten ancestors. The universe, and the earth itself, is unforgiving and without memory. It is only through our works impinging upon the consciousness of men coming after us by which we may be remembered.

In its grandest sense, this desire of each single individual has led, working in conjunction with the desires of other individuals, as Freud points out, to the development of civilization.

The Vulcan, however, takes a more logical view of the world. The desire to have something of himself live on after him, should it at all even exist within him, is not paramount. Having a more pragmatic view of life—and, most especially, death—the Vulcan directs his energies toward ensuring that his life is the very best that it can be during his lifetime. The Vulcan would be more concerned with the quality of his life's work than whether or not that work will be remembered; he, like Shakespeare's Marc Antony, understands that "the good that men do is oft interred with their bones."

The iron control of emotion taught the young Vulcan results in view of his world which must be curiously schizophrenic: He must appreciate beauty and difference and accomplishment and a million other things to the point of adulation, yet he must not allow this adulation to overpower his emotions. A Vulcan may become absorbed in intricate, beautiful music and may appreciate its beauty on many differing levels, but he can never—dares never—be "swept away" by the sheer joy of becoming one with the music itself. This applies to every segment of Vulcan society, as well.

Death, naturally enough, falls under the same guidelines. A Vulcan may feel sorrow, regret, pain at the passing of another, but he may not show these emotions lest he dishonor himself and the memory of the deceased. Vulcans mourn intellectually—they decry the loss to the world, the loss to civilization, to art, to statecraft, to discovery—the loss to anything but the survivors. To feel personal regret, personal loss, would be overemotional, in bad taste . . . possibly considered aberrantly self-centered.

However, we have seen dramatically that death to the Vulcan is not as death to a human. A Vulcan death need not be final; the placement of his *katra* within the Hall of Ancient Thought ensures that some part—indeed, perhaps the most *important* part—of him will survive, perhaps forever. This knowledge, this certainty that the end of physical life is not the end of one's being could account in large part for the Vulcan's calm acceptance of death . . . and life. It would probably be quite easy indeed to look at the world logically and without undue emotion when bastioned by the knowledge that the travails of life are, at best, temporary. A Vulcan whose place in the Hall of Ancient Thought is secure can look at life as a short-time preparation to an eternity of exchanging knowledge and blissful contemplation.

Or so we'd like to believe. The refusion of the *katra* into Spock's Genesis-rejuvenated body is not evidence that the soul of a Vulcan survives intact and whole. Indeed, the explanation that Sarek gives Kirk can more easily be interpreted to mean that a "copy" of Spock's knowledge and personality would be kept, and there is no indication that this essence, this *katra*, would truly be alive. The Hall of Ancient Thought could be nothing more than a depository of knowledge, a psychic Vulcan equivalent of Memory Alpha.

So, if this is true, Vulcans do know death. Spock would know death most of all, for he has served long and well among the humans and other alien species of Starfleet. Although it was not until many years after his entry into the corps that he finally began to allow himself to loosen his tight rein on his emotions and make close friends and relationships, he still must have been hard hit by the occasional swift, unexpected death of a coworker or subordinate. If nothing else, Spock's natural respect for a person who is totally proficient at his work would cause him to feel a certain measure of pain at that person's death; and as Starfleet is certainly filled with such capable persons, we may assume that more than once Spock felt that pang of regret and loss that we humans call grief.

Once having accepted Jim Kirk as his friend (and to a lesser extent, Dr. McCoy, as well), Spock, to protect his own sanity, had to begin letting his emotions show a bit and, more important, to acknowledge their effect upon him. As stated earlier, Vulcans do experience emotion, but strive to control that emotion lest it overcome a logical operative view of life, work, relationships, etc. Spock, never having fully understood such teachings from his father (who has always seemed strangely repressed, even for a Vulcan, where his son was concerned) and having always attempted to deny the existence of emotion within himself, had to therefore construct a completely new and totally individual-unto-himself style of dealing with emotion and the world.

This process, as we have seen, took many, many years, and the cost in pain and severed relationships was very high. The final result, however, should be considered well worth the effort and grief involved, for when the process was completed, Spock was able to acknowledge friendship (and, we may assume, emotion) and was able, for perhaps the first time in his life, to feel relaxed and content in his place in life.

He does not expose himself needlessly to danger, since there are few things for which he cares sufficiently; but he is willing, in great crises, to give even his life—knowing that under certain conditions, it is not worth while to live.

—Aristotle

Aristotle could have been speaking with intimate knowledge of Spock, so appropriate are his words in relation to the Vulcan and his mental conundrums. Even though Spock had, through rigorous mental effort and by dint of self-denial and, eventually, self-realization, reached a point, mentally, at which he was at peace with himself and his world, he still must have suffered from doubt and unease. Spock cared passionately for life—make that Life—but cared absolutely nothing for the trappings of life which we humans carry about with us into every relationship and endeavor. Spock would have thought you insane had you suggested that a person should risk his life for something which paid no dividends in knowledge or beauty.

In short, Spock (or any Vulcan, for that matter) would gladly risk life and limb climbing a mountain for the sheer challenge of doing so and for the beauty which one would surely see when at the peak. What would not interest him would be the reward of felt accomplishment when the mountain is conquered. To risk one's life for a fleeting emotion would be insane. But for a human, the victory often is as important as the doing, if not more so, even though most would vehemently deny this fact.

The death and startling resurrection of Spock force us to look into ourselves in an attempt to reconcile the onrush of emotion and confusion which overtakes logic with the hard and fast knowledge that Spock himself would, should, and probably does take the whole matter right in stride. As many commentators have pointed out, the death of Spock was a grand and noble thing, to have him return in such—in dramatic terms—a casual fashion only serves to cheat us of a heroic sacrifice and cheapen the sorrow with which that "death" was greeted. The sorrow, the pain, was real and heartfelt, and although it is probably matched by the joy and thrill of revival which the return of Spock engendered in many, it seems, somehow, sadly wasted. We were moved and enthralled and saddened and teed off for nothing . . . or so it seems.

What, then, is the profit to ourselves from this? What manner of insights may we gain into our innermost secret souls when contemplating the death and rebirth of Spock the Vulcan? Are we to take unto ourselves a disinclination to view death as an undefeatable entity, an end which must, necessarily, come to us all and which must not be ignored in philosphical terms? Or are we to see death as a doorway to a new life, life which transcends the former realities and gives us spiritual and intellectual philosophical entrée into realms beyond those with which we are intimately, not to say instinctively, familiar? What is the message of Spock? What is the signal given by his death? What is the signpost of his resurrection?

The Democracy of Death.

It comes equally to us all, and makes us all equal when it comes. The ashes of an Oak in the Chimney are no Epitaph of that Oak to tell me how high or large that was; it tells me not what flocks it sheltered, while it stood, nor what men it hurt when it fell. The dust of great persons' graves is speechless too, it says nothing. It distinguishes nothing; as soon the dust of a wretch whom thou wouldest not, as of a Prince thou couldest not look upon, will trouble thine eyes, if the wind blows it thither; and when a whirlwind hath blown the dust of the church-yard into the church, and the man sweeps out the dust of the church into the churchyard, who will undertake to sift those dusts again, and to pronounce, This is the Patrician, this is the noble flower, and this the yeomanly, this is the Plebeian bran.

—John Donne

The Vulcan way is to think of oneself as equal to any man and every man, yet above the passions which tempt every man and any man. Spock, in his too short life and newfound resurrection, found the wherewithal to take the passions of the everyman and the aesthetic of the Vulcan and grind them into one in the crucible of his soul. We, as those who viewed Spock's battle with the forces and passions which daily plagued him and, perhaps more often than we—or he—suspected, attracted him, can readily sympathize with and emphathize with this grinding process, but we can never fully understand nor even appreciate it.

It was a long, arduous process which required that the very being, the very soul, if you will, of Spock the Vulcan be disassembled and minutely examined piece by piece. Then each of those pieces had to be reassembled into a whole again, but with the addition of new pieces—Spock's humanity. The final result, as might be expected, was something quite different from that begun with, yet not so different that it was unrecognizable to us. In fact, the end result, the new reconstructed Spock persona, was probably more recognizable to us than was the old, original persona . . . for was not this "new" Spock, this gift-giving, well-wishing, quip-making Spock, the very same Spock which we had for so long desired to see? Was he not identical to that Spock which we created in our minds, a Spock of giving friendship, of unquestioned loyalty, of unhesitating willingness to die for his friends.

Certainly it was. Our perceptions of Spock as he was during the years of the series, the years of the *Enterprise*'s original voyages, were quite far removed from the reality. Liking the Vulcan, enjoying his uniqueness, his otherworldliness, his satanic good looks, and his cool, calm detachment, we decided that, since we liked him and we were likable people, then he must be likable too, and, of consequence, just like us. Reason told us—as well as Spock, numerous times indeed—that he *was not* just like us . . . he was a Vulcan, he was an alien, he controlled his emotions by choice, he lived the way he preferred and, frankly, found human ways—our ways— almost unbelievably illogical, if not outright repugnant.

However, reason, as the poet says, is not always grounds for thought. We liked Spock, we respected him, admired him, some of us even loved him. How, then, could he *not* feel the things we felt, love the things we loved? And so, because we humans cannot like, respect, admire, or love the things which we do not understand, or the things which we cannot at least slip into some pigeonhole, we allowed our perceptions of Spock to become seriously warped. The Vulcan quickly took on an aura of mystery and romantic tragedy which made him even more attractive, and so the process began to feed upon itself. In short order, we had ourselves believing that Spock was, after all, just like us anyway, kind of reticent, maybe, but a good guy and quite a hunk, for all that.

Spock's occasional emotional outbursts and the ongoing inner turmoil of his search for self-identity gave us ongoing evidence to support our beliefs, gleefully nudging a mental rib, that proves it . . . Spock has feelings, just like us.

It is not at all surprising that we fans should have felt so about Spock, for the "just like us" syndrome has become quite pervasive throughout our society. Star Trek itself did quite a bit to spread the philosophy; the message delivered by most episodes was that they—aliens, Hortas, giant amoebae—are, after all, Just Like Us. This is a far cry from the series' intended statement that all beings, things, etc. are equally valuable and equally beautiful, which is a much more difficult concept to delineate, deliver, and understand. Appreciation and acceptance of difference and diversity is the way to achieve harmony with oneself and with life; shrugging a grudging acceptance that "they are just like us" signals a disdain and even fear of difference, and leaves a door yawning wide open for misunderstanding to come waltzing through.

As a group, we fans didn't—and ofttimes still don't—appreciate the diversity of the Vulcan; we were too concerned with having him be one of us, "the most human" of us all.

Spock is not just an alien, but an alien from a mature, scientifically advanced race whose principles of nonviolence and rejection of emotionalism have given them centuries of peace. Spock is the result of the first successful interbreeding of the Vulcan and human races, was fully educated and indoctrinated in the ways of the Vulcan by his father, but, upon reaching his majority, himself *chose* to continue to act and live as a Vulcan. We may assume that Spock's mother, Amanda, taught him as much as possible about what it meant to be human, and how humans thought and reacted. The lessons were probably no more real to the young Spock than were lessons concerning foreign lands and cultures to us when we were in elementary school; after all, he and his family lived on Vulcan and they (even Amanda) acted as did every Vulcan family. Why then should Spock consider the things he was told about Earth and humans even to be true, much less relevant to his own life? His father was (rather too much so, to judge by some reports) a Vulcan, his mother lived as a Vulcan, he was being educated as a Vulcan, both socially and psychologically, so what was so important about the human part of him?

This is perhaps why the young Spock was so hurt and upset by the tauntings of other youngsters. To be called names when young is bad enough, but to be called names that you know are not true, or that you believe to not be applicable to yourself, hurts all the more. Spock had been taught that while his human half might prove to be somewhat of a handicap when dealing with the control of emotions, it made no difference to what he was and could become. Amanda, and Sarek, too, in his own way, would have made sure of that. But here were other children, full-blooded Vulcans, who seemed to prove that nothing about Spock mattered *except* the fact he had human blood running in his veins.

It must have been a shattering experience. We may assume that Amanda must have attempted to prepare Spock for such childish behavior (Sarek probably considered the entire possibility not worth considering; his kind of pomposity quickly forgets the ways of childhood and expects children to act as miniature adults), but no amount of preparation could have readied Spock for the first sneered "half-breed." Name-calling would have been the first taunts he experienced, and the first to be ignored, but as he and his classmates aged, other, more sophisticated, and therefore more hurtful taunts would have surfaced. Allusions to "human genetic factors," "dilution of the species," and such would have stung terribly, whether they were meant to hurt or innocently overheard. Spock, like any human or Vulcan youngster, was in the midst of the normal teenage identity crisis, and must have had his own insecurity fueled by such comments. It was probably about this time that he began describing himself as having "a female human ancestor"—a half-truth which in the telling must have hurt just as much for the cowardice of it as for the attempt to downplay his mother's heritage.

It is nothing short of a miracle that such a dreadfully unhappy and lonely youngster as Spock ever grew up to be anything more than a competent shadow of his father. Perhaps Sarek expected him to (without really wanting him to), and maybe that is why he was so upset when Spock decided to seek his own fortune and future with Starfleet. . . . The old man may just have been afraid that Spock would fail, and that that failure would be the end of any chance Spock would ever have to be a happy, normal Vulcan. Love was always there between the two, even though unspoken, but maybe fans are wrong when they say that it was Sarek's pride and stubbornness (and Spock's, too) which caused the years-long breach between them. It may have been fear.

Whatever the cause, it eventually benefitted Spock. He successfully graduated Starfleet Academy, then went on to a long and distinguished career which culminated in his appointment as captain of the *Enterprise*, and only ended (?) with his death in the battle with Khan. More important, however, was the progress Spock made in his lifelong battle between his Vulcan and human heritage. Throughout his Starfleet life, Spock formed associations and friendships which changed his outlook on life (and human beings, no doubt); these led to an eventual, but gradual, widening of the doors of emotional response. It was not until his abortive try at achieving *Kolinahr* and his insightful acceptance of the emotionalism within himself and of the importance to such emotionalism for the fullest appreciation of life. In the ensuing years, he became more and more satisfied with his lot and happy with his friends and way of life. By the time of *Wrath of Khan*, Spock was natural and comfortable. He reminded us of his father.

Then he died.

Now he lives.

> The evil that men do lives after them,
> The good is oft interred with their bones.
> —Shakespeare

So what message does *Search for Spock* give to us? We are told it is a story about men who will do anything, sacrifice anything, for a friend. Somehow, however, we cannot help but feel that there is more. Friendship is one of the most valuable commodities which humans—and Vulcans—possess, but is friendship truly what *Search for Spock* is all about?

No. *Search for Spock* is about the need and desire of all men to defeat death. The pompous and ponderous posturings of Kirk at the end of *Wrath of Khan* come home, finally, to haunt him. The memories of Spock felt by him and members of the crew, the scathing attack of Sarek, the inner doubts that he could have done something, anything to prevent the death from occurring in the first place . . . all of these things serve to break down Kirk's carefully constructed cocoon of "acceptance." Kirk has never before in his life accepted death as either a possibility or an inevitability. To suddenly do so, with his long-lost son in his arms, was a denial of everything which he had stood for and everything he had fought for in his life and career. Kirk was more shattered than we knew.

Of all of us, perhaps only McCoy knew how deeply Kirk was disturbed. At the end of *Wrath of Khan*, when everyone else is impressed by the stoicism and dignity with which Kirk is accepting the death of Spock, McCoy is the only one with the acuity to ask not if Kirk is all right, but how he *feels*. He is not put off nor fooled by Kirk's answer that he feels "young"; McCoy knows of Kirk's almost limitless propensity for building self-deluding, but outwardly rational, reactions to stress or tragedy. Kirk wasn't all right, he didn't feel young, or anything much else, for that matter. He was in the midst of his carefully constructed "reaction" to Spock's death, playing the role of the bereaved but brave friend, and all true emotion, all honest grief, was shunted aside.

Once Kirk realized that he had been fooling himself, he acted. The pose of acceptance of Spock's death—of acceptance of the very existence and importance of death—was dropped like a hot potato, and Kirk went dashing off on another of his quixotic and wonderfully daring tangents to find his friend . . . and to prove to himself, one more important time, that death *could* be defeated.

The good that Spock did was not "interred with his bones," of course, but the evil that he did lived on after him and almost destroyed Jim Kirk. In this case, Spock's "evil" was his death, which forced Kirk into the untenable and false position of pretending (to himself as well as others) that he now accepted death. Such an attitude could have resulted in Kirk's own death, for many times in his career, it was only his refusal to give in to the inevitability of death that allowed him and his crew to escape alive.

We must remind ourselves that nowhere in his conversation with Kirk did Sarek say that Spock could be brought back to life. Many fans gleefully overlook this point, instead treating themselves to the enthralling vision of a steely-jawed Kirk battling against the arrayed forces of the universe to regain his lost friend.

No. Kirk heard what Sarek was saying, and he did not, consciously or subconsciously, misinterpret it. He undertook the mission to salvage what was left of Spock, the *katra*, so that his friend could be honored and remembered. A worthy goal, and perhaps one that Kirk would have undertaken under any circumstances. But the thing which impelled him to go to any lengths was the simple fact that McCoy was suffering, perhaps would die.

Now Kirk had a chance to once again cheat death.

It was difficult to do, as always. He had to ensnare conspirators, steal his own ship, make his way to Genesis, pick up Spock's body (which he could not even be sure still existed), make his way back to Vulcan, and, as an almost incidental final topper, get off scot-free. For Kirk, this kind of thing is almost rote. No wonder he looked inexplicably happy when wishing his crew "the wind at our backs."

Imagine his chagrin when this "simple" mission resulted in surprising and, once again, deadly fashion. His son murdered. His ship destroyed by his own hand. Spock alive.

To Sarek's unspoken question "Was it worth it?" Kirk answers an emphatic, unspoken "Yes!" Once gain he has gamed with death, and even though it seems that in this instance death came out ahead, Kirk is not dissatisfied. Not happy by any means, oh no, but not dissatisfied. Triumph and tragedy have always walked hand in hand with James T. Kirk. Indeed, his career virtually has been a series of major victories coupled with small defeats.

This, then, is the ultimate difference between Kirk and Spock. Spock, like all Vulcans, accepts death and defeat as part of life. Time is a fleeting thing, after all, and life must be marked by accomplishment and achievement. Defeat is part of the learning process, and to be cherished as much as, if not more than, success. To dwell upon that which cannot be, is illogical. After all, regrets and bitter emotions are not suitable things to carry into the Hall of Ancient Thought.

Kirk, as you would expect, lives his life by a completely opposite viewpoint. The entire point of life is to win, to build, to explore, to find the answers to the questions before man's three-score and ten run out. Kirk often speaks of a God, but we get the feeling that he doesn't really believe in an afterlife. He's too pragmatic, too concerned with the here and now, too determined to make his mark and make it stick. Growing older depresses him, frightens him, for it means that he will have that much less time to leave that mark, and correspondingly less talent, virility, and power to make it stick. Yet the accompanying fear of failure keeps him "chained to a desk," where, if he can't go out and cheat death one more time, he can at least dodge it for a while longer.

And yet, and yet . . . Kirk and Spock are together again. There is at least one more battle to be fought, one more danger to slickly escape from. In effect, we are back where we started—the brash captain and the half-human first officer ready to take on the universe just for the sake of the Federation, friendship, and maybe a little fun.

Death need never feel cheated by these men. The great game will go on, perhaps forever. Surely Spock will see to it that his *katra* enfolds and protects Kirk's all-too-human soul. In return, Kirk will force Spock's Vulcan heart to occasionally open and reveal a little human emotion. They will continue to challenge death, and continue to win, for as long as we believe in them . . . and in ourselves.

The great end of life is not knowledge but action.
—Thomas H. Huxley

STAR TRIP III: IN SEARCH OF TAXI— A STAR TREK PARODY

by Kiel Stuart

The ship seemed strangely empty.

Wounded, it was limping home. Its captain closed his eyes, shutting out momentarily the images which flickered again and again.

Images that meant sadness and loss, death and destruction, glory and resurrection, heroism and self-sacrifice. A presence that was gone forever.

Suddenly, he leaned forward, pressing the "off" button.

Silence.

"Damn," he said at last, "that was one hell of a movie."

"Ah know," said his chief surgeon softly. "On'y one thang troubles me, Jimbo, an' Ah'm tellin' ya'll, it's a biggie."

"And what's that, McCrotch?"

The doctor's eyebrows played lacrosse on his face. "Just this: How in tarnation are we gonna top this one?"

Captain Jerk said nothing for quite some time. "Oh, we'll think of something," he shrugged.

But his eyes were worried, and he fingered a rabbit's foot in his hip pocket.

"Well," he said, glancing at his watch, "we got about another hour and a half. Wanna watch it again?"

McCrotch shrugged. "Shoot. Ah don't see why not. Got nothin' bettah to do."

Lt. Savvy and Jerk's illegitimate son, Squeaky Sparkus, stood on the observation deck. He knelt to adjust his Topsiders, then rose to face her.

"Gosh," he said brightly, "look at all those stars."

"We are in space, observant one. There are bound to be stars." Then, more softly, "He was my teacher—and my friend. His loss has changed me."

Squeaky blinked. "I'll say. I think I liked the old you better."

"Then you are not alone." Savvy gazed into an Infinity Mirror. It was just like the one her teacher and friend used to have in his cabin. She turned away from it. "I do not think I can remain on this ship any longer. There is too much that reminds me of what I have lost. For one thing, Captain Jerk has that film on continuous loop."

"No he doesn't," said Squeaky. "It just seems that way. But, say, I have a swell idea. Captain Mucho Dinero of the *Cooper* is going to be leaving soon to study what's happening on Genesis II. Why don't you pack a few things and c'mon along with me? Huh? We could explore it together. Won't that be fun? Pretty please?"

"I do not think so. But I will come with you nonetheless. It will give me something to do for the next forty-five minutes." Savvy strode out, Squeaky following, nipping at her heels.

In a somewhat remote sector of space, Cap'n Sleaze of the *Greasy Pirate* turned to his mate, Lieutenant Scumbucket, and snarled, "This better be good. All this rattling around in space on some unholy mission to steal some secret or other has put my digestion off. That Klingfree broad better come through with the moneybags."

Scumbucket's reply was a prolonged belch.

Klinger the Klingfree, wearing several yards of taffeta skirt and a pillbox hat and smoking a cigar, arrived on the bridge. Scumbucket turned at his entrance.

"Hey," he belched in surprise, "I thought this Klingfree was supposed to be a broad."

"So did the Klingfree army," said Klinger, chomping his stogy. "How do you think I got here in the first place?"

"So?" said Cap'n Sleaze. "Where's the money? Where's the dough?"

"On its way," said Klinger. "Heads up, everyone."

All eyes were on the viewscreen where a vast Klingfree fighter ship popped into view.

"Ooh, look," said Scumbucket and Sleaze.

The image of the Klingfree commandant flickered onto the screen.

"Wow," said Scumbucket and Sleaze.

The Klingfree commandant's deep, soulful eyes wandered back and forth vaguely. He opened his mouth to speak, closed it again, scratched his head, and finally uttered, "Gee, Alex, I forgot."

Mumbles came from the background.

"Oh, right." The Klingfree commandant's brow furrowed and relaxed. "Ahhh, hand over the stuff you were supposed to get me."

"Right away, Oh Mighty Ruler." Klinger inserted a small cassette into the MumboJumbo Transmission Unit.

'Hey, Rieger, shoot 'em now." A small, swarthy man, chained to his leader's seat, grinned wickedly as he barked instructions to the first officer.

"I can't shoot 'em now, Mean Louie," whined Alex. "I gotta wait for Lord Jim to say so." His long nose lifted a bit and he turned away.

"Shooting? Who said anything about shooting?" said Scumbucket and Sleaze.

"Shooting?" echoed Klinger. "Great! Is this how you repay a loyal subject of the Klingfree Empire?"

"I notice that ain't no Standard Issue Army Uniform ya got on, Sweet Pea," cackled Mean Louie. "C'mon, Lord Jim, we got what we needed. Shoot 'em! C'mon, before they decide to run away or somethin'."

"Well . . ." The commandant's voice faded as his eyes unfocused. "Ah . . . I suppose . . . gee, Louie, are you sure we shouldn't just, I don't know, give them a citation or something?"

"Shoot 'em, Rieger! We're wastin' time here!" Mean Louie rattled his chain.

"Hey!" protested Sleaze, Scumbucket, and Klinger, just before the Klingfree first officer reduced them to their subatomic components.

"Now ya talkin'," said Mean Louie. "C'mon, Jim, let's go see what we blew dese guys outta de water ta get." He tugged on the chain. "C'mon, c'mon." Just as they rose to leave for the Secret Stuff Room, Mean Louie turned and obliterated a tail gunner.

"Aww, c'mon, Louie, what'd you do that for?" whined Alex.

The commandant turned and blinked.

" 'Cause I was itchin' to try out my new Pocket Blaster, Rieger. Why? You rather I tried it out on you?"

They all hurried to view the tape.

Aboard the *Cooper*, Lieutenant Savvy puzzled over some odd sensor readings.

"Whatcha looking at?" chirped Squeaky.

"You did tell me that there were no life forms on Genesis II," she said, "Yet these readings give every indication of life down there."

"Gosh," he said, "I wonder what that could be." He turned to Captain Dincro. "Can we go down and look, huh, can we please?"

Captain Dinero said nothing, having taken the precaution of sealing off his eardrums before the Genesis II team boarded.

"Well, I guess he'd want us to go down there, wouldn't he?" Squeaky pulled at Savvy's sleeve. "Boy-o-boy, I can't wait to see what's down there, can you? C'mon, let's go, what are we waiting for?"

"We should take a landing party. And weapons. And instruments. And a tank. And a Port-O-San."

"No, c'mon, rilly, it'll be swell. No one'll know we're gone."

Savvy sighed. "That's what I'm afraid of."

Almost home.

Soon the *Enteritis* would dock. There would be a hero's welcome. Captain Jerk could replace the batteries in his Watchman.

"Wowee! Would you look at *that*?"

At the sound of Lulu's voice, Captain Jerk switched off the weakening Watchman and looked at Lulu. Captain though he now was, Lulu's jaw hung open. The rest of the crew followed suit. And, as he raised his eyes to the viewscreen, Jerk joined them.

El Exigente!

The newest, spiffiest Starfleece Heavy Metal Cruiser hung gleaming in space dock. It dwarfed the *Enteritis*.

"Och, Ah hear she can go at speeds exceedin' Warped Twelve," crooned Snotty. "An' thot's only th' beginnin'."

"Fantastic," murmured Jerk. "I hear she can be commanded by thought alone, through a micro-milli Feinberg Drive hookup directly to her captain's brain. Some stuff, huh?"

"And she's mine, all mine," reminded Lulu. "At least, as soon as I bail out of this old wreck."

Jerk idly cuffed him. "Remember, kid, I'm still technically an admiral."

The sound of a foghorn cut short their playful romp.

"Keptin!" Wackov's voice was tense.

"Yes?" Jerk and Lulu answered together.

"Keptin Jerk, I mean, you seely Three Mosketeers groupie. Keptin, somevon hes broken the Sani-Seal on . . ." He gulped. "On Meester Shmuck's cabin!" His knuckles clenched whitely.

Jerk's scowl was ferocious. "Wake up Security," he barked, "And have them meet me there!"

When he arrived, he discovered that someone had indeed broken in. The Sani-Seal was in shreds, the door open and flapping in the breeze.

The security goon, arriving seconds before Jerk, had already fallen asleep. Jerk toed him out of the way, and, fizzer drawn, stepped inside.

It was dark as space.

"Who—who's there?" he faltered.

A deep voice came from the darkness. "I have been, and always shall be, your friend."

Jerk's ears began to twitch. "Awright," he sneered, "now who is that? The Panicky Guy? Don't pull that crap on me, junior. I got a itchy trigger finger, and you just might force me to scratch it."

Again the deep voice from the shadows. "It is illogical to assume that you could hit anything in this extremely low light level, and doubly illogical to assume your aim has improved since your last test scores, when you failed to hit Jupiter with a fizzer bolt at point-blank range."

Jerk whitened. Only one officer knew about the Jupiter incident. And that man was gone.

He leaped for the light switch.

McCrotch sat blinking in a lounge chair.

Jerk did a double-take. " 'Balls,' is that you? Since when did you decide to scale the summit of bad taste—even for you?"

McCrotch rose shakily, staggering over to Jerk. He grasped him by the lapels and swung him around. "Help me, Jim," he croaked.

It was That Voice.

"Take me to Mount Howaya," he whispered, then lapsed into a series of moos, tweets, whistles, and grunts, turned his neck 180 degrees, growled, "Your mother's in hell, Karras," spit up some pea soup, and collapsed.

Jerk scratched his head. "Something's funny here," he commented, and woke the goon to mop up the mess. He checked his watch. He was due in twenty minutes for a date with Admiral Tomorra at Th' Officers' Bar 'n' Grill.

Twenty minutes later, the familiar, glowing red nose of the admiral was winking at him over drinks and pigs-in-a-blanket. "So how's tricks, Jimbo?"

Jerk looked into his Piña Colada and said nothing.

"Well, glad to have the old Honker back, anyhoo. Hic. So what's on the agenda now, boy? A li'l R & R, huh?" He winked and elbowed Jerk in the ribs.

"Actually, I was thinking more along the lines of taking the *Enteritis* out again. Going back to Genesis II. Left something behind there, I think."

"Sorry boy, no can do. The *Enteritis* is being scrapped. The Front Office thinks we've milked the old girl all we can. Besides, Genesis is now a no-no. Strictly off-limits." Tomorra downed his fourth Flaming Death in a gulp.

"But—"

Tomorra tried to rise and sat down again, quickly, feathered tricorn hat askew. "Nice seeing you again, boy. Oh, and tell that Captain Zulu—"

"Lulu!"

"Whatever. Tell him not to have *El Exigente* engraved on his business card."

"What?" Jerk got up slowly.

"Thass right, boy. He ain't gttin' her. Giving it to Hunter. You know, Howard Hunter? Prissbritches?" Tomorra fell gently face-first into the hors d'oeuvres.

Jerk gaped at him.

Lulu and Wackov scurried to his side. "What did he say, Admiral?"

Jerk cleared his throat. "I think we'd all better get drunk first. *Then* we can dip him in battery acid."

The Klingfrees sat around a card table. It was littered with empty beer cans, half-eaten salamis, half-eaten porcupines. Lord Jim gaped blankly into the distance. At last he said, "Ah, well, uhm, Alex and Louie, what do you think?"

Louie leaped onto the table, salivating. "Boss! Dis is de greatest thing ever! I say we take it! C'mon, let's head for dis Genesis what's its name!"

Alex shook his head. "I don't know. Maybe we should all move on to other things."

Mean Louie loosed a greasy laugh. "Hey, Rieger, you wimp, dis is a *gold mine*. I mean, we just saw a doohickey dat could revive all de old series dat ever existed! And we could own all de rights! Not to mentioned da fact dat our names could be in lights again . . . and we wouldn't even have to worry about ratings!" He panted, then fell on the remains of a porcupine, growling and tearing at it.

"What the hey," said Lord Jim. "We got nothing to lose, right? Alex, set a course for Genesis II."

"Gosh, it's cold," complained Squeaky. "Maybe we should have brought parkas or something."

Icy blasts of wind howled along the surface of Genesis II. Minutes before, they had stepped from Death Valley. Before that, a rain forest.

"The climate is, indeed, erratic," said Savvy. "And I can think of a good many things we could have brought." She hefted their one fizzer. "A few more of these might have made sense. Or radiation suits. Or a tank. Or a Port-O-San."

"Aw, where's the fun in that?" He quickened his pace. "C'mon, we're almost at the capsule site."

"One thing is consistent here, though," Savvy continued. "Do you not see all those television sets littering the landscape?" She blinked hail off her eyelashes. "I wonder what that could mean?"

Squeaky said nothing.

They stepped into a clearing, and the climate was once again temperate. Somewhere in the distance rang an ice-cream-truck bell.

The Time Capsule lay completely undamaged. Brushing off the cockroaches and TV dinners, Squeaky popped it open.

"Empty!" gasped Savvy. "What could this mean?"

In his apartment, Captain Jerk surveyed the depressed gang. "Come on. This is supposed to be a party, remember? Script ideas, anyone?"

Wackov stirred his drink. Lulu ate a cheese curl. Uwhora fixed her makeup. Snotty had a soldering iron and was at work on Jerk's toaster oven.

Suddenly, the door swung open and a cloaked figure stepped in.

Jerk beamed. "That you, 'Balls'? Glad you could shake the animal tranquilizers and make it. No need for disguises, though. We're all pals here."

The figure removed his hood and glared.

Psorex. Shmuck's father.

Jerk reddened. "Uh-oh."

Uwhora rose. "Gotta go get my hair cornrowed."

"I hev to read *Var and Peace*." Wackov waved from the door.

"Ran out of solder," said Snotty, edging past.

"I'm going to Benihana's to sulk," said Lulu.

"Ahem," said Psorex, once he and Jerk were alone.

"Well, what can I do for you? said Jerk. "S'matter, didn't you get that Hallmark I sent?"

"That is not why I have come," sneered Psorex. "I must admit that your stupidity astounds me, even allowing for the fact that you are human."

"Hey, bub, ambassador or not—"

"Why did you not bring Shmuck's body to Vulgaris? You have now ruined his chances for what we like to call 'resurrection.' " Psorex flared his nostrils forcefully. "How could you be so moronic as to bungle his instructions to you?"

"What instructions?"

Psorex poked him in the eye, hastily applying the Vulgarian Cheese Meld.

"Oh," he said sheepishly.

They blinked at one another for a few moments, then, hurriedly,

Jerk ran to make a batch of microwave popcorn, and they sat to watch the film again.

"Hold it," said Jerk, near the end. "Freeze frame. What's that little yellow beep box Shmuck is putting into McCrotch's skull?"

"Those are the instructions!" Psorex rose, pointing at the screen. "See? Says so right there in green letters."

"Hmmm," mused Jerk. "So what's why McCrotch has been acting all funny and saying all those dumb logical things."

"True. And you had best bring my son's body back from Genesis II, along with McCrotch, or they will both be doomed forever, and we really mean it this time."

"Okey-dokey," said Jerk. "Shouldn't be too difficult."

"Absolutely not!" roared Admiral Tomorra, when Jerk approached him later. "And if you even think of trying it, I'll have you shot." He downed a jeroboam of straight cough syrup and passed out.

"Well?" Lulu and Wackov crowded around Jerk as he strode out of Tomorra's office.

"Like I said, gang, we'd better steal it. A lot easier." He pulled them both along. "Now here's the plan. . . ."

Squeaky shaded his eyes, looking left and right.

"Down here," said Savvy. "Footprints. Leading away from the Time Capsule."

"Wow," said Squeaky. "They seem to be headed right for the Ice Age. Well, guess this was a bad idea after all. Better call Captain Dinero and go back home . . . nothing to report here . . . heh, heh . . ." He tried to go back, but Savvy blocked him.

"Remember that Captain Dinero still has sealing wax in his ears. He will not hear us. Now stand aside; we must follow those prints."

In the TV-set-littered distance, a baby's wail floated on the wind.

"Listen! What could that mean?" wondered Savvy. She set off in the direction of the cry.

"Uh-oh," blushed Squeaky, "I'm really in for it now." He watched her go, then hurried to follow.

Dr. McCrotch staggered blearily into the Playguy Club, threading his way through fistfights, video games, and tray-bearing bimbettes. At a nearby table, the being he sought had its muzzle deep into a Mai Tai. It saw him and waved a scaly, webbed paddle in greeting.

"So," said McCrotch, sitting at the table. "Here we are."

"Yes," it said, resembling nothing so much as the Creature from the Black Lagoon with a pair of Dumbo ears. "Now, stranger, let us see how close we can come to stealing from George Lucas. Hire you a ship wish to? Money got you?"

McCrotch looked briefly puzzled. "Oh. Right. Yeah, ship wish I to hire. Money plenty I got."

"Where go you wish to?"

McCrotch looked right and left around the crowded bar, then leaned close. "Genesis II take you me to."

The Creature stood. "Impossible. This kind of talking is driving me crazy. I—"

"Excuse me, sir." A baby-faced black man edged the Creature aside and grasped McCrotch's arm. "Lieutenant Hill, Security. You're going to have a nice, long rest. Won't that be fun?"

"No," said McCrotch. "To lie idle at this crucial stage would be illogical."

"Guy talks like a Vulgarian." Hill's slightly overweight partner loomed up on McCrotch's other side. "Come on, you," he said, brushing aside the doctor's feeble attempts at the Vulgarian Nerve Noogie.

Hill and Renko threw McCrotch into a large sack and carried him from the bar.

"Hoboy, Keptin, thees plan of yours sounds exciting." Wackov jumped up and down, clapping his hands.

"Yeah, at last the pace is picking up," said Lulu.

"Oh, don't worry about that," said Jerk. "We'll find a way to slow it down again. Now, everyone all set?"

They nodded.

"Okey-dokey, let's go. Now don't forget: Bowery Boys Routine Number Six. Meet you in five minutes." Jerk hurried away.

He sauntered into the Psych Ward. It was heavily guarded by the usual-issue Conan clones.

"I'm here to see the new wacko." Jerk presented his ID.

"Okay," said the guard. "Me let you in, you no stay long."

He let down the forcefield and Jerk stepped in, winking at McCrotch. "We'll have you out in a jiffy."

Lulu and Wackov were not far behind. "Ho, ho," said Guard One. "How you be, little short peanut?"

"There's a multilegged creature on your shoulder," replied Lulu. While the guard panicked, he took him out with a kendo stick. Wackov took care of the other, hitting him over the head with an unabridged version of *War and Peace.*

"Right," said Jerk. "Too bad we didn't have time for the patty-cake routine. Now let's get a move on."

"Look!" cried Savvy. "Over there on that ice floe. That must be the child we heard before." She scrambled to its side. "Odd. He is wearing Shmuck's burial shroud. I wonder where he could have gotten that?"

Squeaky shoved his hands into his pockets and tried to whistle a nonchalant tune.

"This is very odd indeed," said Savvy. "He appears to be a Vulgarian. See the ears and Secret Decoder Ring, just like the one Shmuck had?" She stared hard at Squeaky. "Did you program this into the Genesis formula?"

He shuffled a toe in the snow, not answering.

"We will get to the bottom of this later," said Savvy. "In the meantime, we must seek shelter." She picked up the child and trudged away through the snow.

Crossing his fingers behind his back. Squeaky followed.

"Whew," breathed Jerk, stretching out in the captain's chair. "Sure is swell to be back on board the old *Enteritis.*"

"Sure is," chorused the others.

"Now look, gang, I know this is a real dangerous and tricky mission we're on, not to mention being illegal as all hell." Jerk paused. "So it's obvious that I can't ask you to risk your lives to save two of our oldest and dearest friends—why, just look at poor old McCrotch sitting over there trying to be logical—so I won't ask you."

"Yeah, okay, sure," said Lulu. "We'll all just hang around here and get our butts thrown in the brig. Come on, Snotty, crank over the starter."

The *El Exigente,* swift, powerful, threatening, was relatively quiet at this hour.

Hill and Renko had the bridge to themselves, and were taking advantage of the opportunity by tossing darts at a poster of "Pissbritches" Hunter.

Suddenly, a moose call sounded.

Renko switched on the viewscreen. "Oh, Lordy—They're stealing the *Enteritis*! Hunter's gonna kill us, Bobby!"

"No sweat, cowboy. This ship is brand-new Super High-Techdom, while the *Enteritis* is about to be melted down to make Cracker Jack whistles. We are *fast*. We'll nail them, you'll see."

Hunter appeared on the bridge, livid. Speechless, he pointed a quivering finger at the fleeing *Enteritis*.

"Don't worry, sir," said Hill. "We'll catch her. This ship is *fast*!"

Jerk ignored the warning sirens as long as he could, then switched on ship-to-ship.

Hunter's voice sputtered. "You get back here this instant, Jerk, or you'll never work in this town again! I'm warning you! Rant, honk, tweet—"

Jerk switched the intercom off. "Snotty, they're gaining on us!"

Snotty only grinned.

"Snotty! That ship is capable of speeds exceeding Warped Twenty-three, and they're getting closer by the second!"

Again, Snotty grinned at Jerk. "Och, dinna worry."

El Exigente zoomed forward like an avenging angel. Then it coughed, bucked, twitched, and rolled over.

One by one, the *Enteritis* crew turned to look at the beaming chief engineer. He held up an empty bag. "Ah put sugar in their gas tank," he explained.

"Full speed ahead, you clever old dog," chortled Jerk. "We have no time to lose in saving both our old friends from doom, and we really mean it this time."

In a cave that looked very much like Superman's Fortress of Solitude, Savvy, Squeaky, and the child were shaking off ice crystals.

"Very clever," Savvy said witheringly, looking around. "Did you design this set, too?"

Squeaky shrugged.

"I have a growing suspicion as to who this young Vulgarian is," said Savvy. She put back his hood and stared. "But look at this . . . I could have sworn the boy was but seven years old when we found him. Now he is smoking Marlboros and drinking beer." She glared at Squeaky. "What explanation do you offer?" Without waiting for an answer, she took the beer and cigarettes away from the boy, searching the robes for other substances that might stunt the youth's growth. She found instead a small book. She read its title; her eyes widened.

"Look!" She sprang upright. "I was correct in my suspicions. See what he was carrying in an inside pocket?" She handed the book to Squeaky and he read its title.

"*Yes I Am Too Shmuck,*" he breathed. "A volume of poetry. Gosh!"

"Explanations?" snapped Savvy.

"Aww, shucks!" Squeaky sat down hard. "Cripes, I might as well 'fess up. I used Plasmatronic Protoids in the dot-matrix tube."

"You what?" Savvy exploded. "How could you, as an ethical scientist, do this? It means that the whole world is unstable, and will soon collapse back into nothing but a pile of demographics!"

"Needed the grant money," he said.

"And that means Shmuck's metabolism is also accelerated. He is aging before our very eyes! In my estimation, it will be mere hours before he is as he was when we knew him." She scowled and glanced at the youth, who was beginning to gnaw at the edges of his book.

"That's ninety-eight to you and me," reminded Squeaky. "Besides, think of all the *pon farrs* he has to go through."

Savvy was motionless. Then, for a brief moment, she grinned broadly.

The walkie-talkie's beep made them all jump.

"This is Captain Dinero. Took the wax out of my ears long enough to hear the Klingfree ship now screaming down on us. You're on your own, kids. But don't worry. I'm sure you'll find plenty of places to hide. Dinero out."

"Uh, oh," said Squeaky.

"You are an untrained scientist," said Savvy. "It is therefore only fitting that I send you off in an unstable wilderness to face a Klingfree invasion with our only weapon." She propelled him out of the cave with the toe of her boot, and watched until she was sure he was well on his way.

Then she went back into the cave and fell asleep.

"Hot dog," said Jerk, "Almost there, gang. We'll just pick up the, er, remains, then scoot back to Vulgaris and fix you up fine, McCrotch."

"Piece of cake," said Lulu.

"Eating sweets is illogical," said McCrotch.

Jerk muttered and opened up the throttle.

Savvy was awakened by a Klingfree boot in her ribs.

Squeaky, flanked by a pair of nasty-looking Klingfrees, waved sheepishly.

"Guess we're in for it now, huh?" he said as they were led out to face a firing squad.

"Go swallow a load of Plasmatronic Protoids," said Savvy.

"Here we are at Genesis, gang," said Jerk.

"Uh, oh,' said Lulu. "Is that a Klingfree ship I see?"

"Shields up," ordered Jerk.

"Er, coptain . . ." ventured Snotty.

"Yes?"

"We left in such a hurry . . . I sort of . . . forgot them. . . ."

Jerk closed his eyes. "Swell."

"Piece of cake, no?" muttered Wackov.

The Klingfree commandant scratched his head, mouth working. "Mean Louie," he called. "There's a Fodderation starship just ahead. Should I . . . ahhh . . . surrender?"

"Naw, you dork!" The communications panel burst into flame. "Shoot 'em, and den threaten dese wimps I got down here. We gotta have dat Genesis II secret!"

"Whatever you say. . . ."

In no time, both ships had managed to do equal damage to each other. "Now what, Louie?" Lord Jim waited, gaping into space.

Below on Genesis II, Mean Louie faced the frightened trio.

"Okay, youse," he said, rattling his chains. "Tell us how Genesis rejuvenates old series, and we kill you nice. Don't tell us, and we kill you mean."

"It does not work," said Savvy, jerking her head in Squeaky's direction.

"Okay, Toots. If we can't romance it outta youse, we do it da hard way." Louie began to sharpen his fangs. "Even as we speak, our fearless leader is getting dat wimpy starship captain ta surrender."

"Captain?" said Savvy. "Captain Jerk?"

"Whoever," snarled Louie, rubbing his hands. "Now, who's first?"

"I can't stand it any longer," sobbed Squeaky. "I'm a bad boy for putting Plasmatronic Protoids in the programming. I don't deserve to live!"

"Dat's right, kid," said Louie. "Here, take dis grenade. You're nothin', you're a weenie, here, lemme help ya, pull da pin like dis." Mean Louie grabbed his chain and ran.

The guards followed. Savvy dragged Shmuck along; he was occupied with pinching her bottom. They dove for cover behind an old *Bonanza* set.

The explosion started an avalanche of TV sets. Savvy took advantage of the situation to grab a walkie-talkie.

"What?" Jerk roared. "My son sat on a grenade?" He shook his fist at the Klingfree ship. "It's really war now," he said. "I mean, we surrender. You Klingfrees can come aboard in five minutes, all righty?"

"Captain," whined the crew.

"Hey, heh, heh," said Jerk, rubbing his hands. "Will we have a welcoming party for them! The *Enteritis* can't move anyway, so I'm engaging the self-destruct program. When they beam over, we'll just beam down to the planet, where it's nice and safe, and watch the fireworks. C'mon, everyone, better hurry up!"

They stood, tears in their eyes, on a trembling precipice littered with TV sets, watching the destruction of their beloved ship. Jerk felt a tap on his shoulder. "Yeah, Lulu?" he sobbed.

"Begging your pardon, sir, but *now* how do we get out of here?"

Jerk stopped crying at once. His face flushed. "Er, I'm sure we'll think of something. I hope." He backed away hastily. "I mean, follow me, gang."

"Something's wrong here,' muttered Lulu. All around them, TV sets were imploding, scenery flats collapsing, fake-front buildings flopping over.

They fought their way through the tangling vines of an old *Tarzan* set, McCrotch growing weaker and more logical by the minute.

"Whaddaya mean, dey blew up dere own ship and our whole crew?" snarled Mean Louie, pausing to scratch some fleas.

"Ahhh, that's right," burbled Lord Jim. "Everyone except me and Alex and you and the guards."

Louie paused briefly to have conniptions.

"Gee, ahh, Louie, you think maybe we should just turn around and leave or something?" The sound of Lord Jim's head-scratching carried over the Klingfree walkie-talkie.

"Naah!" snarled Louie. "Absolutely not! First we kill dis stupid Vulgarian dat's rolling around on de blacktop biting everyone's ankles, den we bring dis chick on board and torture da Genesis II secret outta her. We gotta have it so's we can take over de airwaves!"

"Not so fast!" Jerk and company pounded into the clearing. "The cavalry's here!"

"Gee," said Lord Jim, "maybe I'd better invite them all aboard."

Before Louie could howl a protest, transporter beams whisked away everyone except the guards, Jerk, Shmuck, and Louie.

"No, you cheese brain! Beam dem back down!"

Lord Jim materialized, looking distinctly dazed. "What did you say, Louie?"

Louie leaped forward, gnawing at his commandant's ankle.

Across the steaming rubble of picture tubes, second-draft scripts, and press kits, Captain Jerk faced the Klingfree commandant.

His ship. His son. Gone. And the planet breaking up around them.

He grasped Louie by the scruff of the neck, pulling him free from Lord Jim's leg. "Are you the one who gave Squeaky the live grenade?"

"So what if I did, ya weenie? He deserved it anyway. Hey, ya toup's on crooked!" Louie giggled and snarled. Shards of promo packets rained down on the struggling pair. "Now put me down so's we can get on with da business of ruling de media."

"Ohhh," said Jerk. "You want me to put you down? Is that it?"

Louie nodded, slavering.

"Why certainly," said Jerk, carrying him over to the Chasm of Endless Reruns. "Here you go. Ta, ta."

"Aiieeeee," wailed Louie on a descending scale. The thud of his landing loosed a crop of papier-mâché rocks that tumbled about their shoulders.

"You killed my pet!" The Klingfree grabbed Jerk's lapels, shaking him violently. "That was a very unfriendly thing to do."

They teetered on the precipice. In the distance, Shmuck ran up a tree, barked, ran down again, had a vigorous scratch, chased a rabbit, and went to sleep.

The Klingfree thrust Jerk backward. He slid, stumbled, scratched his way up again, and pulled at the Lord Jim's leg. Suddenly, the Klingfree hung from a frail branch sticking out over the face of the precipice.

Jerk sucked in a deep breath. "You are *canceled*, hairbag!" he roared, and booted the Klingfree out to follow his beloved pet Louie.

Panting, Jerk turned to Shmuck. Crouching over the sleeping figure, he discovered the Klingfree's walkie-talkie lying nearby. He picked it up and opened it.

"Uhmm, Alex, would you, er . . . yeah, beam us up now?"

It was a credible imitation. He materialized on the Klingfree ship, fizzer in one hand, Shmuck in the other.

Alex threw his hands up. "Hey, don't shoot, we can work this out, let's be adults and talk this over,' he whined. "Here, let me show you fine Starfleece people how to work the controls, just don't shoot me, huh fellahs?"

They reached Vulgaris in no time.

The red Vulgarian sun blazed down. Across the stark stone plain, beach bunnies, Greek gods, Vulgarian Elders, Dr. Who, and a parade float of Jacob's Ladders trundled by.

"Wow," said Jerk. "The vulgarian Tomato Surprise Regeneration Ritual." He glanced at McCrotch. The doctor staggered a bit and spoke.

"The whole is greater than the sum of its parts." Jerk moved to his side, then glanced at Shmuck, who stood wrapped in a beach towel, a vacant stare on his face that would have done credit to the late Klingfree commandant.

"Ohh!" said the gang. "Ahhh!"

"I only hope we're in time," said Jerk.

"Hush!" cautioned Psorex. "The mumbo-jumbo begins!"

They took their places.

"Say," Jerk whispered to Snotty, "that Vulgarian Elder—she sort of reminds me of someone—that grace, that noble bearing, that Shakespearean intonation, that brief appearance."

"Och, Ah know, coptain—it's Obi Walk-on Kenobi!"

"Gotcha."

The ritual continued. Jerk began to fidget. "Gosh,' he muttered, "sure wish Dr. Who had brought some of his cute assistants along with him, like Ramona or someone. You realize I haven't even made *eyes* at a chick this whole two hours?"

"Hang on, captain," said Lulu. "Almost there."

"Captain, look!" whispered Savvy. "Here they come now."

Mouths agape, the crew of the late *Enteritis* watched as Shmuck and McCrotch groped out into the hazy red sunlight.

They paused.

They held their breaths.

McCrotch grinned, throwing his arms in the air. "Ah'm okay, everyone! Somebody gimme a mint julep an' a plate o' grits."

"Yay!" said everyone. "It worked!"

Jerk frowned. He hushed the gang up, put a gag on the once more blabberous McCrotch, and slowly approached the towel-clad Shmuck.

"Hey." He poked Shmuck in the ribs. "Remember me?"

"No," said the Vulgarian. "Should I?"

"Whaat?" ranted Jerk. "We risked our stripes, risked our lives to get you back, and you don't even remember who I am? Boy, that's gratitude for you. My son sat on a grenade, I hadda blow the *Enteritis* up, we had a big fight with the Klingfrees, I haven't had a date in hours, that damned Genesis II planet nearly swallowed us all up, and now you don't remember anything. Oh, that's just swell!" Jerk stomped off, sitting on a nearby rock to sulk.

Shmuck blinked a little, pressing a hand to his forehead. "Wait a minute," he said. "Hold on for a brief moment in time. I think, I believe . . . why, yes, it is all coming back to me. Why, hello, admiral, Mr. Snot, Dr. McCrotch, Lieutenant Savvy, Captain Lulu, Mr. Wackov. I trust you are all feeling well?"

"Yay!" said everyone. "Now we know it really worked!" They tossed their caps in the air with a mighty cheer. "Everything's back to normal again! Shmuck's just like he was before, same age and all, McCrotch doesn't have to say 'fascinating' anymore, a terrible weapon that could doom us to reruns forever has been destroyed, and Jerk doesn't have to worry about raising a goofy son!"

"Gosh," grinned Jerk, coming out of his sulk to throw an arm around the Vulgarian's shoulders, "sort of reminds you of the ending to *The Threepenny Opera*, doesn't it?"

In one voice, the gang began to sing the "Third Threepenny Finale," Act Three. "Repriev-ed!" they warbled.

"Hark," said the now-restored Shmuck. "I believe that my discerning Vulgarian ears can detect Kurt Weill and Bertolt Brecht spinning in their graves."

"Aww," said Jerk, grabbing Shmuck once again, "what does that matter now?" He turned to the grinning, expectant crew. "C'mon, gang," he bellowed happily, "it's Miller Time!"

And they all wandered off into the Vulgarian sunset.

Alex, who had converted to Vulgarianism, watched them go. "Wow," he sighed. "Whatta bunch of swell guys!"

MEDICAL PRACTICE IN STAR TREK: CURES AND CATCALLS

by Sharron Crowson

We had the pleasure of finally meeting Sharron Crowson at a convention last year and found her to be a lively, lovely woman, with interests and opinions as diverse as her articles in these collections would indicate. This time around, she turns her attention to medicine in Star Trek. *In her cover letter with this article, Sharron, a registered nurse, said, "Some of the medical aspects of Star Trek were handled so well, I couldn't help wondering about the obvious blunders and outright errors that occurred."*

Medicine plays a big part in nearly every episode of *Star Trek*, It is integral to some stories, plays only a minor role in others, but Dr. McCoy and his staff are essential to developing the themes and magic of *Star Trek*. Like all magic, however, some illusions are spectacular, deserving our hearty appreciation and applause, while others miss, more or less spectacularly, earning jeers and catcalls.

Let's take a look at some illusions that are so believable modern medicine might actually be catching up to them. Computer-aided diagnosis and complex scanners may be a reality well before the twenty-third century. Today computers sort and store more and more data, thereby aiding physicians in their diagnoses. We have scanners, like the CAT (computerized axial tomography) scan, or the NMR (nuclear magnetic resonance), that are very sophisticated and efficient. It seems likely, then, that in the twenty-third century a device like the tricorder, on its own or linked to the *Enterprise*'s on-board computer, would be able to use a remote scanner the size of a salt-shaker to make an accurate diagnosis of internal injuries or disease processes. However, the whole-body scanner capable of analyzing down to the molecular level that appeared in *Star Trek: The Motion Picture* may take a little longer to realize, but is still not outside the realm of possibility.

Many of the "miracle cures" McCoy and his staff pull off seem entirely plausible, given the technology of today projected three hundred years into the future.

In "Miri," one of the best medical episodes, a planet's scientists tried to prolong life by using a series of diseases caused by an altered virus. Calling the changes caused by the viral "diseases" seemed odd, but perhaps understandable, since there were probably violent side effects (fever, rash, etc.) before the virus mutated to its final deadly form. The rationale that the virus would attack at the onset of puberty could be supported, assuming a certain level of reproductive hormones was required to trigger the final changes. Given all the information the landing party found in the ruins of the laboratory, McCoy, working with the biocomp and the *Enterprise*'s labs and computers, isolated the virus and formulated a treatment that would ultimately prove effective. While not standard medical practice, McCoy's decision to test the serum on himself was in perfect keeping with his own personality.

The only jarring note was the rapid disappearance of the blemishes caused by the virus. If they had looked like hives (an allergic reaction), it would have made sense, but those lesions appeared to involve breakdown of both skin and tissue, and so would logically take as long to heal (without some additional topical treatment) as they did to occur.

Another episode with a solid medical basis is "Plato's Stepchildren." McCoy is called upon to treat an infected injury sustained by a remote colony's philosopher-king, Parmen. McCoy matches the bacteria causing the infection to a known strain and comes up with an effective treatment. During the course of treatment, the landing party discovers the inhabitants of this little "utopia" have psychokinesis (all save Alexander, a dwarf). Realizing their need for a physician, Parmen demands that McCoy stay. When the doctor refuses, at Kirk's order, Parmen tries to convince him by using his psi powers against Kirk and Spock.

The solution to this problem is once again McCoy's trusty tricorder and efficient interview techniques by all the members of the landing party. A skilled researcher must learn to ask questions that will illuminate the problem, and listen carefully to each answer. Questioning Alexander, they determine when the powers were first exhibited by the colonists and relate Alexander's lack of power to his deficiency of pituitary hormones, which also cause him to be dwarfed. McCoy distills the psychoactive element, kironide, from available fresh fruit and vegetables, and gives everyone twice Parmen's power level. The effects of the kironide are not instantaneous, which adds a little realism and increases the episode's suspense.

"Miracle cures" occur in several other episodes, and some are more miraculous than others. In "The Tholian Web," McCoy must find something that will help the crew withstand the effects of a "distortion" of the space around them, making them hostile and subject to seizures of uncontrolled fury and paranoia. As McCoy gives his concoction to Spock and Scotty, he says it works by deadening certain nerve inputs. To which Scotty replies, "Any good brand of scotch will do that for you." When McCoy remarks that the drug does indeed work better when mixed with alcohol, Scotty takes the beaker off to see how it mixes with scotch. Mixing drugs with alcohol is a bad idea at any time, since alcohol may increase a drug's effect or cause unpredictable reaction. A drug powerful enough to overcome the serious physical and psychological symptoms exhibited by the crew would probably render them incapable of performing their duties safely.

In "Journey to Babel," the medical section gets a good workout, and some care was taken to make the medical aspects as logical and believable as possible. McCoy diagnoses a life-threatening heart defect in Ambassador Sarek, all the while grumbling about Vulcan physiology. There is a surgical treatment for the defect, but several problems make the surgery risky.

First, McCoy states that he has never operated on a Vulcan. We must assume that most of his training has been in human physiology, with some courses in xenophysiology. And, as he says, that's a lot different from actual surgical experience. You can read, study, watch films, listen to all the lectures, but nothing prepares you for your first sight of a living body under the knife.

Vulcan physiology is different enough from humans for McCoy to be understandably nervous. Organs are rearranged from the human norm, and the blood is the wrong color. While these may seem to be minor differences, their impact could lead to misjudgments and a certain awkwardness.

The open heart surgery proposed takes copious quantities of blood, and Sarek has a rare blood type, T-negative. Spock is the only available donor. The ship does not carry enough Vulcan blood or plasma to start an operation of this type. Spock volunteers to donate the blood, but cannot give enough to supply all that's needed. McCoy and Spock work together with Chapel to research the problem and find a new experimental drug that works on Rigellians to speed up blood production. A drug of this type may be possible in the future, but probably couldn't produce the quantities needed quite so quickly.

McCoy warns Spock that the drug might damage him internally (it would strain the spleen and liver, as well as the blood-producing bone marrow), or it might very well kill him. McCoy's refusal to try it is instinctive, not scientifically deduced, as Spock is quick to point out. He has to use the drug, there is no other way—it's Sarek's certain death against the risk to Spock. McCoy decides to operate.

The operation takes place in the outer room of sickbay. We see Sarek on a diagnostic bed with a metal hood over his chest. This hood must contain lights and the sterile field McCoy asks Chapel to initiate. This field must be very effective, as McCoy wears neither mask nor gloves. Spock is hooked up by plastic tubing carrying his blood for the transfusion. There is a filter to cleanse Spock's blood of its human elements. Sarek does not seem to be getting any kind of anesthesia, certainly not gas or anything we'd recognize. There is no anesthetist, no mask, and Sarek seems to be asleep, but in no way as profoundly anesthetized as an operation of this sort would require.

A nice touch of realism is added by an occasional wisp of smoke coming from under the hood over Sarek. Cautery, or the sealing of open bleeders with heat, is a common practice during surgery, and whether you use electricity or laser, there is always some smoke. Cautery is used because it takes much less time than tying the bleeders off with sutures. (In "City on the Edge of Forever,"

McCoy finds himself in an historical era where they actually use suture. He raves, "Needles and suture, they used to cut and sew people up like garments . . . oh, the pain." McCoy couldn't abide the thought of such primitive aids, that so much pain couldn't be cured without more pain.)

During the operation, the ship is fired on and the sickbay takes a shaking. McCoy is annoyed and worried about the effects on his patients. He says, "One more like that and I'll lose both these men." Now that's about the most tactless thing McCoy is ever guilty of saying. Even considering the pressures of the moment, it does not sound like the McCoy we have come to know and love. Sarek's wife, Amanda, is standing not six feet away, and Spock, while tranquilized, is not unconscious and turns to look at McCoy when he makes his comment. Hearing is the last sense to fade before unconsciousness, and even patients under anesthetic have been known to report things they were not supposed to be able to hear. We can only assume that McCoy is more frantic than his professional facade will let him show.

The operation is a success, both Sarek and Spock pull through, and McCoy finally gets the last word. But the last word on this whole episode may be, "Why?" Vulcans have the unique ability to enter a healing trance and repair or even regenerate organs. True, it takes time and strength, but why couldn't Sarek repair the defect with Vulcan techniques? It may be that healing trances only work after defects have been repaired and are only useful for dramatically speeding up healing. For example, when Spock is shot in "A Private Little War," he's taken to surgery and uses the healing trance afterward to heal himself quickly. However, if you can direct energies to heal organs, it seems that you could direct repairs to a defective heart and save yourself a long, tedious, dangerous operation.

No discussion of medical techniques or medically oriented episodes would be complete without including "Spock's Brain."

A gorgeous female appears on the bridge, puts everybody to sleep, decides Spock's brain is suitable for her purposes, takes him down to sickbay, and removes it. Does Spock die? No, when McCoy comes to, he slaps Spock on life support to stabilize his condition. Spock survives—unassisted!—without his brain for an unspecified period of time. McCoy attributes this to Vulcan stamina. Then the good doctor calls Kirk down and explains that Spock's brain is missing; it's been surgically removed, a real neat job. McCoy also informs Kirk that Spock can only survive twenty-four hours without his brain. Is it possible for Spock to survive without his brain—without life support and/or constant medical treatment? No, it isn't; you can't have it both ways.

Does Kirk accept the reality of the situation? No, he's going to find Spock's brain, even when McCoy explains he can't replace it. Kirk says that if it was taken, the knowledge must exist to return it. Kirk obviously never watched a two-year-old take apart an old alarm clock.

Then Kirk does the most peculiar thing, in an episode of peculiar things. He turns to Scotty and says, "Get him ready." Do Scotty or McCoy ask, "What do you mean?" No, they must know what he means, but we sure don't. And when we find out, we might wish we'd been left uninformed.

Kirk tracks the woman's ship to a bleak, frozen planet. When he's sure he's found the right place, he has McCoy beam down with Spock . . . *Spock*, wearing a zombielike expression and a device the size of stereo headphones on his head just above his pointed ears. McCoy has a tiny box with lights and buttons on it that he uses to control Spock, making him walk, turn, and stop. We must assume that this is what Kirk meant when he said, "Get him ready." It makes you wonder if this is a common technique, or if they'd had to do something like this before. Granted this is three hundred years in the future, granted the Federation seems to have miniaturization down to a fine art, but this remote-controlled Spock is just too much to believe.

The fundamental agreement between the writer and reader for any kind of science fiction or fantasy (for any kind of fiction, really) is the willing suspension of disbelief. When you give your reader something he cannot believe in, you've violated that agreement, and the reader is then free to throw the book at the wall, or the viewer free to laugh and turn to another channel. That Spock could be ambulatory without life support and controlled by some tiny device is ludicrous. There are hundreds of muscles and thousands of nerves needed to receive messages from the brain for even so simple a thing as balancing to stand. Spock would not be able to see, hear, or even breathe. We find out later in the episode that Spock's medulla oblongata, hooked into the planet's main computer, is pumping water, purifying and circulating air, functions as it does in the human body (So the Vulcan brain must be similar to the human brain). So how is Spock's body managing those functions with no medulla or no life support?

The controls on the box are so simple that any one of the party can operate them by twisting a dial. There just isn't any way that so simple a control could have sent all the signals for something as complicated as walking or restraining one of the women.

Spock's stolen brain is functioning as controller for a vast underground complex. Now that's something that just might be possible in the future. Anne McCaffery wrote several stories about disembodied brains that piloted spaceships and made the notion plausible. But Spock speaking to Kirk over the communicator, *in his own voice*, is a lot of nonsense. Even if he could, by some chance, synthesize a voice from inside that black box, it would not sound like his voice. Timbre, pitch, and resonance are all functions of the body, vibrations of vocal cords and chest and sinuses. The body is not speaking, therefore the voice would not be Spock's.

The last portion of the episode is devoted to restoring Spock's brain. McCoy puts a teaching device on his head and learns how to put Spock's brain back, but the knowledge doesn't last. There is no adequate explanation of McCoy's ability to use the teacher in the first place; surely his brain must be different in some essential ways from the priestesses who are meant to use it. There is also no explanation why it would kill him to put it on again when he begins to forget.

The surgery to restore Spock's brain takes place behind a partition that covers only the top of Spock's head. Again, McCoy wears no mask or gloves, and evidently does not have to worry about contamination. No general anesthesia is used, though a local anesthetic might have been. It is possible to use only a local anesthetic in brain operations because the brain itself feels no pain. There is no incision down as far as the neck; McCoy has no access to the base of the brain where the medulla resides. How is he going to put it back?

The most ridiculous part of this implausible episode is Kirk's suggestion that McCoy connect up Spock's vocal cords. Kirk should stick to command and leave medicine to someone who understands it. Spock's vocal cords were never disconnected; they are attached to the inside of the trachea and vibrate to produce sounds. McCoy would have to make an incision in Spock's neck to reattach vocal cords. Spock uses the proper term—speech center—when he begins to talk and direct his own operation. And that's the last straw in this long series of inconsistencies and errors. While Spock might be awake and aware during an operation on his brain (surgery for

Parkinson's syndrome is often done while the patient is awake in order to localize the affected area of the brain), the simple instructions he gives McCoy would have occurred to a first-year resident of the time, and involved several different areas of the brain. Spock did not give technical direction, he made generalized comments.

When Spock sits up after the operation, with not so much as a hair out of place, and begins to rattle on about the fascinating things he discovered, you laugh as much out of relief that the whole miserable mess is over as at the idea of Spock, the jolly raconteur.

"Spock's Brain" was a bizarre idea at best, but it could have been worlds better if even minimal care had been taken to find out some basic facts: how a brain works, which portions perform what functions, how the body and the brain wove together, and, at the very least, where the vocal cords are located. A plausible explanation of how the controlling device they built for Spock might work might have been invented. A computer-synthesized voice for Spock when he was in the black box would have been more believable than using his own voice.

Writers have a responsibility to make every effort to have the technology and facts in their stories at least match what is already known. A writer might bend known facts around at times, but it doesn't pay to ignore or misrepresent them. Failing to make exceptions plausible or neglecting research necessary should get the writer just what he deserves—rejection. In a generally excellent show like *Star Trek*, it's hard to justify such sloppiness.

Many episodes conscientiously try to make even the most alien concepts or practices believable. Nona, the *kanutu* witch woman in "A Private Little War," practices a very strange form of medicine, coupling psychic healing with herbal medicine. She cures Kirk of a venomous bite, but seeks to influence him to give her people advanced weapons by using the "sharing of souls" she experienced as part of the healing ritual. Her rituals and culture are alien, yet there is enough background information to help the viewer suspend disbelief.

"The Empath" Gem certainly does not practice traditional medicine, but McCoy's brief explanation of how her healing might work, and his faith in her, give us the opportunity to believe in it.

In "This Side of Paradise," Kirk figures out how to defeat the spores too-benevolent effect by their failure to affect him: strong emotion creates hormonal shifts that render the spores harmless.

You cheer Kirk and believe in the cure, although it does seem he could have found a less painful way of freeing Spock from their influence. Spock might have killed him in the fight, and everyone would have been trapped on that Paradise of a planet forever.

However, there are also episodes like "Mirror, Mirror," where the viewer is left wondering how Spock-2 could be so close to death one moment and force a mind meld on McCoy the next. Spock-2 is clobbered over the head hard enough to knock him out. If he was damaged enough to endanger his life, he would wake up—*if* he woke up—with one hell of a headache and probably be dizzy and vomiting. His telepathic abilities would probably be severely scrambled for at least a little while, perhaps days.

In *Star Trek II: The Wrath of Khan*, Khan claims the Ceti eels, creatures resembling slugs, wrap themselves around the cerebral cortex and make a person extremely suggestible. Imagine, if you will, three-inch eels wrapping themselves around the gray matter portion of a brain maybe ten inches long and four or five inches deep. Something that ridiculous jars you out of the carefully constructed fantasy back into the real world.

The representation of medical practice is like anything else in *Star Trek*—some of it outstanding, some of it good, some of it awful. At times, the writers use medicine to point up flaws in characters and civilizations, as well as to illuminate what is desirable in them.

Nona, the witch woman, tries to use her healing to gain power; Gem, the empath, uses hers to save life, and, ultimately, her planet. In "Friday's Child," McCoy uses an old-fashioned right cross to the jaw to convince a pregnant woman to let him examine her, but his healing touch and his attempt to persuade the woman to love and accept her child are as gentle as ever.

While medicine may become more mechanized and computerized in the future, Dr. McCoy shows that flesh and blood will always need TLC—tender, loving care, the presence of someone who can listen and respond to the individual, someone who can understand our fears and dreams. No machine can give us that.

McCoy is particularly valuable as the pragmatic, volatile human whose first reaction to almost any situation is sympathetic, sometimes before he even understands what's going on. His instinct is to pit good old human caring and trust against whatever may threaten. This is the most believable aspect of medical treatment aboard the *Enterprise*.

REFLECTIONS ON STAR TREK: PAST, PRESENT, AND FUTURE

by Gail Schnirch

When considering the introduction to this article, we found that we couldn't do any better than to simply quote from Gail's cover letter included with her article:

". . . this article attempts to give a fairly comprehensive overview of the history of the entire Star Trek phenomenon, based on the experiences of one of that huge but ofttimes ignored subgroup of fans known as 'the silent Trekkers.'

"As you are undoubtedly aware, there is much discussion and controversy over the viability of a new Star Trek television series which does not incorporate any of the original characters. I have spoken with many fans who apparently have very mixed feelings on the subject. This article is an attempt to explore the feelings of one of these fans by delving into memories of the original series (the past, as it were); by exploring the emotions brought to life by the movies (present Star Trek); and by taking an in-depth look at Star Trek: The Next Generation *(future* Star Trek*).*

"In order to accurately record my thoughts and impressions, I actually began this article long before the new series premiered. In-

deed, the first several pages were written after seeing only a single advertisement. It was my hope that I would be able to communicate my earliest feelings regarding this new series without the prejudice of having actually seen it. As the premiere movie and the episodes unfolded, I added additional material, relying more and more on the emotional response I felt from watching the new series and comparing it with the original.

"This article is not intended to be an in-depth critique of The Next Generation; *it is rather to be regarded as a summary of the past twenty years of Star Trek and the impressions a relatively obscure fan made along the way. It is, I think, a celebration of a sort—the kind in which one might indulge oneself after having seen a brilliant, but difficult, child finally achieve the recognition due him/her.*

"Star Trek was that difficult child. There were only a few of us (in comparison to the vast horde of fans today) who saw the brilliance and the exciting potential back in the sixties. We were kept busy dealing with the tantrums, the problems, the hardships of explaining why the child was so important to us and to the future. We persevered, calling upon each other for support and encouragement when the going got roughest. We created a bond that has extended through two decades of some of the darkest hours of our mutual history.

"And then, finally, our patience, our perseverance, our faith was rewarded with a breakthrough. The child began to grow, to mature, to look outward, to expand beyond its earlier promising, though dimly perceived, horizons. More important, the world became more in tune with what the child had been attempting to tell it all along. Suddenly there was understanding, where before there had been only doubt and distrust, suspicion and misinformation.

"The child, at long last, was ready for the world. (Or was the world finally ready for the child?) In either event, Star Trek has at last come of age. With the birth of Star Trek: The Next Generation, *we've all 'come home.' "*

We couldn't agree more with Gail, and we feel her article serves as a fine overview of Star Trek and its fandom, and makes an excellent introductory piece to our special section on Star Trek: The Next Generation.

I sit at my typewriter, shivering for no apparent reason. The weather outside is balmy and mild, the temperature in this room quite pleasant. Yet chills run down my spine and my hands are cold and clammy as I contemplate the end of one era and the beginning of a bold, new adventure.

Write, I command myself. Yet still I hesitate to put thoughts into words, and words onto paper, indelibly engraved and beyond recall. Slowly, hesitantly, I attempt to communicate my feelings through this frail human device known as the written word. Nimble fingers that have been known to whip out dozens of pages of precisely typed copy in a matter of moments are shaking so badly that it is next to impossible to type even a single line coherently. I am tempted to give up this venture before it is even begun.

Just thinking about what I have seen is enough to send my heart into my throat. I can feel blood roaring through my veins. Tiny beads of perspiration dot my forehead. I gasp, wondering if I am on the verge of hyperventilation.

The time has arrived. I can no longer deny it. The *event* is upon us!

And what extraordinary *event* could cause an otherwise healthy, normal human being to react in such a manner, you ask? What could make a fearless preschool teacher who daily faces yelling, screeching, charging hordes of two-year-olds to suffer an acute case of the heebie-jeebies?

More to the point, what could cause a stalwart Trekker who sat in a dark, sinister movie house and watched stoically (well, *almost* stoically—if you don't count nails bitten down to the quick, teeth clenched together, and heart palpitations that would make Fred Sanford's "big one" look like a mild case of heartburn) as Spock unselfishly offered up his life for ship and crew in *Wrath of Khan*; who watched impassively (well, *almost* impassively—if you don't count fingernails gouged into the palms of hands fiercely enough to make permanent indentations, "leaking" eyes that required one full box of tissues, and a lump in my throat the size of a golf ball) that lasted throughout the following two years and the entirety of yet *another* movie) as the gallant silver lady of the twenty-third century, our very own *Enterprise*, departed this galaxy in a blaze of glory, disintegrating into Genesis's fiery atmosphere while her crew watched in silent bereavement from the surface of that hapless world.

What, indeed, could cause *any* of the vocal, verbal, vivacious breed of human who has been called "Trekkie," "Trekker," "futurist," and just plain "weirdo" (not to mention other names not nearly so polite) to tremble in apprehension?

The answer, my friends, is simple. I have just seen the first television commercial advertising that long-awaited *event—Star Trek: The Next Generation*. That's right. I *saw* it with my very own eyes. Until that very moment, I think I must have had myself convinced that it would never actually happen. After all, there have been rumors of Star Trek returning to television before. (I discount the animated versions, which offered interesting stories, but simply couldn't generate the same excitement as a real series.) We've all heard the story of the Star Trek that might have been, but never was. And look at the problems Gene Roddenberry had in getting the original series on the air. Not one, but *two* pilots were required and things were rocky from the very start. Remember the foofaraw over having a woman as second in command? Remember the uproar over Spock's satanic features? Television in general, and network executives in particular, were just not ready for Star Trek in the sixties.

Are they ready now? Have they matured enough in twenty years to be a little more receptive toward Roddenberry's vision of a future expressed through modern concepts? To be honest, I was more than half convinced that *Star Trek: The Next Generation* might have ended up as *Star Trek: Another Scrapped Project*.

But I reminded myself that there would be no network interference, no struggle over creative control this time around. Paramount seemed to understand, finally, what we Trekkers had known all along: Star Trek, handled properly, was a Hot Property. In the right hands, Star Trek could well become an even greater phenomenon than it already was.

The Question everyone was asking, of course, was: But is *this* really Star Trek? Or is it something else simply claiming to *be* Star Trek? Is it merely some cheap imitation leaping on the bandwagon, hoping that it would be pulled to success on the coattails of the original? I freely admit that I had my doubts. But when that first commercial flashed on the television screen, I felt the old adrenaline pumping through my body just as it had whenever Star Trek came on the air.

Regardless of the Question, those commercials looked fantastic! The graphics were on the same level as those in the motion pictures. They were so marvelous, in fact, that I found myself cringing a little lest this new series be a complete failure. Oh ye of little faith! I chided myself. The Great Bird of the Galaxy lays *golden* eggs, not failures! Nevertheless, I agonized over the thought of failure—*any* failure, to be truthful, but especially the failure of a philosophy I have taken to heart, and mind, and body, and soul, over much of the past twenty years.

You see (in case you might not have guessed by now), I am one of those strange species known as "first generation" Trekkers. I have been a Star Trek fan since its inception in September 1967. I was thirteen immature years old at the time. I lived in a small town in the Midwest, just about as isolated as could possibly be in the twentieth century. And yet, even in all our isolation and old-fashioned, outmoded ideals, Star Trek reached us. And touched us. Or at least it touched a few of us.

I watched that show faithfully each week, mesmerized by the idea that we Earthlings could actually get along together. In the small town where I lived, there were only white, Anglo-Saxon Protestants. (There was a small Catholic population, but they were, for the most part, ignored. The prevailing philosophy was: ignore them and they'll go away. They didn't, of course. But then, neither did Star Trek.)

How amazing it was to see Kirk (the fearless leader, white and American, of course); Uhura (black, good Lord, and a *woman*!); Sulu (could he possibly be a descendant of the same Japanese who had bombed Pearl Harbor?); Scotty (relatively harmless, and such a lovely accent—but shouldn't he have been out farming potatoes somewhere?); and Chekov (God help us! He's one of them damned Russians!)—not to mention the *real* alien, Spock (thanks to his pointed ears, I have no doubt but that my mother and many others thought he was the embodiment of the Devil himself)—sitting together on the bridge, or in the briefing room, all working together, week after week, toward a common, humanitarian goal. How it revised my thinking and made me aware of others who might be considered "different" but who also called this planet home.

Back in those days I was, I admit it, very close to being a closet Trekker. Oh, I didn't *hide* my attachment to the show, nor would I have denied watching it, had anyone inquired. But the truth is, no one did. There was really no one who shared my enthusiasm for Star Trek. Most of my peers were into other things at the time—smoking cigarettes in the girls' locker room, sniffing glue behind the Methodist church, etc.

I read and loved science fiction, but my closest friends were reading romances and Gothic novels. At that point in my life, nothing was more important than fitting in with the right group. So I plowed through those sickening-sweet romance novels with gritted teeth and saved the sci-fi for the privacy of my bedroom, long after bedtime. I even, on occasion, resorted to subterfuge. For instance, I can distinctly remember hiding a copy of *Stranger in a Strange Land* inside my history book and reading about Valentine Michael Smith while the rest of my classmates studied the contributions of George Washington Carver to American society. Now I have nothing against peanuts, mind you, but it seemed to me that we should be studying the *future* rather than the past. (I have since come to the conclusion that we must learn from the past before we tackle the future, but that's another story. Or, perhaps, I should say, another movie.)

And so the innocent, carefree days of childhood passed. Star Trek was canceled; I entered high school. Robert Kennedy was assassinated; Martin Luther King was murdered; Vietnam escalated. Neil Armstrong took that small step that was so important to so many of us. Vietnam horrified us; Kent State shocked us; Nixon deceived us. I graduated from high school and wondered if I would live to graduate from college.

Somewhere, amid all the turmoil, the resignation, the personal upheaval, Star Trek returned in syndication. It was a breath of hope for many of us, a moment's respite from the pessimism around us. I watched all the episodes again, hardened by my newly acquired sophistication and skepticism. Peace and understanding? What a laugh. Kent State had ended *that* particular fairy tale. Honesty? Take a look at Watergate. Universal brotherhood? Vietnam screamed for attention. I graduated from college and accepted a position in Kansas City—far, far removed, by more than distance, from that small town I had grown up in.

We had absorbed nothing of the philosophy of Star Trek, I told myself bitterly. We had learned *nothing* from our past mistakes. And then I saw "A Private Little War." I agonized with Captain Kirk over his decision to supply arms to his gentle, peaceful friends. And suddenly I knew that life wasn't as simple as I would have it. All was not black or white, right or wrong. There were many, *many* shades of gray.

In my younger years I had watched Star Trek for sheer entertainment. Now I watched for its social commentary. Gene Roddenberry had been pretty smart, I thought. He'd contrived to sneak in a lot of shots at the establishment under the guise of "science fiction." I began to see Star Trek in a different light entirely. I rushed home from work, hastily prepared supper, and ate in front of the television set. I coerced my roommate into thinking that this was actually sane behavior. I got *her* to watch Star Trek with me.

Then, much as I had passed from childhood to adolescence, I now entered the exalted age of adulthood. I met the man I was destined to marry. He was in the army and we were soon transferred to Hawaii. Never have I been so reminded of IDIC as I was there. I met a lot of people who practiced *tolerance* on a daily basis. I "reached" their philosophy, but I must admit that I lost track of Star Trek.

When we returned to the States (somehow Hawaii was never really considered a state), I looked up my sister. I had converted her to Trekism before my marriage, but we'd gone our separate ways since. She introduced me to the Star Trek novels and I began to get reacquainted with my "universe." To my intense pleasure, I found that she and I now spoke the same language. We watched reruns together, went to the Star Trek movies as they were released, and even managed to convince a friend to join us in the fun. (Fun? Or fanaticism? How do you know when you've crossed that line? And what if you discover you don't really care?)

One day we discussed actually going to a convention.

It began as a joke—sort of. I had seen an ad in *Starlog* for the Twentieth Anniversary of Star Trek, to be held in Anaheim, California, in June 1986. Kiddingly, I told my husband that I wanted to go to the convention for my birthday present that year. (My birthday fell on the same weekend as the con.) To my eternal amazement, he took me seriously.

Before I realized it, we had confirmed reservations on the airline, prepaid convention tickets, and hotel reservations. I will never forget that weekend as long as I live. The excitement was unbelievable. The lines were long but people were pleasant and amazingly patient. Some read Star Trek novels while waiting; some visited with other fans; some, like me, simply gazed about in astonishment. It was the dream of a lifetime come true. Leonard Nimoy, DeForest Kelley, Nichelle Nichols, and Walter Koenig were all guests, as were Mark Lenard and Majel Barrett Roddenberry. And so was Gene Roddenberry, the man I had admired for twenty years. I was in seventh heaven, floating so high I feared (hoped?) I might never come down again. That single event was the culmination of a lifetime of hopes and dreams. I discovered not a few, but *thousands* of human beings who believed as I did. My faith in humanity was restored. *Star Trek Lives* became not simply a motto but a way of life.

We picked up on the local conventions in Kansas City and St. Louis, learned of a Star Trek organization practically in our own backyards, and continued to keep pace with all the Star Trek literature blitzing the bookstores. Star Trek, it appeared, had grown from a relatively obscure, commercially unsuccessful television series into a worldwide phenomenon of epic proportions.

Star Trek IV: The Voyage Home was, I think, the epitome of twenty years of Star Trek. Leonard Nimoy had assured us at the Anniversary Celebration in Anaheim that we would love *The Voyage Home*, that it was everything the television series had ever been and more. We left California so anxious to see the movie that I wondered how we would ever survive until its release at Thanksgiving. That last week was one of the longest in my life. I counted down the days, and then the hours, until *Star Trek IV: The Voyage Home* would actually play in one of the local movie houses.

Fortunately, a local radio station picked up on the anticipation stirring through the Trekker population and managed to convince the movie house to preview *The Voyage Home* one minute after midnight the day it was to be released. Tickets to the special preview were given away in a telephone contest and—wonder of wonders!—I managed to be one of the winners! So what if it meant losing a little sleep on a work night? (Actually, it was more like losing the entire night's sleep. The movie wasn't over until 2:00 a.m. and by the time I got home I was far too keyed up to even think about sleeping!) What's a little sleep compared to watching a brand-new, unaired Star Trek movie?

The Voyage Home left me with a wonderful feeling inside, a tingle that said, "This is Star Trek as it was meant to be—funny, warm, touching, and, most important, thought-provoking." It contained a very real message about our future, in terms of what we are doing to it today. I can't think of a better, more timely message from Star Trek than the one which we were given in this movie. *And* to get another *Enterprise* in the bargain? Well, it was certainly, as someone once said, "The best of times."

My euphoria lingered through the winter. By now, of course, I had heard that Gene Roddenberry was definitely involved in a new Star Trek series, set nearly a hundred years after the time of Kirk and Company. I wasn't sure what it was, but *something* definitely stirred me up whenever I thought of a new Star Trek series.

I remember voicing some of my doubts about a series without any of the original cast to my sister. She raised an eyebrow in a remarkable Spock imitation, waggled a finger in my direction, and said, "Come, come . . . Young minds, fresh ideas." She was right, I told myself. Gene Roddenberry created Star Trek in the first place. He could certainly work his special brand of magic a second time.

And there *was* an appalling dearth of decent science fiction on television. This could be just what we needed.

Nevertheless, I still had a knot in my stomach. I tried to analyze my feelings. (Not being Vulcan, of course, this was a difficult undertaking, but I gave it my best effort.) I loved Star Trek. I loved the original series, the movies, the books, the fanzines—in short, I loved *everything* about Star Trek. I might not *agree* with everything, mind you, but I loved its diversity. So why wouldn't I love a *new* Star Trek just as well?

Was I afraid that the new might somehow interfere with the old? Was I so insecure as to think that Trekkers would abandon their twenty-year affiliation with Captain Kirk, Spock, McCoy, and the others in favor of new characters who would, perhaps, be just as heroic, just as marvelous, just as endearing as their twenty-third century counterparts? Poppycock! I told myself. No one could ever replace those dearly loved faces. No one could ever take them away from us. They had tried, you know. There was a period of several years after the series' cancellation and before the first motion picture when the only new Star Trek to be found was that which was created by the fans themselves. But we had persevered and our perseverance paid off in dividends! No, Star Trek could not be taken away.

Could there, then, be room for both? I wondered. Could Star Trek fandom support and nurture both universes—the twenty-third century and the twenty-fourth? Maybe, I responded, almost grudgingly. *Maybe.* But only if the new series remains true to the philosophy of the old. Only if the concepts and ideals which are held in such high esteem continue to permeate the atmosphere of that future *Enterprise*, NCC-1701-D. Only if the values of this new captain and crew remain consistent with those which Kirk, Spock, McCoy, Scott, Sulu, Chekov, and Uhura so gallantly cherished and protected in their lifetimes, only *then* will the hard knot in my stomach melt away. Only then will I agree that the new series has earned the right to call itself Star Trek.

Those were, at least in part, some of my thoughts before I actually sat down to watch the premiere of *Star Trek: The Next Generation*. I got together with my sister and a friend so that we could discuss this new Star Trek after the two-hour movie was over. We turned the television on, tuned in channel 13, and sat back with smiles of anticipation as the opening shot appeared. Planets swirled toward us, familiar despite the fact that none of us landlubbers has ever seen a single one of them in person.

Then we saw her—the *Enterprise*, as sleek and graceful as ever, though her smooth, clean lines were a little different. She was obviously much larger than her namesake, carrying a combined crew/civilian complement of well over twice the number of the original. Still, there was no arguing the fact that she was, indeed, the *Enterprise*. She *felt* right, somehow. She . . . *belonged*, as the poor, luckless, transwarp-driven *Excelsior* never had.

And then, just as we were drinking in the sight of the new vessel, another *newness* hit us in the form of the British-accented voice of Captain Jean-Luc Picard: "Space, the final frontier. These are the voyages of the Starship Enterprise. Its continuing mission, to explore strange new worlds . . . To boldly go where no one has gone before!" A slight shock to hear the beloved words spoken by someone other than Captain Kirk—but then, the precedent *had* been set, if you will recall. Spock had been given the honors in *Wrath of Khan* and *The Search for Spock*. We had all felt that it was appropriate then to hear someone other than Kirk give voice to those stirring words. Perhaps it was appropriate now for Captain Picard to reiterate them. And we were quick to note one other minor, or perhaps *major* difference; the word *man* had been replaced with the word *one*. We agreed this was a proper adjustment for the twenty-fourth century. Surely by then we would have outgrown all forms of discrimination. (At least in *this* twenty-fourth century, there would be no network executive to contend with, thank goodness!)

And in the background, emphasizing the captain's words, warm and soothing, like the voice of an old friend, came the familiar strains of the Star Trek theme song. Although it sounded more like what we heard in the movies rather than in the original series, it reminded us, perhaps more forcefully than anything else might have at that point, that this was, indeed, Star Trek!

The opening credits rolled by. Again, we felt reassured by the fact that "Encounter at Farpoint" had been written by two other old, and very dear, friends: Gene Roddenberry and Dorothy (D.C.) Fontana. From that point on, the two hours zipped past at warp speed. The story seemed fast-paced and well planned. We were introduced to each of the crew members while at the same time being dumped into the thick of the plot.

Midway through the movie, we were surprised and touched to see Admiral Leonard "Bones" McCoy make a guest appearance on the new ship, ostensibly to inspect its medical facilities. As irascible as ever despite his advanced age, he insisted on using the shuttle rather than the transporter when returning to the *Hood*, and he also delivered his own special brand of advice regarding the bold new ship: "She's got the right name. Treat her like a lady and she'll always bring you home."

I admit to a lump in my throat and another "leaky" eye (drat the plumbing, anyway) as Admiral McCoy shuffled slowly down the corridor, Commander Data at his side. Somehow McCoy's presence reassured me even more that this truly *was* the next generation of Star Trek. Somehow seeing that wonderfully dear, familiar face gave the series continuity. Bones's appearance spanned the two universes. Thank you, Mr. Roddenberry, for that very special, and quite unexpected, touch.

I had not expected to see any of the original cast in this new series, chiefly because I had been to a convention in Kansas City in July, and I listened to David Gerrold explain why it would not be "logical" or expedient for any of the old cast to make an appearance on the new show.

The folks at Paramount wanted *The Next Generation* to stand on its own merit, Gerrold had said. They wanted the fans to get used to the new cast without comparing them to the old. Besides, he'd said, this was *seventy-eight* years later. Who, besides the Vulcan Spock, would still be alive? I agreed with each of the points he made. But I was still delighted that he lied (or perhaps he merely "exaggerated") to those of us attending that convention. What a marvelous surprise we had in store for us in the first episode! Somehow I don't believe it would have been nearly so heartwarming had we learned about Bones's guest appearance in advance.

Perhaps, as Mr. Gerrold implied, we should *not* make comparisons between the two. Perhaps we should simply accept each on its own merit. However, human nature—and Trekker enthusiasm—being what they are, comparisons are inevitable.

Therefore, for argument's sake, let us take a quick look at some of the similarities and differences which have appeared thus far. (Please bear in mind that the information presented here has been accumulated after watching the two-hour premiere movie and a handful of episodes. Doubtless, additional comparisons will be possible as more episodes are unveiled.)

The Ship. The *Enterprise* (who is, after all, the real star of past, present, and future Star Treks), as mentioned previously, is a much larger vessel than her twenty-third century counterpart. She is a Galaxy-class vessel (the original *Enterprise* was a Constitution-class starship), and she simply *looks* big, inside and out. Due to the increased length of her missions (fifteen to twenty years), she now carries civilian family members. In order to adequately protect these non-Starfleet personnel, the new ship design provides for the separation of the saucer section from the nacelle-drive section.

When separation occurs, the majority of the bridge personnel adjourn to the battle bridge in the nacelle section. This allows the saucer section containing the civilians to remove themselves from the vicinity of an impending battle. One thing bothers me about this. The saucer section apparently is limited to impulse power only, which perhaps endangers the civilians by reducing the chances that they might reach a starbase or other area of safety within a reasonable period of time.

Additionally, while I find separation a technically interesting phenomenon, I cannot help but wonder what might happen to them if the nacelle section, containing the captain and most of the other bridge officers, as well as the ship's weaponry systems, is damaged by a "hostile." Would the saucer section be left completely unarmed, without means to defend itself should the hostile choose to pursue it?

This possibility worries me, but perhaps some mode of defense is possible and we just haven't had an opportunity to see it yet.

Weapons. The new *Enterprise* seems to possess the same familiar phasers and photon torpedoes we saw in the twenty-third century. In the two-hour premiere, however, we did see that the phasers could be converted into an energy beam, although this beam was not used as a weapon. The torpedoes themselves have a slightly different appearance from the spheres of energy we saw in the original series. Possibly they have greater range and/or destructive capability.

Hand phasers are also in evidence and are still standard landing-party (away team) gear. Again, there appear to be at least two different styles available. The first phaser we saw was a small, box-like creation, and the second presented a more pistollike appearance. Range and effectiveness are apparently still within the norms we might expect with reasonable upgrading consistent with a more advanced technology. (Note: Weapons appear to be used quite sparingly in the new series, perhaps in line with the more nonviolent consciousness of the eighties?)

Equipment. Other familiar equipment includes an updated version of the tricorder, a communicator that is now part of the uniform insignia (detachable, so it can still be lost or stolen in order to strand teams on hostile planets), a revised model of the hypospray for medical use, sensors or scanners that seem to work like their predecessors, and deflector screens or shields, which also seem to have the same basic capabilities and restrictions.

Bridge. The new bridge looks quite different from the old one, even the one we saw on the newest version of the *Enterprise* in the twenty-third century, NCC-1701-A. It is a great deal more spacious, comfortable, and all the bridge stations are highly computerized. Not a single button, toggle, or switch can be seen. The main viewscreen at the front of the bridge is huge. Images that appear on it are larger than life-sized.

Gone are the days of adjournment to briefing room B. Captain Picard has a ready room just off the bridge for such conferences as cannot be handled publicly. (Good thing, too, as we discovered in "The Naked Now." Dr. Crusher said a few things then that probably would have had the poor captain sinking right through the floor of his bridge!) There is also a lounge area just off the bridge. Whether it is an officers' lounge at large or the captain's private lounge isn't quite clear yet.

Engineering. Scotty's beloved engineering section has been completely remodeled. Isolinear computer chips now appear to be an integral part of warp engines. The brief glimpses we have been afforded thus far of the warp drive engine itself ("The Last Outpost" and "Where No One Has Gone Before") reveal an innovative design. The engine is no "wee bairn." It is a huge, pulsating, cylindrical apparatus that simply radiates power.

Sickbay. Medical facilities are also highly revamped, although some familiar items did appear. The hypo-spray has already been mentioned. The diagnostic bed with the panel above showing life-readings is another. (That neat diagnostic table that we saw in *Star Trek: The Motion Picture* with regard to the Ilia probe has never reappeared.) There is, however, a bed equipped with a sort of "iron lung" device reminiscent of the one in "Spock's Brain."

A purely subjective impression is that Dr. Crusher's office seemed larger and tidier than McCoy's, but was somehow sterile and quite impersonal.

Crew's Quarters. These likewise reflect this new atmosphere of luxurious comfort. The bed in Tasha Yar's quarters (briefly glimpsed as she led Data toward it in "The Naked Now") actually looked more like a *bed* than a bunk. My overall impression was of a more homelike atmosphere, perhaps, again, in deference to the expanded length of missions.

Personnel. We are obviously dealing with a larger cast than the legendary seven of the original series. There are seven major characters on the bridge alone: Captain Picard, Commander Riker, Counselor Troi, Lieutenant Yar, Lieutenant Commander Data, Lieutenant Worf, and Lieutenant LaForge. In addition, there is the chief medical officer, Dr. Beverly Crusher, and her precocious son Wesley, which brings us to a total of nine. We have also been given a brief glimpse of two of the chief engineers, who apparently will not play major roles in this new series. (Unlike their predecessor, Montgomery Scott. Good thing, too, as neither of them inspired my trust and confidence the way Scotty did in the old days, despite his propensity for multiplying his repair estimates by a factor of four!)

The female chief seen in "The Naked Now" seemed to be unforgivably pessimistic and unconscionably helpless throughout the entire episode—even when Wesley Crusher hit upon the idea of repulsor beam, I had the feeling she didn't have the foggiest notion of what to do to implement it. In "Where No One Has Gone

Before," Chief Engineer Argyle calmly allowed two complete strangers to do things to his engines that would undoubtedly have had Scotty climbing the walls and uttering Gaelic curses. Fortunately, ol' Wes was once again on hand to save the day. (Why do I have the feeling that we'll be seeing a lot of this young man, standing orders to the contrary?)

Captain Jean-Luc Picard is in command with Commander William Riker as his first officer (referred to, interestingly enough, as "Number One"). They share top billing as Shatner and Nimoy did in the first season of the original series. One might wonder if perhaps one of the other characters will move up to top billing in succeeding seasons, much as DeForest Kelley did in the original.

Picard is quite the opposite of James Kirk. He is a more formal commander and seems much less relaxed around his officers. He appears to be a man who would shy away from close friendships with co-workers. Not a family man, he states quite emphatically that he is not fond of children and doesn't feel comfortable around them. He has a standing order that children not be allowed on the bridge. (Young Wesley Crusher, of course, violated this standing order several times over the course of the first few episodes and was finally promoted to the position of "acting ensign" so that he could be on the bridge *without* violating the captain's orders.) Picard mentions the colors of the French flag as "proper," so we may assume that he is somewhat proud of his French ancestry. Unfortunately, he almost seems humorless except for the episode in which he was acting "under the influence," so to speak. The captain is, no doubt, an excellent Starfleet officer and a fine commander. However, I find myself slow to warm to him, perhaps because he seems to be a colder individual than the captain I'm so used to seeing in command of the *Enterprise*.

If there is anyone aboard the ship who has inherited Captain Kirk's characteristics, I believe it is Bill Riker. He is a warm man who enjoys a good laugh. He smiles more, appears to be more at ease with the crew, and is generally a likable fellow. He considers his primary responsibility to be safeguarding the captain's life, and I think that he will perform admirably in this area. He also, by the way, *likes* kids. Riker has, in fact, been ordered by Picard to help him deal with the children aboard.

In addition to captain and first officer, there is now a "counselor," who seems to function as liaison between captain and crew, and between crew and aliens. In addition, she tries to keep the officers honest with each other and with themselves. She has a knack for going straight to the heart of a matter. Counselor Troi is half Betazoid and half human (another one of those interesting hybrids). She is not totally telepathic, but she senses feelings, or emotions, within others. I get the impression that she has some telephatic abilities that may appear only in times of intense emotion. To wit, her comment whispered to Riker when she was under the influence of the contaminant in "The Naked Now": "Wouldn't you rather be alone with me . . . *With me in your mind*?" Obviously Riker and Troi have had a previous relationship. Whether this unfolds in the course of the series is yet to be seen. It would, I think, make for an interesting storyline. At this point, however, we know little of Deanna Troi's personality.

Tasha Yar is the ship's security chief. Of all the characters, she is the one whose background has been the most thoroughly explored. We know from the premiere that she was born on a world much like Earth of the twenty-first century (post-nuclear war era). She defends Starfleet and commends them for stepping in and saving her world. In "The Naked Now," we are told that she was abandoned when she was five years old but was not rescued until she was fifteen. She managed, however, to avoid the rape gangs during the intervening ten years and she now longs for gentleness, joy, and love.

Lieutenant Commander Data is the true alien aboard the vessel, even more than Worf, the Klingon. Data is an android. Moreover, he is an android who dreams of becoming human. Riker likened him to Pinocchio (the wooden puppet who dreamed of becoming a real, live boy). I found the analogy appropriate. Data is undoubtedly superior to human beings (and is probably superior to every other intelligence represented by the Federation). He very matter-of-factly accepts his superiority and does not hesitate to point it out. However, he is quick to add, quite poignantly, that he would gladly give it all up to be human.

Data is an enigma. He has graduated from Starfleet Academy and is, to all intents and purposes, a Starfleet officer. But who in the galaxy created him? Surely none of the Federation sciences have progressed to the point of creating such an amazing and complex mechanism. In David Gerrold's novelization of "Encounter at Farpoint," we are told that Data was created by an advanced race that no longer exists. Was he the only android they created? Why was he left behind? Is he a machine? A being? Or something somewhere between the two?

I admit that of all the new cast, Data thrilled me least. Perhaps I have too many memories of the androids we saw in the original series. (Remember Ruk and Roger Korby? What about Rayna? And the Mudd androids?) But now that I've had an opportunity to see Data in action, I find that I've reversed my original opinion. With Data as part of the crew, the possibilities are endless. He is, as McCoy pointed out, much like Spock was in the earlier days. His mind is as efficient as a computer, he does not understand human "jokes" or figures of speech, he is intensely curious, he wants desperately to understand and to be accepted.

My gut feeling is that Data and Riker have the potential of developing a very special relationship, not unlike the one that Kirk and Spock came to share. I think it will pay to keep an eye on these two. There is something between them that "clicks" somehow. The chemistry is there, if only the writers will pick up on it.

Worf is the other alien aboard the *Enterprise*. This alien, however, is one that Trekkers are very, very familiar with. Klingons played a large role in the twenty-third-century Star Trek. It is comforting to have them back with us, even as allies! Worf seems to have all the characteristics of his race; that is, he has great physical strength and that wonderful warlike instinct. Worf is always ready to fight, and is often found siding with Tasha Yar when opinions are requested by Picard. He is quite impulsive but also seems willing to adjust to Federation ideals and Starfleet policy.

Worf, like Data, is sometimes utterly confused by humans with whom he serves. He does not understand human slang any better than the android, but, unlike Data, he has no desire to become more human. He is a Klingon and proud of it. He wears the gold sash of the Klingon Empire across his Starfleet uniform. Worf, too, shows great promise. I hope we get to see more of what prompted him to join Starfleet. (By the way, the Klingon ambassador of the twenty-third century swore that there would be no peace while James Kirk lived. Since the Federation and the Klingon Empire are quite obviously at peace, are we to assume that Captain Kirk is no longer with us? Or should we simply believe that the Ferengi menace was so great that the Klingons were ready to ally themselves with the Federation during Kirk's lifetime?)

Lieutenant Geordi LaForge is an interesting choice for navigator on the new *Enterprise*. He's birth-defect blind, but he sees more efficiently than anyone else aboard the ship, thanks to a futuristic prosthetic device which is worn like a visor over his eyes. Apparently there is a certain amount of discomfort associated with the visor. LaForge, like Data, longs to be merely human, with plain old inefficient human eyesight. To see *more*, he explains, is not always to see *better*. An interesting sideline to this character is the fact that he was inspired by a real, live twentieth-century Star Trek fan who was similarly handicapped. Another nice touch on Mr. Roddenberry's part.

Dr. Beverly Crusher and her son, Wesley, are not a part of the bridge crew. They do, however, establish an important link between Captain Picard and the rest of the ship. Dr. Crusher's husband served under Picard years ago. Due to some as-yet-unexplained tragedy, Picard brought Crusher's husband home in a body bag. Wesley was a small child at the time and probably does not remember his father in great detail. Beverly volunteered for the assignment aboard the *Enterprise*, which apparently surprises Picard. He feels that she will constantly be reminded of her husband's death if she serves under him. I think this is an unfair assumption on the captain's part, obviously a result of the guilt he still feels over the loss of a man who once served under him. Dr. Crusher has an inner strength and a stubborn disposition the extent of which Picard is only just beginning to realize. Her Starfleet record must be above reproach since she has been assigned as chief medical officer of a ship as prestigious as the *Enterprise*. She has devoted herself to her career and to her son since her husband's death, and it appears that she has done quite well in both areas.

There is ample room for the development of the relationship between Dr. Crusher and Captain Picard. Their admiration for each other seems mutual and I sense a strong attraction between the two. It will be interesting to see what, if anything, the writers make of this.

Wesley Crusher is the only series regular who is not part of the crew. (This, however, is subject to change. In the last episode I saw, Wes was made an "acting ensign" and was strongly urged by Picard to request admission to Starfleet Academy.) I suspect that a major reason for his existence is to give added dimension to the characters of Picard and Dr. Crusher. Wesley is extremely intelligent and exceedingly interested in starship command. He has already managed to make friends with the ship's first officer, with Data, and with Geordi LaForge. He knows enough about the bridge stations to man one on occasion (quite adequately, too, I might add) and he is even familiar with the captain's chair. He is a friendly, outgoing youth who verges on brilliance. His science project actually saved the *Enterprise* from destruction in "The Naked Now," and he behaved in a more responsible manner than some of the adults under the contaminant's influence. The alien "traveler" in "Where No One Has Gone Before" alluded to his illimitable potential and urged Picard to offer him support and encouragement. I think we should expect to see great things of Wesley in the future. Who knows? He may even change Picard's mind about children!

Something New. Of all the innovations aboard the new *Enterprise*, I am most impressed with the holodecks. While this is certainly not an original idea (I can think of at least one Star Trek novel that utilized the concept), I feel that it is most important to the premise of the expanded twenty-year missions. We have seen two examples of the holodecks thus far. The first was in the premiere, the pastoral scene in which Riker discovered Data whistling "Pop Goes the Weasel." The second was in "Code of Honor," wherein Security Chief Yar demonstrated the martial arts to Lucan. I hope that we will be treated to many other glimpses of these holodecks in the future.

Something Borrowed. "The Naked Now." "Where No One Has Gone Before." Sound familiar? They should. These two episodes of *Star Trek: The Next Generation* are almost direct spinoffs of earlier Star Trek episodes. Oh, the characters are different and the storylines are not exactly the same—but the underlying *theme* is identical. Continuity is a fine thing—and yes, it was something very definitely lacking in the earliest episodes of the original series—but I feel I must take exception to episodes that are so closely paralleled that even the *names* are virtually the same.

I enjoy hearing references to the *Enterprise*'s earlier missions as much as anyone, and I certainly can't deny feeling a definite thrill whenever Kirk's (or Spock's, McCoy's, etc.) name is mentioned in the context of a twenty-fourth-century mission. However, I sincerely hope that the writers will not make a habit of delving into Captain Kirk's logs for story ideas. We've all been looking forward to some completely new and original voyages and I don't feel that rehashing twenty-third-century adventures in a twenty-fourth century setting constitutes originality! Yes, by all means, mention a past mission of the *Enterprise* if appropriate. But please avoid writing another story on the same subject!

(Note: This criticism may ultimately prove to be completely unjust. Simply because two of the first five episodes were related to previous Star Trek episodes does not necessarily mean that two out of *every* five episodes will be likewise related. It may simply be a coincidence brought about by the order in which filmed episodes are being aired.)

What conclusions can be drawn from what we've seen thus far of the new series? What words of wisdom can be imparted to all those Doubting Thomases who fervently believe (as I myself once did) that Star Trek without Kirk, Spock, McCoy, and the others is simply not Star Trek? What can be said that hasn't already been said by Gene Roddenberry, by Dorothy Fontana, by David Gerrold, by Paramount, and, yes, by the fans themselves?

Well, I, for one, think we can say this much, at least:

Star Trek: The Next Generation is not merely a new Star Trek universe. It is an extension of the universe that we have come to know and love over the past twenty years. It continually builds on the premises laid down by Gene Roddenberry over two decades earlier. The United Federation of Planets has in no way become diminished in the seventy-eight intervening years. Clearly it has added many worlds (and perhaps even a few Empires) to the ranks of its member planets and allies.

Starfleet still exists, not as a military organization bent on conquering its enemies and subduing its neighbors, but as a peacekeeping force dedicated to the protection of the weak and the innocent. The Prime Directive is still revered. It may not be the best tool to use in exploring the galaxy, but we're still wise enough to know that we're not wise enough for anything else just yet. Maybe in another couple of hundred centuries . . .

Human beings still have their faults, They admit to them openly (as Picard admitted to "Q"; as Riker admitted to Portal in "The Last Outpost") but they still try to do the best that they can. Peace is still looked upon as the ultimate goal. "Different" does not mean "wrong" or "less." The *Enterprise*'s mission is still the same; to explore, to seek out. Not to change or subvert or influence, but to study, to learn, to *exchange*.

We have yet to see the personal relationships develop as before. I believe the potential is there, but it will be the writers who must make use of the chemistry between the characters. We may never see a friendship as deep and unswerving as the one created for Kirk, Spock, and McCoy. Indeed, we have already seen in one episode that Riker was fully prepared to abandon Captain Picard to an alien consciousness and continue his mission without the presence of his commanding officer. This apparent coldheartedness, or at least indifference, seems far removed from the warm, caring (even if *unvoiced*, at least throughout the television series) friendship that Spock felt for Kirk.

How many times in the original series did *that* first officer sacrifice his career, not to mention his reputation as a "logical" Vulcan, to avoid abandoning his captain in a crisis? As long as there was the slightest possibility that Kirk could be returned, Spock refused to be budged from the spot. Recall if you will the events in "The Tholian Web": Kirk was not only *missing*, he was presumed dead. But Spock drove himself relentlessly, despite his inborn logic and McCoy's badgering, until he retrieved the captain from interphase. Remember, too, that desperate race against time in "The Paradise Syndrome," and Spock's tenacity in locating the captain in "Wink of an Eye" and "Mark of Gideon." There are other episodes in which we see the reverse: Kirk risking his Starfleet career in order to allow Spock the opportunity to return his former captain to Talos IV in "The Menagerie"; Kirk again risking his career to save Spock's life in "Amok Time"; Kirk insisting on a seemingly impossible search for the woman who stole Spock's brain; and the grandest, most moving example of friendship eternal and everlasting expressed in *Wrath of Khan* and *The Search for Spock*.

This is a very special relationship, one that evolved over a period of many years. Yet even in the beginning, didn't we sense the fragile bond developing between the major characters? Wasn't it evident in the gentle teasing on the bridge, the artfully constructed expressions on the faces of these friends, the nuances in their words? Might there not be a trace of something very similar in *The Next Generation*? Only time will tell.

By now it has become obvious that we will never see Kirk's

impulsiveness, his gambling nature, his ways of cheating death, or his "don't like to lose" attitude mirrored in Captain Picard. And that is as it should be, Picard is *not* Kirk. There will never be another Kirk, in this universe or any other. Picard must stand on his own merits. We would not accept him on any other terms.

In the same way, we will never see a Vulcan like Spock aboard the new *Enterprise*. Oh, there are Vulcans aplenty in the background, adequate proof that Vulcan is still a very integral part of the Federation. But there will never be another Spock. Why should there be? He is a unique individual, a never-to-be-duplicated legend. And why should Mr. Roddenberry give us another chief medical officer with the same gruff manner, the same down-home philosophy, and the same endearing qualities as those possessed in such abundance by Bones McCoy?

He shouldn't.

Mr. Roddenberry should not waste his time in re-creating something that was very nearly perfect the first time around. He should create *new* legends. He should breathe life into a new myth.

And that's why we have *Star Trek: The Next Generation.*

Not to repeat what's already been done. Not to attempt to replace the irreplaceable. Not to make *better*. Simply to create *another* legend to stand beside the first. Equal. Separate. Different. But still, when all is said and done, *Star Trek.*

What more is there, after all?

A GUIDE TO STAR TREK BLUEPRINTS

by Michael J. Scott

Michael Scott, or "Scotty" as he is more commonly known in fandom, has been interested in the technical side of Star Trek for many years. Among other accomplishments, he is the designer of one of the original "clone" Star Trek role-playing battle games, and currently designs games for Gamescience and other companies. Like so many others, Scotty began as a fan who just wanted to know more about the Enterprise *and the other ships and technology in Star Trek. Unlike most others, however, Scotty began carefully researching and comparing all of the blueprints, technical drawings, manuals, etc. that began to proliferate as fandom grew. In the following article, he discusses the best and worst of these, and offers his evaluation of which of them should be considered "real" Star Trek.*

Star Trek fandom is one of the most intense subtypes in science fiction. Fans collect every aspect of Star Trek that they can get their hands on, from glossy photographs of the stars to bubblegum cards. I even know a lady in Gautier, Mississippi, who has dedicated an entire room to Star Trek memorabilia. When fans can't get more pictures, stories, and artwork, they create their own. Star Trek fandom has turned out to be most creative and prolific of all science fiction fan denominations.

Of all the stars of Star Trek, perhaps the most popular is the grand lady herself, the U.S.S. *Enterprise*, and a number of Star Trek fans devote their interest primarily to every aspect of the starship and her intricate systems. Initially, the only blueprints and descriptions of the "Big E" were to be found in Stephen Whitfield and Gene Roddenberry's *The Making of Star Trek*, and these were adapted from diagrams printed in the original *Star Trek Writer's Guide*, drawn by Matt Jefferies, the show's set designer (available from Lincoln Enterprises). These blueprints were simple three-view diagrams of the *Enterprise* and comparable drawings of a Klingon battlecruiser and the modern aircraft carrier *Enterprise*, in order to give a sense of scale. There was also a midline cutaway of the starship to give some idea of how the decks were laid out. These same three-views were also printed on the box containing AMT's best-selling model kit of the *Enterprise*.

While of passing interest to most Star Trek fans, the layout, both internal and external, of the U.S.S. *Enterprise* was an object of intense interest among those of us who were model builders and technophiles. The background of the Star Trek universe is one of the things that make Star Trek the most successful science-fiction show in the history of television. And a large part of this coherent background is "realness" of the starships; the idea that there could really be such a spacecraft laid out in just that way. Studying those blueprints would help give the fan the sense of actually being able to walk those corridors and ride the turbolift up the bridge or all the way back to the shuttlecraft hangar bay.

In the early 1970s, Franz Joseph Schnaubelt was amused by his daughter's infatuation with a certain sci-fi television show. Karen had joined the local San Diego division of S.T.A.R. (Star Trek Association for Revival) and Schnaubelt wanted to see what she found so interesting, so he took a look at the club's activities and some of the publications then available. Franz Joseph Schnaubelt is a retired naval architect and designer, and has participated in many top aerospace projects. He became intrigued with the design of the *Enterprise* and decided to see if he could do some realistic drawings of the ship that would make sense, both to the overall external design and to various descriptions of the internal parts of the ship shown and mentioned from episode to episode.

Schnaubelt became more deeply involved in what was originally just an idle inquiry, and eventually ended up visiting Gene Roddenberry and doing extensive research for his drawings. Finally, he ended with a pile of engineering blueprints, showing every elevation of the starship and every detail of her interior, deck by deck. These drawings had the blessing of Gene Roddenberry, whose signature can be found in the credits block. Schnaubelt's work was impeccable. Using his considerable skill as a naval designer, Schnaubelt had managed to locate every room and function of the starship from toilets to tractor beams. The original blueprints saw a short print run and were offered for sale at one of Bjo Trimble's Equicons in 1974. The run sold out immediately. The *Enterprise* blueprints were so popular that they caught the interest of Ballantine Books and were soon released in a beautiful plastic case, in bookstores throughout the country.

Franz Joseph's blueprints were soon followed by the *Star Fleet Technical Manual*, a thick vinyl-bound notebook (recently reprinted in a softcover version), organized much like a military manual, that contained information on details of the Federation from the UFP charter to the rules for 3-D chess. Included in the *Technical Manual* were additional detail deck diagrams and three-view blueprints of other starship types that Franz Joseph imagined might also serve in Starfleet Command. The *Star Fleet Technical Manual* was an instant best-seller and started the flood of fan products that would hit the market for the next decade.

Many fans of Star Trek have a very definite streak of creativity and a goodly number of published artists and authors originally got their start writing and drawing for fan publications. But one thing should be made clear: only those products authorized by Gene Roddenberry and/or Paramount Pictures have any authenticity, and many fans will only accept the original episodes and the four motion pictures as "real" Star Trek. But this has certainly not stopped the fans from writing their own stories and drawing their own original Star Trek artwork and blueprints.

The first fan to really catch on to the idea of adding new material to Franz Joseph's *Technical Manual* was Geoffrey Mandel. A very talented artist, Mandel began a series of technical drawings and articles modeled after the style established by Schnaubelt in the *Technical Manual*. These were fan publications, created and distributed in much the same fashion as hundreds of other magazines.

The difference was that Mandel's work was undeniably professional and only catered to those Star Trek fans who were interested in such details. Mandel is responsible for blueprints of the *Enterprise*'s warp-drive nacelles (somehow left out of Franz Joseph's drawings) and the small freighter depicted in the animated Star Trek episode "Pirates of Orion." He also executed detailed three-view drawings of the Klingon battlecruiser, the Romulan bird of prey, the Kzinti police ship, and a variety of shuttlecraft. Ballantine published Geoffrey Mandel's work in the *Star Fleet Medical Reference Manual* and in *Star Trek Maps* (both currently out of print). Though Mandel's work derived from Franz Joseph Schnaubelt's, he eventually found his own ground and contributed significantly to officially published Star Trek material.

The next official publication of Star Trek technical material, *Star Trek: The Motion Picture Blueprints*, was released concurrently with the film. Executed in the same style Franz Joseph Schnaubelt's *U.S.S. Enterprise Booklet of General Plans*, this set of blueprints was released in an attractive vinyl case, and included technical renderings of all the spacecraft seen in *STTMP*. These included the *Enterprise*, the new Klingon battlecruiser, the Vulcan shuttlecraft, and the travel pod. Also depicted were interiors of the *Enterprise* and Klingon bridges, and details of the tiny workbee. These blueprints were the work of Dave Kimble, who also executed and published one of the most striking Star Trek posters of all time: a complete, full-color, cutaway painting of the new *Enterprise* in orbit over the Earth. Though the drawings were executed by Dave Kimble, much of the original design work had been done by Andy Probert, of Industrial Light and Magic.

But even while this official publication was being offered, a number of other fans had noticed the hunger for this kind of material and followed in the footsteps of Geoffrey Mandel in offering them on the unofficial, fan publication market. The most prolific of these has been New Eye Studios. New Eye Studios had carried some of Mandel's blueprints and, noting their popularity, had searched among fandom for other designers. The best of these was the late Michael McMaster. McMaster's most recognized design works were his complete blueprints and diagrams of the *Enterprise* bridge. These blueprints showed the location of every single button, switch, and viewscreen on the ship's bridge, and also indicated what they did and how they responded. It was a monumental piece of research and work, involving painstaking examination of film clips and stills (this was before the video explosion). Three other notable McMaster works are a complete set of Klingon battlecruiser blueprints, a complete set of Romulan bird of prey blueprints, and a large chart showing all of the various Star Trek ships drawn to the same scale for visual comparison. The Klingon and Romulan blueprints rival Franz Joseph's for depth of detail. While Michael McMaster's work is excellent for detail and drawing alike, it is important to note that none of his blueprints received official sanction except those of the Klingon battlecruiser, which were marketed through Majel Barrett's Lincoln Enterprises mail-order catalog.

New Eye Studios has also marketed a number of other technical publications, none of which has a license or official recognition from Paramount. Indeed, in two cases the blueprints are considered by many to be a violation of Franz Joseph Schnaubelt's copyrights. These blueprints are of the Destroyer/Scout and of the Dreadnought type vessels that Franz created expressly for his *Star Fleet Technical Manual*, and have been used, with his permission, in Gamescience Corporation's *Starfleet Battle Manual* and in Task Force Games' *Starfleet Battles*. New Eye also markets Gorn spaceship blueprints, all of Geoffrey Mandel's blueprints, *Enterprise* construction sketches, new blueprints of starships shown in the motion pictures, and several technical manuals. Many of these works are uncredited and have no reference address other than that of New Eye Studios. Much of the material is comparatively crude and not well-researched, especially those blueprints of vessels revealed in the current movies. It is this uneven nature of New Eye Studios' catalog that should warn the Star Trek fan to be especially careful when ordering. Recommended are any of McMaster's blueprints and any material prepared by Geoffrey Mandel, such as the *U.S.S. Enterprise Officer's Manual* and the *Star Fleet Medical Reference Manual*.

Another entrant in the unofficial blueprint market is Starstation Aurora. Starstation Aurora began by offering a set of space cruiser blueprints, to New Eye Studios, that were based on the spacecraft from the Star Trek episode "The Way to Eden." This craft was a remake of the spaceship model used for the Tholians in the episode "The Tholian Web," and was modified by different lighting and adding a pair of *Enterprise*-style warp-drive nacelles. This ship was referred to as the cruiser *Aurora*, and perhaps this is where the company got their publishing house name. Since then, Starstation Aurora has made a name for themselves by creating blueprints of Starfleet vessels that they think ought to exist. To this end, they have created variants of Franz Joseph Schnaubelt's ships and of the *Enterprise*, based on the new technology shown in the four Star Trek movies. The result is a series of starship drawings showing considerable skill and creativity. The designers at Starstation Aurora have extrapolated all of the Starfleet technology and made a number of quite reasonable and attractive blueprints. The variety of vessels shown rival the different types you would expect to find in a real space service that encompassed several alien races.

Ancillary to these blueprints, Starstation Aurora has also published a book called *Starship Design* that is crafted to the appearance of a typical military magazine of the twenty-third century, much as you would find today at a U.S. Navy base. This "magazine" continues the basis for Starstation Aurora's designs, extrapolating Star Trek movie technology and even depicting new Klingon vessels. Starstation Aurora also publishes a series of technical manuals called the *Federation Reference Series* that show all of the vessels of the Klingons and Starfleet in addition to uniforms and other gear. Both of these publications are highly detailed and well drawn. They are also entirely unauthorized by Paramount Pictures, Gene Roddenberry, or Franz Joseph Schnaubelt (whose designs appear here as well). A good example of Starstation Aurora's method of blueprint production are the plans of the U.S.S. *Excelsior*, the ill-fated battleship seen in *Star Trek III: The Search for Spock*. These blueprints have been produced with meticulous care, with admirable graphics and beautiful detail. They have been marketed in the same type of vinyl pouch that the *Enterprise* and *STTMP* blueprints came in, and, at first glance, would seem to be a good buy. However, Starstation Aurora has decided to redesign the Excelsior Class, and show instead a highly modified ship that they call the U.S.S. *Ingram*, NCC-2001. While superficially of the same general layout as the *Excelsior* seen in the motion picture, the *Ingram* has extensive modifications to her secondary hull with additional weaponry. Thus, what you have *not* bought is a set of *Excelsior* blueprints, but a set of modifications that Starstation Aurora thought made the ship better. Perhaps these changes were done so that Starstation Aurora could market the plans without coming into direct conflict with Paramount licenses.

In direct contrast to Starstation Aurora's publications is the curious release of a set of general plans for the U.S.S. *Avenger* class starships. In reality, these are plans for the U.S.S. *Reliant* seen in

Star Trek II: The Wrath of Khan. The plans are copyrighted by David John Nielsen, but *Star Fleet Technical Orders* included with the plans, are signed by "Fleet Comdre" A. Probert, "Rear Adm." M. Minor, "Fleet Capt." J. Jennings, and "Rear Adm." J. T. Kirk. Michael Minor was the art director of *Star Trek II: The Wrath of Khan*, and designer of the *Reliant*. Andy Probert is the main designer of the new *Enterprise*, and Joseph Jennings was the production designer for *Wrath of Khan*. The signatures included appear authentic and the execution is excellent. I highly recommend these plans, but . . . there is no Paramount copyright, and their origin is somewhat mystifying. If they indeed originated with Industrial Light and Magic, then they are certainly an official part of the Star Trek universe and deserve inclusion in any blueprint collection.

The most recent entry into the Star Trek blueprint field is *Mr. Scott's Guide to the Enterprise.* This is a beautiful book created by Shane Johnson (who had recently published a manual on all the Star Trek uniforms). In the *Guide*, Johnson takes us on a guided tour of the new *Enterprise*, deck by deck, revealing intimate details of everything from airlock procedure to the meals obtainable from a food processing unit. Johnson drew heavily from Dave Kimble's blueprints of the new *Enterprise* mentioned above, and also managed to get the help of Paramount's marketing and publicity offices in obtaining actual set designs and stills to create his blueprints of such places as the recreation room and the warp engine room. Johnson's *Guide* also includes exclusive stills and drawings of the new *Enterprise*, NCC-1701-A, shown at the end of *Star Trek IV: The Voyage Home.* The best recommendation that can be given concerning *Mr. Scott's Guide to the Enterprise* is that it rivals *The Space Shuttle Operator's Manual* and *The Mars One Crew Manual* for detail and subject interest. A definite must-have for a Star Trek technophile. The only thing missing from this book is a set of deck plans for the whole ship. Maybe next time.

Throughout this article, both official and unofficial blueprints have been discussed. I decided that it would not be prudent to go into the intimate details of each publication (since that would take up far too much space) but instead to show the general merits and to suggest guidelines for the fan who wishes to purchase this sort of item. One of the biggest problems of the unofficial blueprints is the lack of continuity with official publications. A good example is *Mr. Scott's Guide to the Enterprise.* Just prior to this book's release by Pocket Books, I purchased another publication called *Line Officer Requirements* from a dealer at a convention. This unofficial book covered much of the same material as Shane Johnson's, but in many cases the two books diverged. Typical areas of divergence were descriptions of transwarp drive and the *Enterprise*'s lifeboats. Obviously, a Star Trek fan would defer to the official publication, but many official, licensed products have used fan publications as sources. A good example of this is the use of McMaster's Klingon battlecruiser blueprints by both FASA and Task Force in their respective game systems, though these blueprints differ wildly from the ones executed by Dave Kimble in his official blueprint set from *Star Trek: The Motion Picture*.

Aside from the legal considerations of supporting non-licensed Star Trek products, Star Trek fans must decide for themselves on the merits of having fan-created blueprints or technical manuals in their collections. Many of these, as has been noted above, are of superior quality and printing, but may vary considerably from official sources such as the motion pictures and licensed materials. In the end, you must decide for yourself how your Star Trek library will be filled.

STAR TREK MYSTERIES SOLVED BY OUR READERS

With Commentary by Leslie Thompson

Leslie Thompson receives a substantial proportion of the mail arriving at the Trek offices, and that percentage goes up every time she publishes a new mysteries article. G. B. noticed that more and more readers seemed to be including their own solutions to both mysteries Leslie had "solved," as well as solutions to questions they themselves asked. We immediately pointed this out to Leslie, who seized upon it as a nifty way to get out of doing the work herself. It wasn't to be that easy for her, however, as we instead insisted that she do a readers' mysteries article in addition to one of her own. Trouper that she is, Leslie eagerly set to work immediately upon our promise to return her firstborn child on receipt of the manuscript.

A while ago, I invited readers to write in with their own solutions to Star Trek Mysteries, either those I had previously "solved" or ones they discovered for themselves. The response, to say the least, was overwhelming. Walter and G. B. presented me with a thick, thick file of letters, and said, "Do something about this . . . you asked for it!" Indeed I did, and I've never had a better time than I had while going through these letters. Your responses and theories are always amazingly creative, and the occasional kind word you throw my way is greatly appreciated.

The following is only a small sample of the response we've received; I only wish we had space for more. Some of them are also a few years old—sadly, I've been too busy to do articles for a while—but they are nonetheless valid and interesting for that. I promise to get back to work! You'll be seeing Star Trek Mysteries and your responses again on a regular basis, as well as other articles by me, both alone and in collaboration with Walter.

Until then, please keep those letters coming in! This mystery game is getting tougher all the time, but it's more fun all the time, too! Thanks again, keep writing, and I'll see you soon!

Carl Brumbaugh
Machias, ME

I have to take exception with two of the "mysteries" you attempted to solve, and would like to offer my solutions.

The first mystery: When Kirk realized that Khan was about to detonate the Genesis Device, why didn't he beam it onto the *Enterprise* and from there into deep space, as he did with Nomad?

The answer to this is quite simple and was evidenced in both the movie and the novelization. It wasn't, as was suggested by you, Leslie, that perhaps the Genesis Wave set up some sort of interference with transporting. It was, rather, where the *Enterprise* was and its condition that prevented Kirk from using the transporter.

We must remember that the *Enterprise* had sustained critical damage to her engineering section. Scotty earlier told the captain that there was barely enough power to transport him and the landing party down to Regulus. And even though some damage had been repaired, the *Enterprise* again suffered damage in the battle in the Mutara Nebula.

Also, as the ship was located in the Mutara Nebula, where dust particles and gases interfered with the sensors, shields, and screens to a degree where they were virtually inoperative. It is also logical to assume that the nebula acted as a shield preventing Kirk from beaming the Genesis Device into deep space.

The second mystery I would like to deal with is why the sensors aboard the *Enterprise* failed to detect Khan's incoming fire and automatically raise the shields?

The ship's sensors detect an object in space and automatically raise the shields. However, in this case, what the sensors indentified was not an unknown ship or object, but a Federation ship. So there was no reason for the computer to order any alert or raise the shields. It seems, then, that the ordering of any alert or raising of shields upon the approach of a Federation or Starfleet vessel is in the hands of the commanding officer. When Kirk ordered "yellow alert," it only put the crew on standby to man their positions, it did not automatically raise the shields.

By the time Khan started firing, he was only a ship's length or two from the *Enterprise*, too late for Kirk to react. In short, Kirk literally "got caught with [his] pants down."

Can't argue with those solutions, Carl. Looks like you did your homework and thought things through carefully.

Michael Parker
Newport Beach, CA

I'm not sure if this qualifies as a mystery, but in every episode, there is a small gold plaque at waist level near the turbolift with the words "U.S.S. *Enterprise*" at the top; the rest is too small to see clearly. The only answer I could come up with as to the rest of the words is from Gene Roddenberry's Star Trek Guide (circa 1965), as quoted in David Gerrold's book *The World of Star Trek:*
U.S.S. ENTERPRISE
Cruiser Class—Gross 190,000 tons
Crew Complement—430 persons
Drive—space-warp
Range—18 years at light-year velocity
Registry—Earth, United Space Ship

This seems like a reasonable answer, yet I'm not quite sure.

It is a reasonable answer indeed, Michael. I suspect your hesitation stems from the fact that some of the phraseology on the plaque isn't quite in keeping with what we know about the *Enterprise* and the Federation. Remember, however, that the *Enterprise* is by no means a new ship when Kirk takes her over, and some of the terminology on the plaque might be outdated or made incorrect by changes in the ship itself. Why wasn't the plaque changed then? Because it is a *commissioning plaque*, placed there when the ship was new and by tradition, not to be removed or replaced until the ship is taken out of commission, no matter how many changes are made. As it was not visible in the redesign, we must assume it was moved elsewhere on the ship, probably down in the rec room near the diorama of the vessels named *Enterprise*. It's just too bad that Kirk didn't have time to remove it before the ship met her untimely death. Or did he take it off and slip it in a pocket on the way, knowing that the search for Spock just might be the last voyage of the Starship *Enterprise*? I kind of like to think so, don't you?

Kenneth Wayne Darden
Marquette, MI
How come the phasers were different in *Wrath of Khan* than in *STTMP*? Just like the guns of today, Star Trek's time may also have many different makes of weapons. We have Colt .45s, .38 Specials, and Lugers, to name just a few. Why can't Starfleet issue phasers like Mark IIs, Altarian Special! The same can also be said of the differences between the communicators in the two movies.

Why wasn't the *Enterprise* refitted in the huge spacedock seen in *The Search for Spock* rather than in the construction rig seen in *STTMP* and *Wrath of Khan*? As we well know, the revolutionary ship *Excelsior*, with its innovative transwarp drive, was probably constructed inside the station, hidden away from potential prying eyes. The *Enterprise* was allowed inside the spacedock only after everything on the *Excelsior* had been declassified.

To hide the *Excelsior* was also the reason for the spacedock doors, as well as keeping any unauthorized spacecraft from entering.

Also, the reason why spacedock didn't use its tractor beams to capture the *Enterprise* was because Chekov, Sulu, and Scotty had sabotaged them, as well.

I'll buy the spacedock theory to a point, Kenneth—I'll agree that Starfleet was trying their best to keep *Excelsior* hidden. I really don't think that construction or even major structural repairs would take place inside the spacedock. The thing is just a glorified garage when you get down to it, and the reason for the doors would be to provide a *controlled* environment free of space debris.

As to the pistols, I think you're right on target. (Ha, ha!) There's probably a couple of hundred different weapons companies making phasers, each one vying for the lucrative Starfleet contracts. Even if the same company gets the contract each time, they would still make sure their weapons reflect changing technology and the advances of the competition.

Edward Jordan
Auburn, NY

In Mark Alfred's article "The Star Trek Films: Variations and Vexations" (*The Best of Trek #10*), I found four "mysteries":

1. Mr. Alfred asked where the nocturnal illumination on Genesis came from, since it had no moon.

As the *Enterprise* approached Regula I, the Mutara Nebula was clearly visible. Since Regula was not destroyed by the Genesis Wave, one must assume that it was visible in the night sky on Genesis, providing the nocturnal illumination.

2. When Kirk and Company came to break McCoy out of jail, why did he act surprised, not forewarned by Chekov?

When Kirk told Chekov to alert Dr. McCoy, he assumed that the doctor was still home resting. However, in the very next scene, we learned that McCoy had gone to a local bar and gotten himself arrested. Obviously Chekov couldn't warn the doctor if he wasn't home.

3. In the same article, Mr. Alfred stated that the *Enterprise*'s transporter-room walls were a dull gray color in *Star Trek: The Motion Picture*. In *Wrath of Khan* they were covered with madly blinking lights. Then again in *Star Trek III: The Search for Spock*, the lights were gone.

This is an easily solvable dilemma. Let's assume that normally the transporter-room walls are covered with little panels that hide the lights. During the battle in *Wrath of Khan*, they were removed for emergency repairs, making the lights visible. Later, after repairs were completed, the panels were replaced.

4. When the *Enterprise* self-destructed in *The Search for Spock*, why did the primary hull explode first instead of the secondary hull where the matter/antimatter intermix chamber is located?

My only answer is that a backup destruct system was used, one that results in the destruction of the bridge and primary hull. Why? Because the heart of the destruct system, the matter/antimatter intermix chamber, which is normally used for warp drive, was knocked out after the duel with the Klingons.

All of your solutions sound reasonable to me, Edward, although I would qualify your first answer by stating where the light the

Genesis Planet reflected came from. My guess is that it would be from the remnants of the Mutara Nebula and the small stars within, as well as the Genesis-created proto-star.

Martin Kottmeyer
Carlyle, IL

Why did Ceti Alpha IV explode only six months after Khan was exiled on Ceti Alpha V? Planets just do not explode without good cause. There must be a nonchance element involved. Two theories:

It's not dead, Jim. The Doomsday Machine had a technology that withstood the blasting of planets. Is a starship blowing up in its mouth really going to kill it? It wandered into the Ceti Alpha system before Starfleet had a chance to reach it. It damages Ceti Alpha IV, which then collapses around it into a miniblack hole, which sensors won't detect when Chekov and company come visiting.

The "Squire of Gothos" starts to track down Kirk because he was such a fun pet. (His parents can't confine him to his room forever, after all.) He followed the trail to Khan's place of exile—Khan was even more fun than Kirk. Egos clash, and before long the Squire crashes his planet into Ceti Alpha IV in a fit of pique, then leaves. Khan deduces Kirk must have known about the Squire, and never bothered to check on him.

Well, Martin, I'm not too sure that's what really happened in either case, but I sure give you ten points for inventiveness!

John McHugh
Alexandria, VA

I think I have the solution to the problem put forth by Nicholas Armstrong in *Best of Trek #8* concerning the use of the *Enterprise* insignia by all Starfleet personnel in the three Star Trek movies. I suggest that rather than being the symbol for the entire Starfleet, the arrowheaded emblem is instead the symbol for a smaller fleet within Starfleet. This fleet, which we'll call Earth Fleet, would be made up of the *Enterprise*, *Reliant*, *Grissom*, and *Excelsior*, as well as all Earth ground personnel and anyone else who is shown wearing the insignia.

Other insignias shown during the series would signify other fleets, so the emblem Captain Tracey wore in "The Omega Glory" might be the symbol for the Vulcan Fleet, and the emblems worn by

Starbase personnel in "The Menagerie" and "Courtmartial" would be the symbol for the Neutral Zone Fleet, and so on. So, just as the U.S. Navy has the Atlantic Fleet, the Seventh Fleet, etc., Starfleet would have smaller fleets as well. This would also explain why Kirk so often referred to "Earth Fleet Command" and the like over the course of the series.

You know, I kind of like that idea, John. It would fall into that category we mystery solvers so often depend on: "the things that are so, you just never heard of them." The only problem would be getting the idea accepted by those fans who like to believe in the idea of "one big happy fleet." Now, we'll hear from someone else who has an answer to one of Nicholas's questions:

Eric J. Hebeling
Broken Arrow, OK
    Nicholas Armstrong asked about the Energy Barrier at the edge of our galaxy. That barrier is no longer there (see Diane Duane's novel *The Wounded Sky*), now allowing us to make the first trip to the Andromeda Galaxy.

Thanks, Eric. At the time I had discussed the mystery, I hadn't yet read Ms. Duane's excellent novel.

Carol Matthews
    The mystery concerning Khan's comment about the *Botany Bay* is a misquote, or, rather, a direct quote from the novelization. In the movie, Khan never claimed that the cargo container was all that is left of the *Botany Bay*.
    To resolve conflicts between novels and movies, or novels and television, we must have some rule of precedence. My own suggestion is that we regard the series and movies as the truth, since it is, after all, what we all observed. Novels and other adaptations are an individual interpreting the actual event and are therefore subject to misinterpretation. I believe you will have problems if you attempt to deal with the novels as if they were also true.
    For example, in *Star Trek III: The Search for Spock*, you will find many conflicts between the novel and the movie. Sure, Kirk was grief-stricken after the mind meld with Sarek, but it was done while both were seated, and Kirk did not collapse into Sarek's arms

after the meld was broken. The discussion between Kirk and Sarek after viewing the tape of Spock's demise from the engineering section was nothing like the discussion between them Vonda McIntyre wrote in her adaptation. Sarek did not ever say that McCoy was having an allergic reaction to Spock's presence, and Kirk didn't chuckle about it.

I found the dialogue in the movie to be more realistic than in the novel. In addition, McCoy didn't collapse when removed from Spock's presence, and he didn't scream and struggle during the restoration of Spock's consciousness. I know. I was there, and saw it happen in the movie.

There are a couple of things in the movie that I found disturbing and inconsistent. The first concerns the mind meld between Spock and McCoy. Spock has always been presented to us as a nonviolent being who does not use force except when absolutely necessary. Why, then, without McCoy's consent, would he implant his consciousness within McCoy's mind? As a woman, I find the concept of rape to be repugnant, and the idea of forcibly imposing one mind on another seems to be even worse. How could Spock do this?

The only reasonable answer I can think of is that it *was* done with McCoy's consent. Agreed, he was not conscious at the time, but we have seen in the past that Spock does the mind meld with the agreement of the other person. (Exceptions: "Mirror, Mirror," where the alternate-universe Spock was able to extract information from McCoy's mind; "By Any Other Name," where Spock was thrown physically when trying to make a simple suggestion at a distance; "A Taste of Armageddon," where, again at a distance, Spock suggested to the guard that they had escaped; "The Paradise Syndrome," where Spock was forced out of the meld, evidently by Kirk.) In addition, I believe that Spock would not perform the mind meld without consent of the other person, even if he could. Where does this leave us with McCoy/Spock in *Wrath of Khan*? It simply means that the transfer of Spock's *katra* was a request by Spock to McCoy. It can be argued that McCoy did not fully understand what he was doing, but I believe that in that last desperate moment, when Spock (mentally) made the request, McCoy's answer was "of course."

Was the Genesis Planet formed from the gases of the Mutara Nebula? It is my own opinion that the central body for the formation of Genesis was Regula I—a planetary body with an illuminating sun, but "essentially a great rock in space." This would seem more logical to me than instant coalescence of the gases into a planetary body. Genesis was not intended to speed up the effects of gravitation. It was intended to modify existing worlds.

Despite the disruptive effect of the explosion, it would still take centuries, and longer, for the gases in the nebula to form a planet or star—and there must have been a star present for the life forms to develop properly; otherwise Genesis would have been a block of ice with the atmosphere frozen to the surface. Remember, Genesis was intended to modify matter with life-producing results; it still required a suitable medium on which to operate.

It saddens me to learn that Spock's body has been regenerated with unstable "protomatter." Now he not only as an unusual genetic makeup, but also an unstable material underlying his already unusual physiology. As far as extrapolating his life span and reaction from Vulcan and human norms, now there is even less basis for comparison. It would seem reasonable that due to all the physiological stresses Spock has undergone, his life span would be considerably shorter than Vulcan norms. I still believe that it is our minds that make us what we are, and it is my hope that Spock's has been restored with a minimum of damage.

Now I'd like to break precedent a little, and include almost the complete text of a letter from Kay Kelly of Albany, NY. Kay's solutions are so well thought-out and nicely written that I just had to include them here.

Dear Leslie:

You'll observe that I'm contradicting the novelizations—which I dislike and do not consider "official"—but not, to my knowledge, anything in the films. I have already advanced my first suggestion in a letter published in *Starlog*.

Q: What form of survival did the Vulcans contemplate for Spock's soul? With body and soul already separated, why did they need the dead body?

A: Any "afterlife" Spock could anticipate with certainty presents problems. If we imagine an existence he would find desirable an eternity of growth and challenge, it dilutes the sacrifice of his death. If we imagine a dismal half-life, it is hard to believe he would want it.

Moreover, it is hard to accept a universe in which the survival of anyone's "soul" could depend on something as amoral as the performance of a specific ritual in a specific place. Add to that the requirement that both body and soul be present, even though the soul has already, apparently, been separated from the body, and we can appreciate Admiral Morrow's disbelief.

I think this is a more acceptable interpretation: Vulcans know reincarnation to be a fact, at least for their species. They have developed a technique whereby the formed personality, and some memories, can be carried over into the next incarnation. What is at stake is not really the Vulcan's "immortal soul"—which would survive, in some sense, in any case—but continuty of identity; the ability in the next life, which might be a century hence, to recall this one and learn from its experience.

The technique involves breaking the link between the physical body and the consciousness—what Vulcans call the *katra*—before the body decays or is destroyed, thus minimizing damage to the *katra*. "Transfer" of the *katra* by mind meld merely weakens the link. But if it is not thus weakened at death, it cannot be broken by a subsequent *katra* ritual.

Spock had never given instructions for the disposition of his remains. He believed that if it was destined to be important—that is, if he has succeeded in transferring his *katra*—someone would know. As a Starfleet officer, he had often faced possible death without attempting a *katra* transfer: either because he expected his shipmates to die with him, or because, if he died, it might be impossible to retrieve his body without risk to others. He attempted a transfer at the end because he was going to certain death, and knew that if the ship survived, his body could be recovered without difficulty or danger. But he had to perform the mind meld in such haste it was only partially successful.

Lieutenant Saavik understood Vulcan death customs. But she, unlike Sarek, realized the dying Spock had been unable to touch Kirk. When no one spoke out against Kirk's plan to bury Spock in space, Saavik was sure there had been no *katra* transfer. That was why—uncharacteristically, for a Vulcan—she grieved deeply enough to weep at the burial service.

Q: How did Spock's coffin come to soft-land on Genesis? David speculated that it happened because "the gravitational fields were still in flux." But if that were true, and he had not anticipated it,

Kirk and McCoy should not have anticipated it, either. They clearly knew the body was on Genesis.

A: Kirk secretly programmed the soft landing. Since he was in command, he knew no one would monitor the trajectory of the tube without his authorization. He picked a landing site where the *Enterprise* instruments showed the surface was solid and level. He further determined that the nearby plants were fragile enough for the tube to slice through or crush them; there was no danger of its coming to rest in a treetop.

Kirk confided that much to McCoy, explaining that he wanted to give Spock a beautiful final resting place. He suggested that they return later, when they could safely beam down, to bury the tube and erect a marker. He said he did not want to tell Carol or David for fear they would object to his "contaminating" the new planet; he could not bear to argue over it. Kirk's emotionalism on the subject contributed to McCoy's failure to remember what they "should" do with Spock's remains.

Kirk had a secret hope he was unwilling to share even with McCoy, for fear of being thought unbalanced. He hoped Genesis might somehow restore Spock to life. ("There are always possibilities . . . and if Genesis is indeed life from death, I must return to this place again.") As a precaution, he had rigged the photon tube to spring slightly ajar automatically in response to life signs within. And he had included a recording of his voice explaining the situation, reassuring Spock, and promising to return for him soon. The recording would also be activated by life signs within the tube. It would then repeat over and over, at intervals of several minutes, until someone shut it off.

He had learned from Carol and David that the area of the landing site would have a mild climate, and there would be no predators. The healthy, rational, adult Spock he was envisioning should have been adequately clothed in his burial robe, and able to subsist for weeks on fruits and berries.

Twenty-four hours after Kirk had deposited the photon tube on the surface, the *Enterprise* instruments still detected no "animal" life readings. Clearly, if something was going to happen to Spock's body, it had not happened yet. And Carol and David had said no one could beam down for weeks. The planet merited continuing study from orbit, but commonsense priorities dictated that Kirk rescue the *Reliant* crew and take them to a starbase medical facility. He could not linger near Genesis without arousing suspicion.

The sight of the new planet had induced a strange euphoria in Kirk; anything had seemed possible. With the planet no longer on the viewscreen, his euphoria faded, giving way to depression and apprehension. The idea that Genesis could restore Spock to life now seemed ridiculous. Kirk was embarrassed at what he had done, and thankful he would never have to admit his folly to anyone.

Subconsciously, he was deeply troubled. What if Genesis restored Spock to life as a mindless zombie? Or restored him, initially sound of mind, in a body still ravaged by the effects of radiation? Those images haunted Kirk in nightmares; but he could not face them, and did not remember them on waking.

When Sarek melded minds with him, he respected Kirk's privacy and "read" no more than necessary. So he only picked up Kirk's memory of Spock's actual death. Kirk later told him the body was intact and accessible, without going into detail.

At this point Kirk abandoned any lingering hope—or fear—Spock might have been restored to life. He unconsciously assumed that if that had happened, Spock's *katra* would have been reunited with his body, even across light-years of space.

When the child Spock awoke on Genesis, he was fascinated by the sounds emanating from Kirk's tape player *cum* communicator. He climbed out of the tube, wrenched the tape player loose, and removed it. Then he closed the tube to sit on it. He eventually wandered away from the landing site, taking the tape player with him. After accidentally shutting it off, he lost interest and discarded it. He had never touched the button that would have opened a communicator channel.

The device that had caused the tube to spring open was so miniaturized David and Saavik failed to notice it. They would have seen the tape player if it had still been near the landing site. But it was not. David may genuinely have been grasping at straws for an explanation when he speculated that the tube had soft-landed because "the gravitational fields were still in flux." Or he may have guessed the truth, and planned to "cover" for his father.

Q: If David used "protomatter" in the Genesis Torpedo, he must also have used it in the Eden Cave Experiment. Why did it cause a problem on Genesis?

A: The cave experiment was rigidly controlled. In the unplanned, uncontrolled planetary "test," normal matter—the photon tube and its contents—were introduced at a critical stage.

Matter and antimatter annihilate one another. Perhaps, at a crucial stage of Genesis, matter and "protomatter" also interact destructively: by triggering runaway aging and evolution! Matter (or, presumably, protomatter) introduced later is unaffected. But the original forms—or, in the case of living beings, their descendants—can only be saved by physically separating them. If it had been possible to remove from Genesis not only Spock, but also the photon tube, the (hypothetical) tape player, the evolved descendants of the microbes, and all organic matter traceable to them, the rapid aging of the planet could have been halted.

In other words—though we can hardly fault him, in light of the results—Kirk actually did "contaminate" and destroy the planet!

Q: Our friends' escape from Earth raises a number of questions. Why did Kirk decide to take the *Enterprise* rather than hire, borrow, or steal a less conspicuous ship? After he and Sulu freed McCoy, they contacted Chekov—who was, apparently, already aboard. Why did he not beam them directly up? Later, why was Uhura left behind on Earth? And what did she mean by saying she would "have 'Mr. Adventure' eating out of her hand"? It would seem she could have left him in the closet and not bothered with him again. Finally, why was there no pursuit?

A: It was imperative Spock's body be taken to Vulcan quickly. Kirk suggested using another ship to test Admiral Morrow's reaction, but he really needed the *Enterprise* for her speed.

Activation of the transporter aboard a supposedly empty, powered-down vessel in spacedock would have triggered alarms and prematurely alerted Starfleet Command. If Scotty, the technical expert, could have boarded hours ahead of anyone else, he could have bypassed the alarms. But Scotty was genuinely on duty board the *Excelsior*: he could not risk leaving early.

Chekov boarded first to begin bringing up the ship's systems. Scotty could have beamed him up via a momentary materialization in the *Excelsior* transporter room, but it would have been risky. Instead, Chekov passed through the transporter room in which Uhura, as part of the plan, had volunteered for "fill-in" duty. He showed his ID to Uhura only, and verbally identified himself as a crewman boarding the *Excelsior*. She beamed him aboard the

Enterprise. (Scotty later beamed himself over—at a "slow" hour, when no one was likely to question his movements or notice the setting on which he left the *Excelsior* transporter.)

When Kirk and his party called Chekov, the ship was still far from ready to leave. Chekov could not risk homing on Kirk's communicator signal and beaming them up from the detention-center elevator.

Kirk, unlike Chekov, could not pass through the "Old City Station" transporter room unrecognized. But even he could have bluffed his way through by pretending to show Uhura an "authorization," and making small talk about his need to visit the *Excelsior*. There was simply no point in wasting time on that sort of charade. Uhura would in any case have had to get the drop on her colleague a few minutes later. The distraction created by Kirk's irregular behavior probably made it easier.

Uhura stayed behind to disable the transporter, so pursuers could not beam aboard the *Enterprise* or pluck Kirk and his party off the ship before it cleared spacedock. There were other transporters nearby, but the one sabotaged would be the obvious choice of pursuing security guards. When they found it disabled, they would not have time to reach another.

Kirk could have had Uhura beamed aboard at the last moment. But he had decided a sixth crew person was not needed badly enough to justify anyone's spending those crucial minutes in communication with her or the transporter room, waiting to beam her up. He was sincere in offering Scotty, Sulu, and Chekov a chance to leave; but he knew them well enough to be almost sure they would decline.

Bear in mind, no one expected this mission to be physically dangerous or demanding. Even a low-speed collision with the spacedock doors would not have resulted in serious injuries. Rather, our friends believed they were risking their careers—probably throwing them away—to do something that would bring them no glory, and not real assurance they had accomplished anything. In that, Uhura was as deeply involved as the others.

She did leave "Mr. Adventure" locked in the closet so he would not be blamed for her sabotage of the transporter. But she spoke with him briefly through the door, and explained enough to make him an ally. He agreed to help her escape—by telling the security guards who would soon arrive that he had been on duty alone, and

Kirk and his two male companions had overpowered him. The guards assumed Sulu had stayed behind to disable the transporter. And while they were scouting the area for an Oriental male, a black female escaped. As for Sulu, if he had decided to leave the *Enterprise*, he could have avoided capture by beaming to maximum transporter range.

It was understood a later check with personnel would reveal Uhura had been on duty. But her colleague was unlikely to be severely punished for having helped her escape. She and her friends meant to turn themselves in as soon as they had witnessed the ceremony on Vulcan.

There was no point in anyone's pursuing Kirk unless he could be overtaken quickly. By Federation standards, both the Genesis Planet and Vulcan were fairly near Earth. Yet even nearby space is too vast to permit patrol ships to be stationed everywhere Starfleet would like. The "ban" on the Mutara Sector was probably being enforced only by a hastily erected system of warning buoys, which would photograph ships that approached from predictable directions and did not turn back.

Scotty's sabotage had cost the *Excelsior* a day or more. And no other ship with a top speed comparable to that of the *Enterprise* was close enough to have a chance of intercepting her. (That is consistent. In *Wrath of Khan*, the *Enterprise* was ordered to respond to the distress call from Regula I, despite having a trainee crew, because no other ship was close enough.)

I realize this effusion is "on the long side.' And I've been restraining myself. So I can just imagine what you're receiving from all sources! Good luck!

Thank you, Kay. Yes, I have received many letters like yours, all of which are equally detailed, involving, and original. I only wish I had the time and space to include them all. Hopefully, I will be able to put together another of these "joint effort" articles very, very soon.

Until then, keep writing, keep thinking, and keep on Trekkin'!

EVEN MORE STAR TREK MYSTERIES SOLVED

by Leslie Thompson

*It's been quite a while since Leslie Thompson has turned her atten-
tions to solving Star Trek "mysteries." You readers have been clamoring for more from Leslie. We've missed her, too, and certainly
miss her around the* Trek *offices. But Leslie is married now and
happily launched on her own career. We're delighted that she found
the time to write another article for us. We would certainly like for
Leslie to rejoin our ranks of regular contributors, and we think you
would, too. If so, why don't you help us try to convince her?*

Looks like it's that time again! Before we get to our questions, I'd
like to take a brief pause to thank all of you who have written over
the past months. I can't think of any kind of Star Trek writing I
enjoy more than this mystery solving, and your support and interest
thrills me beyond words. I really can't say which gives me the biggest kick—letters of praise or letters with toothsome new mysteries—luckily, most of your letters contain both! Again, many thanks,
and keep writing! Now to work . . .

Our first letter comes from Arden Lowe, of South Hadley, MA.
Arden asks, "Every time someone sets foot in the *Galileo*, some-
thing awful happens. First of all, why did they name another shuttle
Galileo after Spock *et al* burned up the first one, and second, why

do they continue to use that particular shuttle? Are superstitions a thing of the past by that time?"

Probably not. Human nature is still in abundant evidence in Star Trek's time, and superstition will always be a part of human nature. One could suppose that a stigma did attach itself to the *Galileo* after the events of "The Galileo Seven," and that its replacement and continued use was an indication of James Kirk's adamant refusal to let superstition have a say in the running of his ship.

Another possibility is that *all* of the shuttles on the *Enterprise* are called *Galileo*. The particular one we see is number seven (a completely different ship from the one Spock lost, just renumbered); there would be at least six more.

The likeliest possibility, however, is that the *Galileo* is the command officer's shuttle, usually reserved for (although not officially restricted to) the use of Kirk and/or Spock. This would account for the fact that it was the ship we most often (okay, always) saw, as well as the fact that a second ship was given the same name and number (either Kirk or Spock had personal reasons for calling it *Galileo*). It would be considered the "captain's gig," kept ready for his use, and probably the only thing onboard he'd really get a chance to "fly." This somewhat exalted status would explain why *Galileo 7* was used by the senior *Enterprise* officers to ferry Commissioner Hedford in "Metamorphosis."

Arden also wanted to know why Mr. Spock did not go into the Vulcan "healing mode" after his surgery in "Journey to Babel." The answer is simple: Spock was concerned about his father, the ship, and Kirk. As the healing mode is a mental state, Spock was able to delay its onset until he had assured himself that all was in order. (Sarek's similar failure to enter the healing mode would be because of like reasons: he was worried about the ship, the conference, and, deny it though he might, Spock.) Chances are that after Dr. McCoy had his famous "last word," both Vulcans slipped quietly and calmly into the trance.

Arden concludes with two questions about *The Search for Spock*: Why didn't the Organians interfere on the Federation's behalf and stop Kruge before he hurt someone? If Vulcans transfer their "beings" into another living being, and then have it transferred back into their own bodies, are there *any* dead Vulcans?

The Organians, having stopped a devastating war in their sector of space, allowed the Federation and the Klingons to go about their business once a treaty was signed. The treaty was always called the "Organian peace treaty" because of the reason it was negotiated; violations probably wouldn't bring the Organians down, only war would. And the treaty was designed to keep that mutually unwanted event from happening. So while the Organians were probably keeping an eye on Genesis (one must assume they, too, once discovered the process), and while Kruge's incursion into Federation space and murderous actions completely violated the treaty, things were not serious enough for them to interfere.

Arden seems to have misunderstood what happens to a Vulcan's *katra*, or soul. It is contained in the mind of another, presumably a close friend or relative, until it can be joined with the souls of millions of others at Mount Seleya. The bodies remain dead, although needed for the ritual, and the individual does not come back to life. Just his spirit lives on in another plane of existence. Although we didn't know it at the time, this "death of the soul" as well as of the body would explain the tortured mental screams that Spock heard in "The Immunity Syndrome."

Scott Osimitz, of Racine, WI, wants to know why Starfleet didn't use the *Enterprise*'s prefix code to take command of it (as Kirk did to the *Reliant* in *Wrath of Khan*) and prevent it from leaving spacedock.

In *Wrath of Khan* you'll remember that Spock worried that Khan might have changed the *Reliant* prefix code; that's exactly what Scotty did to the *Enterprise*. At the same time, he arranged to override *spacedock's* prefix code (we can safely assume all Starfleet ships and bases have such) and ordered the space doors to open wide.

Jerry Modene, Alexandria, LA, has several questions:

1. How come Admiral Morrow says the *Enterprise* is twenty years old? It's closer to forty years old if you add the time Captains April and Pike had the ship before Kirk took over—twenty years ago.

Morrow was undoubtedly referring to the "new" *Enterprise*—the one which had major redesign and refitting at the time of *Star Trek: The Motion Picture*. Sure, that wasn't nearly twenty years in the past Star Trek time, but Morrow seemed to be wrong about everything else, so why not that?

2. Why does Scotty not like the *Excelsior*?

Probably because, it pains me to say, Scotty is getting a little old and "sot" in his ways. I personally believe that despite his confident predictions to Kirk, he secretly feared a decommissioning of the *Enterprise* (knowing so well her extensive damage; damage that internal computer systems would automatically relay to spacedock), and his bitterness just slipped out when he was confronted by "the future."

3. Where does Carol Marcus fit in with Kirk's past? Obvious answer: she has *got* to be that "little blond lab technician" that Kirk almost married, referred to by Gary Mitchell in "Where No Man Has Gone Before."

I didn't like this suggestion at first (a couple of other readers also thought of it), but it's kind of growing on me. On first glance, the time frame seems wrong. Mitchell had to have "aimed" the girl at Kirk while both of them where still in the Academy—the whole idea was to distract hard-nosed instructor Kirk—a good ten, twelve years before Kirk took command of the *Enterprise*. Add that to the fifteen to seventeen that've passed since, and it would seem to make David too young to be the child of "lab technician" and Kirk. But we're not really told David's age, are we? Sure, he *looks* like he's in his early twenties, but looks can be deceiving. If you take into account his degrees, he had to have spent seven or eight years in school, which would make him at least twenty-five anyway. (I'm assuming that while David might qualify as a genius, he wasn't a child prodigy.) So let's say that, yes, Carol Marcus is the woman referred to in "Where No Man," and that David Marcus was the indirect result of Gary Mitchell's machinations.

(Jerry also rightly points out that only sexist pig Gary Mitchell would refer to a (future) Nobel Prize-winning astroscientist as a "little blond lab technician," and that his line about "outlining her whole campaign for her" was probably just bull.)

4. Where did the Klingons get a bird of prey? Why only a crew of twelve?

The Romulan/Klingon alliance might still survive by the time of *The Search for Spock*; but probably not, knowing the Klingon pro-propensity for betrayal. Even so, it lasted a number of years and resulted in an extensive amount of shared technology. For instance, Romulans generally began to use Klingon-design capital ships, and the Klingons got access to the cloaking device.

As the bird of prey motif is definitely Romulan in origin, there's no doubt that the Klingons got the design, if not the ship itself, from them. Probably the Romulans are more skilled in designing small, fast scout ships that would be manned by very small crews. The Klingons, zenophobic though they are, at least recognize quality in weaponry and technology. The versatile bird of prey design (the ship can land on a planet, something the *Enterprise* or a Klingon battlecruiser *can't* do) is ideal for the kind of spying done in *The Search for Spock*. (And if you really think Kruge was acting without the knowledge of the Klingon High Command . . . well, I've got this bridge in Brooklyn for sale. . . .)

5. Could Captain Styles be the same man from "Balance of Terror" or some relation?

Sorry, the spelling is different. It's "Stiles" in "Balance." And, of course, we all know that that Stiles learned his lesson and went on to be a compassionate unprejudiced officer.

Our next letter is from Barry Silbert, of Brooklyn, NY. (Hmmm . . . maybe he'd be interested in that bridge I mentioned . . .) Barry wants to know how, in *The Search for Spock*, could Chekov take part in initiating the destruct sequence?

Even though they were in Federation space, old hands like Kirk and Scotty wouldn't have neglected to reprogram the destruct sequence. Chekov and Scotty were put into the sequence because Kirk knew they would already be onboard, unlike Sulu, who might have been wounded or captured in the escape attempt. (Yes, Kirk or McCoy might have been wounded, captured, or even killed as well, but without them, there wouldn't have been much point in going.)

Christine Pulliam, of Austin, TX, asks how, if my explanation of how the food selector works (*The Best of Trek £5*) is correct, did the tribbles get into the coffee and chicken sandwiches?

The dispenser port in the rec room and elsewhere only serve to deliver the food; the fabricators that prepare it take up considerably more room and are elsewhere. (Probably the cooked food is beamed to the port by a low-power transporter mechanism rather than physically delivered by dumbwaiters or pneumatic tubes or other antiquated systems we have today.) As the tribbles had worked their way into the ship's inner hulls, they had access to the delivery ports and just helped themselves to the meal before Kirk could open the door.

Christine also wants to know why, when McCoy changed history in "City on the Edge of Forever," didn't Kirk, Spock, and the rest of the landing party disappear as the *Enterprise* did. Because they were physically on the planet and under the Guardian's influence—literally removed from time and protected from any changes.

Betty Muller, of Pearl River, LA, has two questions. If Stone in "Courtmartial" was once a starship captain and now commands Starbase 12, why does he wear red and not gold?

The shirt colors represented areas of service—command, science, ships' services—and Starbase 12 is obviously considered a service station (ouch). Seriously, as commander of a base that is probably basically devoted to engineering, Stone correctly wears the red.

Betty also asks why Jim Kirk just doesn't wear contact lenses. Well, Kirk didn't seem to know what glasses were, so one might easily assume that contacts are equally rare. But McCoy had the lenses of the glasses ground to fit Kirk, so the technology still exists. Kirk, allergic to Retinax 5, is probably also allergic to contact lenses or the twenty-third-century equivalent. He's probably not overly handicapped, since his readers etc. could be programmed to compensate, but it must have been a nuisance to have everything within two feet or so be a blur.

Matt "Trekker" Gensert of Columbus, OH, asks several questions, including this poser. In "The Enemy Within," when Captain Kirk was beamed aboard, the insignia on his uniform was missing. The same with his evil twin. But when Kirk went to McCoy's office, it was back on.

Doggone it, I think William Shatner *knew* I would be doing these mystery articles one day, and made a lot of these errors on purpose! Okay, the insignia on Starfleet uniforms are made of a special material that helps a transporter beam lock on to an officer. As the transporter was malfunctioning, the special material in the insignia did not materialize properly for a few moments, more or less literally blending in with the color and fabric of the Kirks' shirts, and only visibly materialized a few minutes later, while Kirk was en route to McCoy's office. (If the transporter operator had been as observant as Matt, all of the trouble might have been avoided.)

Matt also wants to know why, in the same episode, didn't Fisher split into two halves like Kirk and the dog? Because Fisher was the carrier of the magnetic dust that fouled up the transporter in the first place, and it didn't go awry until he had completely gone through the beaming process. It then duplicated the *next* person through—Kirk.

Richard Scarborough, of Houston, TX, wants to know if all Vulcans speak English.

English per se is not what Kirk and his crew speak anyway, Richard. They speak Federation Standard, which is probably based on our form of English (as English has become the standard form of intercommunication today) and quite similar to it, but containing words and phrases from a thousand alien worlds, as well as technical jargon and slang that won't even be invented for another hundred years. It would bear as much relation to our English as the "English" spoken by Chaucer. But to get to the heart of your question: no, probably not. It is likely that the ubiquitous universal translator was around in "Amok Time" and "Journey to Babel," especially. But it is safe to assume that a majority of Vulcans would speak Standard for the same reasons people in other countries learn English today—it is the language of trade and technology, and if you really want to keep up, you have to know it and know it well.

Terri Chick of Garland, TX, has two questions. In *Wrath of Khan*, Saavik was wearing a red stud earring in her left ear. According to *Dwellers in the Crucible*, this is the symbol of an unbonded female. Where did the earring go in *The Search for Spock*?

Many fans would like to believe that Saavik and David became bonded in the time between *Wrath of Khan* and *The Search for Spock*. Not true, I'm afraid. As we all know, Saavik very much changed her "look" around this time, opting for a less severe hairstyle and affecting a more "Vulcan" makeup. She probably opted to stop wearing the earring, either for variety's sake, or, more logically, because she was now on active duty, rather than still in training at the Academy.

Terri also asks why Khan expected the *Enterprise* to have more information about Genesis than did *Reliant*?

Terri is right; any normal, sane person would expect the ship assigned to a mission to have the most information, but Khan was neither normal nor sane. He was seeking any excuse to get revenge upon Kirk and he rightly assumed that if he found the *Enterprise*, Kirk would not be far behind.

Amanda Wray of Camaulla, CA, has a question about "The Paradise Syndrome." She wants to know why Scotty didn't show surprise or happiness upon hearing Kirk's voice after he had been missing for nearly two months?

Scotty was in command up there, and so on his best behavior. Besides, being the faithful officer he is, I'm sure he fully expected Kirk to be alive and well and waiting for them to arrive.

Michael Poteet of Raleigh, NC, wants to know several things. In *Star Trek: The Motion Picture*, Kirk orders Scotty to prepare Order 2005, the self-destruction of *Enterprise*. This would seem to mean it only takes one officer to begin the countdown. Yet this contradicts the series and *The Search for Spock*, in which it took three officers to engage the sequence.

The self-destruct order Kirk tells Scotty to prepare in *STTMP* is obviously a different kind than we see in the series. The one we've seen is a countdown self-destruct, that cannot be reversed after a certain time. The self-destruct Kirk ordered in *STTMP* is probably one that allows the captain to initiate an instantaneous explosion at his discretion, which is what Kirk would have wanted in order to destroy Vejur at the best possible moment. Also, it is unclear if that self-destruct also required codes from other officers—things never got that far.

Michael asks: Can transporters be operated from the bridge? As you'll remember, a woman on the bridge of the Khan-commanded *Reliant* beams up the Genesis Missile from her bridge post.

We definitely know that the transporter can be overridden from the bridge (although that never seems to work, somehow), so it is logical to assume it can be *activated* from there, as well. But I would think the participation of someone in the transporter room itself would be needed. Probably Khan had someone in the transporter room ready to lock on to the missile as soon as they located it, and had the final activation set up on the bridge so he could monitor it closely and simply nod to the woman to do so, rather than saying the order out loud and giving Kirk or someone else a chance to stop the beam or destroy the missile. Khan wasn't dumb, he was just nuts.

Michael adds: In the television series, are the doors operated by those little pushbuttons to the side or are they activated by sensors? I've seen them operated both says.

Those little buttons are privacy seals, requiring a push to unlock (If the person inside verbally agrees, of course). On things like labs, etc., they are probably simple little identifying sensors that approve authorized personnel and allow them in even as they push the button. Naturally, the more sensitive the area, the more elaborate the security precautions, but in most cases, the buttons do.

Michael finishes up by asking the reason why Janice Rand left the *Enterprise*.

All theories about her unrequited love for Kirk aside, the plain and simple unvarnished truth is probably that Janice felt she was at a career dead end. Captain's yeoman isn't exactly the way to fame and fortune in Starfleet. Also, it is quite possible that she was just transferred off as a matter of course—as Kirk had no special reason to keep her around, he wouldn't have interfered. Maybe the poor girl even got a quick, absentminded good-bye from him. Maybe.

Philip Eckert of Edmonton, Canada, asks a question about something a lot of people noticed in *Star Trek III: The Search for Spock*. Why are there Chinese Vulcans? Perhaps Vulcans also have the same diversity of colors and features as we do, but it seems to me others should have been shown before that.

Why? Up until the time of *The Search for Spock*, we saw, what, twenty or thirty Vulcans, tops? Heck, you can wander down the hall in this office building and see twenty or thirty people, and not one of them will be Chinese—or Indian or Black or Mexican. Wander down a hall in Hong Kong, however, and it is a different story. Yes, we didn't know until *The Search for Spock* that there were Vulcans with "Oriental" features, but it makes sense: IDIC would logically have developed among a people very diverse in appearance, custom, language, and life-style. If Vulcans had all been just alike from the beginning, why would they treasure differences?

Glenn Horvath of White Bear Lake, MN (what a beautiful name!) has an "unsolvable" mystery for me: "In 'Space Seed,' Spock reported that Earth did indeed have a nuclear war, a 'third world war in which millions of people died,' but in 'Return to Tomorrow,' Kirk tells Sargon, 'We survived our early nuclear crisis. We found the wisdom not to destroy ourselves.' So what gives?"

Unsolvable, my eye! This stuff is my meat, kiddo! Nuclear weapons were used during the Genesis Wars (also referred to as World War III), resulting in the deaths of millions of people, but apparently cooler heads prevailed before enough weapons were detonated to cause a world-wide holocaust or the theoretical "nuclear winter." Kirk was referring to the wisdom of those who stopped the bombs and made peace, allowing mankind to survive and progress onward.

He was obviously downplaying events a little for Sargon by referring to the wars as "a crisis," but then he was acting as a representative of the Federation and literally negotiating.

Several people have wondered why we see so many white faces onboard the *Enterprise* when a truly multiracial ship would reflect the majority of black, brown, and yellow skin tones found on Earth. Perhaps the Genesis Wars explain that, as well.

It is horrible to contemplate, but very possible that much of the population of Asia and Africa was destroyed in those wars. Khan, after all, was based in Asia, and it is a cinch he and his followers were primary targets. Could the Eugenics Wars have been fought, at least at first, among the "supermen" themselves? It is quite easy to believe so. We could even hypothesize that Khan escaped Asia and ended up somewhere in Europe, where he sought and got pledges of loyalty from a new batch of "Aryan supermen," explaining the strange preponderance of blond hair and blue eyes found in his followers in *Star Trek II: The Wrath of Khan*.

Several questions were asked by Raymond Hoey, somewhere in the armed forces. Raymond first wants to know about phaser settings, wondering which setting was used by Captain Terrell when he killed himself in *Wrath of Khan*, and also asks me to explain the difference between the phaser settings "kill," "stun," and "disintegrate."

Actually, the settings are "disintegrate" (or sometimes "disrupt"), "heat," and "stun." Disintegrate is the highest setting, of course, and the setting a phaser is on when someone says it is "set to kill." There is probably an adjustable range of heat settings; for example, Sulu uses one to heat up a rock red hot, and we've seen them used to cut bulkheads like a torch several times. "Stun" is the lowest setting, an energy burst that hits a person like an electrical charge, knocking him senseless and causing muscular contractions. The word *phaser* itself describes the ability of the beam to phase from one kind of energy to another or use them simultaneously. For example, a phaser beam launched at an opposing starship might be a deadly and effective combination of heat and energy beams, disrupting, melting, and cutting.

Raymond also asks why the crew of the *Reliant* used wrist communicators instead of hand communicators?

Remember that Terrell and Chekov were in bulky environment suits with thick gloves. In those circumstances, wrist communicators, even though serving only as a backup to the suits' internal systems, made more sense.

Finally, Raymond wanted to know why the Klingon bird-of-prey ship's cloaking device left a distortion area Kirk and Sulu could see.

As we all know, Kirk and Spock captured a prototype of the cloaking device way back when, and although Starfleet has apparently never adopted it for their own use, we may assume that their instruments are attuned to it. Klingons and Romulans, uninterested in anything much but weaponry, continue to use and refine the cloak despite its terrific drain on energy and dilithium crystals. The sophisticated viewscreen in the *Enterprise*, even with damaged systems, gave Sulu an indication of *something* moving out there.

Laurie Lu Leonard of Calgary, Alberta, Canada, wants to know why Chekov's eardrum was not broken by the entry of the Ceti Eel, rendering him deaf, and also why the eel came out of Chekov instead of killing him.

Obviously, this tiny, insidious creature does more than simply burrow through the ear into the brain and "wrap itself around the cerebral cortex." Without getting too technical, I would guess the eel doesn't even leave the ear canal, and that a drug it injects into the canal, and subsequently the brain, does the rest. (Khan's "explanation" of how the eel invaded the brain was obviously colored to heighten the *Reliant* officers' fears.) Chances are the eel exiting the canal, as it did with Chekov, was nothing unusual. It is the toxin it leaves that does the damage, and that was probably quickly and efficiently reversed by Dr. McCoy (with drugs unfortunately not possessed by Khan and his people).

Brenda Gallaher of New Braunfels, TX, writes, "I always thought Uhura was Swahili and not Bantu as some novels say. Which is she?"

No great mystery, here, Brenda. Uhura is of mixed ancestry, mostly Bantu. Swahili is a trade language; there are no "Swahili people."

Another of my Canadian friends, Moira Grunswell of London, Ontario, asks, "Why would the Klingon bird of prey have landing capability *and* a transporter? Wouldn't one do?"

No, it wouldn't. The transporter is a way of getting people up or down to a planet quickly and efficiently. But there is still the need to land physically on a planet, for a variety of reasons. Large starships, such as the *Enterprise*, use shuttlecraft for this purpose;

the much smaller bird of prey can operate within an atmosphere and therefore land on its own.

Mimi Brooks of Mermiston, OR, writes: "In 'What Are Little Girls Made Of?' the android Kirk said that George Samuel Kirk had three sons. Yet in 'Operation: Annihilate,' Sam Kirk had only one son. Can you please explain the difference?"

Obviously, the android was in error. The real Kirk skillfully pretended otherwise, not wishing to give Korby any reason to suspect his creation was not perfect.

Ken Crawford of Victoria, B.C., Canada, invites me to choose from a long list of mysteries he submitted. I chose two at random. Ken first wants me to explain how Kirk could have studied Garth of Izar's exploits at the Academy when Garth hardly looked much older than Kirk.

Okay. We know Kirk was about thirty-five at the time of that episode, and he had already established quite a name for himself. Garth *did* look older than Kirk; he appeared to be about fifty. Therefore, when a twenty-year-old Kirk was at the Academy, a thirty-five-year-old Garth could have been out there doing things to make the textbooks and dazzle and inspire cadets.

Ken also asks: "In 'Amok Time,' Spock is terribly ashamed to talk about his mating drive to Kirk, his best friend. Yet in 'The Cloud Minders,' he talks about it casually. Why?"

Probably because once the ice had been broken, so to speak, Spock examined the entire episode logically and found it to be of relatively little importance. Yes, I remember that he said that Vulcans found it difficult to speak of *pon farr* even among themselves, but that is just the point: *Vulcans* might avoid the subject of sex, but humans (and apparently also Droxine) talk about it incessantly. By the time of "Cloud Minders" the subject had no meaning for Spock, and became just one more bit of human babble for him to contend with. And, if nothing else, you have to remember that Spock is, above all, polite . . . in this case, I might even say gallant.

Patricia Dong of Sunnyside, NY, wants to know who was in command of the *Enterprise* when Sulu is suffering from electrical shock and everyone else is down on the planet.

We never saw, but I would suspect it was the faithful Lieutenant DeSalle, who we often saw step in unsung and unflappable in other crisis situations.

Two questions come from Steve Linak of Grand Rapids, MI. He

wants to know why no crew members were affected by the energy barrier at the edge of the galaxy in "By Any Other Name," and "Is There in Truth No Beauty?"?

Simple. Federation scientists had long since identified the unique energy from instrument recordings on the *Enterprise* and constructed an effective shielding against it. Why? Who knows if that energy might not be encountered elsewhere in the galaxy, with equally disastrous results.

Steve also wanted to know how, if Spock was on *total* life support at the beginning of "Spock's Brain," McCoy was able to keep him alive with just a "headband"?

Spock was left for dead by the Imorg female, and McCoy slapped him on full life support to stabilize him. Once the control headpiece was installed, it provided the autonomic functions that kept Spock's body temporarily alive and mobile.

Chris Mullins of Lexington, KY, has a couple of oddball questions about *Wrath of Khan*: "Khan said that the shock of Ceti Alpha VI's explosion shifted the orbit of Ceti Alpha V. Since space is a vacuum, no shock wave could have traveled through it. What is your explanation for this?"

Simple. Ceti Alpha V's orbit was shifted by the change in gravitational forces caused by the absence of Ceti Alpha VI. This could be considered a shock of sorts, but not a shock wave.

Chris also points out that when Terrell and Chekov materialized on Ceti Alpha V, Chekov had his leg bent, resting on a large rock. How did he know to bend his leg?

Chekov, as we all know, aspires to be a hero, like his hero, Admiral Kirk. Therefore, wanting to be a hero, Chekov would, at every opportunity, strike a heroic pose. And, as everyone who's ever seen a Viking movie knows, one leg resting on a rock is definitely a heroic pose. Chekov may be unlucky, but he definitely has heroic style.

Sandra Detrixhe of Ames, KS, wants to know why, in "The Changeling," Spock said, "It's not the Nomad *we* launched from Earth." Does the Federation go back that far?

Spock was speaking generically, as he would if saying, "We believe in peace," when speaking of his friends and crew. The question is notable if only because it reveals how much Spock identifies with Earth and Earth culture, even if he does not consciously realize it himself. Any other Vulcan, even a member of the Federation or

Starfleet, would probably have said something like, "it is not the same Nomad launched from Earth," conspicuously leaving out the "we."

Keith Saturno of Rochester, NY, has three questions, the first two from "City on the Edge of Forever." At the end of the episode, how were seven people able to beam up at one time? Isn't the limit six? And when Kirk asks Spock, "What is this thing, Mister Spock?" the Guardian doesn't respond. But when he asks, "What is it?" it announces that it has waited for a question. Why didn't it respond to Kirk's first question? Don't say because it was directed to Spock; both questions were.

Ah, but the second question did not have the directive "Mr. Spock" at the end of it, therefore leaving it open to interpretation by the Guardian's programming as answerable. As to the beaming question, the seventh person either arrived at one of the secondary transporters aboard the ship or else was held suspended until a pad was open to receive his signal. This is possible, and probably done quite a bit more often than we saw. Remember, we almost invariably saw landing parties and such beam down, and they are usually limited to six or less.

For his third question, Keith wants to know why the parasites in "Operation: Annihilate" needed to have their human hosts build spaceships if they could travel through space on their own. Travel through unprotected space was probably dangerous even for those loathsome creatures, Keith. Additionally, spaceships would allow them to take their human hosts with them.

A quartet of questions were submitted by Fred Schaefer of Wolcott, CT. In "The Naked Time," during Spock's emotional breakdown, he falls back against the briefing-room doors just after he enters them. How?

The sensors aboard the *Enterprise* are sophisticated enough to distinguish between someone walking toward the doors and a person slipping backward against them. It's simply a safety factor.

In "The Conscience of the King," why would Kodos become an actor and parade on stage in front of the whole Federation?

Haven't you ever read Edgar Allan Poe's famous story, "The Purloined Letter"? In it, an important letter was hidden by the simple device of putting it out in plain sight. If it was so visible and unguarded, it couldn't have been important. Kodos used the same reasoning—the "resemblance" of Karidian to

Kodos may have been remarked many times, but who would ever think a famous actor was the notorious mass murderer? No one except Kirk, of course . . .

In "Whom Gods Destroy," Garth was taught dangerous cellular metamorphosis by the inhabitants of Antos IV. Why isn't this planet off limits, just like Talos IV?

Garth was first smashed beyond the ability of humans to repair; he was taught (or given) the power of cellular transformation in order for him to survive. Any other human would have to go through the same trauma, without any guarantee of survival. Seems to me like not too many people would want to go through the trouble. Besides, what makes you think the Antosians would teach the secret to anyone else? Remember, Garth had just saved their planet and they were unbelievably grateful to him.

In "Patterns of Force," Kirk and Spock are injected with transponders. This is a nifty idea; so nifty, why didn't they do it all the time?

The transponders were used because they knew they were going into a situation where the use of communicators might not be possible. You'll also remember that Kirk didn't seem exactly thrilled with the idea—I don't think you would be too thrilled either to have a device with enough energy in it to emit a phaser beam buried in your arm, huh?

I'm getting silly, it's getting late, and my husband is standing at the door tapping his foot impatiently. Before I end this selection of mysteries, however, I must thank all of you who took the time to write and tell me what "NCC" stands for. It is, for course, "Naval Construction Contract," a designation of airplanes used prior to World War II, and placed on the *Enterprise* by former warbird pilot Gene Roddenberry for nostalgia's sake. Many of you didn't know (or forgot, as I did) what "NCC" meant, and offered some extremely creative suggestions. Again, thanks to all of you, and I'll try to keep my rusty little brain in better shape in the future.

Thanks again and please keep those mysteries coming! I can't promise when I'll be able to pen another article, but please be assured I read each and every letter G. B. and Walter forward to me, and that my tired little brain is always busy dreaming up answers to your questions. Much love to you all and I will see you next time! Bye!

STAR TREK: THE NEXT GENERATION—REVIEW AND COMMENTARY

by Walter Irwin

Rumors had been flying fast and furious for months: a new Star Trek series was in the works. One source said that it was to feature the adventures of Captain Sulu and First Officer Saavik, with occasional visits from the other series regulars. Another "insider" said that the new series would feature new actors in the roles of Kirk, Spock, etc., but that all of the stories would be about them in their younger days. Still another rumor swore that the series would simply take up where the last film left off . . . with Kirk and crew heading out in NCC-1701-A. Well, we now know what Gene Roddenberry was really planning. But for a Star Trek fan, the bottom line is simple: is it Star Trek? In the following review, Walter asks the same question, and provides not one, but two answers.

Star Trek: The Next Generation made its debut with a two-hour telefilm titled "Journey to Farpoint." The show qualified as a pilot not only in that it was the first episode filmed, but also in the more prosaic sense that it introduced the major characters and their relationships to each other, as well as setting up the world they inhabit and the rules it works under.

As a pilot film, the episode was entirely successful. We met the crew—Captain Jean-Luc Picard; his first officer, Commander William Riker; the second officer, Lieutenant Data; ship's surgeon, Dr. Beverly Crusher; Chief Helmsman Lieutenant Geordi LaForge; Security Chief Natasha "Tasha" Yar; and Bridge Officer Worf—and got a nice, if incomplete look at the new ship, the U.S.S. *Enterprise*, NCC-1701-D, and its company of Starfleet personnel and their civilian families and friends. We also met, in true pilot tradition, the being who looks as if he (it? she? they?) will become the recurring nemesis of Picard and Company, the enigmatic "Q."

As a story, the film was less successful. The story lines of Q's threat and the mystery of Farpoint were not well integrated. Q's acquiescence to Picard's suggestion that he judge them by their success on Farpoint was too quick, a little too patent for script purposes. Even worse was Q's blatant attempts to force Picard to choose wrongly at the climax of the episode. The last thing needed then was a false infusion of "suspense": we in the audience had already guessed much of the mystery and knew Picard must have, too. The amateurish theatrics that ensued helped to destroy much of the sense of wonder the moment should have generated.

It is a science-fiction axiom that the actions of aliens, being of alien motivation and therefore incomprehensible to humans, do not necessarily have to make sense by human standards. Unfortunately, many science-fiction writers have seen this as license to create creatures/characters that can do literally anything, without the need for reason or explanation.

Such is the case with Q. We—and Picard—are not given sufficient reason why humans are the targets of his rancor. One would reasonably expect that any race advanced enough to perform seeming miracles would be advanced enough to recognize historical evolutionary progression among humans—or, if nothing else, to read the minds and emotions of the crew of the *Enterprise* and see in them that their intentions are benign. Since this does not happen, we are left with only one conclusion: either Q (or "the Q") simply do not want to understand humanity, or they cannot—so much for godhood.

We are left, then, with yet another childish, spiteful, petty tin-plated super-alien, acting like a complete ass by any reasonable standards of behavior simply for the purposes of the plot.

It's old, it's tiresome, and it's been done before, too many times. In fact, it's been done at least four times on Star Trek alone! It was quite disappointing to see Gene Roddenberry and his staff emerge with such a hackneyed plot device for the first new Star Trek episode.

How much more interesting it would have been to have Q be a calm, reasonable being engaging in civilized debate with Picard. Yes, the threat of destruction would still have been there, and it would have been even more chilling. . . . Who wants to think that he would fail a test of ethics when judged fairly and impartially? Especially if such failure would result in the confinement of your entire race—a confinement that would, sooner or later, result in the death of that race.

The second plot of the pilot, the mystery of Farpoint Station, was not a lot more original, but it was at least handled more effectively, if only because the *Enterprise* crew members went about solving the mystery in a scientific and methodical fashion that smacked of realism. If they didn't catch on any too soon, well, that happens in real life occasionally. And the proper scientific method is to investigate all possibilities before making a hypothesis.

My only complaint with the Farpoint mystery scenes is the overly histrionic fashion in which Groppler Zorn acted and the offhand manner in which he and everyone else described the methods of "construction." It is hard to believe that the Federation would have decided to build a Starfleet station without knowing *how* it was to be built; simple security and integrity of construction would demand more than a cursory examination, if nothing else. And if Groppler Zorn and his people acted in the same sullen, evasive manner to Starfleet negotiators as they did to Picard and Riker, the real mystery is why Starfleet ever accepted the deal in the first place.

The ending did manage to mesh the two plots effectively enough. The scenes of the alien "jellyfish" creatures reuniting were well done and quite moving. And it did bring back a little of that old Star Trek spine tingle to hear Picard say, "Let's see what's out there!"

There is no doubt that Patrick Stewart as Captain Jean-Luc Picard is the star of the show. Although not a particularly impressive physical specimen, he has a presence that literally takes command of every scene, the same kind of presence an actual Starfleet starship commander would have.

Stewart's Shakespearean training is evident with every line he speaks. And the viewer has to be careful these days . . . Stewart holds to the time-honored British tradition of "throwing away" the occasional line. Let your attention wander, and you just might miss something.

The ship is new to Picard, but not brand new. He is still finding his way about and around her, but does not lack for confidence in either himself or his ship. That he is uncomfortable with children comes as no surprise—the surprise is that he feels it a flaw, and makes sure it is one that is corrected before it hampers the operation of his ship.

This scene, as well as the one in which Picard orders Riker to manually dock the ship, tell us that Picard is a perfectionist, expecting nothing but the best from himself as well as others. But he is not a martinet; he understands the necessity for families aboard the *Enterprise* (although he may not agree with the policy) and works to make the best of what he sees as a bad situation. Picard is the kind of man who tries to plan for every eventuality, and I suspect that if he has any qualms and second thoughts about his command, they come from the things he feels he should have foreseen and did not.

He's not a physical man. We will not see Picard leaping from his command chair to rush down to an unknown planet, nor are we likely to see him in one-on-one combat with an enemy. He is a cerebral captain given to consideration of a problem before acting, taking all possible available advice, waiting to see rather than waiting for the main chance. Picard may act wrongly, he will never act impulsively.

The problem with such an approach is twofold. First, Picard probably is not a gambler. Risks are part of the job, but Picard will believe more in preparedness than bluff. Although this is probably a realistic view of what a starship captain would be like, it does tend to downplay the thrills and fun a little bit. We Star Trek fans have been conditioned to want our captains to be a little bit roguish and unpredictable.

Second, a thinking captain is more likely to capitulate than an "action" captain. Not out of cowardice or a conviction that he cannot win, but out of a desire to make the best of a situation. In the pilot, I felt that Picard surrendered a little too quickly to Q. Yes, he was protecting the families in the saucer section, but maybe it would have been better to put up at least the pretense of a fight. If Q would have been savvy enough to pick up on the importance of the saucer, he would have made for it instead of the engineering section.

In all, however, Stewart's Picard is a worthy addition to the ranks of starship captains. He manages to combine dignity and authority with just the right touch of idealism and enchantment with space to be believable. The ultimate test is passed: we would not mind shipping out under Captain Picard.

We cannot yet be quite so sure about Jonathan Frakes's Commander William Riker. Frakes got to do very little in the way of real acting in the pilot, and his scenes as Riker, although plentiful once he was introduced, had nothing to particularly impress or endear him to us. The only memorable scene, in fact, was his short idyll in the forested rec room when in search of Data. I hope that plans call for Riker and Data to become friends, as they interacted very well here, and it was during these scenes that Frakes seemed most at ease.

Obviously, Riker will carry the brunt of whatever action is to be found in this new series (by all reports, there will be less in the way of violent, physical action than in the original series and the films), aided and abetted by "away team" regulars LaForge and Data. As we now have a reflective captain, we can only expect to have a first officer who is more a man of direct action, and who will counsel same when asked.

It is nice to see Riker acting as Picard's first officer—officially issuing commands, serving as his liaison with the crew, taking responsibility for the day-to-day operations of the ship. Again, it is one of those touches of reality so desperately needed in a science-fiction series. (Of course, if Riker really did fulfill all the duties of a first officer of a ship of the line, we would hardly see him. He certainly wouldn't be beaming down; he'd be far too busy.)

Although Roddenberry and Paramount publicity have constantly reiterated that "There will be no Big Three" in this series, because "everyone is a star," events of the pilot immediately give the lie to what we all knew was patent nonsense anyway. Picard and Riker sit alongside the ship's counselor, Deanna Troi, in an arrangement that brooks no argument about who is in command and who is important. (Actually, given the likely high visibility of Dr. Crusher, we will probably end up with a Big Four on this show—kind of a *Bob and Carol and Ted and Alice* in space.)

Picard and Riker must, of course, be involved in every major decision, and even though the series postulates that Captain Picard will consult his entire staff whenever possible, making for scenes in which all the regulars put their two cents in, when push comes to shove, there will be two or three figures that the show will focus on.

Focus on, not feature. Everyone will be featured before very long—they are all interesting characters, designed to have a vital element of mystery and excitement that piques our interest. We will, sooner or later, learn more about Yar and Worf and LaForge. But in no way will they become the stars of the show.

But Data just might. Dismissed before the series began by many fans as "the worst idea about the show," Data looks to be his own man, if you'll pardon the expression. There's certainly nothing new about android characters—the original series had its share, and so did another Roddenberry project, which we'll discuss in a moment—but it somehow seems right that this new Star Trek, with its unspoken devotion to IDIC, feature a character, and, more importantly an *officer* who is not only not human, but isn't even "alive."

Brent Spiner, the actor portraying Data, is completely engaging, yet still transmits an intelligence and sensitivity that we immediately respond to. A number of fans have remarked on his scenes with the aged Dr. McCoy in the pilot as sure evidence that he is intended to be the "Spock" of this new series, but I believe otherwise. I think that Roddenberry saw immediately that Data has more in common with McCoy than Spock, and that is why he was chosen to speak with the admiral. Gene Roddenberry isn't saying, even in private, but no less of an authority than Majel Barrett Roddenberry has her suspicions that Data might just be one of the last of the Questor androids, left by advanced aliens to guide and protect mankind, as seen in Rodenberry's aborted TV pilot, *The Questor Tapes*.

Data looks completely different, true, and there is no other evidence to support such a suspicion, but it's kind of nice to think that Star Trek is connected with the world of Questor.

We also got a brief look at how Geordi LaForge's optical visor fits on, and a hint that wearing it causes him constant pain. It is refreshing to see that LaForge's "handicap" is not played as such—either way. His vision is used as a tool when necessary; his lack of vision is not used as a story point.

Many fans do not know that the character Geordi is based on a real person, George LaForge. George was an avid Star Trek fan who, although quadriplegic, attended many Star Trek conventions in the early 1970s. His unfailing good humor, bright smile, and quick wit caught the eye and earned the friendship of Gene Roddenberry. Sadly, George died in 1975, but the memory of his intelligence and courage lives on, thanks to Gene Roddenberry and Ensign Geordi LaForge.

A number of fans have dismissed the presence of young Wesley Crusher as a sop to teenage boys, but if I were still a teenage boy, it wouldn't be Wesley I'd like . . . it would be Tasha Yar. I know that when I was thirteen or fourteen, there was nothing I liked better than a good-looking, tough woman. Of course, I'd probably have been scared to death had I met one. . . .

All kidding aside, Roddenberry probably didn't give over-much thought to that aspect of Tasha Yar. What he wanted to give us was a young, tough security chief, a woman who combined beauty and a certain measure of femininity and vulnerability with determination and sheer grit. We learned that Tasha (short for Natasha) is a native of an Earth colony that somehow went wrong and became what might be best described as a planet-sized ghetto.

(As much as we want to learn more of Tasha's origins, the tale of how her planet slipped into such an awful state and why the Federation did nothing to solve the problems, might make for a story that would be just as interesting, if not more so, than hers. To pose only one question the scenario raises: do Federation colonies fall under the restrictions of the Prime Directive?)

I have heard fans comment to the effect that Tasha acted too impulsively in the pilot; other comment says she seems scared or nervous when faced with a security challenge. I must agree that Denise Crosby could have handled some aspects of her character a little better (I personally feel the ever-intense expression and short, chopping sentences grow a little grating), but, like everyone else, Tasha is still growing both as a character and as a member of a team. The intensity she displays now might just, in the future, form the basis of an episode in which that intenseness—or the lack of it—is pivotal to the survival of the ship and crew.

Talking about Tasha reminds us of Worf. They seem to be part of a miniteam working on the bridge, both involved with weapons and scanners. They are also both of a temperament.

Worf, true to his Klingon heritage, is quite ready to fight at all times, and has no hesitancy about speaking out. One of the most interesting moments of the pilot was Worf's anger at being ordered away from the ship before a pending battle. He referred to himself as a Klingon, of Klingon heritage—and although he has obviously taken a vow to serve under and obey Starfleet rules and regulations (and restraints!), he *thinks* of himself as nothing but a Klingon, as well.

We don't yet know Worf's story—scuttlebutt before the series began had it that the Federation and the Klingons were now allies, which is why Worf (and eventually) other Klingons would be seen onboard the *Enterprise*. Other, later rumors state that Worf was rescued from a crashed Klingon ship as an infant and raised in the Federation. His attitude would seem to refute that scenario, but it is possible. Worf was a latecomer to the original cast—although an extremely welcome one—and was therefore not as completely fleshed out as the others.

I'm going to give Deanna Troi short shrift in this review. Mainly because I feel that she, of all the characters, is the one that Roddenberry and his staff will change the most over the next few months, and what she may become might be different enough to dispel any complaints I might have here. Suffice it to say that I very much disliked both the character and her part in the show.

The most background we got on a character in the pilot was that of Dr. Beverly Crusher. Her husband was killed when serving with Picard, a fact that causes continuing tension between them. Beverly is competent, a little bit sassy, and darned good-looking. If there is to be a continuing romance on the show, I would prefer it to be between her and Picard rather than between Riker and Troi. It would be nice to see a starship captain who came "home" every night to relax and maybe just talk things over with a friend and lover.

Wesley Crusher I really don't know about. He seemed like a pretty normal, likable kid, even though of genius level. There's little enough to say about him now. . . . The danger in Wesley lies in allowing him too much screen time. As I stated before, youngsters who watch Star Trek won't be looking for someone to identify with, so there's no need to feature Wesley each week—certainly no need to allow him to become a "Will Robinson" character who is always right while the bumbling adults are always wrong. Too, there is the danger that Wesley will come across as just a little wimpy. The best way to avoid this is to keep him interacting with other kids his age—both boys and girls, Gene!—and show him growing and learning slowly but surely, as we all did (and do).

There is much to admire about *Star Trek: The Next Generation*. The ship is beautiful; the special effects are wonderful (although the shift to videotape is sometimes a little jarring); the production values, sets, and props first-rate; and the actors all competent, with a few outstanding. Roddenberry and Paramount have promised to maintain this level of quality, and with the great number of stations running the show, and the consequent influx of money to the episode budgets *The Next Generation* should remain the best-looking show on television.

The eclectic mix of crew did not work totally in the pilot, but such a large cast needs time to shake out and fall into their respective roles. There is enormous potential among these characters—in Picard, Data, Yar, Crusher, and Worf, especially—and with care and slow development and nurturing, they should become worthy successors to our beloved original crew.

So, the question remains: Is it Star Trek? The answer is a definite yes. *Star Trek: The Next Generation* is completely true to the principles and ideals of the original series. It is also a logical development of both technology and socio/military attitudes in the Federation, the kind of extension of the Star Trek universe many fans have always imagined. No, it is not *Wagon Train to the Stars*—but it *is* an extension of Gene Roddenberry's dream, a continuation of the things we know and love and cherish about Star Trek and what it stands for.

There's another yes, however. *The Next Generation* is also the Star Trek of special effects, aliens (and alien monsters, eventually), glitzy weapons and ships, costumes, and weird-looking beings all over the place. Eventually, it will also be the Star Trek of the books and records and comics and toys and coloring books and pajamas and lunch boxes and . . . And conventions. And jokes. Wisecracks. Snide remarks. The typical dual attitudes of "If it's popular, it can't be good," and "I hate Trekkies" that we despise so and have so sadly become accustomed to.

Yes, my friends, *Star Trek: The Next Generation is* real Star Trek. And once again, we will have to take the good with the bad. Gene Roddenberry and his wonderful staff, along with Paramount Television, have presented us with a wonderful and—to be honest—long overdue gift. But, as always, we are the bottom line: it is up to us to keep the show alive, to make it so much more than even Roddenberry imagines it could be, to make it part of our fandom, our universe, our lives.

When you get right down to it, friends, it doesn't matter if *The Next Generation* is "real Star Trek." It doesn't matter because *we* are the real Star Trek.

SAME SEXISM, DIFFERENT GENERATION

by Tom Lalli

In *Star Trek II: The Wrath of Khan*, as Saavik takes the *Enterprise* out of space dock, Kirk becomes so nervous that McCoy offers the Admiral a tranquilizer. We're amused, but it's unclear *why* Kirk is so agitated. Sulu, as has been pointed out, is not about to crack up the ship no matter who's in command. But if we look at James Kirk as the alter ego of his creator, Gene Roddenberry, this anxiety is understandable. This, after all, is the first time in live-action Star Trek that a female is permitted to command a Federation starship.

Any discussion of the ideology behind Star Trek must begin and end with Gene Roddenberry. As Benjamin Svetkey wrote in his review of *Star Trek: The Next Generation* (in *Rolling Stone*), "you can practically see (Roddenberry's) fingerprints on every frame." Few in history have communicated their personal world-view as effectively to as many people as Gene Roddenberry. His vision is of a united, future Earth free of war, poverty and injustice, whose inhabitants live well into their hundreds. The original Star Trek was so far ahead of its time that it (with *The Next Generation*) is *still* the only memorable television series to portray a positive future for

300

humanity. And it is because Gene Roddenberry is such a remarkably forward-thinking man that Star Trek's sexism is so jarring.

I have long considered sexism to be Star Trek's one great flaw. I was therefore very disappointed when *Star Trek: The Next Generation*, instead of correcting this fault, proved to be nearly as sexist as the original show. Gene Roddenberry had the courage and foresight to propose a female first officer in 1964 (in "The Cage"), but he has not taken similar risks with his new show. Indeed, *The Next Generation* does not keep pace with the strides made toward sexual equality in the last two decades. Gene Roddenberry gets much of the credit for Star Trek's success, and deservedly so. It is becoming painfully clear that he also deserves much of the blame for Star Trek's sexism.

It is often said that Mr. Roddenberry did his best to include women in the original series, but was defeated by the interference of NBC, and the prejudices of the time. This is one of the many excuses that have been offered for Star Trek's sexism and, like most of them, it has some validity. Mr. Roddenberry wanted a crew which was 50 percent female, but the network insisted on only one-third women: Also, Star Trek was produced before the height of the feminist movement (but after the height of the Civil Rights movement, which helps to explain why blacks fared somewhat better on the show than women). The consensus seems to be that the series was actually progressive for its time. But the premiere of *The Next Generation* has cast doubt upon the notion that Star Trek's sexism was due solely to the social climate of the sixties, and it is appropriate to reevaluate some long-held assumptions.

Gene Roddenberry's decision to include women in the crew of his starship was not motivated purely by egalitarian concerns. For dramatic purposes, it was necessary to have women aboard the *Enterprise*. It would have been very cumbersome to "beam up" a female guest star every time sexual tension was required, every time Kirk wanted to flirt, or comfort a frightened "lass." As David Gerrold pointed out in *The World of Star Trek*, women are traditionally seen as a necessary reward for the hero of a story. Star Trek, though set in the future, is in as many ways an old-fashioned show. Its characters are traditional heroes (not anti-heroes), and Roddenberry was influenced by "Horatio Hornblower" and Westerns as much as science fiction.

Historically, in times of crisis or urgency, women have been allowed to temporarily occupy male roles (the settling of the American West and World War II are recent examples); the place of women in Star Trek derived from this tradition as much as it anticipated the feminist movement.

Certainly, Gene Roddenberry went beyond what was then considered necessary when he included women such as Number One and Uhura in Star Trek. Indeed, the pilot that sold the series ("Where No Man Has Gone Before") included only one recurring female character, the forgettable Yeoman Smith. Still, Star Trek's reputation for progressiveness is due more to its *suggestion* of a future society devoted to equal rights than to what was portrayed in the show. In other words, the supposed sexual equality of the Federation was left largely to viewer's imaginations.

Mr. Roddenberry's descriptions of the ship's crewwomen are telling. The *Star Trek Writer's Guide* (from 1967) describes Uhura as a "highly female female off duty." The obvious implication is that, though her career is "unfeminine," Uhura is not the "walking freezer unit" you might expect her to be. A 1977 update of the *Writer's Guide* includes this same description of Uhura. Yeoman Rand, the *Guide* says, is treated equally by her male colleagues "during duty hours." In *The Making of Star Trek*, the "Captain's Yeoman" is described as having "a strip-queen figure even a uniform can't hide." She also dreams of serving her captain "in more personal departments." It is a short step from the captain's yeoman to the "captain's woman" of "Mirror, Mirror."

For Gene Roddenberry, a woman's gender is almost always her definitive trait (though she may resist this). He often describes his female characters as "disturbingly" or "mysteriously" female; most of them have "*very* female bodies." The *Next Generation Writer's Guide* describes both Tasha Yar and Beverly Crusher in such terms: Beverly's "natural walk resembles that of a strip-tease queen." Of course, Mr. Roddenberry's female characters are not defined solely by their sexuality. Still, it's not surprising that such an approach to women has undermined some of the progressive ideals of Star Trek.

Most fans stop short of blaming Star Trek's creator and producer for its sexism. We all feel a great deal of fondness, gratitude, and respect for Gene Roddenberry. He has given us so much that it seems almost a betrayal to level strong criticisms at him or his creations. This feeling, though understandable, is overly defensive.

This article is not an attempt to tarnish Mr. Roddenberry's great accomplishments. Its purpose is to shed light on the attitudes underlying the inadvertent but persistent sexism of his productions. Now that he is producing weekly episodes again, it is important to understand these attitudes, and the reasons for fan tolerance of them.

Despite its progressive ideals, from the beginning Star Trek was especially vulnerable to the encroachment of sexism. Starfleet's mission consists mostly of military and scientific duties, two of the last bastions of male dominance. Even today, many people are very uncomfortable with women serving in the military (when we fear for our safety, we fall back on comforting traditions). And though combat is infrequent in Star Trek, deep-space exploration can be equally terrifying. The fact that Starfleet is a quasi-military organization increased the resistance to sexual equality in Star Trek, and has a significant effect on viewer perceptions, making both Star Trek and *The Next Generation* seem less sexist than they are. Another reason fans have traditionally accepted or belittled Star Trek's sexism is simply that, until recently, there's been little alternative. Most fans came to the show after the last (original) episode had been produced. There was no way to change what had been filmed, so we responded to errors in the show by adjusting Star Trek history in the name of consistency. Some reacted to the show's sexism in this way, often by elevating Yeoman Rand and Nurse Chapel to positions of great importance on the *Enterprise*. Others have found the sexism of the show too severe and offensive to gloss over. These opposite reactions have resulted in wildly divergent views of Star Trek's female characters.

Janice Rand, for example, is a space-age stewardess created by former airline pilot Roddenberry to wait on Captain Kirk. On the other hand, as Beth Carlson wrote in *The Best of Trek #4*, "Starfleet would not have accepted her" if she weren't "a highly proficient and duly qualified professional." This circular logic says that since Rand is in Starfleet, she cannot be a featherbrain, no matter how many times we see her act like one. In *The Star Trek Compendium*, Allan Asherman stresses Rand's "courage, resourcefulness, and loyalty."

Much of the confusion surrounding Rand and Chapel stems from the fact that Star Trek is sexist without being misogynistic. Star Trek insists that most women remain in traditional roles, but within those limits it does provide positive, likable female characters. Because of this, and because Grace Lee Whitney and Majel Barrett make them appealing, we are compelled to defend these women. It's true that Janice Rand and Christine Chapel are trivial characters, present mainly to serve their male superiors, and as potential love partners for Kirk and Spock, But they are not inherently offensive; such women could conceivably be found on the *Enterprise*.

The problem, simply, is that Star Trek discourages deviation from traditional female roles. Women who attempt to do so are almost always punished, though some ("Mudd's Women," Nancy Hedford, Elaan) are redeemed by a return to tradition. And instead of the promised future world of total equality, we see contemporary gender divisions projected into the 23rd century. Excluding the pilot episodes, we never see male communications officers, yeomen, or nurses; these "feminine" positions are reserved for women who choose to serve in male-dominated Starfleet. Although Star Trek challenges many of the "slogans and superstitions" of modern times, its approach to gender roles is distinctly conservative.

In addition to assistants, servants, girlfriends, and wives, Star Trek presents women as helpless victims (Aurelan Kirk, Lt. Arlene Galway, "Wolf in the Fold," Lt. Mira Romaine, Zarabeth); male fantasies ("Shore Leave," Spectre of the Gun"); traitorous femme fatales (Lt. Marla McGivers, T'Pring); witches (Sylvia, Nona); mantraps (Nancy Crater, Vina, Leila Kalomi, Deela, Odona, Losira, "The Lorelei Signal"); mistresses or prostitutes ("Mirror, Mirror," "A Piece of the Action," "Bread and Circuses"); mindless nonpersons (Andrea, Lethe, "The Changeling," "I, Mudd," Shahna, "Spock's Brain," Reena); shrews (Stella Mudd, Elaan); cats (Sylvia, Isis, M'Ress); "cargo" (Mudd's Women"); and even slaves ("The Menagerie," "Gamesters of Triskelion," "Whom Gods Destroy"). (For an overview of women in the original series, see Pamela Rose's "Women in the Federation" in *The Best of Trek #2*.)

Gene Roddenberry has some very old-fashioned ideas about women. But he is also a futurist, a man deeply concerned with ethics, morality, and the fate of humanity. This results in an odd contradiction: Spock is sexist, yet there is also a strain of feminism in the show. The sexism is predominant, but the feminism is never entirely vanquished. Mr. Roddenberry realizes the inevitability of change, and he wanted Star Trek's portrayal of the future to be as realistic as possible. He therefore included (or allowed the inclusion of) a number of strong women in Star Trek. By taking a closer look at these characters, we can better understand why such portrayals were not more common.

Apologists for sexism in Star Trek usually offer the character of Number One as proof of Gene Roddenberry's commitment to sexual equality. The description of Number One in the *Star Trek Format* (from 1964) is of "an extraordinarily efficient officer . . . probably (the captain's) superior in detailed knowledge of . . . the vessel." She is also described as "glacierlike," someone who "enjoys playing it expressionless, cool." In "The Cage," however, Number One does not seem to be enjoying herself. Instead, she is melancholy and distant. Number One was intended to be a symbol of future equality, but she was also the first of many coldly efficient women in Star Trek: (including) Dr. Elizabeth Dehner, Nancy Hedford, Dr. Miranda Jones, and Chief Engineer McDougal (of "The Naked Now").

Though the idea of a female first officer was ahead of its time, this character is also tiresome and sexist. She possesses the stoic nature of Mr. Spock, but without the alien ancestry that would explain her emotional repression. The implication is that a normal woman could never have attained such a high rank in Starfleet. Only by denying her female nature, if not her humanity, has "Number One" (she was never given a name) risen to her post. The idea that women can function professionally only by repressing their natural drives and emotions recurs in Star Trek. And had a one-half-female crew been permitted, it's likely that such stereotypes would have been just as prevalent. (According to Stephen Whitfield's *The Making of Star Trek*, and contrary to popular belief, Gene Roddenberry agreed with NBC's decision to get rid of Number One; not surprisingly, test audiences had reacted negatively to the character.)

Among the more impressive crewwomen in the original series is Dr. Helen Noel, of "Dagger of the Mind." Helen has been criticized because her mind is not on her work during the investigation of the Tantalus penal colony. Though Dr. Noel is a psychiatrist, it is Captain Kirk who uncovers a psychological "chamber of horrors." However, I don't find this particularly sexist, since Kirk is usually one step ahead of everyone else. Actually, Helen Noel is one of the few truly liberated women in Star Trek. She combines intelligence and professional achievements with aggressive, healthy sexuality.

In "Dagger of the Mind," Helen performs heroically in a crisis, killing a man (without using a weapon) and saving Kirk's life. She openly desires Kirk, and (in a fantasy sequence) doesn't mind if his interest in her is purely sexual. She is not ruled by her passions, however, and properly resists Kirk's advances after his mind has been affected by Dr. Adams. Helen is not an emotional cripple like most professional women in Star Trek, and is therefore a threat to Kirk: she dares to compete with him intellectually while challenging his ability to control his own sexuality. To Kirk, such a woman had "better be the best assistant I ever had."

James Kirk (in the series) finds it difficult to cope with a woman who is at once attractive, strong-willed and professional. Thus, many of the stronger female characters in Star Trek are women to whom Kirk would not be sexually attracted. Some are the wrong age (Miri, T'Pau, Amanda), while others are the wrong race (Uhura, Lt. Charlene Masters, Yeoman Tamura). No matter what their personal convictions, 1960s television viewers would instinctively know that Kirk could only become involved with white women of a certain age (even the interracial kiss in "Plato's Stepchildren" is forced by a group of perverts); therefore, the sexual tension which would otherwise exist between Kirk and (for example) Uhura is diffused. Uhura is free to be more liberated than a white woman, since she cannot be a threat to Kirk's dominating sexuality and ego.

"City on the Edge of Forever" is the only episode in which Kirk consciously falls in love with a woman. This necessitates a very unusual story in which the *Enterprise* vanishes and Kirk escapes into the distant past, freed of the urgency of command (most of the episode consists of Kirk and Spock waiting for McCoy to appear). Only in these fantastic circumstances, including the inevitability of his lover's death, can the character Kirk succumb to a woman. Edith Keeler is a strong female character—she must be, to make Kirk's love convincing—but she is far from realistic. She is a fantasy projection (of Kirk's feminine ideal), a stereotype (woman as angel of mercy), and even supernatural (a Christ figure). Kirk, in a state of dreamlike infatuation, doesn't see her as an equal; he puts her on a pedestal (he is often seen gazing up at her). Though "City" is a powerful tragedy, the character Edith Keeler is not a departure from traditional female stereotypes.

Lt. Uhura, of course, is Star Trek's most impressive female character (for a list of her admirable traits, see G.B. Love's "She Walks in Beauty" in *The Best of Trek #4*). Nevertheless, we know less about Uhura as a person than any other regular character; we learned more about Janice Rand in nine episodes than we learned about Uhura in 78. Our love and respect for Uhura owe more to the dignity, charm, and talent Nichelle Nichols brought to the role than to any dialogue or scenes she was given.

She has even inspired the belief in some fans that Uhura is fifth-in-command of the *Enterprise*, but this is blatant revisionism. In "Catspaw," when Kirk, Spock, Scott, and Sulu are detained on the planet, it is Mr. Desalle who takes command. Uhura's one chance to command the ship came during the height of the feminist movement, in the 1973 animated episode, "The Lorelei Signal." Even here, however, she takes command only because the male crew have been imprisoned by alien sirens (who feed off the men's vitality and cause rapid aging). Uhura is never formally given command, nor is she seen in the captain's chair.

The character Uhura was an afterthought. Joseph Sargent, director of "The Corbomite Maneuver," has been quoted (in *Files* magazine's "The Undiscovered Star Trek, Vol. 2") as saying that a black female communications officer was his idea. Mr. Roddenberry agreed to add the character for one reason: to symbolize the futuristic equality of Star Trek's world. Like Number One (and Sulu), Uhura was never given a first name or personal history, and her sexuality is rarely acknowledged. Roddenberry helped to create Uhura, but he could not imagine what would motivate such a woman; she is a career Starfleet officer, yet she is neither brittle nor frigid. Uhura is an anomaly in Star Trek's world, and thus cannot be developed or explained. She is indeed a mysterious female.

Nichelle Nichols makes us forget that Uhura is a symbol, but even she could not escape the sexism of her environment. Uhura's "Captain, I'm frightened," is probably the quintessential example of sexism in Star Trek. Uhura says this because, as the only woman present, she must express the fears of everyone, thus allowing the men to maintain a pretense of fearlessness. As Nichelle Nichols said in *The Star Trek Interview Book*, the show's creators had her provide "female gentleness, tenderness." (Incredibly, such stereotyping is just as evident in *The Next Generation*, twenty years later).

Carolyn Palomas, in "Who Mourns for Adonais?", is not particularly impressive; she seems more the breathy coed than a Starfleet officer. She is remarkable, however, in that the story requires her to *pretend* to be a feminist ("I'm no simple shepherdess you can awe," she tells Apollo). And the only way Kirk can convince her to act as a feminist is by acknowledging the essential sameness of men and women: "Man or woman, it makes no difference—you're *human*." There is great irony here, since Kirk is forced to admit female equality in order to save his ship. It's no wonder he seems pained during this scene.

The original (censored) ending of "Who Mourns for Adonais?" had Carolyn pregnant with her and Apollo's child. This ending would have necessitated her leaving the *Enterprise (The Making of Star Trek* specifies that pregnant women must leave the service, at least temporarily). In "Space Seed" Marla McGivers also left Starfleet, going into exile with Khan. She also held her "female drives" in check long enough to save Kirk and the *Enterprise*. Again, the suggestion is that women can remain in Starfleet only as long as they suppress their natural instincts, or until they find the right man. This not only flatters the male ego, but reduces women's liberation to a form of foreplay.

Most of the women in Starfleet seem to be searching for husbands. Fertility is a recurring theme in Star Trek, and several times we hear references to the human instinct to colonize and populate new territory. Taken together, these facts suggest that Starfleet approves of crewwomen *because* most of them will leave the service to raise a family. The goal is to spread the human race throughout the galaxy, and child-rearing is seen as a woman's proper destiny. (And if the crew is stranded on an alien planet, the presence of women will allow them to begin a colony.)

Star Trek's males resist settling down. In Gene Roddenberry's original pilot, "The Cage," Christopher Pike is captured as "breeding stock." In a perversion of traditional courtship, the temptress Vina (who is in reality deformed) tries to lure him into fathering a human colony. Pike, like Jean-Luc Picard, is much happier traveling the galaxy, and has no use for family life. James Kirk takes this one step farther, living out a male fantasy ("love 'em and leave 'em") by conquering (and probably impregnating) numerous women on countless planets. Many of these women pine away for Kirk for several years afterward. Gene Roddenberry's lyrics to the Star Trek theme are sung by such a woman; she sings of a man on an endless "star trek" who finds "strange love a star woman teaches." The song ends with the words, "tell him while he wanders his starry sea, remember, remember me."

In "The Naked Time," James Kirk laments his lack of a "flesh woman to touch, to hold." In retrospect, this seems silly, considering the number of "flesh women" he's had the pleasure of touching. The original conception of Kirk may have been that of a lonely commander, but he soon became a womanizer, albeit a charming one. As was documented by Walter Irwin in "Jim's Little Black Book" (*The Best of Trek #2*), Jim Kirk can love, seduce, and manipulate women, but he cannot trust them as friends. Star Trek justifies this mistrust by giving many of Kirk's love interests questionable motives.

(Janice Rand is often praised for her "good sense" in transferring off the *Enterprise* to prevent a romance with her captain. It's more likely that Janice and Jim had a brief affair, after which Kirk initiated her transfer. This would be more consistent with what we see in the series; Kirk has little need for his lovers after his passion is gone, and in "The Menagerie" he is embarrassed when word of his sexual exploits catches up with him.)

Since its stars were male, most of the major female roles on Star Trek were played by guest stars. Karin Blair discusses this in her fascinating book, *Meaning in Star Trek*:

"In almost every episode we have a different female guest star, which usually guarantees that . . . she is alien and disposable. Most often she dies, disappears, or remains at the service of a father-figure, if not her actual father."

(On the *Inside Star Trek* record, Gene Roddenberry asks William Shatner why Kirk needed a different girl every week. Shatner jokes that "he uses up the old one!")

Friendly interaction between women is almost nonexistent in Star Trek. Ms. Blair observes that we rarely see a mother-daughter relationship (Deanna Troi and her mother may be the first). Star Trek's typical female character lacks a mother who could "nurture her and defend her right to live"; she "has little existence or identity apart from what the father has created." (The popularity of Edith Keeler and Amanda is partially due to the scarcity of positive maternal figures in the series.) Most of the women in Star Trek are present only to interact with male characters. They are "projections of the masculine psyche," and "allow Kirk to relate to the unconscious feminine side of his own psyche."

Ms. Blair also illustrates how Star Trek represented women through male characters. Dr. McCoy, especially, represents the traditionally feminine side of humanity (such labels, of course, will ultimately seem arbitrary and sexist themselves). McCoy is emotional and compassionate, he dislikes machines, and he "mothers" the crew (he can also tolerate a female assistant). With this in mind, it is not surprising that *The Next Generation*'s two surviving females, Dr. Crusher and Counselor Troi, share what were once McCoy's duties. Also, the fact that Star Trek's all-male "triad" convincingly includes virtually every human characteristic proves that few traits are exclusive to one gender.

Karin Blair's book is remarkable in that it describes the extent of Star Trek's sexism while also explaining why the show offers so much to women. This is reflected in her statement, "Spock . . . is more important to women than Number One could ever have been." Spock's importance to women, which is not limited to his being an object of sexual fantasies, helps to account for their tolerance of Star Trek's sexism.

Though traditionally masculine in many ways, Spock has the ability to communicate with and understand a variety of females, both human and alien. Blair writes, "In reaching out to the feminine, Spock neutralizes the myths and stereotypes that have kept it underground as diabolical or on a pedestal as heavenly." One of the ways to interpret Spock is as a man attempting to acknowledge and commune with the feminine (or "human") side of himself. In "The Naked Time," Spock "learns how to cry"; this has since become the stereotype of the liberated man. Significantly, it is most often McCoy who tries to draw out Spock's emotions (Uhura also does this in McCoy's absence). Spock's struggle to forge an identity from two opposite "selves," in defiance of traditional categories and labels, is an inspiration to those who would free themselves from divisive stereotypes, sexual or otherwise.

Just as rare in Star Trek's universe as a mother-daughter relationship is a truly egalitarian society. Though we'd expect the Federation (based on justice), and particularly Vulcan (based on logic), to practice equality, neither seems to. We see countless patriarchal societies (including those in "Return of the Archons," "Friday's Child," "Bread and Circuses," and Vulcan in "Journey to Babel"), and a sprinkling of matriarchal societies (Vulcan in "Amok Time,"

Roddenberry's pilot "Planet Earth," and *The Next Generation*'s "Angel One"), but never true equality.

NBC is said to have rejected a half-female crew because they thought it would suggest a lot of "fooling around" on the *Enterprise*. But Gene Roddenberry's own failure to portray sexual equality, even on alien planets, surely stems from this old-fashioned idea, that men and women cannot work closely and equally without sex interfering (witness Kirk's discomfort with female assistants, and Ilia's effect on the men in *Star Trek: The Motion Picture*). This "either/or" approach to societal dominance also reflects (and encourages) men's fear that liberated women will bypass equality and "take over."

Indeed, this is what happens in Roddenberry's television pilot film, "Planet Earth." Set in a post-holocaust 22nd century, it portrays a sadistic matriarchy in which men are slaves ("Angel One" is a toned-down version of this story). To maintain order, the women must regularly administer a drug which turns men into cowards (thus implying that women could not dominate men without the aid of an artificial accomplice). "Planet Earth" makes explicit the message that was often implicit, the message that liberated women are ultimately unbalanced, unnatural, and emasculating.

Gene Roddenberry was less involved with Star Trek during its third year. Perhaps it is not coincidental that the third season saw a greater number of female writers employed, and a noticeable improvement in female roles. Of course, the show continued its internal struggle between its ideals and its sexism. We meet several very powerful women in the third season, including the female Romulan commander, Natira, and Elaan. Unfortunately, they are as unhappy as their predecessors, and neglect their duties in order to pursue a man.

The third season tended toward stronger female characters (Miramanee, Miranda Jones, Mara, Deela, Gem, Odona), and flirted with more progressive ideas. "Requiem for Methuselah" can be read as a feminist parable of a woman-child (Reena) who experiences a "consciousness raising," realizing she need not be a mere extension of her father (Flint) or her lover (Kirk). Of course, she dies almost instantly, an ending which would argue for a conservative approach to women's liberation, at best.

The final episode of the original series is crucial to any discussion of sexism in Star Trek. Although it is not a bad episode, I suspect I am not the only fan who wishes "Turnabout Intruder" had never been made. For it is in this episode that we learn that women are not allowed to be captains in Starfleet. Although some have tried to obscure this fact, watching the episode closely makes this conclusion unavoidable.

This episode suggests another excuse for sexism: Star Trek had to portray sexism in order to comment upon it. In other words, Gene Roddenberry compromised his vision of the future in order to explore this timely issue (just as he'd compromised by making many of the Federation's ambassadors so obnoxious). Though it may not be applicable elsewhere, in reference to "Turnabout Intruder" this excuse serves mainly to obscure the sexism of the show. Janice Lester is another woman whose "hatred of her own womanhood" (i.e., desire for a career) has resulted in pain and bitterness. That Dr. Lester's goal is to command the *Enterprise* is intended to emphasize the depth of her irrationality: any woman who wants to be a starship captain must be insane. Kirk (and Roddenberry) sees a female captain as an obscene invasion of what is properly a masculine domain (represented by Kirk's own body). And when Kirk says of Janice, "Her life could have been as rich *as any woman's*" (my italics), he implies that reasonable women accept their traditional place in society. "Turnabout Intruder" is one of the few episodes in which Uhura does not appear. It's almost as if her presence would be intolerable in a story that dramatizes the credo, "a feminist is just a woman who wants to be a man."

Several episodes deal with the "demons" lurking within James Kirk, including "The Enemy Within," "The Naked Time," and "Obsession." In these stories, aspects of Kirk threaten to free themselves from his will, and he must reintegrate them. In "The Enemy Within," Kirk becomes stronger by embracing his "evil" self; in "Turnabout Intruder," Kirk must expel a female invader and regain pure masculinity. "Turnabout Intruder" denies the existence of valuable femininity within Kirk. (Not surprisingly, the original story ended with a homophobic scene in which Kirk worries that his manhood may have been contaminated by Janice Lester. He knows that all is well when he finds himself gazing appreciatively at a female yeoman.)

The source story for "Turnabout Intruder" was written by Gene Roddenberry. When Kirk agrees with Dr. Lester (*sotto voce*) that

Starfleet's treatment of women "isn't fair," is this a comment on contemporary society, or is it a reluctant admission of Star Trek's own sexism? Like James Kirk, Mr. Roddenberry believes in equal rights for women as theory, but he has not incorporated this belief into his life and creations. The following is an exchange between Gene Roddenberry and Majel Barrett in an interview for *People* magazine (March 16, 1987):

" 'Majel often questions my ideas about sexual equality,' says Gene, 'but it's something that I've always believed in. I think they're silly little creatures, but . . .'

"He believes in the equality of women,' interrupts Majel, 'as long as it doesn't interfere with his home life.' "

Despite the vast amount of literature published on Star Trek, we are still without a biography of Gene Roddenberry. However, he did write the novelization of *Star Trek: The Motion Picture*, which is full of insights into his views on Star Trek, fandom, and other subjects. The novel and the film also constitute a compendium of many of the ideas of the original series.

Correspondingly, Ilia is an exaggeration and combination of several of the female types we see in the series. She is Deltan, from a planet where sex is a constant part of life; she views humans as "sexually immature." She is the ultimate "mysterious, disturbing female"; her effect on the crewmen is at least as profound as that of "Mudd's Women." Ilia, though, is sexually too advanced for any human male to handle . . . and that is too much for the male ego to handle.

Ilia's sexual powers aggravate men's suspicions that women are in some ways superior to men. This tension is relieved when Ilia (in uniform) is exchanged for the Ilia-probe (in a miniskirt). Ilia becomes yet another frigid, mechanical female who, like Andrea, Kalinda, and the others, requires a strong man to humanize her, to "access her memory banks" and evoke the feelings she cannot reach herself.

After his mind meld with Vejur, Spock explains, "Each of us, at some time in our lives, turns to someone: a father, a brother, a God. . . . Vejur hopes to touch its creators." Ilia, at first a proud, talented officer, comes to represent a "child" looking for its father, and is a mere pawn in the power struggle between Vejur and the *Enterprise*. Trapped inside the probe, she is no longer any threat to the male dominance which is implicit in Star Trek.

A recent twist, which begins in *Star Trek: The Motion Picture*, is that the female officers all seem to have known one of their male colleagues. Just as Ilia knows Will Decker, so Deanna Troi knows Will Riker, and Beverly Crusher has a history with Jean-Luc Picard. (It's unclear whether Tasha Yar knew Picard before joining the *Enterprise*; the *Star Trek: The Next Generation Writer's Guide* states that Picard had visited her barbaric home planet.) It is never implied that they used these connections to obtain their assignments, but it is unusual that such past encounters are now a virtual prerequisite for the female characters. (In the original show, it was usually the female guest star who had known one of the male officers.)

The promotions of Chapel, Rand, and Uhura, although welcome, are strictly cosmetic improvements. The underlying sexism of *Star Trek: The Motion Picture* is well illustrated by the reactions of Decker and Chapel to being replaced, respectively, by Kirk and McCoy. Captain Decker, of course, is shocked and angry. In the novel, Doctor Chapel responds to her demotion by proclaiming, "I have never been so pleased and relieved over anything in my life."

Gene Roddenberry's novel gives us details on Kirk's relationship with Vice Admiral Lori Ciani. She is certainly the first female admiral (or captain, for that matter) in Star Trek, but, like Ilia, she soon shifts into a more familiar role. Once he realizes that Admiral Nogura has been using Lori to placate him, Kirk labels her "Nogura's staff whore." An earlier description of Lori as "perfection—lover, wife, friend, mother . . . " shows that she is not a realistic woman, but another fantasy projection. In the movie, Lori becomes the ultimate "disposable female," killed off by a transporter malfunction before we even meet her (her punishment for manipulating Kirk).

The two other important women in *Star Trek: The Motion Picture* are not women, but machines. The *Enterprise*, of course, is Kirk's first love; this metaphor is stressed in the novel. When Kirk takes over from Decker, Uhura sees "that look that comes into some men's eyes when they've just won a woman and she lies there ready to be taken." Scotty sees Kirk's arrival as "the herd bull returning to find a young usurper rutting there." In this hypermasculine context, it is understandable that Gene Roddenberry finds a *female* captain virtually unthinkable.

Despite the references to Vejur as "it" or as "an infant," the cloud creature can also be seen as a symbolic mother. Karin Blair described how, in such episodes as "Obsession," "The Immunity Syndrome," and "The Doomsday Machine" (and the animated "One of Our Planets Is Missing"), the devouring creature is a projection of what she calls "the monstrous mother," the smothering female that consumes her young (literally or figuratively). To this group we can add Vejur. The visual imagery of the film, with the *Enterprise* traveling through Vejur as a sperm seeking an egg, supports this. That Decker and Ilia merge with Vejur, instead of destroying her, indicates an evolved conception of the "omnivorous mother" of the series. This ending also allows Will Decker to symbolically have sex with Ilia; his compensation for losing the *Enterprise*.

I find it significant that Gene Roddenberry (writing as Admiral Kirk) uses the first paragraphs of his book to explain why Kirk uses his father's surname:

" . . . the fact that I use an old-fashioned male surname says a lot about both me and the service to which I belong. Although the male surname custom has become rare . . . it remains a fairly common thing in Starfleet. We are a highly conservative and strongly individualistic group. The old customs die hard with us. . . .We are proud that . . neither temptation nor jeopardy is able to shake our obedience to the oath we have taken."

This passage tells us two important things. First, that Gene Roddenberry wants to address the problem of (what many perceive as) sexism in Star Trek. And when he defends the male surname custom by connecting it to the pride and loyalty of Starfleet personnel, it reflects his reluctance to concede the unfairness of male domination in Starfleet. (This stubbornness was to become even more apparent in his approach to women in *Star Trek: The Next Generation*.)

In *Star Trek II: The Wrath of Khan*, the first thing we hear is a captain's log entry . . . spoken by a female. Although it turns out that Saavik is in training, and not yet a captain, the point has been made. This signals the beginning of what Harve Bennett calls "the middle years" of Star Trek. One of the distinguishing features of *Star Trek: The Motion Picture*, *Wrath of Khan*, *The Search for Spock*, and *The Voyage Home* is that they are decidedly less sexist than Gene Roddenberry's Star Trek.

In *Wrath of Khan* we meet two strong female characters, Saavik and Carol Marcus. Lt. Saavik immediately impresses us as a bright young officer. Though she is an unemotional alien, she is able to "let her hair down." She exudes pointy-eared sex appeal, but this in no way detracts from her competence, or from that of her male colleagues. Her scenes in the captain's chair further distinguish Saavik from all past crewwomen.

Carol Marcus is, simply, the first realistic love interest James Kirk has ever had. Neither a fantasy projection nor a stereotype, Carol is refreshingly believable as a Federation scientist, mother, and Jim's former love. Like Gillian Taylor in *The Voyage Home*, she is deeply involved in, and proud of, her work. (Nicholas Meyer, who contributed to the scripts of *Star Trek II: The Wrath of Khan* and *The Voyage Home*, wrote and directed *Time After Time,* in which Mary Steenburgen's character tells time-traveler H.G. Wells, "My job *is* my life, just as it is for you or any other man.")

Star Trek II: The Wrath of Khan does not portray the sexual equality which would obtain in a real 23rd-century Federation. Most of its characters are men, Khan's women followers are mere window dressing, and Star Trek (like our society) is still sexist. However, Harve Bennett and Nicholas Meyer (and later Leonard Nimoy) have updated Star Trek, and their treatment of women is, at worst, not embarrassing. Considering that the films must inevitably focus on the male stars of the series, they have done a fine job of including women (as well as blacks and other minorities) in the action.

Star Trek III: The Search for Spock continues this trend, although not as impressively as did *Wrath of Khan*. Carol Marcus does not appear, and Saavik is now played by the unconvincing Robin Curtis (although she does have a tender scene in which she takes the sexual initiative with young Spock). The presence of Valkryis suggests that Klingons entrust important missions to capable females, although her courage seems motivated more by her love for Kruge than by any personal goals (she, too, also proves to be *very* disposable). This film also gives us Uhura's "Mr. Adventure" scene, and the Vulcan matriarch T'Lar.

Significantly, when Harve Bennett deemed it necessary to eliminate a continuing character, it was a man, David Marcus, who was sacrificed. (One could argue that David's fall from grace encourages the belief that a "fatherless" child cannot succeed.) It's also interesting that when Admiral Morrow reviews the young crew at the beginning of the film, a surprising number of the cadets are female . . . surprising because most of the same crew in *Wrath of Khan* were male. Admittedly, the filmmakers probably felt less comfortable using women in *Wrath of Khan*'s violent combat scenes.

In *Star Trek: The Motion Picture*, James Kirk spurns his protégé Will Decker with relative impunity. Since then, however, Kirk has paid dearly for his indulgences: Khan comes back to haunt him, resulting in the loss of his son (a virtual stranger to his long-absent father), his ship, and (temporarily) his best friend. Also, since *STTMP*, Kirk depends more than ever on the help of his friends.

The first three Star Trek movies each feature a male character who threatens Kirk's power. Decker is a square-jawed hero we can easily imagine in Superman's cape. Khan has lost the charisma he had in "Space Seed"; although still a fascinating character, he is obviously insane. Commander Kruge's actions in *The Search for Spock* border on incompetence. This increasingly negative view of macho characters is another distinguishing feature of the middle years of Star Trek.

In "Assignment: Earth," we met Roberta Lincoln, Star Trek's idea of the sixties woman (a bubble-headed secretary). In *The Voyage Home*, we see Star Trek's first eighties woman, and the difference is staggering. We also finally see our first female Starfleet captain (Captain Alexander of the *Saratoga*), and Nichelle Nichols has a substantial role. In terms of its treatment of women, *The Voyage Home* is Star Trek's finest hour.

Dr. Gillian Taylor is secure, strong-willed, smart, and every bit Jim Kirk's equal. It is a delight to hear her call him "Robin Hood," "landlubber," and "farm boy" in quick succession, and accuse him of being a "dipshit" and on a "macho" mission. This irreverence is funny because it is the opposite of the awe or lust with which women traditionally view Kirk. Though we are not seeing her at her best (she is mourning the loss of her whales), Gillian refuses to be a simple answer to Kirk's fantasies or a pawn in his plans. And although she likes Jim, she does not pursue him; she is the first woman since the Vulcan-trained (and blind) Miranda Jones to resist Kirk's charms.

The importance of Gillian Taylor is that, unlike Edith Keeler or most other women who have encountered Kirk, she is real enough and strong enough to break into his world of Starfleet. She is not a fantasy projection, who would have to remain in the past, like a dream. When Gillian grabs onto Kirk and is beamed aboard with him, this symbolizes women taking their long-denied, rightful place in Star Trek. And when she smoothly adjusts to the 23rd century, is posted on a science vessel, and tells Kirk, "*I'll* find *you*," it is a deliberate reversal of the sexism of the original show.

As likable as Gillian is, neither she nor any other female Star Trek character has attracted as much attention in such a short time as the late Tasha Yar. Tasha was *Star Trek: The Next Generation*'s major concession to sexual equality, a character designed to carry the burden Uhura bore in Star Trek. Yar was tough, a fighter, the *Enterprise*'s aggressive security chief . . . she was also likable, vivacious, and sexy. By forcing the death of this immensely appealing character, *The Next Generation*'s sexism became willfully self-destructive. Tasha Yar may become a martyr to the cause of sexual equality on Star Trek.

"Skin of Evil," a lackluster and distasteful episode, was a fitting conclusion to the shabby treatment of Tasha Yar. (Her death is not even deemed worthy of a commercial break.) Although the final scene was moving, we are left with the feeling that her death was unnecessary. In retrospect, Yar's death seems inevitable. She almost died in several episodes, and she lacked a crucial survival skill for women in Gene Roddenberry's Star Trek: the ability to fade into the background. In terms of this world, Yar began with two strikes against her: she was security officer (notoriously a "dead-end" job), and she was an unapologetically strong woman.

She was also the only *The Next Generation* character who could be described as flirtatious. She was seen flirting with an older man (Picard), and several aliens (including Worf), and seducing an android (Data). To an older generation, such behavior could easily earn her the label "loose woman." It's therefore tempting to interpret her execution by a shape-changing, phallic monster (which also traps Deanna Troi) as symbolic retribution. Tasha was killed (rather than transferred to another ship) for the same reason gay characters are often killed off in films and TV: as penalty for her sexuality.

Tasha Yar was originally conceived as a "masculine kind of woman" (*Starlog Yearbook #3*), a product of a horribly violent childhood. (A healthy childhood, presumably, would result in a properly feminine woman.) Denise Crosby not only made this potentially embarrassing character believable, but also brought an electric presence to the *Enterprise*. It was disheartening to watch her fade from a co-starring role (she was originally billed fourth) to, as she put it, "a glorified extra." Although I will miss the character, I applaud Ms. Crosby's courage and sense of self-worth—she did exactly what Tasha would have done.

The original Star Trek began with eight continuing characters, two of whom were women. One of these, Yeoman Rand, was replaced by Nurse Chapel midway through the first year. *The Next Generation* began with nine continuing characters, three of whom were women. With the first season over, two of them are gone. Tasha Yar and Beverly Crusher—like Janice Rand, Ilia, and (Kirstie Alley's) Saavik before them—disappeared before they could truly become a part of the Star Trek family.

Doctor Crusher, in her brief tenure aboard the *Enterprise*, several times exercised her option to give Captain Picard an order. Most often Picard was successful in resisting such orders, reflecting Gene Roddenberry's resistance to female equality. (Consider Beverly's resemblance to Majel Barrett's Nurse Chapel.) It is a tribute to Gates McFadden that she was nevertheless able to project authority and experience. Beverly Crusher was not a flashy character, but she was a believable adult, and her dismissal is further evidence that *The Next Generation* cannot accommodate strong female characters.

The sole returning female character, Deanna Troi, does little to alleviate *The Next Generation*'s sexism. She is submissive, even childish, and stereotypically at the mercy of the emotions of others. Though intelligent, she is not a well-rounded officer, and seems to be present largely because of abilities she was born with. And despite her sensitivity, Deanna rarely expresses her emotions (she binds her hair and body as tightly as her feelings). She cannot acknowledge the opposite side of herself, and must therefore remain near those who can physically protect her.

The extent to which unconscious sexual stereotypes inspire Gene Roddenberry's characters is clear when we consider Deanna's ancestry. Betazeds, we learn in "Encounter at Farpoint," can read minds. Deanna is only half-Betazoid; her father (male, thus logical) was human, while her mother (female, thus emotional) was a Betazed. Naturally, Deanna is able to sense only emotions. Presumably, if her father had been the Betazed, she would read only thoughts. That would be "unfeminine."

Now that women are questioning traditional roles, it seems that their right to participate in Gene Roddenberry's Star Trek is jeopardized. Excluding the regular cast, *The Next Generation* has presented very few memorable female characters. (The exception is Lwaxana Troi in "Haven.") Women such as Lisa Akim "Home Soil"), Minuet ("11001001"), and Roshalla ("When the Bough Breaks") are unimportant, peripheral characters, who are at best inoffensive. Gene Roddenberry is obviously more comfortable with male characters, and includes women only when it is necessary (as in romantic scenes), or when self-consciously making an effort to promote equality.

In "Angel One," we visit what Captain Picard describes as "an unusual matriarchal society . . . which is considered most sensible and natural." (What's truly unusual is that all of the planet's inhabitants seem to be under thirty.) This episode follows a familiar pattern: strong, liberated women turn out to be sexually frustrated. (The fact that human males attract the Mistresses "like no man ever has" makes no sense in terms of the evolution of the planet.) Still, "Angel One" is an effective, if simplistic morality play. Predictably, a matriarchal society was chosen as the target (are the many patriarchal societies we've seen any more "natural"?), and the episode shows little appreciation of the complexity of the issues surrounding sexism. But "Angel One" is Mr. Roddenberry's most successful attempt so far at promoting sexual equality. The problem is that *The Next Generation*'s capacity for feminism seems to have been exhausted by this one episode.

The unabashed machismo of Picard, Riker, and Worf forms a bulwark against true equality in *The Next Generation*. The show is carefully structured to prevent women from commanding the *Enterprise*. Tasha Yar was too young and impulsive to take command (except very briefly in "The Big Goodbye"), while Counselor Troi and the chief medical officer are outside the chain of command. Our attention is distracted from this by the fact that the command chores are (mostly) divided between two men, rather than four or five as in the original series. (We know Data is third in command only because we are told he is.) We have seen a boy, Wesley Crusher, in the captain's chair, but Gene Roddenberry is still very reluctant to show a woman in the "center seat."

One of the larger bones thrown to feminists by *The Next Generation* was the appearance of Captain Tryla Scott in "Conspiracy." She reached the captaincy, we're told, "faster than anyone in Starfleet." (Picard has the audacity to ask her, "Are you really that good?") In this same scene, however, we learn that Walker Keel's first officer and chief medical officer are both men, and that women in the 24th century *still* take their husband's surnames. And, predictably, Tryla Scott is one of those absorbed by the parasitic invaders. These facts lessen the impact of such token appearances, which are meant to suggest that Starfleet practices equality, even if *The Next Generation* does not.

One of the most common excuses for Star Trek's sexism is the idea that the "spirit of the show" promotes equality, even if what we see is sexist. Nichelle Nichols expresses this view in *The Star Trek Interview Book*, saying, "whether I ever took over the ship or not is immaterial. . . . I was capable of it." The fact that Ms. Nichols' role in Star Trek led to her association with NASA, recruiting women and minorities into the space program, is itself an example of the positive influence the original series has had. Ultimately, the love, hope, and tolerance of Star Trek has made it easier to overlook its sexism. With the premiere of *The Next Generation*, however, this excuse has lost its power to persuade.

Richard Arnold, assistant to Gene Roddenberry, in a response to my letter to Roddenberry, wrote, "the philosophy of the show is more important than the gender of the lead roles." This suggests that the gender of the lead roles is somehow separable from the philosophy of the show. Clearly, what we see in *The Next Generation* is in direct contradiction to what we have been told about the Federation and the 24th century. With the excuses of societal prejudice and network interference no longer viable, it does not surprise me that *The Next Generation* is feeling pressure from women and minorities to practice what it preaches. In terms of sexual equality, the "philosophy of the show" is little more than a promise that has been broken.

Gene Roddenberry *has* kept his promise to use men, as well as women, as sex objects. The presence of a variety of attractive males in Star Trek makes its sexism easier for women to tolerate; whether this strategy works as well for *The Next Generation* remains to be seen. Data's presence, certainly, makes up for some of the "mechanical geishas" we saw in the original series. (As the android is fond of pointing out, he is "fully functional," the implication being that this is a vast understatement.) Data also continues the tradition of using male characters to represent the "feminine" side of humanity. The *The Next Generation Writer's Guide* states, "Data has needs not unlike that of a female crewperson—in other words, Data needs very much to be needed."

Mr. Roddenberry also continues to portray women as sexually aggressive, with mixed results. When the crew become intoxicated in "The Naked Now," the women pursue the men. Yar's seduction of Data is funny, and mostly believable. Beverly Crusher's giddy pursuit of Picard might also have worked, had she not been required to apologize for her lust, whining, "I'm a woman without the comfort of a husband, a man." Beverly, we are asked to believe, has remained celibate while on the *Enterprise* (with its crew of over a thousand), hiding her loneliness and her desire for "Jean-Luc" (just as Number One hid her attraction to Captain Pike). Deanna Troi's attempt to distract Will Riker is simply pathetic.

We are left with the impression that all three female characters, like so many of their predecessors, are sexually frustrated. Female sexuality is portrayed as incompatible with success in Starfleet because it is thought to lead inevitably to domesticity, the antithesis of exploration. Again, the unconscious message of Gene Roddenberry's Star Trek is that the traits of a good officer come naturally to men only.

Dr. Crusher's transfer off the *Enterprise* is hard to accept, especially considering her interesting relationship with Capt. Picard. To understand this, we must return to the attitude that men and women cannot work together without romance interfering. Though *The Next Generation* is as sexy a show as Star Trek, sex among the continuing characters is still discouraged (witness the fate of Tasha). If sex among the characters is forbidden, but abstinence is also considered impossible, it's obvious that none of the female characters can be allowed to remain on board for very long.

Considering the speed with which they pair up in "The Naked Now," it's hard to believe these supposedly 24th-century adults are satisfied with holodeck fantasies. Yet there's an odd strain of puritanism in *The Next Generation*, expressed by Picard's statement, "I think we shall end up with a fine crew, if we avoid temptation." In Star Trek, there were "no regulations against romance." If this has changed, the reasons for the change should be explored. If not, for the sake of realism, at least one of the lead characters should be involved in a "shipboard romance."

Ironically, considering the disciplinarians who now run the *Enter-*

prise, The Next Generation is a self-congratulatory program. A self-righteous tone reared its head in "Encounter at Farpoint"; one example is Tasha Yar screaming, "This court should be down on its knees worshiping what Starfleet represents!" This tone continued throughout the first season. A certain amount of pride among Starfleet's finest is understandable, but the finger-wagging of Picard, Riker, et al., has been nearly a constant. This is especially offensive in reference to the supposed sexual equality of the Federation. We have seen several alien races who were surprised at the status of women on the *Enterprise* (the Ferengi are amazed by "clothed females"); Yar's fighting skills usually taught them a lesson. Such scenes dare the viewer to accuse *The Next Generation* of sexism. By stridently insisting on its own progressiveness, *The Next Generation* gives itself away; the show protests far too much.

Messages that would have been laudable in the sixties are now exercises in "preaching to the converted"; for example, few viewers of *The Next Generation* would think twice when seeing a female police officer (Yar's contemporary counterparts), yet are expected to be impressed by a female security chief. Equally ridiculous was the marriage/career conflict of Troi in "Haven" (in which Wyatt Miller rejected her because she was not the blonde of his fantasies), and Yar's yearning to "be feminine without losing anything." Both are more evocative of the 1970s than the 2300s.

"The concept of equality should have been presented in a very straightforward manner; a fact of existence with no preaching concerning the evils of hate or prejudice. The existence of female starship captains . . . or any other possible kind of starship captains should have raised no eyebrows or garnered no double takes."

These comments, from Steven Satterfield's "Star Trek: Concept Erosion" in *The Best of Trek #5*, apply even more to *The Next Generation* than to Star Trek. *The Next Generation* could have portrayed total, un-selfconscious equality between the sexes, and included a female captain or first officer, thus gaining instant credibility as a futuristic program with a progressive message for its audience.

Obviously, this would be an ideal situation. Now that *The Next Generation* is a commercial success, its makers are not about to kill off popular male characters in the name of sexual equality. Indeed, our growing attachment to Picard, Riker, and their male colleagues—and our love for Kirk, Spock, and McCoy—is another

324 THE BEST OF THE BEST OF TREK® II

important reason for fan tolerance of sexism. Any criticism of sexism in Star Trek implicitly threatens the right of the male characters to exist. It implies that some of them should not have been created, or even that they should be done away with. (I am not suggesting this; I like Data, Worf, and Geordi as much as anyone.)

A passage from the *Inside Star Trek* record illustrates how strongly both Star Trek and *The Next Generation* reflect their creator. Gene Roddenberry is discussing his troubled childhood when he says, "How lovely all your daughters are inside, how fearless all your sons . . . if only you could see." This brief quotation indicates the man's great sensitivity and gentleness, his optimism and intelligence. It also reflects another belief we see in Star Trek: that some traits are male and some female.

Gene Roddenberry's sexism is neither intentional nor malicious. It is the sexism of stereotypes, a learned set of beliefs which exaggerate the differences between the sexes, and ignore differences among men and among women. Stereotypes require that men and women behave in certain prescribed ways, expressing "male" and "female" emotions. They also make it difficult to accept women in any but the most traditional roles (of which there are very few in Starfleet).

Gene Roddenberry's attempts at feminism, though halfhearted and sporadic, speak of his good (conscious) intentions, and have been enough to satisfy most of Star Trek's very loyal fans. To this day, most fans insist on blaming the show's sexism on everyone *but* Mr. Roddenberry. (Some fans are able to ignore the show's sexism because their mental picture of the Federation takes precedence over the episodes themselves. Also, it must be said that there is no lack of well-intentioned sexism in Star Trek fandom (see Patricia Lee Johnson's "The Twenty-Third Century Woman" in *The Best of Trek #11*).

After the original show went off the air, and its sexism became increasingly obvious, it was natural for fans to assume that this flaw was due to network short-sightedness. (Even if he had wanted to, Roddenberry could not have portrayed complete equality in the sixties.) They also assumed that if the show ever returned to production this flaw would be corrected. This was an incorrect assumption: the idiosyncratic sexism of Star Trek is very evident in *The Next Generation*. The sexism of the original series did reflect American society in the sixties, but it is now clear that it also reflected the beliefs, however unconscious, of the Great Bird himself.

The Next Generation, like Star Trek, is very much Gene Rodden- berry's show. By all reports, he is involved in every aspect of pro- duction, including the selection and rewriting of scripts. His priority remains the faithful and consistent presentation of his personal vi- sion. As he was quoted in *Star Trek: The Official Fan Club* (maga- zine) #57, "even if it has to be the continuity of my errors, at least it must have continuity."

Gene Roddenberry's views are scrutinized much more closely than those of most people, of course. Born in 1921, he is of a generation not known for producing male feminists. That he has escaped most of the prejudices of his contemporaries is in itself very impressive. He worked in male-dominated fields (in the military, and as an airline pilot, policeman, script writer, and producer) before becoming the patriarch of the vast world of Star Trek. In fairness, it is not surprising that his fictions reflect these life experiences. Mr. Roddenberry has said that "sexual equality is as basic as any other kind of equality." His efforts to implement this belief have been blocked by some "very human imperfections" in his ideology. Like Christopher Pike, he "just can't get used to having a woman on the bridge."

Nevertheless, no matter how innocent or unintentional Star Trek's sexism may be, it should not be excused or ignored. Gender- based roles, though they may have been useful earlier in human evolution, are now outdated and destructive. In order for individu- als, and humanity, to mature and grow, we must be free of sexual stereotypes. The differences between men and women will manifest themselves naturally, without conformity to exaggerated concep- tions of "masculine" and "feminine." We can each find within our- selves a working balance of strength and sensitivity, discipline and compassion, logic and emotion.

Gene Roddenberry realizes that growth requires the integration of opposites, of course; this concept is dealt with often in his pro- ductions. At the end of *Star Trek: The Motion Picture*, male and female (human, alien, and machine) merge, giving birth to a new race. Unfortunately, Mr. Roddenberry seems to have lost interest in visualizing this "next step in our evolution" (as he did with Spock). Consequently, he is being left behind by an audience which has learned to question traditional sex-based roles.

It's true that most Hollywood productions are sexist to some degree. This is partly due to the fact that they are inspired by old films as much as by reality; *The Next Generation* is particularly susceptible. But sexism in a supposedly progressive context can no longer be overlooked. *The Next Generation*'s commitment to sexual equality pales beside that of recent shows such as *Hill Street Blues* and *Cagney and Lacey* (both of which, unlike *The Next Generation*, had to contend with some degree of "network interference"). Because Star Trek is inspired by such high ideals, and because it demands a questioning intelligence of its viewers, it must inevitably be judged by high standards. (While writing this article, I was reminded of those Catholics who are frustrated by the prohibition of women priests. The analogy is appropriate, as the similarities between Star Trek and religions become ever more apparent. Star Trek, of course, has always discouraged the rigidity of dogma and scripture, and our Great Bird has certainly never claimed infallibility.)

I urge all Star Trek fans to express their views on the issues raised here to Gene Roddenberry and his staff. *Star Trek: The Next Generation* promises to be a long-running program, and there is ample time for changes to be made. Though the show may never be on the cutting edge of sexual equality, we can ask for more and stronger female characters, and for the addition of more women to *The Next Generation*'s mostly male creative staff. Instead of being overwhelmed by feelings of nostalgia (for the original show) or self-satisfaction (now that a new series is finally in production), I hope fans will uphold the tradition of vocal involvement that began with the letter campaigns which saved the original series. To criticize *The Next Generation* is not disloyalty, but an expression of the hope that the show will fulfill its great potential. After all, the corollary to Star Trek's theme of "the continued striving for greatness" is that there is always room for improvement.

YOU HAVE THE CONN: THE STAR TREK VIDEO AND COMPUTER GAMES

by Dan Skelton

Video and computer games are unique forms of entertainment. What other kinds of play permit you to become the main character in a television program, then allow you to control the outcome of the story? If you've ever seen a Star Trek episode in which you wondered, "If only Captain Kirk had done this . . ." you're a prime candidate for computer-gaming.

The history of video and computer games is a short one, as they did not even exist until 1970 saw the birth of Atari's original *Pong*. Within eleven years of their introduction, video games had overtaken all other forms of entertainment in popularity. Indeed, for a brief time in 1981, video games were taking in more money than movies, records, tapes, and books combined.

The bubble burst in late 1982, as consumer attention and dollars shifted to computer-gaming, though that bubble itself burst in 1984. However, in 1987, their popularity rose again. Video and computer games poised to take their place as mature media in the universe of popular entertainments.

With the introduction of *Star Trek: The Next Generation*, we saw just how completely computer-gaming had become accepted as mainstream entertainment. When Paramount announced their promotional plans for the new show, in addition to the standard crossovers into comic books, models, toys, and novels, a mention was made that the new crew would be featured in "innovative computer software." It is important to note that such a statement would not even *have been possible* in 1966, when the original series premiered.

But this was far from the first time that Star Trek had been featured in the video game media, for the history of Star Trek in computer and video games goes almost as far back as computer games have existed—for me personally, back to my very first exposure to a computer of any kind.

In 1975, I attended a science and engineering seminar at the United States Naval Academy in conjunction with my work on a marine biology science fair project. I had never seen a computer. All attendees were given free time on the Academy's Univac system. It wasn't too long (i.e., minutes) before someone entered the fateful command "list games." One game immediately jumped out from the list. It was called "Startrek."

This seminal interpretation of Star Trek in computer form immediately became the most popular form of after-hours recreation for the attendees. Of the 90-plus terminals on the system, a survey of them at any moment found more than 80 running *Startrek*. Most of the terminals that weren't running *Startrek* were those locked in private offices, unavailable to seminar participants.

This heavy usage rapidly became a problem, because these were not the standard video computer terminals to which we all have now become accustomed. These were Teletype terminals, which printed messages on rolls of yellow paper such as Mr. Spock pulled from the *Enterprise*'s computer. We were chewing through the Navy's paper supply by the ream.

What was so fascinating about the game? It was unlike any other entertainment we had ever experienced. We were in control of the Starship *Enterprise*, hopping from quadrant to quadrant, saving the Federation from ultimate destruction, blasting Klingons to smithereens.

The format of the game was simple: The galaxy was a 10 × 10 grid of smaller areas called quadrants, each quadrant in turn 10 × 10 units. At the beginning of the game you were told how many starbases were in the galaxy and how many Klingons, but you were not told their locations. Your mission was to eliminate these Klingons in a specific number of star dates.

You could travel around the galaxy using warp drive or impulse power, warp drive simply being any distance of one quadrant or more and impulse power being anything less than one quadrant. You could use your short-range scan to view the current quadrant, long-range scan to approximately examine adjacent quadrants, and you could call up a galactic map of previously scanned quadrants from the ship's computer. This method of scanning was so intuitively useful that many Star Trek computer aficionados may not be aware that differentiation between long-range and short-range scan was never made in the original television series.

Klingons could be destroyed by phaser or photon torpedo. Phasers were less efficient and less likely to destroy an enemy, but they always locked on target. Photon torpedoes, while usually fatal, had to be specifically aimed. The strength of the *Enterprise*'s shields and the intensity of phaser barrages were expressed in energy units. Energy units could be transferred from shields to phasers for attacks, and would decrease when the *Enterprise* was hit by enemy fire. You could replenish your energy and torpedo supply by docking with a starbase. The game did not take place in real time; that is, if you sat and thought about a particularly difficult move for an hour, no game time would pass.

The most unusual sidelight to this game came if you tried to maneuver past the 10 × 10 grid of quadrants. The game would tell you that you had run into the energy barrier surrounding the galaxy, had suffered severe damage, and you were thrown back to a random location. Luckily for you, there was evidently no Gary Mitchell on your ship. A second incursion into the barrier was fatal to you, causing you to lose the game.

At the end of the contest, you were graded on how well you had performed your mission, from a top ranking of "admiral" to a low of "ship's cook."

As a Star Trek fan, this game was pretty close to my ultimate fantasy: I had the conn. The fate of the Federation was in my hands. As Star Trek, though, the game lacked several important elements. For one, there was no Kirk, Spock, or McCoy with whom to interact. The subspace communications weren't relayed by Uhura, and Scotty wasn't there to complain about his engines (and in my first few games he would have been complaining loudly).

But more than that, the fundamental thrust of the game was wrong for Star Trek. The Klingons were endlessly violent, and your mission was not to "seek out new life and new civilizations"; your mission, simply put, was to kill, kill, *kill*! Unfortunately, this would continue to be true of most, but not all, of the Star Trek games to follow.

This original format Star Trek computer game rapidly made its way into the computer systems of academia and business, where it flourished. I next encountered the game during my college study at Tulane University, where several versions of the game again dominated after-hours computer usage. Some wrinkles were added to the game. Now, in addition to Klingons, you had to destroy Romulans in your quest to rid known space of all galactic vermin. Like their television counterparts, the Romulans had a cloaking device, but unlike previous incarnations of the device, they did not have to de-cloak to fire. At any time during the course of the game, a star could go nova, destroying an entire quadrant (and you, too, if you didn't move quickly!). This could be to your advantage, as you could fire a photon torpedo into a star, causing it to go nova, then warp out leaving the Klingons and Romulans behind to fry.

When I entered the working world, I encountered the biggest, most elaborate version of the game yet. On an IBM mainframe computer, this game sported planets to be explored. The exploration was limited to a simple beam-down, beam-up process, but it was definitely a step in the right direction. Your survey parties could bring back anything from alien riches to spare dilithium crystals to a plague which would kill your crew.

The most interesting strategic innovation in the game was the introduction of Klingon "Supercommander" Kang, a direct computer-controlled adversary for you. He would move from quadrant to quadrant, attacking starbases. In this game, unlike previous versions, you could lose your valuable bases.

Though on our business computer, we were permitted to play the game during our lunch hour and after work. I missed more than one bus from being intensely involved in *mano a mano* battle with

Kang. Eventually, the game was taken off the system because it (and our "saved game" files) were taking up too much disk space.

Shortly after the game was taken off our system at work, I bought an Atari 2600 home video game console. One day, while browsing the game cartridge section at Sears, I ran across a game I'd never seen, one sold only through Sears under their *Tele-Games* label. It was the old Star Trek computer game—and a very simple version at that! It was called *Stellar Track* to keep Paramount's lawyers happy, and the principal players were renamed, as well.

With the advent of home computers, many different public domain versions of the game sprang up. "Public domain" meant that anyone could copy the game for free, so no one made any money from it—the computer software equivalent of a fanzine. There were versions of this game for literally every computer, most of them less sophisticated than the one I'd played at Tulane. They had almost-generic names like *Trek, Strek*, and *Startrek*, and this kind of star battles game became known as the "Star Trek" genre.

The next step in the evolution of this type of game was commercialization. Several smaller computer game publishers saw a distinct market for this kind of game, if it was done well. This would mean adding game features reminiscent of the IBM mainframe program, using color effectively, and adding music and sound effects. Some of the games which sprang up at this time included Miklyn Development Co.'s *Starship Challenge* and Eagle Computer Consulting's *Starship Valiant*, but easily the most successful of these games was Interstel's *Star Fleet I*.

When the genre became commercialized, Paramount finally took notice and threatened lawsuit against those products infringing upon its Star Trek copyright. *Star Fleet I* author Dr. Trevor C. Sorensen wisely opted to consult Paramount prior to programming and releasing his addition to the field. What he found out was that he could not use names and references specific to the Star Trek universe, such as character names and the names of alien races. Music and graphic representations of Star Trek elements were, of course, out of the question. Boiled down to its essence, he was told that if the game was such that the player believed himself to be in the Star Trek universe, Paramount would consider it copyright infringement.

So the Klingons became the green-skinned Krellans, the Romulans became the insectoid Zaldrons, and the *Enterprise* was removed from the available fleet of ships. The focus of the game, whose fans included science fiction author Jerry Pournelle, was shifted to the accumulation of a service record. The program followed a player's career from Starfleet Academy through promotion to the admiralty.

The program became a best-seller for Interstel, and was eventually picked up for national distribution by software giant Electronic Arts. The game has spawned at least one sequel of its own, *Star Fleet II—Krellan Commander* (you get to be the bad guy!), with more to come. As with all media, the influences of Star Trek will extend far beyond derivative products.

Though *Star Fleet I* was the ultimate example of the "Star Trek" genre of computer-gaming, the earliest example of Star Trek in the video game field can be found in one of the first arcade games, the Vectorbeam cult favorite *Space War*. The game was a battle between two players whose ships traveled around a star or a black hole. Though this game had little to do with Star Trek, one player's ship (as well as the artwork on the side panel of the game) bore more than a striking resemblance to the *Enterprise*.

One rather obscure Star Trek product bridged the gap between toys and video games. *Star Trek Phaser Battle* by Mego unfortunately was released just as home video game consoles were reaching the market. It was a stand-alone battery-powered unit which used LED's to represent attacking Klingon and Romulan battleships. Decidedly low-tech by the standards of the *Captain Power* era, it used a motorized spinning perforated disc to flicker ambient light when explosions occurred.

The player was required to use a joy-stick to aim phaser blasts at enemy ships shown on the back wall of the game. If the player missed, a split second was permitted to raise the *Enterprise*'s shields or face destruction. Though not a true video or computer game, this was definitely a precursor of the two major video game offerings which followed.

Finally, in 1982, over 12 years since Atari's *Pong* and over seven years since I played *Startrek* at the Naval Academy, a true video game burst upon the scene which could proudly bear the name Star Trek, could use Klingons, Romulans—anything in the Star Trek universe—without fear of infringement. The name of the game? *Star Trek: The Motion Picture* by General Consumer Electronics for the Vectrex home arcade system.

You say you've never heard of it? Well, during the height of the video game boom, with Atari 2600 sales approaching 12 million units, with several million Mattel Intellivisions sold, the first product to bear the authorized Star Trek trademark appeared for a fledgling system which came and went without ever making so much as a ripple in the video-gaming pond.

The Vectrex home arcade was elegant, a self-contained unit with a vector-scan picture tube, one which did not hook up to your television. Instead of forming screen images by rapidly displaying a series of horizontal lines as a television does ("raster" lines, they're called), vector scan tubes draw short, straight lines on the screen in any direction. The best-known game to sport this type of screen was Atari's arcade classic *Asteroids*. The G.E.C. Vectrex attempted, unsuccessfully, to bring that technology home. That it failed to do so was not the fault of the unit or the picture (both were excellent) or the games themselves (likewise of high caliber), but because the unit sold for nearly three times as much as the Atari 2600, which had roughly 20 times the game library that the Vectrex did. And where the Vectrex was black-and-white with colored plastic overlays, the Atari 2600 sported up to 256 colors.

But what of *Star Trek: The Motion Picture*, the game? It was exciting, the first game to give you a first-person view from the *Enterprise*'s main viewscreen into deep space—from which you were still being attacked by those same mindless, unmotivated, kamikaze Klingons and Romulans who populated the earlier Star Trek computer games. The sharply drawn line graphics added a clarity and excitement to the game, as did the muticolored plastic overlay (actually, some of them were so good that you forgot the game was black-and-white). The Klingons and Romulans were graphically accurate, though the Romulans weren't using their cloaking device.

A couple of things did stick out like sore thumbs in this game (as in, did the person who designed this ever watch Star Trek?). For one thing, you were fighting through eight levels of play to reach a battle with the Klingon "Mothership." Now, I remember Cylons having "Base Stars," and I remember a really big "Mothership" hovering over Devil's Tower, Wyoming, but for the life of me I cannot recall any mention of a Klingon "Mothership" anywhere in Star Trek. The very reference sounds wimpy in Klingon terms, but I guess this was the best they could do since the term "Death Star" was already taken.

If you wanted to accelerate play, you could call up a black hole, enter it, and be transported instantly to the Mothership confrontation. In real terms (and in the Star Trek universe, which did strive for scientific accuracy) if you flew into a black hole you would be crushed to death, and the game and your life would be over.

A couple of things could have been done to bring this more in line with *The Motion Picture*. Instead of calling up a black hole, the player obviously should have been required to enter a wormhole. To exit the wormhole sequence, the player would have fired photon torpedoes at asteroids in the wormhole, with the number of asteroids destroyed determining how many levels of play would have been skipped. And the final confrontation should have been with Vejur, or at least his energy probes surrounding the Earth. A little attention to detail would have made this a better game, and better Star Trek. The two are not mutually exclusive.

However, this does bring up a good point. Real Star Trek does not lend itself particularly well to the traditional video game format, as does a property like Star Wars, whose basis and appeal are much more in line with the "shoot-em-up" nature of traditional video games. (Quick digression: Why was there never a *Battlestar Galactica* video game? If ever a property lent itself perfectly to interpretation as a video game, it was *Galactica*.)

But in 1983, Sega expertly balanced arcade action with the elements of Star Trek in their *Star Trek Strategic Operations Simulator*, easily the best interpretation of Star Trek in a video game format. Though this was a traditional arcade "shoot-em-up," it was made palatable by being presented as a combat simulator used to train Starfleet Academy cadets. The sit-down version of the game was especially nice.

The gameplay centered on a two-window view of combat in space. One window looked at the playing field from overhead, and the other provided a first-person viewscreen image. A rotary control changed ship direction and buttons controlled impulse power (slow thrust), warp speed (fast thrust), phasers, and photon torpedoes. The remainder of the color vector scan screen was devoted to a status display which indicated phaser power, photon torpedo supply, and shield strength. Though the first person viewscreen implied a third dimension, all conflict actually took place in a single plane. If you ever wondered why Khan was crippled thinking "two-dimensionally" in *Wrath of Khan*, he probably trained on this simulation.

When you began play, you were greeted by the "captain on-board" whistle as used in *Wrath of Khan*. A Spock-like voice announced each sector of gameplay (I never could figure out if it actually was Leonard Nimoy). In each sector, you faced a number of Klingons surrounding, and some attacking, starbases. You could destroy the Klingons one at a time using phasers or you could use photon torpedoes to take out several at once. If you were running low on ammunition or shield energy, you could dock at a starbase for resupply. If you saved a starbase from destruction without docking at it, your score would be greatly increased. The visual representation of incoming fire striking your shield, reminiscent of the Tholian Web, was especially effective.

At higher levels of play, you were pursued by an alien saucer of unknown origin. If you contacted this saucer, your shield energy would be drained until you destroyed it. After two levels of play you would be required to navigate an asteroid field to dock with starbases, replenishing your supplies until you ran into an asteroid. And before advancing to the next major level of play, you would face a blast from Star Trek's distant past: Nomad!

No longer searching for Jackson Roykirk or attempting to sterilize imperfect lifeforms, this little metal monster (which was graphically true to "The Changeling") raced across the video screen, scattering mines in your path. In the most pleasant surprise of the game, if you destroyed Nomad you were treated to a few bars from Alexander Courage's TV theme (the portion that wasn't used for *The Next Generation*).

This was a very enjoyable game, which allowed you the action of a fast-moving, exciting shoot-a-thon without the guilt associated with mindlessly destroying in the name of Star Trek.

The *Star Trek Strategic Operations Simulator* came home in several versions, for the Atari 2600, Atari 5200, Coleco Vision, and most popular home computers. I have played several of these myself, and personally prefer the Atari 5200 version, primarily because its excellent use of the 5200's multiple buttons mimics the arcade console quite effectively. Of course, any time an arcade game has more than one button, translations to home systems can suffer.

Several years after Sega's ultimate Star Trek video game, the first *real* computer games based on Star Trek began to appear.

By 1985, the format of computer games had radically changed from the first games discussed in this article. Larger memory, better graphics, and faster processors combined with the increasing skills of programmers weaned on our favorite television series to produce games that were exciting, involving, but, best of all, true to the spirit of Star Trek.

Their format, though, derived from another of the earliest types of computer games, the "text adventure" genre. With its roots in the mainframes and micros of academia, this style of gameplay evolved at about the same time as the Star Trek genre. In a text adventure, the player would type English commands into the computer, and the computer would respond with an English description of what transpired. These games, like those of the Star Trek genre, did not take place in real time, so poor typists were not penalized.

The point of the earliest text adventures was simply to visit the entire world contained in the game and collect as many valuables as you could find. Later, though, as players tired of picking up diamonds, the games became complex puzzles to be solved. Unfortunately, some of these puzzles were convoluted scenarios of illogic, in which the only aim seemed to be "try and think like the programmer and type what he wanted you to say at this point." The better text adventures contained challenging and interesting puzzles, consistent and believable characters, and required intense concentration to solve.

Commands entered by players in the earliest games usually consisted of a verb followed by a noun, such as "take axe" or "kill dragon," and movements were usually expressed with a single word, such as "west" or "up."

The simplistic command structure limited the range of situation possible within these games. As the genre progressed, the computer interpreters of English commands (called "parsers") became more sophisticated. So the player could now type, "Take the gun from Mrs. Robner, then call the police" and expect the computer to understand all that was said.

Oddly, though, the first authorized Star Trek text adventures took a step backwards in the sophistication of their command structures. The first, *Star Trek: The Kobayashi Alternative*, by Simon and Schuster for most popular computer systems, used a command language that was little deeper than the two-word parser of the earliest adventure games. Though the syntax could be more complex, the vocabulary of the game was quite limited. In fact, the puzzle of the game proved so difficult to solve within the limited vocabulary that a special supplement was printed which listed all the words the player could use. The alien races the player encountered understood only nine phrases, one of which was "Hello," which made communication with them difficult. One unusual aspect of the game was that everything typed in was interpreted as speech. Entering commands such as "go north" would be interpreted by those near you as a request that they leave.

The premise of the game was quite interesting, however, and very true to Star Trek. In a confidential transmission to Admiral Kirk, it was revealed that three Starfleet Academy cadets had beaten the *Kobayashi Maru* test within the previous year, and only one of those by reprogramming the simulation. Therefore, Starfleet decided to drop the test and substitute another.

The new test would not be a "no-win" scenario (who would want to play such a game?) but would be a solvable puzzle. Based on an incident in the history of the starship *Enterprise*, the recovery of the USS *Robert A. Heinlein* during the second five-year mission, this would more accurately simulate that "gray area" between the no-win scenario and the no-lose attitude.

The *Enterprise* was ordered to the 145 Trianguli area to investigate the disappearance of a ship under the temporary command of Hikaru Sulu, who had been recommended for the assignment by Kirk. The game booklet contained a cryptic transmission of the last moments from the ship's flight recorder. Ending in disaster, the transcript revealed that the *Heinlein* evidently had been attacked by twelve ships of unknown origin. Given a description of the planets in the Trianguli area, you were ordered to investigate all possible whereabouts of the *Heinlein*. That's right. *You.* Because in this game, you played the role of James T. Kirk.

If bopping around the galaxy in the early Star Trek games was pretty close to my ultimate fantasy, this was even closer. I was cast in the role of Captain Kirk, with all the attendant possibilities and limitations. I had to fit the part of Kirk, because if I didn't, the other crew members could relieve me of duty.

Movement in the game was accomplished by entering coordinates in Starfleet parlance, and by traveling to those locations by transporter, shuttlecraft, or on foot. The *Enterprise* of the game was fairly complete, containing a bridge, engineering, sick bay, transporter room, turbolifts, and corridors. The layout of the ship was familiar, the commentary provided by the crew was appropriate and in character, and Dr. McCoy even responded to "Bones" when addressed.

The comments of the characters as well as information received from computers and scanning devices was relayed to the player in an innovative series of text windows. This added to the slickness of the presentation, and set *The Kobayashi Alternative* apart from other such games. The planets to be explored ranged from Class M worlds of beauty and flora to harsh and hostile environs. Unfortunately the designers tried to force some traditional adventure game elements such as medieval settings and wizards into the Star Trek universe. They didn't fit. As stated in the writer's guide for *The Next Generation*, fantasy and magic have no place in the Star Trek universe.

Another irritant in the game was the introduction of new members of the crew for the game (though one of them was Ensign Naraht, the Horta who has figured in Diane Duane's novels and comic book stories). Although it is always tempting for a writer to try to create new, interesting characters to add to the Star Trek universe, in this game it was not appropriate. It was difficult even to remember that the new crewmembers existed while playing the game. Further, some of them were necessary to solve the puzzle, and my first inclination was to ignore them as potential "red shirts" and take only the tried and true characters from the original series. After all, I wanted to spend some time with Scotty, Bones, and Chekov, not Lieutenants Renner and Kerasus.

Since the rescue of the *Heinlein* took place between *Star Trek: The Motion Picture* and *The Wrath of Khan*, it was no surprise that Sulu would be found. However, finding him is the point of the game. It wouldn't be entertaining to look for his remains. The hints contained in the supplement pointed the players in the directions of the necessary clues. This hand-holding was necessary because of the very open-ended nature of the game. If you could wander anywhere in the universe, there was no guarantee that you would ever stumble across the information needed to solve the puzzle.

That the game was true to Star Trek philosophy was due in large part to the contributions of Diane Duane, whose work on this computer program makes her the most varied creator in the history of Star Trek (novels, computer software, and scriptwriting). The characters acted like the people we have come to know and love over the past twenty years and the documentation was written in the same "semi-official" format that made the original *Technical Reference Manual* such as winner. Duane was credited with text and story as part of the design team, and in a computer text adventure, that's the most important part.

The story was good. The characters were real. The puzzle was too hard.

By contrast, the second authorized Star Trek game from Simon and Schuster, *Star Trek: The Promethean Prophecy*, was exactly what I was afraid would happen when I first heard that Star Trek text adventures were being written.

Though the characters were on target, the game itself was much more of a standard computer text adventure, in which the plotline of the story was fully thought out for you, and you were expected to type certain things into the computer at certain times and hope you said what the programmer expected.

Example: The first time I played, Ensign Berryman did a terrible job of analyzing the attack at the beginning of the game. I didn't find out the attackers were Romulan until I called Spock to the bridge to relieve Berryman. So, after dying, I decided the next time out to call Spock to the bridge to relieve Berryman immediately. Instead of getting Spock to the bridge, I was merely informed that he was inspecting sensors, and I would be able to contact him shortly. I would be forced to endure the ineptitude of Berryman until the program decided it was time to permit me to make progress. Pointless! But that's all supposed to be part of the fun. . . .

So is destroying the Romulan, accomplished by repeatedly unloading photon torpedoes at the mirror image paralleling the Romulan's attack. One of the most frustrating things in any adventure game is being forced to repeat the same command over and over, with the program not responding correctly until you have entered the command a predetermined number of times.

Surprisingly, this frustrating section at the start of the game was completely superfluous to the main plot of the program. This was merely an excuse to contaminate the ship's supply of food, so that I could be forced to beam down to a planet's surface for an even more standard adventure, involving a legendary race of beings who held the key to replenishing the *Enterprise*'s food supply.

The upshot of *The Promethean Prophecy* was that the majority of the time playing the game was spent battling the parser to try to get the game to do something, then being prodded along by the other characters in the game when my progress was too slow. The parser did not understand simple phrases such as "go to," and the documentation did not clue me in as to the phrases required to accomplish many things. Example: the book said that to transport down to the planet's surface, we must stand on the transporter, then give the command "energize." So I entered the command, "stand on transporter." The computer responded by telling me that the word "on" seemed out of place.

Much more irritating was the predilection of the program to use a certain word in a description, then be completely unable to understand it when used by a player. I could understand some of that (otherwise the descriptive prose would be limited to the game's working vocabulary), but when Uhura told me that we were receiving a transmission from an unknown source, and asked me if I would like to put the transmission on the screen, I expected the command, "Uhura, put transmission onscreen" to have more of an effect than generating the message that the computer did not understand "transmission" or "onscreen." Though I initially thought the documentation for *The Kobayashi Alternative* was too explicit in its list of vocabulary and phrases, the alternative as found in *The Promethean Prophecy* was less enjoyable.

Probably the most enjoyable aspect of *The Promethean Prophecy* was its documentation, another fine package from Simon and Schuster. The top-rate illustrations included a letter from Sam Kirk on Deneva to his brother in San Francisco (as a philatelist, I'm glad to see they'll still be using stamps in the 23rd century). Photos of the original crew were utilized in the margins, and the two prose sections, a short introduction to the story and the transcript of a speech given by Captain Kirk on effective starship management, were both well written. Overall, the effect was less technical than *The Kobayashi Alternative*, and more like a professionally produced fanzine.

Both of these programs may pale in comparison to the third offering from Simon and Schuster, *Star Trek: The Rebel Universe*. Immediately available for the Atari ST, and not yet available for a computer on which I could play it (as I write this), the reality of *The Rebel Universe* will be enhanced by the use of digitized graphics and sound effects from Star Trek television and movie productions—and the opening will be spoken by William Shatner! The plot of this third adventure will center around a rebellion against the

Federation, which the *Enterprise* will be sent to quell. There will be more than 4,000 possible planets to explore, so the emphasis on exciting adventure in unknown worlds seems to be right on target. But best of all, rather than requiring the user to enter commands from a limited vocabulary of possible words, the program will be more graphically oriented, with the user pointing at items to use, and selecting actions for those items by mouse clicks.

This method of gameplay has been made possible by the advent of even more powerful computers such as the Atari ST and the Commodore Amiga, whose capabilities actually exceed those of the mainframes on which the original Star Trek games were developed. On those earlier machines, many users shared the resources of a single computer. On these newer machines, that same power is harnessed to provide a single user with graphics and audio beyond anything a mainframe could accomplish.

And this newest game will more correctly live up to the original hopes I had for a Star Trek computer game. With such an interface, the player will be much more like the writer/director of a Star Trek movie—manipulating characters and situations which will add up to a brand new Star Trek adventure on your desktop. This is the latest step in the long path that will inevitably lead to something much like the holodeck which has featured so prominently in *The Next Generation*.

Each of the more than 20 games mentioned in this article expands the Star Trek universe slightly, as does each novel, comic book, or fanzine story that you may read. But video and computer games expand that universe in a way that simply cannot be done by any other media: by beaming *you* into the 23rd century as an active, living character in the Star Trek universe. When you play a Star Trek video or computer game, *you* have the conn. Starfleet wants you! Enlist at your nearest arcade, video game console, or home computer!

THE MEN AT THE HELM: CAPTAINS KIRK AND HORNBLOWER

by Mark Alfred

(First Semester Essay for "Military Theory and Theorists," SA 203, Starfleet Academy)

Since this paper is not intended to be a biography of Captain James T. Kirk, I will briefly mention only a few facts before presenting my thesis and its documentation.

James Tiberius Kirk was born in Riverside, Iowa, and was surrounded by a farming atmosphere during his early years. His brother George Samuel, "Sam," elder by four years, left Earth as a colonist when Jim was fourteen. Sam's action crystallized the yearnings for adventure Jim had experienced since early childhood. His father, George Sr., was often away from his family due to his posting as Starfleet Security Supervisor, an occupation filled with excitement and danger in young Jim Kirk's imagination. He also absorbed his mother Winona's love of reading, and treasured the tactile pleasures of holding and reading an old-style printbook.

As mentioned in his autobiography, *Where No Man Has Gone*

Before, and as also referred to in his *Strategy and Tactics*, a text for this very course, Captain James Kirk is familiar with the twelve "Hornblower" books of Cecil Scott Forester (Earth, 1899-1966). These eleven volumes of fiction and one of commentary chronicle the life of Horatio Hornblower, a fictional member of England's navy around the turn of the 18th century. In his autobiography, Captain Kirk admits to having read the adventures more than once, and in his text he makes several passing comparisons of space tactics to nautical warfare as practiced by actual sea commanders such as Wellington and fictional ones such as Hornblower.

As the young Iowa farm boy absorbed the nautical images of Captain Horatio Hornblower exploring the seas of Earth for king and country, his imagination wakened, sparking the beginnings of his desire to explore the final frontier—space.

It is plain, from a dual examination of the Hornblower books and Captain Kirk's record as a space commander, that the character of Horatio Hornblower did indeed serve, at least in part, as a role model whom Kirk intentionally emulated. In fact, some incidents in Kirk's life entirely outside his control find an eerie resonance in Forester's work.

For example, in *Mr. Midshipman Hornblower* (1948), the 17-year-old youngster, posted to his first ship and completely unfamiliar with seamanship, comes under the rule of John Simpson, the *Justinian*'s senior midshipman. "He was diabolically clever at making other people's lives a burden to them" (Chapter One). This sounds amazingly similar to Captain Kirk's reminiscences of Bruce Finnegan, his "personal tormentor" at Starfleet Academy. In Forester's tale Hornblower manages to get Simpson into a duel, whose rules he changes to make the odds more advantageous to him, just as Cadet Kirk changed the odds of his second *Kobayashi Maru* examination. The dueling pistols misfire, and it ensues that Hornblower is transferred to another ship.

Upon reaching command of his own ship, Captain Kirk must have seen many similarities between his function and that of Hornblower in Earth's nautical past. For example, in the 18th and 19th centuries, before the invention of wireless radio, a ship was effectively out of contact with the Admiralty upon weighing anchor, unless it chanced upon a ship with later news from home.

In the same way, the great galactic distances traversed by the *Enterprise* in her patrols rendered even subspace radio communication a long series of delayed replies, of little use in an urgent situation. As in Hornblower's day, the lack of a speedy, reliable communications link placed a special burden of power and responsibility upon the captain of a Ship of the Line.

It is hard to underestimate the extent of that power. Not only do Captains Hornblower and Kirk command a force not to be encountered lightly in battle, they are also constrained by that very power to use it constructively and responsibly to further the goals of the Commands each serves.

The rigors of rank and command placed a lonely burden upon a ship captain in England's fleet. Sometimes operating under sealed orders, or under strictest secrecy (as in *Beat to Quarters*, published in 1937), always responsible for decisions whose facts might remain ever unknown to his subordinates, Hornblower deliberately cultivated a personal reputation for calculation and aloofness.

While Captain Kirk's manner, to all reports, is more accessible than Hornblower's is described to be, none can doubt that he has undergone enough experiences to provoke somber reflection on the demands of his role as a commander of men. Who knows but that occasionally he might wish for the serenity of a quiet beach to walk on, freed from care and responsibility—but he knows he cannot escape the loneliness and solitude of command.

At various times in his adventures, notably in *Commodore Hornblower* (1945) and *Lord Hornblower* (1946), Forester's hero is shown regretting that he cannot confide in his second-in-command or in his lieutenants, but must order his men to risk their lives with no explanation other than their captain's bidding. It is much the same in today's Starfleet, when in an emergency situation the discipline of the service may require uninformed obedience.

After visiting Gamma Hydra IV, Kirk and other crewmen began aging rapidly after exposure to low-range radiation from a renegade comet. One of Kirk's symptoms was a forgetfulness that Starfleet Code Two had been broken by Romulan Intelligence. After treatment for the radiation poisoning and in the midst of a Romulan attack, Kirk ordered the use of Code Two for a message to Starfleet, despite a reminder as to Code Two's status. As became clear, Kirk used Code Two deliberately to put the Romulan force off-guard, broadcasting what is familiar to tactics students as a variation on "the Corbomite maneuver."

This sort of insightful deceit of an enemy is another character trait the young Kirk may have admired in Hornblower's exploits. As described in *Ship of the Line* (1938), Hornblower's ship, the *Sutherland*, "had the round bow given her by her Dutch builders, the same as nearly every French ship of the line, and unlike every English ship save three or four" (Chapter Ten). A French brig indeed takes *Sutherland* for French, and hoists the signal flags "MV," which Hornblower correctly interprets as the French secret recognition symbol for ships at sea. Hornblower subsequently harasses French forces up and down the French and Spanish coasts, using "MV" to come close enough for attack before baring *Sutherland*'s true colors.

Similar tactics have been followed by Captain Kirk time and again, the aforementioned Corbomite bluff comprising an excellent example. Likewise, when the refitted *Enterprise* came under Khan Singh's sneak attack from *Reliant*, Kirk temporized while in fact accessing *Reliant*'s command codes and dropping Khan's shields out from under him.

One use of the *Sutherland*'s Dutch construction was the capture of the aforementiond French brig, the *Amelie*. While transporting Federation ambassadors to Babel I, stardate 3842.2, Captain Kirk used a similar tactic to lure a dangerous opponent into striking range. After receiving repeated phaser strikes from an Orion suicide vessel, Kirk ordered a sequenced power shutdown. The Orion approached for the kill, certain it had disabled its opponent, and dropped its shields. Suddenly *Enterprise* burst into action and fatally damaged the other: a tactic virtually identical to Hornblower's in inception.

When Jim Kirk was eight, his elder brother Sam helped him build a treehouse—actually a wooden fort on legs—which the boy immediately christened *Lydia*. A family flatphoto, published in Shaw and Van Cott's *Kirk*, shows the grim-faced boy standing at the top of the fort's ladder, wooden-lath sword at the ready as if to repel hostile boarders. The photo's caption states that the fort was "named after a ship in an old movie."

Indeed. In 1951, Warner Brothers Studios released the flatfilm *Captain Horatio Hornblower*, which in the space of two hours condenses the action of *Beat to Quarters*, *Ship of the Line*, and *Flying Colors* (1938), into one heady narrative. Considering that it is a flatfilm recorded on acetate in 2D and monosound, *Hornblower* is an exciting experience, and Gregory Peck in the title role embodies all the captainly virtues to be admired by a preadolescent, starry-eyed farm boy. With all due respect for Captain Kirk and the peoples of Elan and Troyius, Hornblower even falls in love with Barbara Wellesley, a noble lady entrusted to the *Lydia* for transportation to her appointed wedding.

As shown in the film, the *Lydia* prevails against the *Natividad*, a ship greatly outgunning her, but only after a hellish, protracted combat that exacts a fearful toll. One of the casualties is a youth, Mr. Longley, shown previously as an earnest and precocious young officer, as eager to learn seamanship as Cadet First Class Peter Preston some 450 years later was eager to learn engineering aboard the *Enterprise*.

After sinking the *Natividad*, Hornblower descends to sickbay to find Lady Barbara Wellesley tenderly caring for the dying lad, who in his death fever believes her to be his mother. Hornblower assists her in allowing the lad to die restfully and at peace. Such also was Kirk's compassion and nobility at the deathbed of Peter Preston, who was mortally wounded by Khan's attack on the *Enterprise*. With a myriad other responsibilities clamoring for his attention, Kirk took time to attend and comfort a crew member fallen in the line of duty. What might be perceived by some as a waste of the cadet's life was redeemed by the valor with which he surrendered it for his comrades. Captains Kirk and Hornblower alike did not shirk the duties of command as they paid tribute to their fallen crewmen.

Toward the middle of the movie, Hornblower makes a fateful decision. Showing the "MV" signal to the fort atop the cliffs of Rosas Bay, *Sutherland* safely enters; with her cannon she dismasts four French ships of the line before she is severely damaged.

It becomes apparent that *Sutherland* is doomed, as she absorbs round after round of cannon shot from the French ships as well as the Rosas embrasures. Knowing his ship must sink or be captured, Hornblower decides, "Let's sink her where she'll do the most good—in the center of the channel," to block the passage of any other French ships. His strategy, though desperate, is sound: he cannot save his ship, so it is best, given the circumstances, that her loss do the greatest possible damage to the enemy.

The correlation here to Captain Kirk is obvious. The drama of Hornblower's fictional act of final strategic defiance is surpassed by the real-life actions of Kirk when attacked by the Klingon Kruge's

Bird-of-Prey. Kruge's stealthy approach while cloaked and subsequent dishonorable sneak attack disabled *Enterprise*'s autosystems, leaving her defenseless. Kirk's son, Dr. David Marcus, was then murdered to coerce Kirk to surrender his ship. Who can say whether the desperate yet intuitively correct actions of Hornblower, his childhood hero, did not come to Kirk's mind as he searched his memories and experiences for a way—any way—to strike back at Kruge.

The *Enterprise*, in design as well as spirit Starfleet's finest ship, could not under any circumstances be surrendered to Klingon military intelligence. Both regulations and Kirk's training and common sense dictated he must scuttle her. But how to give her loss its utmost value? How to "sink" her where it would do the most good?

Kirk pretended to surrender, asking for two minutes to inform his crew. In that time he armed the *Enterprise*'s secondary self-destruct mechanism and beamed down with his four companions to Genesis. Kruge's boarding party, nearly his entire crew, materialized aboard the *Enterprise* moments later, too late to prevent their doom as the *Enterprise*, Starfleet's finest and best, fulfilled her last and most noble role. Kirk's actions turned the loss of his vessel into a masterstroke of strategy that changed the odds of the confrontation to his eventual favor. Just as Hornblower had used the inevitable loss of *Sutherland* to inflict the greatest damage to his enemy, so Kirk forged from the destruction of his own ship a fighting chance to survive. Kirk not only survived, he prevailed, bringing his crew home in a captured ship, complete with Klingon prisoner.

I have endeavored to show the influence of C. S. Forester's Horatio Hornblower on James Kirk's Starfleet career. We have seen not a slavish imitation or a superstitious reenactment of an idol's exploits; rather, Kirk has taken from what might be considered a worthless diversion a new perspective on his duties. As with his studies of Earth's 20th-century conflicts and the United States' Civil War, Kirk has utilized the brilliance of past warriors to prevail in the present. As the great tactician he is, Kirk realizes that the key to victory is not in outgunning an opponent, but outthinking him.

I shall conclude this survey by describing Hornblower's triumphant return from supposed death in France after the loss of the *Sutherland*. Recall, if you will, the recent return of Captain Kirk and his crew from Vulcan in their captured ship, and the manner of Kirk's final disposition as captain of NCC-1701-A. Now, at the conclusion of *Flying Colors*, also used as the closing of the flatfilm, Hornblower has retaken the British ship *Witch of Endor* from the French and sailed her home to England. The English public believed the *Witch of Endor* had been a prize to the French for nearly a year, and Captain Horatio Hornblower had been dead six months (Chapter Fifteen).

As England reacts to Hornblower's arrival home, "Somebody was cheering. Hundreds of voices here cheering . . . Precious few other captains have ever been cheered by all the ships in the fleet like this" (Chapter Eighteen).

Need I add that seldom has a starship captain been awarded such richly deserved acclaim as was Kirk at the conclusion of his court-martial?

And now Captain Kirk is once more at the helm of the *Enterprise*. None can doubt that this legendary ship, her crew, and her commander will encounter new exploits to be appreciated by students of military theory and by the public the *Enterprise* serves. Captain Horatio Hornblower is a fictional character whose adventures are experienced as at the most an inspiring diversion. The courageous deeds of James T. Kirk are a real demonstration of the best our Federation has to offer, a shining example of the worthiness of honor, valor, and public service.

Hail, Hornblower! Hail, and thank you, Captain Kirk!

WALKING THE DECKS OF THE REAL ENTERPRISE

by Sally Jerome

Basically, I am a quiet, reserved, introverted person. Until someone mentions Star Trek. Then my antenna goes up and starts whirling around. I am always ready to set up a display of my collection somewhere or promote Star Trek any way I can.

This was the display to end all displays. And what came about because of it, I would never have dreamed possible.

WXXV-TV, channel 25, asked me to help them promote the then new *The Next Generation* series by placing one of my displays in their Star Trek Day in the Mall promotion. I was more than happy to do so. The Day was such a huge success that the wonderful people at WXXV called Paramount and arranged a private tour of the Star Trek sound stages for me and a party of two. I took my son, Lon, and his friend, Paul Felix.

It was raining when my plane landed. Lon met me at Los Angeles Airport and we drove out to Edwards Air Force Base to pick up Paul. By the time we got back to L.A. to check into the Ambassador, it was a monsoon! As we exited the freeway, we saw cars stalled in deep water in the outer lane. A Highway Patrol car was off the road in a ditch, totally covered with mud. The only thing

349

you could see was its antenna sticking up. When we got settled in our hotel room and turned on the late news, we saw on the TV screen the scene we had just passed, mud-covered patrol car and all. The officer had gotten out of the vehicle in time and wasn't injured. What a way to start our weekend!

It was a dark and stormy night, but the day dawned clear and bright! (I always wanted to say that. Does it sound Hollywood enough?) The morning *was* beautiful as we picked up our pass at Paramount. They give you ten minutes to get your pass at the Pass and I.D. Building just behind the Melrose Avenue gate, or you're off the lot! We drove the car to the parking lot and walked the couple of blocks to the left where the William S. Hart Building is. The only four-story building on the lot, it houses the Star Trek offices. Richard Arnold's office is on the fourth floor; that is where we were heading. There was an elevator at the back of the long hallway, but we walked up, stopping at every floor. That way we got to go by all the rooms and peek into the offices through the open doors.

From the start of our day in Richard Arnold's office, to eating in the Commissary, to the company store, where you can buy souvenirs, to walking the studio streets over to the sound stages, everything was better than we ever could have imagined! It was a special unexpected treat to see all of the Oscars and Emmys displayed in a window showcase outside of the Commissary. We even walked past the old sound stage where *King Kong* was filmed (the original, with Fay Wray).

While we were standing outside the gift shop, Ted Danson walked by with a coffee cup in his hand and a briefcase under his arm. He waved and said, "Hi." It didn't take long to realize that if you saw someone you thought was somebody, they probably were. Meredith Baxter drove by in her neat white car and waved, too. Probably at our guide, Richard Arnold. He's head of public relations for Star Trek. But it's nice to think that she was waving at all of us. I don't think she was doing the seven mph speed limit, either. Stardom has its privileges.

Before we got to the sound stages, we went by the city streets sets from *The Untouchables*. They've been used in some of the Star Trek episodes, too.

The first sound stage we entered was Stage 16. This is the Planet set. It was all the space they need to build any planet surface they might want, and the lighting system to make it any color they choose. There is a huge tank that can be filled with water to create a lake. It can be drained and used for caverns and tunnels, as in "Encounter at Farpoint." The police station for "The Big Goodbye" was set up on this stage. It was painted to make the walls above the railings and woodwork look soiled, giving them a used appearance. I know they do things like this all the time, but we were impressed. Even Paul said he was impressed, and he's usually noncommittal.

Mr. Arnold went to all the doors of Sound Stage 6, but it was "locked down," so we didn't get to see the *Next Generation* bridge. Mr. Arnold told us that someone had taken visitors on the set and they had turned all of the electrical systems on and had blown some fuses and wiring. It could have started a fire, taking a great deal of time to rewire and repair. I can't imagine anyone doing anything like that! It's almost sacrilegious.

The first Star Trek sound stage on the lot is Stage 9. It has the permanent sets from the movies on it, and they are used as part of *The Next Generation Enterprise* as well. The bridge is the "battle bridge" for the new series. Dixon Hill's office for "The Big Goodbye" was set up in a corner of the stage that wasn't used as part of the permanent sets.

What can you say about walking the decks of the *real Enterprise*? Except that it makes the hair stand up on the back of your neck! Especially when you enter the sound stage and start down the corridor and you realize that the person walking just ahead of you is Patrick Stewart! Captain Jean-Luc Picard himself! It's all there, too. The corridors, crew quarters, transporter room, bridge, "new and just completed" conference room with its gorgeous 3-D Federation emblem, medical sickbay with the "mahogany" diagnostic table, and next to it, the engine room! That was really something else in a whole tour that was *all* something else to begin with!

The engine room is really fabulous: three stories high with a working elevator. When you stand at the railing in front of the main engine and look down, it's painted to give the illusion that it goes on and on. The main engine reminds me of a very high-tech potbellied stove. I mean that as a compliment, because it seems to be somehow very familiar and something you can relate to, and at the same time "outer-spacy." They still have six of the pedestal chairs left from the original series. Now they're blue. Some of the technicians who are working there worked on the original series. The man who pulled the doors open when they went "whoosh" still does.

Gene Roddenberry came on the set while we were there and asked the sound man (also an original) if there was anything they needed. The sound man told Mr. Roddenberry that they needed a new roof. It had rained a deluge the night before and there were buckets sitting around to catch the drips. I'll bet they got their roof!

A closed set doesn't just mean that you can't get onto it without a pass, it also means that the actors can't leave it in their Star Trek uniforms, either! So they eat on the set. Lunch was brought in by a catering service while we were there and they asked us if we wanted to eat with them, but we had already eaten in the Commissary. We did have a snack, though, and this way we got to do both. I wouldn't have missed a chance to eat in the studio Commissary!

There were boxes of Cheerios on the serving table, too. At the time they had their *Next Generation* promotional stickers inside. One of the extras gave me one of them. One was the new *Enterprise* sticker and I didn't have it yet. I was thrilled to get it. Especially at that time, from that place. I hate to tell you how many boxes of Cheerios I bought, trying to win a little plastic *Enterprise*! I never did. A friend of mine needed a box of cereal and he bought Cheerios so I could have the sticker, and he won a little *Enterprise*! With one box! He gave it to me. Some of the extras are "permanent extras," so they will appear in the background of several of the episodes all year long, giving the series a look of continuity. They work as doubles and stand-ins for the cast as well.

We watched them for a couple of hours setting up the scene and getting the lighting just right. The actors rehearsed the scene twice, then the director called, "Clear the set," and the people who had just wandered in and were standing around, left. There weren't many. We were about the only outsiders around that day and we didn't have to leave. Some of the extras were sitting at a table playing cards to pass the time between scenes.

A bell rang loudly and the director called, "First team," and all the actors filed in to do the scene, right past us! And I brought binoculars with me so I would be able to see them! The director said, "Lights," and they flooded the scene with blinding light. Then "Camera," and a man held up a clapboard to record the number of the scene and the take. Then he said, "Action," and they did the scene. I'll never forget one word of the dialogue. They're all very professional and *very* good.

While the sound man was setting up his recorder, a piece of

plastic broke off something inside the machine. I couldn't see from where I was standing exactly what it was. He scrounged up a tube of glue from one of the other technicians and fixed it, put the cover back on, and was ready to do the scene. The reel-to-reel recorder was about the size of my old Beta VCR. It didn't look new, but it did look like it was a very expensive unit. The man operating the microphone boom during the take would swing it so fast from one actor to the other that I was afraid he was going to bop one of them on the head, but of course he never did.

Walking down the corridor of the *Enterprise*, I noticed one of their "alien" potted plants sitting to the left of one of the doorways. It was the one with lavender-colored, saw-tooth-edged leaves. I had seen it in some of the episodes that had already been shown on TV, and it was all so familiar, I felt right at home, but at the same time totally in awe of it all. A roll-about clothes rack with costumes for the cast hanging on it was just outside the conference room. One of the beds from sickbay was in the corridor. They store some of the equipment they're not using in the room of the permanent sets that they don't need for that particular episode or scene. It was a real trip to brush by the clothes rack and even get to touch the plant and those six chairs from the original series!

I was amazed at all the cables and electrical equipment all over the place. It's really dangerous and you could trip over something and have an accident if you didn't watch your step. But all that equipment is what makes our *Enterprise* fly! The one thing that sticks in my mind in this high-tech, special-effects age is that they have to push the camera manually on smooth wooden planks while filming. That really surprised me, although it's nice to know that there are still some things machines can't do.

When it was time to leave, we went out the opposite side of the sound stage from where we'd entered. The door opened up onto a group of trailers for the cast. They had all put their personalized hand-drawn signs on the doors. Gates McFadden was in her trailer waiting to do her next scene. She was dressed in a beautiful pink suit that looked like it was straight out of the 1940s. It was. She said that every time she rehearsed the scene in it and knelt down, it would wrinkle and she'd have to call wardrobe to steam press it, and that was hard on her legs and nylons.

I hadn't really said much all day and I figured I could ask one personal question without getting into too much trouble. Besides, the tour was all but over and there was no way they could take my day away now! So I asked her why she had changed her first name from Cheryl to Gates. Her answer really surprised me! She told me her mother's maiden name was Gates. My mother's maiden name was Gates, too!

She had always wanted to use it as her stage name, and the role in the series gave her that opportunity. Were we both surprised to have the name Gates in common. The time frame of "The Big Goodbye" put her at about my mom's age in the Forties, and she looked so much like her in that pink suit, it was uncanny. As we said our good-byes, she commented on how much she liked the brown leather bomber jackets Lon and Paul were wearing.

Just to the right of the cast's trailers was the makeup trailer. The makeup man was just starting to put Data's makeup on as we walked by.

My day was over. What can you say about a dream (that you never even dared dream about in the first place) come true?

Outstanding?

Doesn't do it justice.

Nothing could!

Thank you, Richard Arnold! Nobody ever taken on a tour enjoyed or appreciated it more than I did.

Postscript.

During the time we were walking around the sound stages, I wanted to reach down and pick something up off the floor. A sliver of wood, peeling paint, dust, anything! There probably was nothing there. I didn't look to see. It was just a thought, and I'm surprised it had even crossed my mind. It's just not something I'd do.

While we were on the sets, Mr. Arnold told us to stand back and be very quiet. We did, and we were. When we left, I discovered I had paint all over the back of my jacket! I'll never wash it! I couldn't take the chance of washing out the paint! I got my souvenir!

This is my official thank-you to WXXV-TV 25. I could fill all the paper in the world with thank-you's and it still wouldn't suffice.

We had a wonderful weekend and did some memorable things, but they all pale beside walking the decks of the *real Enterprise*!

THE DISAPPEARING BUM: A LOOK AT TIME TRAVELS IN STAR TREK

by Jeff Mason

"Everybody remember where we parked."

Jim and his shipmates left the park and entered the city at dawn. The sun burnished adobe houses with gold and burned away the fog. Long, fuzzy shadows shortened and sharpened

Jim had not walked through his adopted home in a long while. Climbing the steep hills, he began to wish he had come on the voyage in a pair of good walking shoes instead of dress boots.

Ground cars and pedestrians crowded the streets and sidewalks. Jim's tension doubled as everyone around them gave them more than a second look. His group was suddenly surrounded by a forest of pointed fingers and running people. Spock, in particular, seemed to receive special notice. Jim's alarm grew; the rest looked bewildered as a crowd formed a tight circle, pushing and shouting good-natured gibberish. More people got out of ground cars, some of the vehicles stopping so fast that only luck prevented several minor accidents. Others ran weaving through traffic to join the swelling mob.

A small notepad and what Jim assumed to be a writing instrument were shoved into his hands. Behind him, the others, too, were under a barrage of paper, everything from bound books to paper satchels. At the same time they were bombarded with unintelligible questions, to which they responded with a blank look or "Eh?" "Um?" or "Er?" To Jim, his crew looked to be more frightened by this than by any of the space monsters they'd faced or combat situations they'd been through together.

A long-haired, pimply youth popped up through the human wall and managed a reasonable facsimile of the Vulcan nerve pinch on the shoulder of a startled Spock.

"Live long and prosper, man!" the youngster said with a smile and a Vulcan salute.

Spock gently pushed away a small book called *Come Be With Me* proffered by another hand, and arched an eyebrow at Kirk.

"Fascinating."

The crowd around him laughed and clapped.

Kirk, not knowing what else to do, agreed with a young woman that his costume was indeed "authentic-looking," and then signed his name "James T. Kirk." The woman looked delighted.

Then the questions poured down on his head.

I've just written a revised version of a portion of Chapter 6 of Vonda McIntyre's novelization of *Star Trek IV: The Voyage Home*. I won't apologize. I'm just using it as an example to point out what would seem to be an obvious problem:

Just where the heck is *the* star trek in Star Trek? Where's the show, the movies, the entire sub-culture that grew around the Great Bird's creation? In all of the episodes or movies or novels that present Captain Kirk's past—our present—everything is exactly the same as in our reality, except for that one important cultural artifact: Star Trek. One of the most important and influential television shows in history is missing in Kirk's past. The mob scene I invented did not take place in McIntyre's novel, but why did it not take place?

In the first two editions of *The Best of Trek*, James Houston, Walter Irwin, and Mark Andrew Golding fought a very technical skirmish over the mechanics of time and time travel in the Star

Trek universe. I get out of my depth very quickly in some of their arguments, especially those of Mr. Golding, but the ones I was able to wade through made it obvious that one of the major unsolved issues left alive after a run through the idea mill was the question of whether the Star Trek universe is one that runs on linear time, where events follow one after the other, unchanging and unchangeable, or if the Star Trek universe runs on time lines, those devices beloved of science fiction writers, in which time can be split into multiple realities by events called cusps.

Time lines are a lot more fun, as they can be split like firewood, tied or looped in fancy knots like ribbon, or erased altogether in mind-scrambling paradoxes in which you end up swallowed by scabrous green genealogical beasties of your own making. Under the rule of time-lines, Adolf Hitler could just as easily have been blown into a thousand oily pieces in the trenches of World War I as he could have become a frustrated artist who emigrates to America as he could have been dictator of Germany.

The absence of Star Trek the television show in the 1987 depicted in *Star Trek IV: The Voyage Home* conclusively proves the parallel-time-line theory of the Star Trek universe. If this is the case, then there must have been a cusp event that split our reality (hereafter called time line 1) from the "reality" that will become the universe in which the United Federation of Planets will exist, what we fans call the Star Trek Universe.

During the entire run of the TV series, and in all of the films, there is no mention that anyone else has attempted time travel to visit Earth's past. Therefore, I contend that the split between time line 1 and time line 2 was caused by the inadvertent intervention and/or outright carelessness of the crew of the *Enterprise*.

The crew is well aware that critical cusps affecting time don't have to be major, earth-shaking events—Edith Keeler proved that to them. But could something else just as seemingly minor, perhaps even more so, have caused a cusp that would, amazingly, protect the founding of the Federation by destroying its TV image in the twentieth century?

In "Tomorrow Is Yesterday," Kirk gets an A in temporal damage control; no new time lines were created. But as no one recognized him as a member of the *Enterprise*, we may assume that the split took place earlier than the 1960s. The same thing is true of "Assignment: Earth." Therefore, we must look to the earliest time to which the *Enterprise* crew traveled: the 1930s of "City on the Edge of Forever."

Throughout the episode Kirk and Spock work to identify and fix the damage done to time by McCoy in his drug-induced madness. The cusp, of course, is the life or death of Edith Keeler: If she lives, the Federation is washed from time's blackboard; if she dies, Kirk's and Spock's future is guaranteed. In this case history is like a time-line marshaling yard: it's up to Kirk and Spock to guide the train onto the right branch line before McCoy arrives and slides it onto a deadend siding. Kirk, at immense cost to himself, rights the wrong to history. They return to their present, appearing to have corrected every change in the time line that has been caused by their presence.

Or have they?

There is one event, caused also by McCoy's intervention, that is *not* rectified when the trio returns through the Portal. This event is odd in that it seems to have no relation to the other happenings in the episode. It occurs, and nothing that follows appears affected by it. But it seems McCoy inadvertently found a new branch siding and switched the temporal express right onto it.

Scene: McCoy has just crossed through the Guardian. The first person he sees in the streetlamp light is a bum, a nobody like thousands of others belched out of the guts of the Great Depression. His evening meal is in his hand. McCoy screams and rages, obviously out of his mind, so the bum freezes, hoping the madman will just walk back through the wall again.

He stands petrified as the doctor questions him and examines his skull, then stands surprised as the crazy collapses in a gibbering heap. He gets over his astonishment fast enough to rifle the pockets of the unconscious lunatic. He doesn't find any recognizable swag, but comes up with an oblong black box that fits nicely in his hand. The vagrant doesn't know what it is, but he's sure he can sell it downtown for next week's flophouse money. But first, what do these buttons do?

A bright, human-shaped glow and the bum is dead, atomized. Another nexus has been created, another fork in time that can't be fixed because even McCoy doesn't remember it happening. Even Edith's later death doesn't change this one. To show how important this is, we'll look at the original problem created by McCoy's rescue of Miss Keeler.

Only two time lines are involved so far. If Edith lives, the pacifist movement she leads in the U.S. permits the Nazis to win World War II with atomic weapons; the Federation is prevented from existing on that line. If Edith dies, history should follow its familiar channel. Familiar in this case includes the airing of Star Trek the television series from 1966 to 1969. This causes a problem.

If Star Trek is allowed to exist on the time line that will eventually produce the Federation, the very existence of the show and subculture in the twentieth century will paradoxically negate the universe of the *Enterprise* that we are familiar with in the twenty-third, as modeling an interplanetary government and defense force on a three-hundred-year-old video show would be considered ridiculous. The Federation might exist on such a line, but its form and name would be radically changed. Another break in the time stream must have happened to create both our time line and the *Enterprise*'s line 2.

When Kirk lets Edith die, he thinks he is preserving the integrity of time line 1, the prime line. But even as she becomes one with the pavement, they are all unaware that they are riding on time line 2, which I argue was born with the death of that nameless bum.

Jim's subsequent actions here are understandable: He is so distraught at the loss of Edith, and so relieved to have restored the time fabric at the same time, that his judgment and command faculties are not at their best. But it still remains that he failed to examine their actions completely to ensure no other damage was done, and if found, to somehow prevent that bum's death from the overlooked phaser blast. Therefore, if Edith's end creates two possibilities, two separate lines, McCoy's accidental killing of the bum creates *four* different potential realities.

One: The bum is killed. Edith is hit by that truck. Result, Nazis lose, Federation comes into being.

Two: Bum dies. Edith lives (we assume that Kirk is unable to prevent McCoy from saving her, or that Jim cannot allow her to die). Nazis win, Federation winks out.

Three: Bum lives (does not find phaser or does not experiment with any buttons). Edith dies, Nazis lose, Federation is founded.

Four: Bum lives. Edith is saved by that dashing young captain from the future. Hitler takes it all, Kirk and Edith die in nuclear strike on New York City in 1943. Spock ends his days repairing mechanical rice pickers, and McCoy goes to work on the railway.

(I *am* an engineer, not a doctor!) Federation dies a horrible temporal death, squeezed off into more exotic dimensions.

Fine. By the above list it seems it doesn't matter doodly squat
whether the bum glows in the dark or not. But it stands that Star
Trek the series, the movies, the throngs of Trekkers would track
down and corner Kirk, Spock, and the others at penpoint were they
to show up in the San Francisco of 1986 (or the 1968 of "Assignment: Earth"), do not exist on Kirk's time line 2.

I'm going to engage in speculation, whether you like it or not. I
mentioned earlier that the bum was heretofore unnamed, so let's
call him George. The fact that George dies because, and only because, of McCoy seems important. What happened as a result of
his "untimely" demise?

We can guess that George was one of many unemployed workers
with a family to support, as he is middle-aged and most likely married. Stealing and begging to try to feed his children became his
full-time job. In spite of this he would try to be a good father, and
inspire in his kids hope for the good times he remembers, and that
will come again. We can say his children loved him and leaned on
him a great deal, as George drew support from them.

One, a boy in his early adolescence, is shattered by his father's
sudden disappearance. Not knowing of George's death, he comes
to the conclusion that he and his siblings are victims of desertion.
He grows resentful and rebellious.

The young man is drafted in 1942, but is given a dishonorable
discharge for a drunken attack on an officer. He then wanders from
one menial job to another, finally falling onto the welfare rolls.

In 1953, after an epic pub crawl on the last of his welfare money,
George's son runs down and kills a police sergeant in Los Angeles.
No one saw the late-night hit-and-run, and the drunk speeds off,
driving until he runs out of gas. A few years later, still in fear of
being caught, he dies of alcohol poisoning in a Chicago hospital.

So? It happens that that policeman in his spare time moonlighted
as a television scriptwriter, one who was getting very good at what
he did. His name was Gene Roddenberry.

Thus, Star Trek would have never been shown. It is not exaggeration to say that without the social impetus of the idealism behind
the show, concern for the environment and other aspects of the
human condition would be blunted. Interest in the space program,
acceptance of space-oriented research, or pursuit of any outward-

looking policy was discouraged. The pessimism of the Sixties generated by the Vietnam War, and the worldwide invitation to a nuclear
barbecue, was not countered by the optimism and hope generated
by the original voyages of the *Enterprise*, and by Roddenberry's
own world vision. This mood was not helped any by the syndication
and endless reruns of *Lost in Space*.

In TV and perhaps elsewhere, racial integration would have been
set back years, as well as concern for endangered species like humpback whales, all in part due to the absence of Roddenberry's
ground-breaking. This is the reality of time line 2, a world exactly
like ours except without Star Trek, all resulting from the accidental
death of a bum in the 1930s. This cusp is just as important as Edith's
death, and in conjunction with it gives new importance to the four
separate time lines I listed before. We'll look at them again.

One: The bum is killed. Edith dies as well. The show Star Trek
does not air. Lack of ecological concern helps humpback whales as
well as other animals to become extinct. The Federation is established, and the *Enterprise* undertakes its famous and well-
documented five-year mission. Add Eugenics wars, Colonel Green,
Tribbles, Klingons, etc., shake well, and you've got time line 2.

Two: The bum is vaporized but Edith lives. The Nazis use A-
bombs to conquer the world. Presumably the whales die out and in
consequence the probe destroys a planet full of fifteenth-generation
National Socialists.

For obvious reasons Star Trek never aired on this line, as the
state-run stations only showed the *Adolf and Eva Variety Hour*.

Three: The bum doesn't find the phaser and survives. Edith becomes a New York City traffic statistic. The Allies whip the Hun.
The Great Bird of the Galaxy, alias Gene Roddenberry, produces
his cult favorite from 1966 to 1969. The humpbacks manage to
survive, albeit in small numbers. A body that might well vaguely
resemble the Federation could be down the road, but there is not
a recognizable *Enterprise* and James T. Kirk winds up as captain of
the Saturn-Earth tourist shuttle.

This is our reality, time line 1.

Four: George lives to scrounge another day, and Edith is saved
just in time. The landing party on the Guardian's planet, desperate
for food, wind up eating (who else?) the hapless security men.
Otherwise, treat as Two above.

Note in only one of the possibilities does Roddenberry get to make Star Trek. This is also the line on which is the greatest possibility of survival for the whales: therefore on line 1, the probe will not need to pencil in a side trip to Earth. If McCoy's phaser had *not* done in the vagrant and Edith *had* died, Kirk, Spock, and McCoy would have gone back through the Portal to find themselves still in a chronological mess, except this time they'd be on line 1, no *Enterprise*, an unrecognizable Federation-like organization, and a Saturn-bound shuttle with a missing captain. But when the Guardian told Kirk everything was back the way it was, it knew of what it spoke. McCoy *had* to cause George the Bum's death in order for the following cusp of Edith's death to have its desired effect.

Because the crew of the *Enterprise* never journeyed further in the past than the 1930s, we can assume that as far as the Federation is concerned, before George's death time was running on only one major line (all other cusps of importance happening so far in the past that they resulted in alien realities, as would have occurred if for some unknown reasons Europeans had never colonized the New World). If you accept this, it follows that McCoy as a matter of historical continuity *had* to inject himself with cordrazine in order to charge through the Portal and effect the change that would ensure the future of the Federation on line 2. The reality of the *Enterprise* and its universe could not stand it otherwise. The cusps McCoy provoked had to happen in their particular sequence for the future to remain as he remembered it, George's death being in this case just as important as Edith's.

The irony of this, of course, is that by saving the Federation, by destroying Star Trek, and condemning the whales, McCoy has guaranteed the deadly visit of the probe, which requires that he and his friends once again use time travel to save their future reality.

This is all supposition, of course, but in order for everything to return to the way it originally was, as the Guardian saw it, the bum's killing was a vital necessity. Otherwise, at the end of "City," the Guardian wouldn't have told the captain that everything was patched up again. (It would have told the captain, in that dignified ten-commandments voice, that McCoy had fumbled the goose pâté again, and with whipped-puppy expressions the trio would have trooped dutifully back through the gateway to try it one more time.)

While this argument may not have the number-rattling, theory-twisting complexity of Mr. Golding's or Mr. Irwin's, it proves the time-line theory of the Star Trek universe. It can be seen that the show does not exist in the realities that Kirk visits in the past, and I assert the reason for this is the death of George, the unsung bum. This death spawned two different time lines, ours and the *Enterprise*'s.

I leave it to the experienced Star Trek authors to come up with some interesting plots involving the two lines, something gauche involving the return to kill Gene to save the future . . . or maybe a plot line that's a little more elegant, as in . . . I know, Jim and Spock masquerading as NBC executives in 1964, discouraging a hopeful Gene Roddenberry from developing his really neat idea for a "Wagon Train to the Stars":

Kirk adjusted the uncomfortably thick glasses on his nose and fingered the thick manuscript. An anxious Roddenberry looked on.

"It'll never fly. Nobody would believe it. Right, Mister, er . . . Spocknik?"

Spock stopped trying to perfect his necktie knot.

"Check, Capta—Chief."

STAR TREK'S THIRD SEASON: A WORTHWHILE MIXTURE OF SUCCESS AND FAILURE

by Gregory Herbek

As stated in Allan Asherman's *Star Trek Compendium*, "Continuity is the raw material of anything." One of the primary arguments derogating Star Trek's third season is its loss of continuity with the program's previous two seasons.

In that final year, characters take on personality traits contrary to those already established in the series, and as a result of this change, they react to situations differently than expected by viewers, given the previously determined standards. The changes are radical enough that ultimately a definite gap between the first two seasons and the last has formed. But given the circumstances of specific stories, how much differently are the characters really acting? More important, are their actions justified in light of those circumstances?

In David Gerrold's *The World of Star Trek*, criticisms are leveled against the third-season episode "For the World Is Hollow and I Have Touched the Sky"—criticisms specifically against the characterization of Doctor McCoy, who is supposedly "so out of character, he really isn't Dr. McCoy at all. He's someone else with the same name."

In the episode, the doctor has contracted a fatal disease. Upon beaming into an asteroid/spaceship, he meets Natira, the priestess of the "planet," who falls in love with him. She essentially asks McCoy to be her husband, and eventually he agrees.

It is hardly out of character for McCoy, a dying man, to choose this option. We know his only marriage to have failed and have seen the tragic end of his relationship with Nancy Crater ("The Man Trap"). There is no reason why he would not want to spend the last year of his life with a beautiful woman who really cares for him and has a true desire to learn more about him.

No matter how well one knows a person, one can never be sure how that person will react when suddenly faced with death. McCoy felt he could best confront his dilemma with a woman. Although some would like to have seen him turn to his friends for support, one can't condemn him for his choice. If any character should be scolded, it is Kirk, who refuses to accept his friend's decision. But, like McCoy's decision, Kirk's reaction is realistic. When one stops thinking of these characters as all-perfect heroes and starts thinking of them as human beings with faults and personal needs, the reality of "uncharacteristic" situations sometimes becomes apparent, and one's feelings toward the characters in those situations are heightened.

In the end, of course, the doctor is miraculously cured and returns to the *Enterprise*. Having regained his life, he remembers where his duty lies and that he cannot stay with Natira. If upon being cured, McCoy had refused to leave her, or had even had second thoughts, his actions *would* have been contrary to his previously established personality traits. Instead, he makes a sacrifice not unlike those of Captain Kirk on "City on the Edge of Forever" and Mr. Spock in "This Side of Paradise." All three men, in their respective episodes, have an opportunity to experience true happiness, which none of them his been able to experience before, due to various circumstances. They give up that happiness because of their devotion to duty and each other.

Although instances of seemingly uncharacteristic behavior can sometimes be justified, there are several events and scenes in Star Trek's third season which can be neither explained nor excused.

In "The Cloud Minders," Spock explains the Vulcan mating cycle to Droxine, an acquaintance on the cloud city Stratos. Spock's sexual drive, a subject too personal to discuss with his best friend, Jim Kirk, only a year before in "Amok Time," is relegated to common conversation with a virtual stranger with whom Spock becomes all too intimate. The Vulcan acts similarly uncharacteristically in "The Enterprise Incident." Spock's wooing of the Romulan commander is explainable as a necessary part of his duty, and would be entirely excusable were it not for the final lines:

Spock: All the Federation wanted was the cloaking device.
Commander: The Federation . . . And what did you want?
Spock: It was my only interest . . . when I boarded your vessel.
Commander: And that's exactly what you came away with.
Spock: You underestimate yourself, Commander. Military secrets
    are the most fleeting of all. I hope that you and I exchanged
    something more permanent.

Whereas in the first two seasons, Mr. Spock never displayed sexually oriented emotions, unless under the influence of an outside factor, he does so in "The Cloud Minders" and "The Enterprise Incident," with nothing to account for the change in his behavior.

Occurrences like these only hastened the general deterioration of Star Trek, taking place all too often throughout the third season. The scenes appear, for the most part, in scripts which are poorly written to begin with, and are a result of other actions in those scripts. Therefore, rather than loss of character continuity, the real problem with Star Trek's final season was its shortage of quality scripts and the abundance of those less imaginative and sometimes even childish.

Perhaps it was an omen that NBC chose "Spock's Brain" as the third-season premiere episode. Probably the worst segment of Star Trek, "Spock's Brain" is definitely the least imaginative and disregards the importance that Star Trek always placed on Believability.

Up through the scene in sickbay, when McCoy informs Kirk that Spock's brain has been removed, the episode looks to be a promising mystery. From there the script goes completely downhill, ultimately evolving into little better than a *Space: 1999* episode. Such poor writing is surprising, at least from Gene L. Coon, who had provided such fine scripts as "Devil in the Dark" and "Metamorphosis" in the first and second seasons.

Besides supplying generally inferior stories in the third season, Star Trek's writers relied more than ever before on clichés and even reused story lines, as if they were running out of ideas. One of the worst offenders of rehashed plots is "All Our Yesterdays." Although not a poor story in itself, its similarities to "City on the Edge of Forever" are all too apparent. Other, less flagrant examples include "Plato's Stepchildren," which bears some resemblance to "The Gamesters of Triskelion," and "Requiem for Methuselah" and "Whom Gods Destroy," which borrow plot devices from "What Are Little Girls Made Of?" and "Dagger of the Mind," respectively. The reuse of previously utilized ideas even took place within the third season itself, as Captain Kirk is missing or presumed dead five times that year alone.

These unnecessary similarities are due either to the laziness of the author or the loss of Gene Roddenberry's guidance in the final season, and in most cases, they could have been avoided with a little imagination.

Although the quality of stories presented in Star Trek's final year deteriorated to a certain degree, Star Trek did not lose itself totally. One of the most important aspects of the show, though not at all its best, was still present throughout the third season—the writers continued to incorporate a moral, sociological, or philosophical message into their scripts. Unfortunately, these messages are sometimes too blatant and/or thinly disguised, and some, although well woven into the scripts, are unsuccessful due to a poor story. This is one reason why Star Trek's final year is the least popular of the series. Unlike most first-season segments, in which all aspects of the episode fit together to produce an overall fine drama, something is too often missing in a third-season script. The story is either ill conceived but contains a fine comment, or vice versa.

"The Cloud Minders," for example, unsuccessfully tackles a serious problem of the sixties—and today—race and class division. In the episode, a world inhabited by two "races" is presented. The "superior" people live in the cloud city Stratos, far above the planet's surface. They engage in intellectual pursuits while the "inferior" race, the Troglytes, work in the caves on Ardana, the harsh planet below. Their inferiority, however, is not inherent, but due rather to an invisible gas natural to the caves in which they live.

The idea of individuals being influenced by their environment was a new theory in the 1960s. A commission appointed by President Lyndon Johnson to examine the race riots late in that decade agreed with the theory and ultimately presented two solutions to race conflict in America: the enrichment of ghetto conditions or the integration of ghetto inhabitants with the rest of society. The latter promised eventual equality for all and the commission supported it; unfortunately, Star Trek did not. "The Cloud Minders" agreed that environment shapes the individual, but did not illustrate the course of action necessary to reverse the widening gap between classes in America. At the episodes' end, the Troglytes are given special masks to filter out the harmful effects of the gas, but are still not allowed to share the benefits of the beautiful cloud city—they continue to live in caves. Whether or not the author's intention, the disheartening statement which the episode ultimately makes is that ghetto conditions can be improved, but those who live there will never join the larger society.

"Turnabout Intruder" suffers from similar problems. The episode blends an interesting concept with a compelling drama, but while exploring the issue of feminism, whether intentionally or not, it conveys a chauvinistic message, contrary to Star Trek's previously established beliefs.

However, for every one of Star Trek's third-season mistakes, there is a triumph. Several of that year's episodes do meet the high standards set by the show's earlier installments.

"Let That Be Your Last Battlefield," despite all complaints of obviousness and blatancy, stands as Star Trek's finest editorial against racial hatred and violence. The issue is brought right out in the open when the *Enterprise* encounters two warring aliens from the planet Cheron. Their faces are divided down the middle, one side black, the other white, the coloration of each side of the face opposite that of the other race.

The parallel to blacks and whites is intentionally unmistakable; the viewer immediately relates the hatred on Cheron to the hatred in America, and therefore does not spend an hour deciphering the episode, but rather continually compares the fictional world it presents with the world he or she lives in. Although this format is inferior to Star Trek's usual disguising of modern-day issues, it works to the advantage of this particular episode.

The aliens, Bele and Lokai, are introduced merely as enemies—the latter and his people supposedly oppressed the former and his people. Not until halfway through the story is it revealed that their different pigmentation is the root of their hostilities—a detail that Kirk and Spock, and the viewer, either do not notice or deem significant until the following discourse:

Bele: It is obvious to the most simpleminded that Lokai is of an inferior breed.

Spock: The obvious visual evidence, Commissioner, is that he is of the same breed as yourself.

Bele: Are you blind, Commander Spock? Well, look at me . . . Look at me.

Kirk: You're black on one side and white on the other.

Bele: I am black on the right side. Lokai is white on the right side. All of his people are white on the right side.

That their intense hatred could be caused by this trivial difference is incomprehensible to Kirk and Spock, who are totally perplexed after the above conversation. Earlier in the episode, when Lokai pleads with Kirk to kill Bele, the captain incredulously says, "You're two of a kind!" As the aliens continue to bicker and battle, the viewer adopts Kirk's attitude of incomprehension and sadness. He or she eventually realizes the absurdity and futility of the aliens' hatred and cannot help but carry at least a little bit of that attitude into the real world.

"Day of the Dove" also deals with war and violence. In this story the crew of the *Enterprise* and that of a Klingon battle cruiser are unknowingly forced to fight by an energy being which lives off the hatred and violence of others. In time Kirk and the Klingon commander realize that their true enemy is not each other, but rather the being which is controlling them. They join together in a successful effort to defeat it by laughing it off the ship.

The human capacity to destroy evil through emotions is a concept also explored in the underrated "And the Children Shall Lead." This episode illustrates how evil misleads the innocent and preys on people's fears to achieve its purpose, and how anyone can defeat it once its true identity and intentions are identified.

"Is There in Truth No Beauty?" is another of the finer segments of Star Trek's last season. A study in human emotions, it deals with jealousy and prejudice. The episode explores Larry Marvick's jealousy, which eventually drives him to attempted murder but, more specifically and importantly, it examines Dr. Miranda Jones' jealousy of Mr. Spock.

For years Miranda, a telepath, has been studying on Vulcan with hopes of becoming the first non-Vulcan to achieve mind meld and, in turn, become the first being to meld with a superior mental race called the Medusans. After Miranda has boarded the *Enterprise* with the Medusan ambassador, with whom she has fallen in love, the ship is plummeted into another dimension. The only way to pilot the ship home is to utilize the ambassador's advanced knowledge of star navigation. Since Medusans have no corporeal form and cannot verbally communicate, the only way to utilize the ambassador's knowledge is by telepathy—the Vulcan mind meld.

Spock is chosen to perform this act rather than Dr. Jones because of his technical knowledge of the *Enterprise*. Unfortunately, by establishing a mind-link with the Medusan, Spock executes the very action which Miranda has devoted her life to achieving. Her dream shattered and her lover's mind, in her opinion, invaded by Spock, she houses intense feelings of jealousy and anger for the Vulcan. With Spock on the brink of death after the meld, the question is whether Miranda, unlike Larry Marvick, will find the courage to overcome her jealousy and aid Spock. She eventually does so and saves the Vulcan's life.

"The Empath" also delves into human emotions, specifically the love that Kirk, Spock, and McCoy feel for one another. In the episode, aliens trap the three officers on a strange planet with plans to use them in a brutal experiment. Also on the planet is a mute empath named Gem, on whose account the experiment is being staged. She is an inhabitant of one of two populated worlds in a doomed star system. Unfortunately, the aliens have the power to save only one of the planets, and are using the men of the *Enterprise* to determine whether Gem's race is the one more worthy of being saved.

They torture Kirk and send him back to Gem, who has the power to alleviate his pain by empathically transferring it to herself. She helps the captain and later risks her life to save McCoy, who has been tortured to the point of death. Gem shows the aliens she has learned compassion, and they judge her planet worthy to be rescued.

Just as each of the men would rather endure the pain than have one of their friends subjected to it, Gem, who doesn't even know the officers, would rather transfer that pain to herself than watch them suffer.

"The Tholian Web" uses a somewhat clichéd plot device as its focal point—death of a main character. The problem with this event lies in the viewer's knowledge that a main character in a continuing television series doesn't die, at least not permanently. Therefore, a story which employs this concept must be engaging enough to hold the viewer's attention even though he or she knows the eventual outcome—that the character will be saved or, in this case, will recover. "The Tholian Web" fulfills that requirement and emerges as one of the best episodes of Star Trek's last season.

The apparent death of Captain Kirk kindles some of the finest dramatic interplay between Spock and McCoy in the entire series, revealing much about the Kirk/Spock/McCoy relationship. Although it was obvious before the events of this episode that Kirk is the stabilizing influence in the friendship, that fact has never been illustrated as clearly as in "The Tholian Web," which reveals the condition of Spock and McCoy's relationship with Kirk (they think) permanently missing from it. Though the doctor truly cares for Spock, without Kirk their friendship would never flourish.

Although other third-season segments, such as "Elaan of Troyius" and "The Savage Curtain" are entertaining, they are not as intellectually stimulating as those cited above or earlier episodes such as "Balance of Terror" and "The Doomsday Machine." So it is true that many third-season installments cannot measure up to Star Trek's earlier accomplishments. But the failures of Star Trek's final year are too often identified and criticized by writers who don't bother to also identify the successes.

In *The World of Star Trek*, David Gerrold writes, "Star Trek's best stories were those that were about people; one or two individuals caught in a trying situation." Miranda Jones, Gem, and Bele and Lokai are such people. They, however, are ignored by Mr. Gerrold. He simply damns the third season and harps upon the excellence of the first, ignoring *its* faults.

Star Trek fans and writers can overlook the inconsistencies and problems in a first-season episode for two reasons: (1) Because, on the whole, that season is representative of the series' best, and to criticize it would be close to sacrilegious; (2) because there is usually enough worthwhile material in a first-season script to compensate for any worthless material.

In "Operation: Annihilate!" for example, neither Spock nor McCoy can remember that one of a sun's properties is light. After Kirk has pointed this out to his scientists, McCoy subjects the Vulcan to a potentially lethal experiment before all preliminary test results have been compiled, needlessly resulting in Spock's blindness. These are professional errors far from "in character" for the best medical mind in Starfleet. The episode would be a total failure were it not for the look at Kirk's family and an excellent example of his strenuous command responsibilities.

In "The Menagerie," Spock shows compassion and practices outright deceit, disobeying Starfleet orders and stealing the *Enterprise* for the sake of his former captain. This flaw in Spock's character, however, is ignored, as "The Menagerie" is otherwise excellent Star Trek—and excellent science fiction.

Like the seasons that preceded it, Star Trek's third contains mistakes—perhaps more than its share. However, it also contains too often overlooked quality drama and science fiction. The episodes commended above are only a few examples of the interesting, sensitive, and important scripts which make it worth looking past the mistakes of the third season to its positive impact on the history of Star Trek.

UNIFORMS

by Lieutenant David Crockett

Through television and motion pictures Star Trek has presented to us nearly thirty years of Starfleet and Federation history. In a time period that long, change is inevitable. The Starfleet we see today only remotely resembles the fleet of Captain Christopher Pike. There are different ways in which one could examine the many changes, but one of the easier and more definitive ways is to examine the uniforms of Star Trek.

Uniforms have always been a staple of organized military life, and Starfleet is no exception. Although the primary mission of the *Enterprise* and like vessels is that of scientific exploration and alien contact, starships cover a host of secondary missions military, diplomatic, etc.—and their organization illustrates this fact. Starship crew members progress through an established rank structure in specific branches. Uniforms reflect that progression, for they tell us both the rank of an individual and his branch of service, roughly equivalent to one's area of expertise.

The uniforms of Star Trek have changed much over the years. By examining this evolution from the days of Captain Pike to those of Captain Spock, we can learn much about the careers of the *Enterprise* crew, the organization of Starfleet, and the fleet's changing role over the years.

Let us start at the beginning, and the beginning of Star Trek rests with what seems to us now to be an almost ancient *Enterprise* under the command of a young Captain Christopher Pike. There are only two prominent uniform colors during this time—blue and golden yellow—but there are at least three specific branches, or divisions. The insignia of the *Enterprise* herself is the familiar arrowhead shape. The branch symbols are found in the middle of this insignia. Command is represented by a star, sciences by a three-dimensional ring, and support services by a jagged spiral. At this time, those branched sciences wear blue shirts, while those in command and support both wear the yellow. Captain Pike and First Officer Number One are both branched command. As science officer, Spock is naturally branched sciences. The same is true for Phillip Boyce, the ship's Chief Medical Officer. Lieutenant Tyler, who mans the helm, is in support.

Rank designation at this time is very general. This is evident when one notices that Captain Pike, Number One, Doctor Boyce, and Lieutenants Spock and Tyler all wear one solid gold stripe to indicate rank. Captain Pike is the acknowledged senior officer, but his rank does not reflect this. The single gold stripe probably indicates the very general designation of officer. This differentiates them from the plain cuffs of the crewmen.

The uniforms of this early voyage tell us some interesting things about Starfleet. From the episode "The Menagerie," we know this to be thirteen years prior to Spock's trial; it is a full twenty-eight years before the *Enterprise* herself is destroyed. (Admiral Morrow's comment in *The Search for Spock* about the *Enterprise* being twenty years old is a gross underestimate. She's at least thirty.) The Federation at this time seems to have just commenced a new era of widened exploration and expansion, and the *Enterprise* is its finest ship. She is undoubtedly a fairly new vessel, possibly having just completed her shake-down cruise under her new commander, Robert April. The division of branches indicates that Starfleet is well established and organized, but the simplified rank designation makes it apparent that it is a young organizational structure. Captain Pike represents the beginning of that era in Starfleet when the starship and her crew enjoyed the utmost flexibility and independence from Headquarters—a true Horatio Hornblower in space, brought to its highest level by James T. Kirk.

About twelve years later, the *Enterprise* finds herself under the command of Captain Kirk. Neither the ship nor the uniforms have changed much since the early days of Captain Pike, but some things should be noted, as they set the stage for the first five-year mission under Kirk.

In "Where No Man Has Gone Before," Spock is seen wearing the command branch insignia on a yellow shirt. This is the first indication of an essential fact: As members of any military organization advance in rank and responsibility, they must attend advanced schooling to remain qualified. Sometime in the recent past, perhaps even while Pike was in command, Spock was made first officer of the *Enterprise*. This greatly increased his duties, since he remained science officer as well. In order to fully qualify for both jobs, Spock probably attended an advanced command course. He then transferred from sciences to command for a time. This placed him irrevocably on the road to an eventual command of his own. Now that he is command-qualified, he will soon transfer back to sciences, his true vocation.

This episode also marks the entrance of Sulu and Scotty. Sulu is head of the astrosciences department and is branched sciences, while Chief Engineer Scott is branched support. As chief medical officer, Doctor Mark Piper is also head of the Life Sciences department and branched sciences. That position will soon be filled by Doctor McCoy. Finally, Chief Navigator Gary Mitchell is branched support.

One annoying thing about this episode, which must be taken into account for those who pay great attention to detail, is that the sciences and life-support insignia are reversed from the rest of the series. That is, scientists Sulu, Piper, and Dehner wear the jagged spiral of support, while support personnel Scott, Mitchell, and Kelso wear the three-dimensional ring of sciences. Though it is perhaps best to ignore this inconsistency, there is a feeble explanation that can be given for those who insist on rationalizing such things. For an unknown reason, probably the birth of modern Starfleet bureaucracy, sciences and support switched their insignia sometime during Pike's command, only to switch them back during Kirk's command. . . . Perhaps we should just forget it.

Rank insignia at this time is only slightly more specific than before. Sometime during the few preceding years, Starfleet decided to set apart the commander of the ship. As captain, therefore, Kirk now wears two solid stripes on his sleeve as opposed to the single stripe worn by his officers. As first officer, Spock has been promoted to lieutenant commander, but his uniform still bears a single stripe.

The first major change in modern Starfleet history takes place immediately following "Where No Man Has Gone Before." The *Enterprise* herself undergoes a thorough refitting. There are internal changes, and the crew complement is more than doubled from the 203 of Pike's command to the 430 of Kirk's. The biggest change is in the uniform.

The three major branches remain, their insignia intact. Now, however, uniform color is directly related to branch. Yellow shirts correspond to command, blue shirts to sciences, and the new red shirts to support. Spock therefore has completed his transfer from command back to sciences; Sulu has completed a transfer from sciences to command as he takes his position at the helm. Uhura very early on is seen branched command, but she soon transfers to support. Doctor McCoy takes his place as chief medical officer, and is joined by Nurse Chapel, who brings evidence of yet a fourth branch in Starfleet, the medical branch. This is indicated by the red cross on her *Enterprise* insignia. It would seem, then, that the chief medical officer, because he is also head of Life Sciences, is normally branched sciences, whereas strictly medical personnel have a separate branch to themselves. Their slightly different uniform style supports this statement. Finally, it should be noted that Yeoman Rand begins her career in support.

Rank insignia has also become more specific. Lieutenants Sulu and Uhura wear one solid stripe, while Lieutenant Commanders Scott and McCoy wear one solid and one broken stripe. Chekov, when he first appears as an ensign branched command, wears no rank insignia. As captain, Kirk wears two solid stripes surrounding one broken stripe. Spock, meanwhile, poses a problem. He wears two solid stripes, indicating his eventual rank of commander, but early on he is clearly referred to as a lieutenant commander. This same situation exists for Records Officer Finney and Security Chief Giotto. All three men are identified in episodes as lieutenant commanders, yet all three wear commander's stripes. It is certain that the rank of commander is a step above lieutenant commander and not simply a title honoring position. Probably these three men hold brevet ranks, awaiting Starfleet action to become official. Spock is soon a commander in rank as well as position.

The most startling uniform change at this time is that of the female uniform, for better or worse, depending on your point of view. This inexplicable change from trousers to short skirts is never adequately explained or justified. Perhaps it marks either the beginning of Starfleet's decline or the culmination of its ascent. The debate continues.

Let us now see what the preceding changes tell us about Starfleet at the time of the first five-year mission under Captain Kirk. Just as there is an upgrading of technology, so there is a change in organization. This is most noticeable at the helm. Before this time the helm positions were manned by officers in support. Now, however, the helm is a command position. Sulu's change from physicist to helmsman indicates an ambition to eventually command a starship. Because the reorganized Starfleet specified that the helm would now be a command position, Sulu takes this opportunity.

It is now clear that branch determines job, but note should be made that there are exceptions to this in the operational procedures of the *Enterprise*. All officers on the ship are cross-trained so they can perform several jobs if necessary. Thus, both Uhura and Kyle are seen manning the helm at times. Chekov is being trained in sciences, for he is often seen at Spock's station. There are many times when a primary officer of the bridge crew is missing, even during a red-alert emergency. When such cases occur, the officer in question is elsewhere on the ship, performing alternate duties or manning backup systems. There also occur occasional instances in which branch assignment seems incongruous with job. For instance, Doctor Anne Mulhall, an astrobiologist, is branched support. Under normal circumstances she would be in sciences, but apparently her job aboard the *Enterprise* is support-oriented.

We now know something about the normal career progression of Starfleet officers. It is easy to see that they are cross-trained in the fundamentals of several jobs. This is an obvious necessity for the bridge crew, whom we see most often, and an indication of their special level of skill and expertise. It seems that young officers are marked for a specific assignment upon commissioning, but there is also a certain flexibility concerning job and branch that enables one to pursue the development most suited to that person. Spock, Sulu, and Uhura all change their positions in Starfleet one way or another, and it will soon be shown that other changes also occur.

Starfleet now appears more centralized and bureaucratized than before, and it is beginning to threaten the independence of the Hornblower-minded Kirk. Several times he runs up against the wall of Starfleet organization. Nevertheless, the ensuing five-year mission of the *Enterprise* is one of unprecedented discovery and expansion for the Federation. It is also one of unprecedented disaster for Starfleet. The primary mission of the *Enterprise* remains to explore and contact alien life. Consider the contacts made in less than five years: Talosians, Thasians, Metrons, Vians, Excalibans, Lactrans, Organians, Melkotians. Include also Trelane, Apollo, Sargon, Kukulkan. Include also the giant space amoeba and the doomsday machine. Alien life of such power is bound to give any military mind concerned with Federation security a massive headache, despite the fact that many of the above proved either benevolent or remarkably disinterested in the rest of the galaxy. A few pose enough of a threat to be potentially devastating should they ever turn truly belligerent.

As the *Enterprise* pushed back the boundaries of the Federation, she also pushed back the feeling of security provided by the expanse of space. In addition to the alien life mentioned above, consider also that of the twelve or thirteen *Enterprise*-type ships in the fleet, three were completely destroyed—*Constellation, Intrepid, Defiant*—and two rendered devoid of life—*Exeter* and *Excalibur*—in little more than a year. To put this in perspective, imagine the United States losing five of its nuclear aircraft carriers or five of its army divisions. It is a major disaster for Starfleet, for it is a loss of over a third of the starship fleet. It is extremely difficult to absorb the loss of over two thousand starship personnel. In the face of these events, we can only increase our admiration of Captain Kirk and his crew for bringing in the *Enterprise* relatively unscathed. We have grown accustomed to thinking of the *Enterprise* as representative of Starfleet; that view perhaps gives too much credit to the fleet and not enough to the character of the *Enterprise* crew and the people who lead them.

Nevertheless, it is obvious why at the conclusion of this famous five-year mission, Starfleet again undergoes a tremendous change. The results are seen almost three years later, as Vejur heads menacingly toward Earth. The *Enterprise* has been refitted again, this time dramatically so. Starfleet uniforms are also greatly changed. There are several styles: long-sleeved or short-sleeved, one-piece or two-piece, brown or blue, or otherwise. Uniform color is no longer pertinent to branch, and they are unisexual once again. Rank insignia remain the same, and most of the old *Enterprise* crew have been promoted one rank.

The major changes occur in branch selection. By this time the old branch insignia have been replaced. The star of command has become the universal insignia of the *Enterprise*. Branch is now indicated by the background color of the new *Enterprise* insignia. A white background indicates command, red indicates engineering, yellow indicates support, and green indicates medical. Special notice should be taken that engineering has been reorganized into a separate branch.

Admiral Kirk and Captain Decker both wear the white of command. Lieutenant Chekov, absent from the *Enterprise* during the latter part of its mission to train for his present assignment as security and weapons officer (demonstrated by his absence from the animated series), is also branched command. Doctor McCoy, following his "forced induction" back into the *Enterprise* crew, has transferred to the medical branch. This may be due to his extensive research into the applications of Fabrini medicine. Lieutenant Commander Sulu, however, has been transferred from command to support. When Spock rejoins the *Enterprise*, he is branched engineering, as are Chief Engineer Scott and Transporter Chief Rand.

The positions of Ilia, Sulu, Chekov, and Spock are evidence of more organizational change in Starfleet. The helm positions held by Ilia and Sulu were support positions in the early days of the *Enterprise*, but during Kirk's first command they were changed to command positions. Now they have returned to their former branch. This is Sulu's third known branch. While diverse training is good, it must also be complementary. Constant branch changing, particularly while holding the same job, can lead to bureaucratic nightmares, and is not conducive to rapid advancement. Starfleet reorganization quite possibly costs Sulu an early starship command, a position he certainly merits but does not receive until it is too late. Chekov's position, on the other hand, indicates that the security forces of Starfleet have been moved from the support branch to command. Chekov's wide experience and continuity in the command branch structure certainly contributes to his promotion to first officer of the *Reliant* years later.

As for the engineering branch of Spock, the explanation lies in the nature of the refitted starship. Due to the highly advanced nature of the engineering, the new transporter, and new pulse-warp drive, the refitting involved many scientific problems and theories. The engineering section, at least that of the *Enterprise*, became a branch separate from support. When Spock rejoins the *Enterprise*, the engines are the major source of concern. Though he is listed as the ship's science officer, for the rest of this voyage and the remainder of the refitting he is technically branched engineering. This situation is similar to that mentioned earlier concerning Dr. Anne Mulhall's peculiar position.

This is a good time to mention yet another indication of Starfleet's reorganization. When Kirk is promoted, he is not promoted to the rank of commodore, which is the next highest rank after captain, but to the rank of admiral. The commodores of Starfleet, represented by such people as Commodores Stone, Mendez, Barstow, Decker, Stocker, Wesley, and April bore three solid stripes to designate rank. They commanded starbases, fleet task forces, and held high-level staff positions. What seems to have happened in the reshuffle at Starfleet is that the rank of commodore has been eliminated, to be replaced by another grade of admiral, of which there are several. This is not that unusual, for the United States Navy did the same thing following World War II. As a result, there never was a Commodore James T. Kirk.

At the end of *Star Trek: The Motion Picture*, the Star Trek universe again seems to be in order. Kirk is again in command of the Federation's finest crew on Starfleet's finest vessel, prepared for another five-year mission. The mission of the *Enterprise* continues to be one primarily of science. By the time Khan Noonian Singh and Commander Kruge arrive to wreak havoc on all, however, this has completely changed. We know that the death of Spock and subsequent destruction of the *Enterprise* takes place nearly eight years after the Vejur incident. This is very apparent when one considers the dramatic change in uniform style and the fact that the *Enterprise*, at the cutting edge of Federation technology a few years prior, is now only fit (ostensibly) for the scrap heap.

The uniforms have now undergone their third major change. They are much more military in style than any of the previous ones. The *Enterprise* insignia is universally present on all belts. This includes members of other starships and starbase personnel. There was a time, during the series, when fleet personnel not assigned to a starship bore a different insignia. In fact, even other starships sported unique designs. Now, however, the *Enterprise* symbol is omnipresent. The old rank stripes have been replaced by metallic insignia worn on the right shoulder. Finally, branch is now identified by the color of the right shoulder strap and the color of the underlying sweater. Command, support, sciences, and medical still retain their colors—white, yellow, blue, and green, respectively—while engineering has returned again to support.

Admiral Kirk remains in command, but he is now joined by Captain Spock, who is the new commander of the *Enterprise*. Other commanders—Terrell, Styles, Esteban, Morrow—also wear white. It is interesting to note that in the brief glimpse we have of Janice Rand, she is ranked a commander and is branched command. Considering her origin as a yeoman just fifteen years ago, this is a remarkable achievement. In the meantime, McCoy remains branched medical. Commander Sulu remains in support, but, if we are to believe the movie novelization and the assumption of a promotion to captain for him, he will soon change to the white of command. This is also assuming his career survives the hijacking of a starship. Scott as well rejoins the support branch, and maintains it even as captain of engineering of *Excelsior*. Commander Chekov, in his new position as science officer of the *Reliant*, has been transferred to sciences. This is hardly surprising, considering his close work with Spock when he first joined the *Enterprise* bridge crew. It has long been known that he is well trained in this area. Joining Chekov on the *Reliant* is Commander Kyle, one-time transporter chief of the *Enterprise*, also now branched sciences. Commander Uhura, after fifteen years in support and several more years before that in command, is now branched sciences.

The one remaining person, Lieutenant Saavik, poses a problem. In *The Wrath of Khan*, she and her fellow trainees wear both red and black collars. This could simply designate status, black representing perhaps Academy cadets (midshipmen) or ensigns, and red representing young lieutenants training for their first starship assignment. Saavik, being a lieutenant, wears red. In *The Search for Spock*, however, she wears the white of command. Her duties on the *Grissom* indicate that she should be wearing the blue of sciences. It is possible that her assignment to the *Grissom* is intended to be only temporary, for the duration of the Genesis expedition. Her situation would not be unlike that of Anne Mulhall's or Spock's during the Vejur incident.

It is obvious that Starfleet has undergone yet another reorganization, this one more drastic than the last. The communications specialty, represented with great skill by Uhura, has been completely transferred to the sciences branch. This is perhaps due to the nature of modern communications, particularly with the development of the so-called transwarp drive. The position of Scotty as captain of engineering on board the *Excelsior* indicates something else about the new direction Starfleet is taking. With the advent of larger and apparently more powerful starships, department heads like engineering, life sciences and astrosciences will now hold the rank of captain, while remaining in that specific branch, and be under the overall command of a senior captain, such as Captain Styles.

This new Starfleet bears little resemblance to the organization that pioneered galactic exploration thirty years ago. Indeed, the period of wide and rapid exploration seems to have ended. Starfleet has now taken on the role of military protector. Interstellar politics have stripped starship commanders of their independence. One only has to examine the actions of Captain Styles and Captain Esteban, as well as Admiral Morrow, to realize that this is so. Captain Kirk, had he been on the *Grissom*, would never have "checked with Starfleet" before beaming up a Vulcan child in a snowstorm. The lack of initiative and general malaise, reaching to the highest level, is glaring. The presence of vessels like *Reliant* and *Grissom* suggest that the scientific mission of the *Enterprise* has been transferred to others. The *Enterprise* herself has been relegated to the role of training vessel. The existence of the *Excelsior* brings with it the possibility of a new era of intergalactic exploration, but its full potential still remains to be seen.

What, then, does the future hold for the former crew of the starship *Enterprise*? Assume they are not all brought to trial for mutiny, aiding in the escape of a Federation prisoner, the disabling of one starship, hijacking and then destroying another, and breaking the quarantine on the planet Genesis. Assume they do not flee to deep space to become benevolent pirates. Assume instead that somehow all is set right and they even get a new ship, perhaps even a new *Enterprise*. What then? Professional advancement cannot be ignored.

At the present time, the following situation exists among the legendary crew: Admiral Kirk, acting always like a captain and never an admiral, certainly wants a command. Mister Spock, however, has already been promoted to captain. To continue, Scott has also attained the rank of captain, as has Sulu. Chekov is a first officer, just one step away from being a captain. Uhura is a commander, just one rank below a captain, though it is uncertain what her next career move might be. At any rate, of the seven major characters, four are already captains or higher, with two more close behind. We can safely assume that Doctor McCoy will stay away from command—unless he becomes "Captain of Life Sciences." An interesting, even fascinating idea.

Shall we have a crew run by a group of captains? As the fourth movie approaches, the future of our favorite crew remains much in doubt. Considering the path the stories have taken, Starfleet and its uniforms will probably not change significantly in *Star Trek IV*. The characters, however, have reached the point at which some tough decisions must be made. It will be interesting to see what direction they will take.

About the Editors

Walter Irwin has been writing professionally for almost twenty years, and has authored over one hundred articles, features, and short stories. He became active in *Star Trek* and comic book fandom in 1970, culminating in the publication of *Trek* in 1975 with G. B. Love. He is currently script editor and head writer for Mediaplex Film Corporation. In addition to editing *Trek* and coediting the *Best of Trek* volumes, Walter continues to publish short fiction and novels. He married longtime *Star Trek* fan Lauren Johnson on Halloween in 1987, and they currently live on a ranch in Valley Lodge, Texas, with hordes of horses, dogs, and cats.

G. B. Love was one of the founding fathers of comics fandom and was also a *Star Trek* fan early on. He began publishing the seminal fanzine *The Rocket's Blast* in 1960, and eventually became one of fandom's first entrepreneurs, organizing some of the first comic and *Star Trek* conventions, and publishing over one hundred books and magazines. G. B. began editing *Trek* in 1975 with Walter, and continues to coedit the *Best of Trek* volumes to this day. G. B. is happily single and lives with his faithful dog Rip in a house full of comics, books, and toys in Pasadena, Texas.

Both together and separately, Walter and G. B. are currently planning several new books and magazines.